Augustus Baldwin Longstreet

Master William Mitten

A youth of brilliant talent, who was ruined by bad luck

Augustus Baldwin Longstreet

Master William Mitten
A youth of brilliant talent, who was ruined by bad luck

ISBN/EAN: 9783337120740

Printed in Europe, USA, Canada, Australia, Japan

Cover: Foto ©Andreas Hilbeck / pixelio.de

More available books at **www.hansebooks.com**

MASTER WILLIAM MITTEN

OR,

A YOUTH OF BRILLIANT TALENTS,

WHO WAS

RUINED BY BAD LUCK.

BY THE

AUTHOR OF "GEORGIA SCENES."

MACON, GA.:

BURKE, BOYKIN & COMPANY.

1864.

BURKE, BOYKIN & CO., BOOK AND JOB PRINTERS, MACON, GA.

TO

DOCTOR HENRY HULL,

OF

ATHENS, GEORGIA.

—————

ALLOW ME, MY HIGHLY ESTEEMED FRIEND,

TO

INSCRIBE THIS UNPRETENDING VOLUME TO YOU.

YOU WILL APPRECIATE THE INSCRIPTION

BY

THE SPIRIT WHICH DICTATES IT, AND NOT BY THE MERIT OF THE WORK.

THE AUTHOR.

PREFACE.

In 1849, I resided for a few months in Jackson, Louisiana. During my sojourn in that place, two meritorious young men, who had established a Press in the village, earnestly solicited me to write for it. I agreed to do so; and as a College and a number of admirable schools graced the village, I framed the story of Master MITTEN, to induce the youth of the place, to improve the opportunities which these institutions afforded them of becoming useful and distinguished men. Master MITTEN and his mother, are both imaginary characters; but who that has had much to do with the instruction of youth, has not seen both, at least in their leading traits?

I LAID the scene of the story in Georgia, and took the liberty of introducing into it, the names of several of my Georgian friends, giving a very slight touch of their characters in the conduct and language which I ascribe to them. This I did, to increase the interest of the story to them at least, should it ever reach the State of Georgia. I deem it proper to mention these things, for the story having been broken off at the fifth chapter, by my departure from Louisiana, when it was resumed in Georgia, for the *Field & Fireside*. Many finding these names in it, with some of the characteristics of those who bore them, supposed it to be a veritable history, which it is not. Master MITTEN is introduced to Doctor Waddel's celebrated School in Willington, Abbeville District, South Carolina, just as it was, from 1806 to 1809, inclusive. SPRAGUE has given us a brief sketch of the Doctor's biography, in which his merits as a Teacher and a Divine are gravely portrayed. MITTEN shows the reader the man at the head of his school in its palmiest days.

MASTER WILLIAM MITTEN;

OR,

A YOUTH OF BRILLIANT TALENTS, WHO WAS RUINED BY BAD LUCK.

CHAPTER I.

MANY years ago there lived in a small village in the State of Georgia, a pious widow, who was left with an only son and two daughters. She was in easy circumstances, and managed her temporal concerns with great prudence; so that her estate increased with her years. Her son exhibited, at a very early age, great precocity of genius, and the mother lost no opportunity of letting the world know it. When he was but six years old, he had committed little pieces in prose and poetry, which he delivered with remarkable propriety for his years. He knew as much of the scriptures as any child of that age probably ever knew; and he had already made some progress in geography and mental arithmetic. With all this, he was a very handsome boy. It is not to be wondered at, that his mother should be bringing him out in some department of science, upon all occasions; of course, she often brought him out upon very unsuitable occasions, and sometimes kept him out, greatly to the annoyance of her company. Not to praise his performances, would have been discouraging to Master William Mitten, and very mortifying to his mother; accordingly, whether they were well-timed or ill-timed, everybody praised them. The *ladies*, all of whom loved Mrs. Mitten, were not unfrequently thrown into raptures at the child's exhibitions. They would snatch him up in their arms, kiss him, pronounce him a perfect prodigy, both in beauty of person and power of mind; and declare that they would be willing to go beggars upon the world to have such a child. Others would piously exhort Mrs. Mitten not to set her heart too much upon the child. "They never saw the little creature, without commingled emotions of delight and alarm; so often is it the case that children of such

B

wonderful gifts die early." Her brother, Capt. David Thomson, a candid, plain-dealing excellent man, often reproved Mrs M. for *parading*, as he called it, "her child upon all occasions."

"Anna," said he, "you will stuff your child so full of pride and vanity, and make him so pert and forward that there will be no living with him. From an object of admiration he will soon become an object of detestation."

"No danger, brother—no danger;" she would reply, "I take special care to guard him against these vices."

At eight years of age, William was placed under the instruction of Miss Smith, the teacher of a female school, into which small boys were admitted by courtesy. Here he continued until his tenth year, when Miss Smith told his mother that he was getting too old to remain in her school, and that she could keep him no longer. Here Miss Smith whispered something to Mrs. Mitten which drew a smile from her, but which has ever remained a secret between them. It took about the time to deliver it, that it would take to say; "the truth is, he is too pretty and too smart to be in a female school."

William being now out of employment, his mother took six months to deliberate as to what was next to be done with him; and in the meantime she sent him in the country to stay with his grandmother. On his return she determined to place him under the tuition of Mr. Markham, one of the best of men, and best of instructors. Accordingly, she conducted him to the school room of his second preceptor.

"You will find him, Mr. Markham," said Mrs. M., as she delivered over her son to the teacher's charge, "easy to *lead* but hard to *drive*."

"If that be the case, Madam," said Mr. Markham, "I fear that your son will not do well under my government."

"Why, surely, Mr. Markham, you don't *prefer driving to leading*."

"By no means, Madam—by no means. I much prefer *leading*; but no child of his age can be *always* led. Withal, a teacher must govern; by fixed rules, which cannot be relaxed in favor of one of his pupils, without rendering them worthless, or unjust to all the rest."

This took Mrs. Mitten a little by surprise; for she supposed that Mr. Markham would be proud of such an accession to his school as William. She acquiesced, however, in the soundness of his views; but flattering herself "that he would never find it necessary to *drive* William," she turned him over to the teacher and withdrew.

William made his debut at school in a dress which was rather tawdry for Sunday, and extravagant for the school-room. The first ten or fifteen minutes were spent by William and the school boys in interchanging looks of admiration, which Mr. Markham indulged, under pretence of not observing. At length a pretty general titter began to run through the school at William's expense. Mr. Markham now interposed, with a sternness that instantly brought all to order but William, who tittered in turn, at divers persons and things. But this Mr. Markham *happened* not to notice. The object of William's *special regards* and *amusement* was John Brown, whose clothes seemed to have been made of remnants of old bed-quilts, so numerous and party-colored were their patches. John's *attitude* was as curious as his dress; he seemed to have derived it from the neck of a crane at rest. His head was flat and bushy, his feet were large and black, and his face bore a marked resemblance to that of a leather-winged bat. In all his life, William had never seen exactly such a thing as this; and he laughed at it, without stint and without disguise. John soon became indignant, and raising his book between his face and the teacher, he set his mouth to going as if repeating all the vowels and consonants of the alphabet in quick time, and shook his fist at William with a quiver of awful portent. According to the masonry of the school-room these signs meant: *"Never mind, old-fellow, soon as school's out I'll make you laugh t'other side of the mouth."*

"Come here, sir," said Markham who always saw more than he seemed to see. "Who are you shaking your fist at, sir?"

"Mr. Markham, that fellow keeps laughing at me, sir."

"And did'nt you laugh at him first?"

"I—I—laughed at him a little bit; but he keeps at it all the time." He don't do nothin' else but keep'n' on laughin' at me all the time."

"Well, if you laugh at other people, you must let them laugh at you; and now, sir, go to your seat; and if I catch you shaking your fist at anybody in school hours again, or *using it upon anybody afterwards*, who has only paid laugh with laugh, I'll *shake* you."

There was a little spice of equity here, that John had entirely overlooked; and he went to his seat much cooler than might have been expected.

"Come here, William!" continued the preceptor. William did not move; and the whole school was electrified at disobedience to Mr. Markham's orders.

"Come here, William!" repeated Mr. Markham but with no better success. Whereupon he rose, and commenced " *leading* " him, in quick time, to his seat. Having stationed him by it he said to him : " William I know you have been indulged so much that you hardly know the duty of submission to your teacher's orders, or I would correct you for not coming to me when I called you. You must do as I tell you ; and I tell you now to quit laughing and get your lesson—*you*, John Brown, are you tittering again already ? Put down your feet and come here, sir !" Here Mr. Markham, by way of parenthesis, gave John three cuts, which sounded like a whip-poor-will, and made him dance a jig, a minuet and a polka all in less than a minute. He retired, crying, and limping and rubbing and shaking his bushy head like a muscovy drake in a pet ; and Mr. Markham proceeded : "I tell you, William, you must obey me "—

"Yes, sir," said William, pale as a sheet.

" I can have no little boys with me who won't do as I tell them "—

" No, sir."

" If you will be a good boy, and mind your book and your teacher, you need not be afraid of me. Go now and take your seat and quit laughing and get your lesson."

William obeyed promptly, and hardly took his eyes from his book until the school was dismissed.

During the recess he begged his mother to take him away from Mr. Markham's school. He said Mr. Markham whipt his scholars, and he "didn't want to go to a man that whipt children."

" But," said his mother, " you must be a good boy, and then he will not whip you. I've entered you now, and paid your first quarter's schooling, and you must go to the end of the quarter."

William returned to school, and for several weeks did remark. ably well. He was put in a class with George Markham, son of the preceptor, a promising youth, but equal to William in nothing but attention to his studies. As William could get his lessons in half the time allowed him for this purpose, he soon began to neglect them, until the last moment from which he could commit them, and then to some time beyond the moment ; and here was the beginning of his *bad luck*. As he grew remiss, Mr. Markham counseled him, lectured him, and threatened him ; but all to no purpose. At length he told him that the next time he came to recite without knowing his lesson, he would correct him. This alarmed William a good deal ; but not quite enough to stimulate his industry to con-

tinued exertion ; and after ten or fifteen lessons he came up deficient
again.

"Why have you not got this lesson, sir?" said Mr. Markham
with terrific sternness.

"I—I—was sick, sir!"

This was William's first falsehood ; but it saved him from a whipping which he awfully dreaded ; for though Mr. Markham knew
that he had not told the truth, he deemed it best to admit the excuse, at least so far as to withhold the rod of correction for the
present.

As he dismissed the school, he told William to remain a few moments, and when they were alone he thus addressed him :

"William, I very much fear you told me a falsehood to-day. I
saw you all the morning before you came to recite, idling, and
whispering, without any appearance of sickness ; and since the recitation, I have seen no sign of sickness about you. Still I may possibly
be mistaken, and I hope I am ; but remember, if ever I find you
telling a lie to hide your faults, I will punish you more severely than
I would without the lie." He then proceeded to counsel him kindly
and affectionately against the danger of lying.

William went home in sadness and in tears, for his conscience gave
him no rest. His mother sought in vain for the cause of his distress.
The next day he went to the school and acquitted himself well for
that and the four succeeding days, for which Mr. Markham gave him
great credit and encouragement. On the fifth day he got permission
to go out, and as he remained out an unusually long time, Mr. M.
went in quest of him, and found him in the act of concealing his
book among some rubbish near the school house. He was unobserved by William, and he withdrew to the school room. Just before
the recitation hour William made his appearance. What he had
been doing during his absence, was not known ; but that he had not
been studying was manifest from his conduct, and still more manifest
from his ignorance of the lesson when he came to recite.

"What have you been doing, William," said Mr. Markham, "that
you know nothing of this lesson?"

"I lost my book, sir, and I couldn't find it."

Mr. Markham passed the matter over until he dismissed his school,
when he detained William, told him where his book was, repeated
his lecture upon lying, and enforced it with a pretty severe flogging.
William had never experienced the like of that before, and probably
would never have experienced it again, but for the imprudence of his

mother and her friends. He promised his preceptor that he would never repeat his offence; and he went home with a countenance and manner indicative of a fixed purpose to keep his promise. He told his mother nothing of what had happened, nor did she find it out for four days afterwards. In the meantime, William was all that she or his preceptor could wish him to be. It so happened, however, that Thomas Nokes had lingered about the school-house, and seen all that had transpired between William and his teacher. He went home where he found Mrs. Glib, one of Mrs. Mitten's most devoted friends—as she proved by carrying to her all news that was likely to affect her peace. Mrs. G. had stopped on her way to her brother's in the country, to bid Mrs. Nokes farewell, and had actually risen to depart, when Tom stept in, big with the events of the day.

"I tell you, what!" said he, "Mr. Markham give Bill Mitten *jorum* to-day!"

"It isn't possible," exclaimed Mrs. Glib, "that Mr. Markham has whipt that dear, sweet, lovely boy."

Mrs. Nokes tried to catch Tom's eye, that she might stop him; but his whole attention was directed to Mrs. G. and he went on—

"Yes he did—and he linked it into him like flugins. I'll be bound he made the blood come."

Here Tom caught his mother's eye, which was darting lightnings at him, and he concluded, "*but I don't reckon he hurt him much though!*"

"Oh, the brute!" muttered Mrs. Glib, as she left the house for the carriage.

On the afternoon of the fourth day from her departure, she returned to the village, and immediately hastened over to Mrs. Mitten's. Mrs. M. met her at the door very cheerfully and very cordially.

"Oh," ejaculated Mrs. Glib, "how happy I am to find you so cheerful! I was afraid I should find you in tears."

"In tears! For what?"

"Why, for the unmerciful beating which Mr. Markham gave to your dear, sweet, lovely little William, last Friday."

"Surely there must be some mistake Mrs. Glib. William never said a word to me about it: and not fifteen minutes before you came in, Mr. Markham was here congratulating me on the progress my child was making in everything that was good."

Here Mrs. G. looked as if she had taken an emetic which was just about to operate; and after a short pause she proceeded:

"Well, I hope it is a mistake; but it came to me from an eye witness. You know I don't send *my children* to Mr. Markham; because I don't choose to have *my children* cut and slashed about like galley-slaves, for every little childish error they commit—breaking down their spirit, and teaching them sneaking and lying, and everything that's low and mean. Mr. Toper never whips; and I don't see but that *my children* get along under him as well as other people's children." (Here Mrs. M. covered her face with her handkerchief, either to hide her grief, or a smile which grief could not extinguish, or blushes of conscience; for she had warned her son against ever associating with the Glibs.) "But you know how strict Mrs. Nokes is with her children; one of them would as soon put his head in the fire as tell a lie—specially before her. Well, Thomas told me, right in her presence, that Markham whipt William till he drew the blood from him!"

"Mercy on me!" groaned Mrs. Mitten, "why didn't William tell me of it!"

"Oh, that is easily accounted for. My George Washington Alexander Augustus says that John Brown told him, that 'if anybody went to carrying tales out of Mr. Markham's school, he'd make 'em dance *juba.*' Poor William dare not tell of it. John said, moreover, that Markham dragged him from his seat the first day that he went to school, and would have whipt him then, if he had been in school a little longer."

"I fear," said Mrs. Mitten with streaming eyes, "that I offended Mr. Markham when I placed William under him, by telling him that William was easy to *lead* but hard to *drive.* He immediately showed some reluctance at receiving him. But I only meant to apprise him of the child's disposition. Poor child, with all his talents, I fear he is doomed to *bad luck.*"

"Oh, no, madam; I can explain the matter better than that. George Markham was given up on all hands to be the smartest boy in school. Now everybody knew what a prodigy William was; and old Markham knew that as soon as William entered the school, his *beloved darling, precious George,* would have to come down a notch. All the boys say that William is smarter than George, and yet that old Markham is always pecking at him. Who can't see the reason?"

Just at this moment William made his appearance with a bright and joyous face; and holding up a most beautiful edition of Sanford and Merton. "See, ma," said he, "what Mr. Markham gave me to-day for keeping head of George three days. And he says if I'll keep head of him eight days more, he'll give me a book worth twice as much, and I mean to do it too."

"What hypocrisy!" exclaimed Mrs. Glib. "He's got wind of it!"

"William," said his mother, "did Mr. Markham whip you last Friday?" In an instant his countenance fell, and his eyes filled.

"Yes, ma'am," whispered William. "But I don't think he will whip me again, for I mean to be a good boy."

"Poor, blessed, little innocent angel-lamb!" sighed forth Mrs. G. with honest sympathy.

"And haven't you always been a good boy, my son?"

"Ye-e-s m'm."

"Then what did he whip you for?"

"He said I told a lie, and wouldn't get my lesson!"

"Oh, shocking, shocking—worse and worse!" vociferated Mrs. Glib. "I'd stake my salvation on it, that child never told an untruth in all his life."

It was very *unlucky* for William, that Mrs. G. made this remark; and still more *unlucky* that his mother did not suspend her examination here, until Mrs. G. retired.

"William, it would break my heart to discover that you had told a lie; but if you have told one, confess it, my child, to your mother!"

William paused and pondered, as well he might; for having Mrs. Glib's salvation and his mother's heart in one eye, and Mr. Markham's awful lie-physic in the other, he was in a most perplexing dilemma.

"Don't you see, Mrs. Mitten, that the child is actually afraid to deny that he told a lie? He knows that if it gets to Markham's ears that he denied it, he'd beat him to death. Didn't he whip you very severely, William?"

"Yes, ma'am."

"Where did he whip you?"

"On the calf of my legs."

"Well, now, do let us examine them! I lay the marks of the whip are upon them to this day."

William's pants were rolled up, and at the first glance, his legs seemed as white and as spotless as pure alabaster. But a glance did not satisfy Mrs. Glib. She was confident that William had received "*jorum*," and that marks of it might yet be found. Accordingly, she put on her specs and squatted down to a close examination of William's legs, beginning at the left."

"Look here, Mrs. Mitten," said she, after a short search, "isn't this the mark of a whip?"

"N-no," said Mrs. M. carelessly, "I believe it's nothing but a vein."

"It's no vein, my word for it; it's too straight for a vein. I'm told that whip-marks, just before they disappear, can hardly be distinguished from veins."

Proceeding from the left leg to the right, she examined for some time with no better success. At length, however, on the right side of the limb, she found the palpable marks of "*jorum*." For reasons that need not be given, I hold myself perfectly competent to explain this matter with unquestionable accuracy. *Jorum* is always administered with a scarificator; and in receiving it, it is almost impossible for the patient to keep his legs still. The consequence sometimes is, that the scarificator, which is made and intended to act simultaneously and equally upon both limbs hardly scratches one, while it spends all its force (double force) upon the other. William had obviously "danced juba" under the operation, and in three of his movements he had so distracted the instrument, that the end of it pressed much harder upon the flesh in these places than the operator intended, and of course it left its most permanent mark where it pressed hardest. Nor is it true, as Mrs. Glib was informed, that its mark retire in likeness to a vein, but with a greenish, straw-color, as the case before her proved.

Mrs. Glib had no sooner discovered these marks, than she went through divers evolutions of horror, better suited to the Inquisition than to this occasion. At length she became composed enough to speak.

"Oh, Mrs. Mitten, see what your dear lovely, brilliant boy has suffered. Think of when it was done!"

Mrs. Mitten looked and burst into tears afresh. Just at this point her daughters made their appearance, and the matter being explained to them they burst into tears; and William seeing his mother and sisters weeping, he burst into tears. In the midst of this affecting scene, David Thompson, Mrs. Mitten's brother, made his appearance, and he didn't burst into tears.

"Why, what's the matter—what's to pay?" enquired he, with no little alarm.

The ladies all answered at once, with different degrees of exaggeration, but all to the same point, namely, that Markham had beaten William most unmercifully.

" Why, nothing seems to be the matter with him that I can see."·

" Look at his legs !"

" Well, I see nothing the matter with his legs."

" Look at his right leg."

" Well, I see nothing the matter with his right leg."

" Look on the right side of his right leg."

" Well, I see nothing on the right side of the right leg."

" Look *here*, Mr. Thompson," said Mrs. Glib—" bend down a little
—do you see these marks ?"

" *Psh-e-e-c-t!* Why surely you have all run crazy ! Is it possible
you're making all this fuss over these three little specks ?"

" Those *specks* as you call them, brother, are the remains of what
was put on my child's tender flesh *four* days ago."

" And have you all just made up your minds to cry about it !"

" We did not know of it, brother David, before."

" Why, didn't William tell you of it ?"

" No, poor child, he hardly dare talk about it now. He is completely cowed. Since he went to school he seems to have been
buried; nobody notices or speaks of the child any more than if he
were dead."

" Yes, there it is ! you have been feasting upon his praises so
long, that you cannot live without them. What did Markham whip
him for ?"

" The *charge* was, telling a lie, and neglecting his lessons."

" Well, are you sure he did not tell a lie ?"

" Oh, brother, how can you ask such a question right before the
child's face ! Yes, I'm just as sure of it as I can be of anything.
I never detected William in a lie in all my life."

" No, nor you never will, the way you're going on, if he told a
thousand. Now, if Markham whipt him for lying, I vouch for it he
told a lie, and Markham knew it; for he never moves without seeing
his way clear."

" I think he has a prejudice against William, and I think I
know the reason of it."

" Prejudice ! He's incapable of prejudice against anybody, much
less against little silly children. I'll go over and see him and learn
the whole truth of the matter."

" No, you needn't trouble yourself, brother, I shall not send
William to school to him any longer."

" Why, Anna, you surely are not going to take your child from school without hearing from Mr. Markham the particulars of this matter?"

"I don't want any particulars, more than my own eyes have seen. Suppose the child actually did tell a lie, (which nobody who knows him will believe) it wouldn't justify Mr. Markham in beating him to death."

"Beating him to death! He's certainly a very natural looking corpse! And when you take him from school, what are you going to do with him?"

"I'd rather send him to Mr. Toper than have him cut and slashed to pieces by Markham."

"Toper! what that drunken booby who hardly knows B from bull's foot."

"Good morning, ladies!" said Mrs. Glib—"Good morning, Captain Thompson." ₄

"Why, brother! How could you talk so of Mr. Toper? Don't you know that Mrs. Glib sends her children to him? She'll go right off and tell him what you said."

"No, I don't know, nor don't care where she sends them. All I know about them is, that Toper is a drunken fool, and that her children are perfect nuisances to the town, and that if you mean to send your child to the devil, Toper is the very man to carry him for you. Mrs. Glib may tell him all this too, if she chooses; and then if he opens his mouth to me about the matter, I'll kick him out of the town, as a public charity."

"I only said I *had rather* send my child to Mr. Toper than have him beaten so. I think I shall employ a private tutor."

"And pay ten times as much as is needful for your child's instruction; and then have him not half as well taught, as he will be, by Markham! Anna, I beseech you, I implore you for your child's sake, don't act at all in this matter under your present feelings. Let the matter rest until I can see Markham and learn the whole history of it. I know more of boys than you do. They do many things at school that they never do at home, for the plain reason that they are under many temptations at school which they are not under at home. You are probably now at the turning point of your child's destiny, and a false step here may ruin him forever."

Strange to tell, William listened to his uncle with a kind of approving amazement, and as soon as he had concluded, said:

"Ma, I'm willing to go back to Mr. Markham now; I a'nt afraid of him; I don't think he'll ever whip me again."

"That's a brave boy," said the Captain. "Every word in the sentence is worth a guinea. No good boy fears Mr. Markham."

"Ah, poor child!" said Mrs. Mitten—"he knows little of the world's duplicity. He little dreams of the undercurrent that is at work against him."

"What undercurrent? Is it possible, Anna, that after nine years acquaintance with Markham, you can suspect him of duplicity and secret hostility to such a child as that—*your* child—*my* nephew!"

"Mr. Markham's not *perfection*, if what I've heard of him is true," said Miss Jane.

"No," said Miss Ann, "and if I was ma, I'd die before I'd send brother William back to him to be beaten like a dog!"

"And if I was ma, I'd learn you to hold your tongues till your counsel was asked for."

"Oh, do, brother, let the girls express their *opinions*. I should suppose that one might have an *opinion*, of even Mr. Markham, without having their heads snapt off."

"Well, Anna, I see your mind is made up to take William from Mr. Markham's school."

"Yes, I'm resolved upon it."

"And without one word of explanation from Mr. Markham!"

"Yes; I want none of his explanations."

"Ma," said William, "let me go back to the end of the quarter."

"Bravo, Bill! Go back, my son—be a a good boy, and learn your book, and you'll be a noble fellow by and by."

"Brother David, do you think it right to encourage a poor little ignorant child to run counter to his mother's wishes?"

"No, Anna; but I supposed that the wishes of the child in whom you are so much wrapt up, might save you from rash resolutions concerning him."

"Well, it is not necessary to debate the matter further. I vow he never shall go back to Mr. Markham's school, and that is the long and short of it."

Captain Thompson wheeled off and left the house as if to get something of importance that he had left in a dangerous place. In about a half hour he returned:

"Well," said he, "I have seen Markham, and heard the whole matter explained"—and he gave it from first to last, just as it occurred. Still Mrs. Mitten adhered to her resolution. He argued, he entreated, he implored, he forewarned, he remonstrated, he used every means that he could think of to change her mind, but to no purpose. The truth is, Mrs. Mitten would not place her son where he was liable to be whipt. Her brother left in a storm. I have been thus particular in giving this part of William's history, because it proved in the end, as the sequel will show, to be remarkably *unlucky*, and fruitful of wonderful consequences.

CHAPTER II.

The reader will remember that we left Mrs. Mitten resolved to remove Master William from Mr. Markham's school. Her resolution was carried into effect; and she forthwith began to look out for a private teacher for her son. But *unluckily* no such teacher was just then to be found; she was constrained, therefore, to adverfise for one; and though she placed her advertisement in three Gazettes, of pretty general circulation, three months rolled away before any one proffered his services to Master William. In the meantime our little hero was a gentleman at large; and having formed many acquaintances at school, common courtesy required that he should give them as much of his attention as he could. Accordingly he was with them at every intermission of their studies, and took great pleasure in attending the evening parties of such as were smart enough to do without evening study. These soon became so frequent that William entirely neglected his mother's parties for them; by means whereof his mother and her friends lost the entertainment which he used to afford them upon such occasions. She often demanded of him explanations of his discourtesy to his old admirers, which he promptly gave to her entire satisfaction. Sometimes he was at the Juvenile Debating Society; at others he was at a Prayer Meeting; at one time he "went to hear Parson Deleth's Lecture." (On the importance of the Oriental Languages to the student of Theology.) At another he went to hear the Euterpean band; and at all other times he was taking tea with good boys, or engaged in some laudable employment. As the young Glibs had rather more leisure than any other boys in town, and as their mother had charged them to cultivate a close acquaintance with Master William, they were frequently thrown together. At first William was rather shy of those acquaintances; but as they forced themselves into his company, pleading their mother's order for so doing, he could not well refuse to take them under his moral training. Accordingly they soon became very intimate; and William was pleased to find that they were by no means as bad boys as his mother took them to be. Withal he soon discovered that they were possessed of a vast fund of information, which they communicated to him freely; first to his astonishment, and afterwards to his delight. They knew who had the best apples, peaches, plums, cherries and melons in the town and neighborhood—what gardens contained the most strawberries, raspberries, grapes, figs and pomegranates—who had the earliest and latest fruits—what time bad dogs were turned loose at night—where hens, guinea-chickens, ducks and turkeys, were in the habit of laying. They were masters of all culinary matters, except the higher branches of cookery. They were abolitionists of the most generous stamp; disdaining the distinctions of color, and holding out the most liberal encouragements to slave industry, by promising the most liberal prices for such little dainties and curiosities as the poor slave might have to dispose of. Nor were these young gentlemen without personal accomplishments, corresponding with their vast mental endowments. They were the most expert climbers of trees and fences in the country. They were good riders and better runners. Though one of them was two months, another fifteen and another thirty-seven months older than William, they could slip through gaps that he feared to attempt. They could heel a game-cock, whet a jack-knife, and shoot a pistol, with unrivalled skill—their age considered. They could recognize people in the dark with the eye of an owl; and run half-bent in gutters and ditches, faster than William could, on a plain. They could perform many amusing and ingenious tricks with cards; and smoke segars, chew tobacco and drink cordial, apple-toddy, egg-nog and the like, with marvelous grace and impunity.

At the end of three or four weeks from the time that William left school, Mr. Markham's examination came off, and most of the town attended it. The visitors were, as usual, liberal in their praises of such as did well; and these, William, who was present, heard with painful emotions. They were praises which made his tea-party-compliments seem insignificant. Here was competition, and not one was praised, of whom he did not know himself to be decidedly the superior. The examination closed with an allotment of prizes to the best in the several classes, by judges appointed for that purpose. William saw one and another distributed with increasing dejection and self-reproach. At length George Markham was called out on the stage, and Judge Dawson advancing to him with a large silver medal, suspended by a crimson ribbon with tasteful decorations, observed: "Master George, in the course of the examination you have labored under some disadvantages; for the judges, from an apprehension that their high respect for your teacher, might be unconsciously transferred to his son, have been more vigilant of inaccuracies in you than in any of your school mates. So well have you acquitted yourself, however, that you have entirely relieved us from all apprehension of doing you injustice on either hand, and we presume there will not be a dissenting voice in this large and respectable assembly, to our judgment, which awards to you the first honor in your class; in token of which we present you this beautiful medal. Remember," continued Judge Dawson, as he placed the loop of the ribbon over the head of Master George, and dropt the medal on his breast—"remember as often as you look upon that medal, that on the day you received it, you raised the highest expectations of your future distinction, and resolved never to disappoint them." As the judge concluded, the house thundered with applause. William dropt his head and wept bitterly; for he felt that all this would have been his, had he remained at school.

In the afternoon the usual exhibition came off. We may not dwell upon the performances of each of the students respectively. For reasons which will be hereafter observed, we notice but two.

The fourth speaker called out was MASTER JOHN BROWN! John stept out so completely metamorphosed, that William himself hardly knew him. His hair was combed down straight and slick. The lard-gourd had obviously been laid under contributions for it. His feet were disguised under shoes and stockings. His suit was all new and of course all of one color. His mother had tried herself upon it from the spinning of the first thread, to the fitting of it on. But nature had decreed that John should be a funny looking fellow in spite of dress; and as he stept to the centre of the stage, as if laboring under a slight founder, (for shoes manifestly pestered him) an involuntary smile diffused itself over every countenance. He made his bow, and in a clear, distinct audible voice he began:

"Ladies and Gentlemen: You will not be surprised that I should have selected as my theme for your entertainment this afternoon the incalculable advantages of *personal beauty*."

Here it seemed that the house would be knocked to pieces. Men, women and children laughed and thumped immoderately; and even Mr. Markham could not preserve his usual gravity. Mrs. Brown plainly showed that her trouble in rigging out John was repaid by the very first sentence. With almost every other, the same scene was renewed; until at length all respect for order seemed to be for-

gotten; and such commendations as these might be heard in under-
tones all over the house: Well done, flat-head! Hurra short-neck!
Bravo pug-nose! I tell you stiff-leg is *some.* Give me homespun
at last. John concluded, and had it been allowable, he, doubtless,
would have been encored at least three times. He owed most of his
credit to the patient and careful drilling of his teacher, but there
were few in the school who could have improved good drilling as
well as John did.

Next to John's speech, the most amusing thing in the exhibition
was a dialogue between George Markham and David Thompson,
which elicited great applause. At the conclusion of the exercises,
honors were a second time distributed, and young Markham was
again complimented with a prize. Brown got one, of course, which
was rendered doubly complimentary, by another peal of applause as
he received it.

All this was slow murder to William Mitten. Nor did his tortures
end here. Seeing his uncle and Mr. Markham in conversation as
the company retired, he flattered himself that they were negotiating
for his return to school, and he drew near to them unobserved by
either, and overheard this conversation:

"That little fellow Brown is an odd looking fish, Mr. Markham,
but there's some *gumption* in him after all."

"He's rough material to polish, but he has some talent; and if he
can be made to study, he may be a man of worth yet."

"I congratulate you on the very handsome manner in which your
son acquitted himself in everything."

"He may thank Mrs. Mitten for his honors of to-day, for had she
suffered her son to remain at school, George would not have touched
a single honor. When William studied (and he had begun to study
well) he was vastly superior to George in everything. The dialogue
was written on purpose to show off his wonderful dramatic talent.
George's part was designed for him, and your son's for George; and
I'll venture to say, that I can take William and read over the part to
him but once, and he will perform it decidedly better than George
did. He spoke before me but three or four times while he was with
me. The first time, I read over his piece to him after he had repeated it, and made him deliver it again; and I was amazed to see
how exactly he followed my reading in every respect. Take him
altogether, I think he is decidedly the smartest boy I ever had in my
school." Here the conversation was interrupted by the congratula-
tions of several other gentlemen.

William went home in tortures, and hardly slept a wink that night. He would have given the world for the honors and praises which George Markham had received that day; and he would have been willing to have changed persons with John Brown, for the trophies which John had won.

The next morning he recounted to his mother all the events of the day, and particularly the conversation which he had heard between his uncle and Mr. Markham. She was now stung nearly, or quite as deeply as her son. But what could she do? Her vow was out and it must be kept.

"Well, my child," said she despondingly, "all this only goes to show that you are born to ill-luck. But I hope it is all for the best. Those who are unlucky in youth are apt to be lucky in old age, it is said—and I hope it will be so with you."

"Ma, when you get your private teacher will he have any exhibitions?"

"No, my son, he will have no scholar but you."

"Then I don't want to go to a private teacher."

"But remember my child, that as he will have but you one to attend to, he can teach you a great deal better, and bring you on a great deal faster than Mr. Markham could, who has so many in charge. And study well, and you will soon enter college, where you will have an opportunity of showing off your talents not simply to a village, but to a whole State!"

"And how long will it be before I can go to college?"

"With your gifts, and a private teacher, I have no doubt you will be prepared to enter college in four years at the outside."

"Why, Ma, I'll be dead before four years!"

"Oh, I hope not; they will roll round before you are aware of it."

As the private teacher had not yet been found, William had nothing to do for the present, and he resumed his attention to public and devotional exercises, in fellowship with the young Glibs, and others of their stamp.

A few days after this Parson Turner was announced as wishing to have a few minutes private conversation with Mrs. Mitten. He was ushered into the parlor; and Mrs. Mitten soon followed him.

"Mrs. Mitten," said the Parson, "I have called on you to beg of you to keep your son at home on Wednesday nights. He and the Glibs come to the church where we hold our prayer meetings, and sometimes at the door, and sometimes in the gallery, keep up such a

c

laughing, bleating and groaning, that it is next to impossible for us to proceed with our devotions."

"Why, Parson Turner, you must be mistaken! I have always taught my child to treat religious services with the most profound respect; and for reasons that need not be mentioned, I am confident that he is hardly acquainted with the Glibs."

"No, madam, there is no mistake about it. We all know him very well."

"Well, Parson Turner, I will enquire into the matter, and, if I find it so, I will see to it that my son disturbs you no more."

"Whether you *find it so* or not, I assure you madam it is so." So saying he took his leave. He had not been gone long when William came in.

"William," said his mother, do you associate with the Glibs?"

"They sometimes come to where I am, and then I can't get rid of them; but I don't go where they are."

"Well, now, I strictly forbid you from associating with those boys. They are very bad boys and unfit company for you. Parson Turner says you go with them to the church, and behave very rudely during prayer meeting. Is that so, William?".

"'Twasn't me, Ma, it was the Glib-boys."

"How came you there with the Glib-boys, at all?"

"I said I was going to the prayer meeting and they followed me."

"Well, my son, I'm very glad to learn that *you* didn't misbehave at the meeting. Brought up as piously as you have been, I didn't think it possible that *you* could treat religious services with contempt. When you go to such meetings, (which I am glad to find you disposed to do) take your seat near the leader of them, and bad boys will not follow you there. Never have anything to do with boys that can trifle with sacred things. It's the worst sign in the world."

Mr. Turner went from Mrs. Mitten's to Mrs. Glib's, and repeated his story.

Mrs. Glib received him with a careless chuckle, and said to him: "Oh, Mr. Turner, I wouldn't mind little thoughtless boys; they *will* have their fun; but they'll quit these things when they grow older. I'm very cautious against reproving my children for little childish freaks in church, lest I should excite in them a dangerous and lasting prejudice against religion."

Mr. Turner, after sitting petrified for about a half minute, rose and abruptly left the house.

About noon on the following Thursday, Mrs. Glib came over to Mrs. Mitten's, in a great flurry. "Oh," exclaimed she, as she entered the house, " do you know, Mrs. Mitten, there's a warrant out against all our children ! I got wind of it and hid my children; but I'm told they've got William "—

" A warrant !" shrieked Mrs. M. "In mercy's name tell me what has my child been doing to have a warrant out against him ?"

"Oh, nothing of any consequence—don't be alarmed—nothing but disturbing a prayer-meeting. Squire Crumb says there's no law for it; and if there was, throwing stones at a house and setting off squibs at the door would not be against the law; and if he was employed, he'd blow it all up. But Judge Dawson says there is a law against disturbing worshipping assemblies. I was afraid of this, when Turner went about complaining of the boys for their little sports. You know such things always make them mad and worse than ever."

Mrs. Mitten was nearly distracted; for her head was filled with jails, and punishment, and eternal disgrace, which she supposed the invariable accompaniments of warrants. Her brother David was sent for, post-haste; and he was soon at Mr. Justice Easy's office, where William was under arrest. A short interview between him and Parson Turner settled the matter amicably. The latter told him all that had transpired and said he saw no other way of stopping these hopeful youths; but that if Mr. Thompson would pledge himself that they would disturb the meetings no more, he would stop the prosecution. The pledge was given, and the matter was settled.— This done, Mr. Thompson proceeded with William to his sister's, where he found the two mothers.

" Where are your children, madam ?" said Thompson sternly to Mrs. Glib.

" Why, they—I expect they are—that is, I think likely—which one of them ?"

" Why, all of them, madam."

" Oh, I have not seen one of them since quite early this morning. What did *you* want with them, Captain Thompson ?"

" *I* wished to know from their own lips whether, if I get them out of this scrape, they'll let people pray in peace hereafter."

" Oh, yes, yes, yes—I'll engage for them; and I will consider myself under everlasting obligations to you Captain, if you'll get them out."

" I must have the pledge from their own lips."

" Well, I'll run over home and see if they are not there. I've
no doubt they are, for they always come home about this hour—what
o'clock is it?"

" Half after twelve."

" Oh, if it's as late as that, I'm sure I shall find them at home.
Stay a minute, Captain, and I'll run over and bring them."

She soon returned with her three boys, who were placed with
William before the Captain.

" Do you know, young gentlemen," said he with great solemnity,
" that you have violated the laws of your country? That a warrant
has been issued against you, to vindicate the offended majesty of the
people's laws?" (Here the ladies looked much alarmed.) " That,
unless somebody will befriend you, your mothers are liable to be
mulct in *pounds* of money; and that you are liable to be cast in
prison *for ten long days and nights*, with nothing to eat but bread
and water, and nothing to sleep on but the hard floor and a few
blankets? Then be dragged to a court of justice, before the eyes of
the whole world, and there to be tried, by a jury of twelve men duly
empanelled to pass between you and your injured, insulted country?
Then, when convicted, (as you are certain to be,) that you are to be
turned over to Judge Dawson, (who always respects religion, and
whose wife is a most excellent member of the church,) to be dealt
with according to the law in such case made and provided? And
do you furthermore know, that all four of you are posting to the
devil just as fast as he would have you go? Do you know all this,
my hopeful young friends?" .

" Yes, sir," answered the boys.

" Very well. .Now, I am disposed to befriend you all; but I desire to know what I am to expect from you, if I do; for I don't wish
to get myself into any more trouble on your account. If I can be
certain that you will never get into any more such scrapes, I'll hush
up all this matter, as I know I can; but I must have a promise from
all of you that, if I do, I shall have no more such matters to hush
up. As for *Bill* there, I'll manage *him* myself: and if he goes to
disturbing religions meetings again, after the trouble he has given
me, and after I have snatched him from the clutches of the law, I'll
give him the timber myself, harder than Markham did, mother or
no mother, objection or no objection."

" In such case, brother David, I think you would be perfectly
justifiable, after you have stood his security and "—

" Certainly, certainly," said Mrs. Glib; " and in such case, I would not think of opening my mouth, if he should whip my children too."

"Well, will your children make the promise, or will they prefer going to jail?"

"Why, Captain, I would not own them if they refused. They are too high minded and honorable to refuse so great a favor upon such easy terms."

"Very well. *George Washington Alexander Augustus Glib:* Do you promise me here, in the presence of your mother and Mrs. Mitten, that if I stop this prosecution, so that it shall not harm you or your mother, or your brothers, that you will never disturb another religious meeting while you live, either by mouth, foot or hand, inside or outside of the house; and that you will show no rudeness, in any form or way, to Parson Turner, at any time or in any place? Do you?"

"Yes, sir."

"*Thomas Jefferson Napoleon Bonaparte Glib:* Do you make the same promise that your brother has just made?"

"Yes, sir."

"*Benjamin Franklin Pulaski Lafayette Glib:* Do you make the same promise?"

"Yes, sir."

"Well, remain here five minutes, and if in that time I do not return, you may be *certain* that the matter is satisfactorily settled." So saying he retired.

"Oh, Mrs. Mitten," said Mrs. Glib, " what an excellent, excellent man, that brother of yours is. I shall love him as long as I live."

"Brother David has a good heart, though he is sometimes rough in his manner. Was ever child so unfortunate as mine? It is an old maxim, that one had better be born lucky than rich, and I believe it. Brother David will probably settle the *suit;* but who is to wipe out the stain from my child's character?"

"Dear me, Mrs. Mitten, the thing will be forgotten in a week! Everybody knows that it was but a childish frolic, that nobody but old Turner would have noticed; and I shall make it my business to give him my mind upon it very freely, the first time I meet him. *I'm* under no promise, if my children are."

"I cannot blame Parson Turner, Mrs. Glib, and I hope you will not."

The five, and even ten minutes rolled away, and, Mr. Thompson not returning, Mrs. Glib moved off with her sons, looking very little like their namesakes.

CHAPTER III

Mrs. Mitten now determined to keep her son at home of nights; she therefore charged him, "upon pain of her sore displeasure," not to leave the house at night without her permission. William promised obedience, of course; and like a good boy, kept his promise for two nights and a half, without ever asking leave of absence. On the second night she seated him at the stand to read to her and his sisters. He had proceeded about a quarter of an hour, when three strange whistles were heard near the house. They were not noticed by Mrs. M. as yet; but the first had no sooner sounded, than William began to read horribly.

"Now, William," said his mother, "you've got tired of reading already; and you're trying how bad you can read, that I may make you stop!"

"No, I declare I a'nt, ma."

"Well, what makes you blunder and halt and miscall words so? What does that incessant whistling mean?"

"That's the way the boys whistle at school," said William.

"How do they do it! for it sounds like blowing in large phials."

"They do it by blowing in their hands."

"What are they blowing about here for? they never did it before. Go out William, and beg them to desist."

William obeyed promptly, and it seemed gladly. The whistling ceased as soon as he went out; and in a few minutes he returned.

"Who are they?" enquired Mrs. Mitten.

"A parcel of school-boys," said William, "but they said they wouldn't whistle about the house any more." He resumed his seat, and read pretty well until his mother excused him.

The next evening the whistling was renewed; but at such a distance from the house, as to attract the attention of no one; unless, perchance William from the events of the preceding night, was led to notice it.

"Ma," said he "mayn't I go to the Juvenile Debating Society to-night?"

"Certainly, my son; but come home as soon as the Society adjourns."

He set out, but happening to fall in with Ben and Jeff' Glib, by the way, (so they were called for short) they proposed going by Squire King's garden, and getting a few June apples. Ben said, "that Lawyer King was a very clever man, and didn't care who took his apples, if they didn't break his trees; and only took what they wanted to eat." Jeff said that he knew "that to be a fact; for he heard him tell William Strain, his wife's little brother, that very day, to go in with his playmates, and eat as many as they wanted, but not to break down his trees."

"Well, if that's the case," said William, "Ill go; but I wouldn't *steal* apples for anything in the world."

"Neither would I," said Ben. Law, no! Not for the world."

"Oh, it's nothing like stealing," said Jeff. "Sposen you was to lay down anything, and say you didn't care who took it, if. they didn't break it, and I was to come along at night, and take it, and not break it, would that be *stealing?*"

"No," said Ben, "it's no more stealing than picking up a chip."

William had attended the Juvenile Debating Society too long and with too much profit, not to feel the full force of Master Glib's logic, and consequently his scruples were immediately removed and the boys proceeded to the garden. The fence was easily ascended, and they were soon under the best apple tree.

"William," said Ben in a whisper, "this is a good place to learn to climb. The limbs are low and I can push you up to them. When you get in the tree, shake down the apples, and brother Jeff and I will pick 'em up; but don't shake down more than we can eat; for Mr. King wouldn't like that, and I should hate to do anything he don't like. Don't shake hard. The best way is to get on a limb, and hit a little *stomp* with your heel, and if they don't come stomp a little harder."

Thus instructed, William, with Ben's help, ascended the tree. He stampt limb after limb until he thought enough had fallen to satisfy the company, and was about descending, when Jeff said, "Don't come down yit—we an't got enough yit—I can eat a bosom full. Here, go out upon this limb and fetch it a pretty hard stomp or two and that'll do."

William went out on the limb as directed, and at the first stamp, missing the limb, he fell, and broke his arm just above the elbow. His pain was great, and his alarm was greater, but he bore them with little complaint until he cleared the garden. He then broke forth in heart-piercing groans, sobs, and lamentations; but not loud enough to disturb any of the villagers; "Oh, my arm does hurt me

so bad ! Only see how it swings about ! Oh, my poor dear mother;
it will kill her. My Heavenly Father, forgive me this one time, and
I never will do the like again ! I don't want *you* two boys to go
home with me. If you *please* don't go home with me."

His cries announced his coming before he reached home ; for they
became louder as he approached his mother's door. His sisters flew
to him, and his mother rose to follow them ; but her strength failed
her and she fell back in her chair. They could not learn the cause
of his wailing until he entered the house ; when advancing to his
mother, he sobbed out, " Oh, my dear mother, look at my arm!"

" What, is it broke ?"

" Yes, ma'am, I can't move it."

" Oh, my God, was ever a child doomed to such misfortunes !
Ann send for the Doctor immediately—I have not strength to move.
Send for Doctor Hull and Doctor Barden both."

The doctors came, and set the arm.

Of course the enquiry was from all, how the accident happened.

" I was going to the Society," said William, "and was standing
by a tree, and one boy said he'd learn me to climb, and he pushed
me up the tree, and I fell down and broke my arm."

We will not detain the reader with the many questions which this
explanation provoked, and the answers to them which William gave.
Suffice it to say that Doctor Hull fetched a little grunt of equivocal
signification, and took a chew of tobacco upon it, with as little interest in it as if he had set a thousand arms broken in this way ; but
Doctor Barden was as particular in his enquiries into the case, as
though he meant to report it to the Philadelphia Medical Journal.

The next morning Squire King came over to enquire " how poor
little William was." He expressed, and no doubt felt, tender sympathies for the boy ; but any one to have marked his eye, would have
supposed that his sympathies gathered about William's *feet* rather
than his *arm*.

This might be accounted for without discredit to the Squire's
heart ; for being a great hunter, he had contracted a habit of examining tracks, and track-makers, which beset him at times, and
sometimes upon improper occasions, as in this instance.

" William," said the Squire with a small dash of waggishness in
his tone and countenance which Bill seemed to think very ill-timed ;
" was it a smooth-barked tree, or a rough-barked tree ?"

" I——forgot ;" drawled out Bill a little crustily.

" Did you get up to the limbs before you fell, or just fall from the body ?"

" I——got to the limbs—"

" Did you take off your shoes?"

" No."

" Aye, that's the way the accident happened. You went up with your shoes on. You should always take off your shoes when you climb. The Glib-boys, who are the best climbers I know, always take off their shoes and stockings both. I hope, my son, you will soon be well. Mrs. Mitten, if there's anything that I have that can minister to William's comfort, it is at your service. I have some very fine June apples, and I will send him over some; little boys commonly like such things."

" Thank you—thank you kindly, Mr. King. I know he will prize them very highly—William have you no thanks to give Mr. King, for his kindness?" Mr. King retired.

" William," said his mother, it seemed to me you were a little rude to Mr. King."

" I know him," said Bill sulkily.

" Well, you know a most excellent, kind-hearted man."

" He's always poking his fun at people."

" I'm sure there was nothing like fun in what he said to you. It was all tenderness and kindness."

William's arm kept him, for the most part confined to the house for five weeks or more; during which time he was quite lucky; for nothing happened to disturb his, or his mother's peace. He had been so long kept from the Juvenile Debating Society that he had become very anxious to attend it; and his mother's consent being obtained, he departed once more for the arena of youthful polemics.

He did not return until the family retired to rest; and in passing to his room he made such a noise among the chairs, as to wake up his mother.

" Is that you William ?" said she.

" Yes."

" Is that the way you answer your mother?"

" Who put all these chairs in the entry ?"

" There are no more there, than are always there."

" It's a lie."

" Oh heavens, my child is deranged ! My child ! my child ! That arm, that arm !"

Mrs. Mitten sprung from her bed, and before she even lighted a candle dispatched a servant to Doctor Hull with the request that he hurry over immediately; for that her son was out of his senses. She had hardly got a light and a loose-gown thrown over her shoulders, before the Doctor was at the door. They met in the entry, just as William had come the fourth time to a chair which had been *heading* him ever since he entered the house. He seized it (for it had naturally enough exhausted his patience) and slung it with all his might as far as he could send it.

"Oh Doctor!" exclaimed Mrs. Mitten in the deepest agony of mind, "can you do anything for my poor unfortunate boy!"

"Oh yes ma'am—yes ma'am. Don't be alarmed. I pledge myself to have him sound and well before nine o'clock to-morrow morning."

"Oh Doctor how can you speak so confidently without ever feeling the child's pulse."

Just here, William having got hold of a small table that stood in the entry, and which he probably mistook for a wash-basin, poured out upon it a villainous compound, of heterogeneous elements, which it would have required a stronger head and greater *capacity* than Bill possessed, to keep together in peace for a single night.

The Doctor grunted, as usual; but with unusual indications of sympathy for *Master Mitten*.

"Why, Doctor, it seems to me," said the good lady, "that I smell peach brandy!"

"It seems so to me too," said the Doctor, "and segar smoke to boot."

"It's a lie," said Bill. "He tells a lie, and you tell a lie."

"Do you think my child is drunk, Doctor?"

"No doubt of it in the world, madam. Nothing else is the matter with him."

"Then my fate is sealed. I am doomed to wretchedness for life." And she sobbed and shrieked by turns.

"Retire to your room, madam. I will put him to bed, and stay with him until he gets sound asleep; and he will be well in the morning."

She did so; but it was to walk her room in tortures through the live-long night—not to sleep.

It was late in the morning before William rose. He had learned from a servant all that passed on the preceding evening; and it was an hour after he rose before he could venture from his room, to face his mother. At length he came, and mingled tears of contrition with her tears of sorrow—confessed his fault and promised never to smoke another segar, or drink another drop of liquor, while he lived.

About noon, on this day, an elderly, good looking gentleman made his appearance at Mrs. Mitten's and introduced himself as Mr. Judkins Twattle. He said he had seen Mrs. Mitten's advertisement, and had come to offer his services as a private teacher. Mrs. Mitten desired him to call again at ten the next morning, when her brother would be present, whose counsel she wished to have in the matter.

At the appointed hour the parties met.

" Have you any certificates of character and capability Mr. Twattle ?" said Captain Thompson.

" More, I presume, sir, than you will be willing to read."

Whereupon he produced a large bundle of certificates, running by long jumps through twenty years, and growing colder and colder. with very few exceptions, from the first to the last. They all agreed however in representing Mr. Twattle as fully competent to teach all the ordinary branches of an English education, with Algebra, Geometry, Latin and Greek. The two first were very flattering, and spoke in unmeasured terms of his skill as a teacher, his talents, attainments, gentlemanly demeanor, and spotless moral character. The two last merely testified that " *Doctor* Twattle was a good scholar and fully able to teach Latin, Greek, Mathematics, &c., &c.; the one almost a literal copy of the other. The first and second were from Vermont —the third from Pennsylvania—the fourth from Vermont—the fifth from Virginia—the sixth from New Hampshire—and the seventh from Kentucky—the eight from Vermont—and the rest were from various places, under the designations of " Bethel Seminary," "Bethesda Institute," " Pineville Lyceum," " Buckhead Atheneum," " Goosepond Literary Parthenon," " Big Lick Acropolis of Letters," " Tickville Emporium of Literature and Science," &c.

Captain Thompson knew nothing of Mathematics, Greek, or Latin, but he could understand certificates as well as Newton, Demosthenes, or Cicero ; and he spared no pains in studying them upon this occasion. After he had looked them over until he wore out the patience of his sister and Dr. Twattle, he observed :

" You seem to have been a great traveller, Doctor."

" Yes, sir. I early conceived a desire to settle in the sunny South ; and as soon as I raised money enough to bear my expenses, I left my native State for Pennsylvania ; but my health failing, I had to return. As soon as I recovered my health, I set out again for the South ; but

my health again failing, I was again constrained to seek a Northern
clime. And thus I went on until, advancing in years, I found that
I could not only endure a Southern climate, but that' it was now
more congenial to my constitution.than a Northern one. Thenceforward, I have always resided in the South. Having no aim but to
spread the lights of science through our favored country, and no disposition to accummulate money, but a strong propensity to travel and
see the world, I have so ordered my life as to fill the measure of my
wishes. I teach from place to place, for longer or shorter periods, as
I like or dislike the people; but never make an arrangement for more
than two years at a time. Thus it is, sir, that you see so many certificates from different places."

"What gave you such a strong desire to visit the South?"

"At first, nothing but my inborn roving disposition; but after
residing awhile at the South, particularly in Virginia, I became so
much enamored with Southern manners, customs, talent, spirit,
generosity, hospitality and vivacity, that I determined to fix my
abode here as soon as I could do so without rushing, with my eyes
open right into the jaws of death."

"Emph-hemph!" nosed out the Captain, ponderingly. "What
are your terms, Doctor?"

"Six hundred dollars a year, if I have to board myself and visit
my pupil twice a day, and sometimes at night, (for 1 expect to teach
Astronomy) through all seasons, and all weather; or two hundred, if
I board in the family with my pupil."

"Why, that is a vast difference, Doctor."

"So it is; but I detest taverns so much, that I would rather
sacrifice twice the price of board than board in one at any price."

"But you can find private boarding in the village, in genteel
houses, for much less than four hundred dollars."

"Well, if you prefer it, get me board in a genteel private family
and add to the tuition as much as it may be less than four hundred
dollars; and send the pupil to my room, instead of requiring me to
go to his."

"Why not let the tuition stand at two hundred dollars, and we
pay your board?"

"No objections in the world, if you will allow me to board where
I please, and allow me every accommodation that I could have at a
tavern, and send the pupil to me. I understand that Mrs. Norton
is a nice woman, and takes boarders. I will board with her and

pledge myself that my board shall not cost you over three hundred dollars."

"Mrs. Norton's is the dearest boarding house in town, and fully one mile from my sister's."

"Well, if too far for the scholar to walk, how much harder for me to walk! Nor can you expect me to let you choose my boarding house, and fix the price that I shall pay too! Allow me to board at Mrs. Norton's and I will knock off fifty dollars from the tuition."

"Or, I suppose, allow you to board at my sister's and you will do the same."

The Doctor looked as if he had committed a terrible blunder; and after a little halting and smiling, he replied : "Well, sir, you've got me where the owl had the hen : so that I can neither back nor squall —of course I will."

"Are you willing to contract for six months on trial at those rates ?"

"Perfectly willing—perfectly willing—provided you will engage not to turn me off capriciously at the end of six months; and allow me to fix the time of our connection, by our next contract, if I deport myself to your satisfaction. Dining one day with Thomas Jefferson, and Nathaniel Macon, the latter made a remark which I have often proved the value of since : "In making a contract," said he, "always have a *little of it* on your own side."

"Are you acquainted with those gentlemen ?"

The Doctor looked provoked at himself, for having made the remark, and replied in a courteous but hurried manner : "No sir— that is not—no sir. no. The circumstances which brought us to the same table, were purely accidental. Neither of them, I am sure, has *now* the most distant recollection of me ; though we did interchange some words upon that occasion."

"Well, Doctor, my sister and I will confer upon the matter in hand, and if you will call at three o'clock, this afternoon, we will let you know our decision."

"I will call at the hour," said the Doctor rising, "but to avoid any unkind feelings, it is proper that I should apprise you of my views of negotiations of this kind. When I made a proposition, which is not immediately accepted, I do not consider myself bound by it afterwards. If time be claimed to deliberate upon a proposition of mine, I claim the same time for retracting it if I see proper."

"That is all perfectly fair, Doctor—perfectly fair."

The Doctor withdrew; and he had hardly cleared the door before

Mrs. Mitten begged her brother to call him back, and close the bargain immediately. "He sees," says she, "where you entrap him, when speaking of Mrs. Norton, and his last remark was made on purpose to help him out of the difficulty."

"Anna," said the Captain, "my advice to you is, to have nothing to do with this man. If he is not a pickled villain, I'll give you my head for a foot-ball. A man of his age and accomplishment running about the country with a batch of old rusty, ragged certificates in his pocket, gathered through twenty years, not one of which ten years old, says a word about his moral character—willing to teach for the pitiful sum of one hundred and fifty dollars, and confessedly with no money in his pocket! Down from Vermont, and then back again—then South, then North, then here, there, and every where! He's a rascal—as sure as you're born he's a rascal."

"Oh! brother David, what uncharitable beings you men are! Every objection you raised he answered, as if by accident, before you raised or even thought of them. He has accounted most satisfactorily and nobly, for the cheap rate at which he holds his services—"

"—P-h-e-e-e-w! He from Vermont and care nothing for money! A literary apostle to the Southern Gentiles, moved by pure love of their wondrous virtues! So devoted to them, that sickness can't drive him away from them! Stuff, smoke, nonsense! He'll breed mischief in your house as sure as you take him there."

"Brother David, are you going to let slip this favorable opportunity of getting a teacher for my child at this critical period of his life,"—

"No, I'm going to let you do as you please. If you want him, you shall have him; and I'll do the best I can with him, for you; but once more I pray you to let this man alone; save the expense of him and the danger of him, and send your son to Mr. Markham, and beg him to whip the devil out of him, that has been getting into him ever since he was taken from school."

"I have said again and again, and I now say once for all, that my child shall not go to Mr. Markham."

"Very well, I'll engage Twattle. Take him for six months first, and you will be sure of his doing well, for that time at least; but look out for squalls, afterwards."

This was agreed to, and Mr. Twattle was employed upon the terms and conditions already intimated. That is to say, for six months, at the rate of one hundred and fifty dollars per annum—Mrs. Mitten to board him, and he to fix the terms of his next engagement.

Dr. Twattle deported himself to the entire satisfaction of Mrs. Mitten for six months. He had not been in her house one month, before he completely captivated the whole family. So dignified and easy was he in his manners, so neat in his person, so courteous and respectful to the ladies, so rich in knowledge, so pleasant in anecdote, so attentive to his business, and so careless of sordid lucre—in short, so perfectly did he come up to the Mitten-standard of the gentleman and the scholar, that he was soon admitted to all the rights, privileges and immunities of a near connection, in the family. The girls called him *Uncle Twatt.* William called him *Father Twaddly.* And Mrs. Mitten called him *Good Man,* and *Good Doctor,* and burdened him with delicacies for the palate. The Captain watched him closely; but was constrained to say, greatly to the delight of his sister, that he didn't know but that he had misjudged the man. "Certainly," added he, "if he is an imposter, he is the most accomplished one that I ever met with; and I have seen not a few."

"And now, brother," said Mrs. M., "I hope you'll acknowledge that *for once* in your life, I was right and you were wrong."

"Not yet, Anna. Any rogue may be clever for a few months. I will admit, however, that he does better than I expected, even thus far."

The Doctor's first quarter's salary was paid; and he laid it nearly all out in presents for Mrs. Mitten, her daughters and son.

"Good Doctor," said she, "if you could turn these things to any use, I would insist on your keeping them; for it looks like down right robbery to take them from your scanty means."

"I only regret that my scanty means *in hand* will not allow me to double them, Mrs. Mitten."

"How would you do in case of sickness or misfortune?"

"I have had for many years a little fund laid up to meet these contingencies—some ten or twelve thousand dollars, or such a matter. This, small as it is, will bear me through a long spell of sickness gently to the grave; or keep me above want, should I linger on the shores of time after I become too old to be useful, or to labor in my vocation. When thrown upon that fund, I shall change my character—my liberality will end; but until forced upon it, why desire to iucrease it. So little do I think of it, while I am able to make a living without it, that I hardly count it as a part of my estate. It might as well not be, for I shall probably die before I need it, and I certainly never shall touch it until I do need it. For several years I have not even drawn the interest upon it."

"Suppose you were to die suddenly, to whom would you leave it?"

"To some of the many beloved pupils whom I have taught; or to some one that I might be teaching when death arrests me."

"Have you no near connections, Doctor?"

"None nearer than fourth cousins, madam; and these are so profligate and abandoned, particularly the one who bears my name, that I never wish to see them again."

"Were you never married, Doctor?"

"Yes, madam, for a short time; but———"

"Pardon me, Doctor, for touching that tender chord. I see that I have inadvertently revived long buried griefs."

"You are very excusable, madam—your question was a very natural one in its place. At another time I will give you the history of my married life, as long as my dear Anna lived. For the present, suffice it to say that the little pittance of which I was just speaking came by her; and upon her death, I set it apart as a consecrated fund, never to be touched, while I could live without it. You have here another and the principal reason why I never speak of that fund as my own. But I have yet another: If the world knew of it, I should be harrassed and have my feelings lacerated incessantly and insufferably, with idle questions about my manner of life, while I have the means to live without labor, as though it were not every man's duty to labor in some useful calling, while he is able to do it."

"I fully approve your conduct, Doctor; and I shall keep sacred the secret which my reprehensible curiosity has dragged from you."

"Thank you, madam; but pray take no blame to yourself for your curiosity; it rose as naturally from the current of your conversation as the bubble rises from the agitated fountain."

Mrs. Mitten possessed too kind a heart to receive presents from the Doctor without returning them with interest.

At the end of the first month, Mrs. Mitten proposed to give a large tea-party, for the express purpose of introducing the Doctor to the villagers, male and female; but he begged her not to do it. "I cannot," said he, "reciprocate hospitalities, and I should be pained to receive attentions which I cannot return. I am fond of company, but for the reason just given, with others, I rather avoid company than seek it."

"I have noticed that, Doctor. You hardly ever leave the house in the day time, while you often take recreation-rambles at night."

"Just so, madam; but there is a better reason than that: the day is yours, (or your son's); the night is mine."

Considering that William never rose till breakfast time in the morning, and was out almost every night to a late hour, he made very rapid progress in his studies under Doctor Twattle. His mother had committed him to the entire direction of his teacher, and as night was the recreation hour, he could not object to his pupil's following his example.

A little incident occurred in the first month of the Doctor's tutorship which must not be passed over in silence, as it produced important results in the end.

One morning Mrs. Glib called on Mrs. Mitten, and, after the usual salutations and interrogatories, said:

"I am told Mrs. Mitten that you are delighted with your new teacher."

"I am, indeed," said Mrs. M.

"Well, I've come over to see if he can't take my boys too. They and William have become so much attached to one another, that it seems a pity to separate them. I have discovered" (lowering her voice to a confidential pitch) "that Mr. Toper drinks. That good brother of yours spoke but too truly when he charged Mr. Toper with drinking. Now, I will pay three-fourths of Dr. Twattle's salary if he will take my boys in with William; and that will bring William's tuition down to almost nothing."

"But will you board the Doctor three-fourths of the time?"

"Certainly I will."

"But he will not be willing to teach four boys for the price he gets for one."

"Well, I'll let his wages stand at what they are; and I will double them for my three boys, and board him half the time."

"But how will we do? I can't consent for William to go to your house to be taught."

"Well, the teaching may all be done at your house."

"But I know that Doctor Twattle would not be willing to come from your house to mine to teach."

"Well, then, he may stay altogether at yours, and I will pay part of his board."

D

'" Oh, Mrs. Glib, I couldn't think of taking pay for board from you."

" Well, what plan would you suggest. It's cruel to part the boys, for they can hardly live out of each other's sight."

" I really do not see how it will be possible to arrange it—I don't think it can possibly be done."

" Suppose you invite him down, Mrs. Mitten; and let us talk over the whole matter, and see if we can't fix it so that the boys may be together."

To this proposition Mrs. Mitten readily assented, for she was very confident that Doctor Twattle would not, upon any terms, consent to take the young Glibs. Accordingly, he was invited down, and introduced to Mrs. Glib.

" I have called, Doctor," said Mrs. Glib, " to see if you would not be willing to take my three boys under your instruction with Master William. Mrs. Mitten and I are like sisters, and our children like brothers, and if you would consent to take my children, you would greatly accommodate us all round."

" Certainly, madam," said the Doctor, " if Mrs. Mitten desires it, I will take them with pleasure; but being under contract with her, I can of course do nothing without her consent."

" But how could it be arranged, Doctor?"

" Just as you and Mrs. Glib may choose."

" Would you be willing to board part of the time with Mrs. Glib?"

" I would rather not change my boarding house; but if Mrs. Mitten desires it, I will even do that."

" Oh, no, Doctor, I do not desire to put you to that inconvenience; besides I should feel that I was violating my contract if I did not board you all the time!"

" Well, then, Doctor, how would this suit? You board here all the time, and I pay Mrs. Mitten half your board?"

" Very well, indeed, madam. I should prefer that to moving from house to house."

" But I couldn't take money from Mrs. Glib, Doctor, for board. And suppose we were to make that arrangement, how would it be as to tuition? I suppose you would ask four times as much for teaching four as you do for teaching one."

" That would be equitable; but I will not stickle about prices, if I can accommodate the friend of one who has been such a kind friend to me, as Mrs. Mitten has been."

" But where would you teach, Doctor? At my house or Mrs. Glib's?"

" Just as you may say, Mrs. Mitten."

" So you see, Cousin Mit," (so Mrs. G. in her playful moods called Mrs. Mitten) " that the whole matter is in your hands, and you are to say whether my poor boys are to get an education or not."

" Just here, when Mrs. Mitten was getting into an inextricable entanglement, a bright thought struck her, which relieved her from all difficulty, and in the transports of which she compromised her piety a little.

" Well," said she, " we can arrange this matter satisfactorily, provided brother David will give his consent that Doctor Twattle shall take other children under his charge besides William. But *you* know, Doctor, that he has had the whole management of this business in his own hands, and I would not dare to move an inch in it without his consent. I will submit the matter to him, and if he consents, I will most cheerfully consent that you take Mrs. Glib's sons under your instruction."

" Oh, well," said Mrs. Glib, " I have no fear but that he will give his consent. You know Mrs. Mitten he stepped forward, unasked, to assist my children, upon no other condition than that they gave him a promise : and that promise they have all kept most honorably and *religiously.*"

" Very well; whatever brother David says I will do Mrs. Glib; that I will promise you."

" And whatever Mrs. Mitten says," said the Doctor, " I will do."

" I shall see brother David to-day, Mrs. Glib, and let you know to-morrow what he says."

Here the company separated, all perfectly satisfied.

" Well, certainly," soliloquized Mrs. Mitten, when Mrs. Glib left the house, " that is the most trying woman that ever was born. She keeps me everlastingly in hot water. *Cousin Mit !*"

It was not until the next morning that brother David appeared at his sister's. He had no sooner arrived than Mrs. Mitten made known the desires of Mrs. Glib.

" Oh, yes," said he, " take the angels by all means !"

" But I wish you to be serious, brother. Mrs. Glib has my pledge that the matter shall be submitted to you, and I have promised her to abide by your decision."

" You have ! Well, tell Mrs. Glib that I am perfectly delighted at the idea of having my nephew in constant association with her

lovely boys, and nobody else! That rather than lose so fine an
opportunity of advancing the interest of my nephew, I will send the
young gentlemen to school every day in my carriage—Good morning,
sister."

"Stop brother—if you have any regard for me, don't leave me
with such a message to Mrs. Glib"—Lord bless my soul and body,
yonder she is coming now! Brother David! Brother, if you have
one particle of love or respect for your poor widowed sister come
back."

"Well, what do you want?"

"Do you seriously desire me to bear that message to Mrs. Glib?
I know you do not. Then speak with your usual frankness."

"Well, you are certainly the strangest woman that ever was born.
You are forever asking my advice, and never taking it. I had almost resolved to give you no more advice; but as you seem afflicted
by this, I'll reverse it; which I do seriously. Tell Mrs. Glib that I
object to Twattle's taking any more children while he is under contract to teach William alone—I will not have his attentions divided.
And tell her, moreover, that I had just as lief see a polecat, a rattle-
snake and a hyena come into the house as her three children."

"Now, you've gone too far again! Do, my dear brother, revoke
the last part—see, she's most here"—

"Very well, I revoke it. Good morning!"

He had not left the house two minutes before Mrs. Glib entered it.

"Well," said she, "I saw your brother retire as I came up, and
I suppose you know his will concerning the boys?"

"Oh, yes, Mrs. Glib; and he won't hear to the Doctor's taking
any more children while he is under contract to William. He
wishes William to have all his attentions."

"He *does!*" said Mrs. G., biting her lip and patting her foot.

"Yes, ma'am. He seemed very positive."

"I suppose that gives *you* very great pain—Good morning, Mrs.
Mitten!"

"Why, you're not going so soon!"

"Yes, madam; I just run over to know Capt. Thompson's *edicts.*

"Now, we've to have new trouble?" mused Mrs. M. as Mrs. G.
left the house. And she hit it exactly. In less than three months
after this date, a very strange report was whispered about in secret
places of the village. And what, gentle reader, do you think it was?
"Why that Twattle was courting the widow Mitten." No, that was
not it; but that the widow Mitten was courting Twattle!! It was a

slander, of course. The widow Mitten was not the woman to court anybody—*i. e.*, matrimonially.

About a month before the first term of Doctor Twattle's service expired, he spent several evenings with Mrs. Glib, who, the reader has long since discovered, (though I believe I forgot to tell him so,) was a widow too. Her given name was Bridget; but not liking it as she grew up, she added an "*a*" to it, so as to make it more romantic. She was rich, and for her years remarkably handsome.

In these visits Mrs. Glib offered the Doctor many inducements to close his contract with Mrs. Mitten at the end of his engagement, and make a more advantageous one with her. How the Doctor received her overtures is not known; but it is certain that Mrs. Glib cherished the idea that after another short engagement with Mrs. Mitten, he would be at her service; an idea that was strengthened by the fact that when he came to renew his engagement he limited it to only four months.

It was not without alarms that Mrs. Mitten observed the growing intimacy of Mrs. Glib and Dr. Twattle; and when he limited the time of his second engagement to four months, instead of a year or more, as she had expected, her alarms were increased. No change, however, was observed in the Doctor's conduct; and nothing of higher interest occurred for the first two months, than, that Mrs. Mitten in taking one of Master William's coats to mend, found a pack of cards in one of the pockets, which discovery she reported to his teacher, who promised to cure him of all love of cards by parental reproof and kind counsels.

The third month of the second term had just passed, when a report spread all over the village that Doctor Twattle and Mrs. Mitten were certainly engaged to be married. It no sooner reached her brother's ears than he hastened to her, to put her upon her guard, lest in her well known admiration of the Doctor, she might say or do something tending to encourage the report. To his surprise, he found her unmoved by her brother's disclosure. "If people choose to talk about me," said she, "let them talk. It would be no discredit to me to marry such a man as Doctor Twattle, I'm sure, for he has every quality that any woman could desire in a husband, and not a fault that I have been enabled to discover."

"Where is he?" said the Captain, "I'll pack him off, if it costs me my life."

"And if we were going to be married, do you think that would stop it? I assure you it would not."

"Very well, take your course! I see plainly the report is true. I have one piece of advice to give you, and it is the last that I ever expect to give you. Have your property secured to yourself and your children. If you don't, every shilling of it will go to him as soon as you are married; and do not beggar yourself and them to enrich a stranger."

"Rest assured, if we get married, that will be done; and if it were not, the good Doctor would not touch one dollar of it without my consent. Of this I have the most satisfactory proof. But I have heard him say, that if he should ever marry again, while he would have no woman who would not trust her property, with her person to his care, yet that when both were committed to his charge, he would always consider the wife as his, but the property as hers; and for fear of accidents, he would immediately afterwards settle her property on her. Not before, because there would be no merit in doing it then, and great demerit in his betrothed to request it."

"Why, Anna, he's a scoundrel as sure as you are born, and I feel strongly tempted to cut his throat. If you're bent upon marrying him, as I see you are, let me bring a lawyer here and have your property secured to you immediately."

"What is the use of doing that, when it is certain that he'll make no such contract?"

"And, therefore, you're going to marry him without one?"

"Yes, but I'm not going to lose my property for all that, brother. I know Doctor Twattle much better than you know him; and if I were at liberty to give you his history, you would not even ask me to require a marriage-contract of him—I know you would not."

Just here the young ladies, who had overheard the conversation, made their appearance in tears.

"I would," said Miss Jane, "rather Ma should marry Uncle Twattle than anybody else, if she will marry, but I never can see my poor dear father's place————"

"Hold your tongue!" said Mrs. M., sharply.

"Ma, you can't blame us," said Miss Ann, "for not wishing to see our dear departed father's————"

"Hush, I tell you! and speak when you're spoken to."

"Oh, sister," said the Captain, "do let the children have their *opinions*. I should think they might express their *opinions* of even Mr. *Saint* Twattle, without having their heads snapped off."

Mrs. M. was in no humor for this retort just at this time, and she showed more independence and temper than she had evinced for many long years.

"Well," said she, "*I'm* my own mistress, and I'll marry who I please, if all the brothers and children in the world should oppose it." So saying she hurried from the room.

"Well, young ladies, I hope you've got a teacher to your liking now!" said the Captain.

The girls each seized a hand of the Captain, and begged his forgiveness for opposing his advice to their mother, and promised more for the future than the Captain could have required. He withdrew his right hand from Anna's embrace, and turned his eyes away from them, as if looking for something that he did'nt wish to find, and with his middle finger pressed something from both, that he manifestly wished to conceal.

"Oh, my dearest, dearest uncle," said Jane, "our father, our only, our best counsellor! Will you not do something to stop this match?"

"I don't know what I can do," said the Captain, striving to dissipate or hide his feelings by rough words, "unless it is to cut the scoundrel's throat, to which I feel strongly tempted."

"No, uncle, no. Use no violence———"

Here William came in whistling "*Yankee Doodle.*"

"You young scoundrel!" said the Captain, "you've brought things to a pretty pass! Would God you had died at your birth."

"Why, what have I done, uncle?"

"You've filled your mother's heart with anguish ever since you quit Markham's school; and you've brought into the house a man who is going to beggar her and all her children."

"I did'nt bring him, uncle. You know I was willing to go back to Mr. Markham."

"Well, to do you justice—but what have you been at ever since! Disturbing prayer-meetings, you——little rascal, and running into all manner of iniquities! You'll come to the gallows as sure as your name's *Bill Mitten*, you young dog! Do you know your mother's going to marry Twattle?"

"Yes, sir; he told me about it long ago; but said he would'nt do it if I objected———"

"If *you* objected! If *you* objected. And I suppose your Royal Majesty gave your consent?"

"I told him," said Bill, with humility, for he had never seen his uncle in such a terrific state of mind before, "that if he loved Ma, and Ma loved him as much as he said they did———"

"Clear out of the house, you young rascal, or I'll———" (Bill scampered.) "Don't you see the deep, designing knave and hypocrite, in everything he does! Using a child—his pupil———. I'll smoke the viper out of his hole!" so saying he rushed up to Twattle's · room amidst the screams of the girls.

He knocked at the door, but received no response.

"You may as well open the door, Mr. Hell-cat, for I'll come in if I have to break it down."

After a short pause, and no voice from within, he forced open the door; and behold, the Doctor was not in! He went in search of him, but luckily did not find him till his fury abated. He went home and took his bed; for the excitement had brought on a smart fever.

CHAPTER V.

At the close of the last chapter, the reader will remember that we left Mrs. Mitten resolved to marry Twattle, against the wishes of brother and daughters—Capt. Thompson sick in bed. from over excitement—his two nieces in tears—Billy comfortable, and his teacher missing. How did Twattle happen to be out of his room in the day time? Doubtless, Mrs. Mitten had advised him to take an airing, while her brother was swelling. Current as was the report of the intended marriage, and strengthened as it was by what had passed between Capt. Thompson and his sister, Mrs. Glib did not believe it.

"Mark what I tell you," she would say, with a great deal of self-complacency, " it will never take place."

Her visits to Mrs. Mitten had not entirely ceased from the last which we have noticed; but they had become much less frequent, and much less cordial than before. And when she heard of what had passed between Thompson and his sister, at their last meeting, she appeared rather pleased than pained by it.

Captain Thompson had kept his bed two days, when the Postmaster of the village visited him with a letter in his hand, and mystery in his face.

"I have come over," said the Postmaster, "to make enquiries of you concerning Mr. Twattle. Here is a letter from a Mr. Charter Sanders, written at *Athens*, mailed at *Lexington*, and requesting an immediate answer directed to *Washington;* enquiring, whether there is not a man here by the name of Twattle; and whether he goes by the name of John, Jacob, Joseph, James, Jeremiah, or any other given name beginning with a 'J;' and requesting a particular description of him. The writer begs me to say nothing about this letter; but as I hardly know Twattle, I have come to you for the information required, as well as to let you know that there is probably something wrong in this Twattle, whom report says your sister is about to marry."

"The dirty scoundrel!" exclaimed the Captain, "it now occurs to me that every certificate which he produced, I believe without a solitary exception, save two which *Doctored* him, was in behalf of 'J' Twattle; and the rogue's going through the country under every name that 'J' is the initial of. Set down here, and answer it immediately; and don't whisper a word about that letter to any one else."

It was done accordingly; but unfortunately, the gentlemen had not noticed a servant girl who was in attendance on the Captain; during the conversation, and before the answer was finished, the servant informed Miss Jane that Charter Sanders, "who lived in Washington, had written about Mr. Twattle, and said his name was John, Jim, and a heap more names, and that he was a dirty scoundrel." Miss Jane hastened home, and conveyed the information to her mother, and her mother to Twattle.

He received it with a smile, mingled with a little indignation, and observed:

"That worthless fourth cousin of mine, Mrs. Mitten! He keeps me making explanations wherever I go. I hope Sanders will find him, and bring him to justice. Now, I must post off to Washington, to see Mr. Sanders, or lie under the suspicions of the town until he comes here. Is your brother able to leave his bed yet?"

"No sir; but he is better, and I hope to see him out in two or three days."

This day, and the next, the Doctor was out more than usual; and the day following he was missing.

About this time, the impression became general that the Doctor had run away. Mrs. Mitten became very uneasy; and Mrs. Glib came over *to console her.*

"Did he make no explanations to you?" said Mrs. Glib.

"None about *leaving;* though I know what took him away."

"Why, he explained the whole matter to me."

"That is very strange!"

"You may rest perfectly easy, Mrs. Mitten; he will return next Thursday week."

"Why, it should not take him that long to go to Washington and back."

"Washington! He's not gone to Washington; he's gone to South Carolina to receive a valuable rice plantation, which his lawyer writes he has recovered for him in that State."

"How did he go?"

"I sold him a horse. I offered to loan him one; but he said he never borrowed a horse for more than a day. He could have no peace on a journey of a week, upon a borrowed horse, for fear of accidents and delays that might injure the animal or incommode the owner."

"What did he give you for him?"

"More than I asked, by fifty dollars; and when I objected to receiving more than my price, (which was up to the full value of the horse,) he begged me to accept it, 'as an earnest of further and larger favors that he meant to show me;' so he gave me his note for two hundred dollars."

"His *note!* Why, he had *money*, I know."

"Yes; he told me you had been kind enough to advance him thirty-two dollars and a half since the last contract with him; but that, he said, would hardly bear his expenses to Charleston; so I loaned him three hundred dollars to pay his lawyer's fees."

"Mrs. Glib, he's an imposter; and we have both been made the dupes of his villainy, as sure as you live."

"Now, how it would distress you if I were to tell the Doctor that, on his return, cousin Mit."

"No, it wouldn't in the least. He'll never return, unless he is brought by Mr. Sanders."

"What Mr. Sanders?"

"Why, haven't you heard of the letter from Mr. Sanders, inquiring about him, and representing him as a scoundrel, and I know not what all?"

"Why, no. Is there such a letter in town?"

"To be sure there is."

"Well, if *I* had known of such a letter, Mrs. Mitten, I would have told *you* of it."

"I have had no opportunity of telling you of it."

"But I can hardly think him an imposter, after all, Mrs. Mitten. Have you any reason to think him so?"

" Yes, abundant reason. On the day he left, he borrowed two hundred and fifty dollars of me—all I had—telling me that he had just discovered where a distant relation of his was, who under his name, was imposing upon people everywhere, and constantly bringing him into discredit; and that, if he could borrow five hundred dollars, he would conduct Mr. Sanders to the rogue, and take all the expenses of prosecuting him on his own shoulders. As I had a deep interest in the matter—that is, in seeing all rogues brought to justice—I advanced him two hundred and fifty dollars, to get legal advice, a horse, &c., that he might be prepared to set out with Mr. Sanders, as soon as he arrived, in quest of his rascally fourth cousin, of whose iniquities he had long before informed me. I concluded he had gone to Washington to meet Mr. S."

" Well, he told me about that cousin, too; and a long cock and bull story about the death of his dear wife Bridgeta. I told him I didn't think there was a woman in the world, besides myself, who bore that name——"

" Did he say her name was *Bridgeta?* Why, he told me her name was *Anna.*"

" Why, the hypocritical, lying scoundrel! I'll make brother John cut his ears off at sight, if he prove to be the villian I fear he is."

Brother John, nor brother David, will ever get sight of him."

" Well, if he has taken my best horse, and choused me out of three hundred dollars, I'll spend a thousand dollars but what I'll bring him to justice."

" Well, now, Mrs. Glib, we have both been imposed upon ; our best way will be to keep the whole matter to ourselves."

" No ; I am determined to expose him, and to seek legal redress. I can't sit down quietly under a loss of a fine horse, and three hundred dollars, without making some effort to save them. Let people say what they may, I'll try and get hold of this rice plantation at least."

" Believe me, that story about the rice plantation is all a fabrication. Did he tell you about the fund that he got by his dear Bridgeta ?"

" Oh, yes. It amounted to what he called the insignificant sum of ten or twelve thousand dollars, and was held sacred, and all that rigmarole ; which, he said, nobody in the world knew about, but me; and which he didn't wish to have known."

" Precisely what he told me !"

"The infamous rascal! If I was near him, I'd claw his eyes out. I'll pursue him to the end of the earth but what I'll have satisfaction!" So saying she left in a great hurry and a great flurry.

In a few days, Mr. Sanders arrived. His report was that Twattle had two wives then living, whose property he had squandered. That he had courted many widows and old maids, all of whom he had fleeced to a greater or less extent; and some of whom he had treated even worse. That his title of *Doctor* was assumed by himself for purposes of villainy. That he passed under every given name that "J" would suit; with much more that need not be repeated.

Captain Thompson recovered rapidly after Mr. Sanders' letter reached the village. As soon as the latter had told his story, the Captain visited his sister, whom he saluted very pleasantly.

"Well, sister, have you heard Doctor Twattle's history?"

"As much of it as I wish to hear of."

"When does the wedding come off?"

"When men cease to be scoundrels."

"But surely you don't think ' *Good Doctor Twattle* ' a scoundrel; you, who know him so much better than any body else knows him."

"Well, brother David, if you men will be such infamous, hypocritical, lying villains, how are we women to find it out?"

A very proper question, Mrs. Mitten! We can excuse Captain Thompson for a little raillery, under the circumstances; but we cannot excuse the indifference of mankind generally to the iniquities of men, and their want of charity for the errors and weaknesses of women. Many a man in high life is in the daily commission of crimes which would blast a woman's reputation forever! By what law is this distinction made between the sexes?

How comes it to pass, that men are not only indulged in their own dereliction from virtue, but in laying siege to the virtue of the better sex? And why is man allowed to avail himself of the most lovely traits of woman's character—her warm affections, her unsuspecting confidence, her generous hospitality, her admiration of what is noble in human nature, and attractive in human conduct—to ruin or to swindle her? If there be no better world than this, where more even-handed justice is meted out, than this, God help the women! But to return from this digression—

Mrs. Mitten's question stumped the Captain, and he turned the subject:

"And what are you going to do with William, now?" said he.

"Heaven only knows, brother David. I regret my vow not to send him to Mr. Markham; but it is out, and I must keep it."

The Captain tried to convince her that her vow was not binding, but without effect. Fortunately, a young man of liberal education and good character opened a school in the village, within three days after Twattle left, and William was sent to school to him.

William had just got into his new quarters, when the Captain visited his sister, bearing with him a letter from the Post Office, to her address.

"Anna," said he, as he entered the house, "did you lend Twattle two hundred and fifty dollars before he went away?"

"Yes," said she, blushing blue, "but I've got his note."

"Oh, well, if you've got his *note*, that will make you just as safe as if you had got his tooth-pick. I do hope I'll come across the scoundrel yet, before I die. You would do well to set down and calculate how much your tenderness for Bill's legs have cost you in actual cash, to say nothing of trouble. Who is your letter from?"

She opened and read as follows:

AUGUSTA, March 4th, 18—

"*Mrs. A. Mitten:*

"Having recently understood that you have procured a private teacher, we have ventured to stop your advertisement, *though ordered to continue it untill forbid*, under the impression that you have probably forgotten to have it stopped. If, however, we have been misinformed, we will promptly resume the publication of it. You will find our account below; which as we are much in want of funds, you will oblige us by settling as soon as convenient. Hoping your teacher is all that you could desire in one,

"We remain, your ob't. serv'ts,

"H—— & B——"

"*Mrs. A. Mitten to Augusta Herald, Dr.*

"18—
"Mar'. 4th.   To 47 insertions of advertisement for private teacher from Mar. 4, 18——, to date, $1.00 for the first, and 75 cents each, for the remainder, ... $35 50

"*Rec'd payment.*"

"Why, brother," said Mrs. M., as she closed the letter, "I can't surely be compelled to pay this bill, which has been running on for nine months after I got my teacher."

"Yes you can, sister; unless the stoppage of it in the village paper, where it first appeared, required them, by the custom of printers, to stop it. I stopt it here as soon as you got Twattle; but I know nothing of this advertisement; and don't remember seeing any order, through this paper, to other papers to publish it."

" No, I wrote to H. & B. to publish it in the Herald, and to Dr. C. to publish it in the Argus."

" Well, you'll have to pay both for publishing it until you order it stopped. So put down seventy or eighty dollars more to account of love for Bill's legs; and then hang him up by the legs, and whip his back for a week, if you'll allow nobody else to do it."

" Brother, how have you taken such a prejudice against my poor, unfortunate child? If you'd talk to him kindly, and advise him, I have no doubt he would do well; for he loves and fears you, both."

" No, Anna; if you had let him follow my advice when he wished to do it, he would ever after have done it, and in the end he would have been an honor to the country; but he won't follow it now."

" Well, brother, after all, I don't see that he is so very bad."

" Well, I know him to be very bad from men who would not deceive me."

" I've very little confidence *in men.*"

" So have I; but there are some honest ones among them; and even dishonest ones may be trusted when they tell of bad boys who infest the village. I will go and stop the advertisement in the Argus; and much as I sympathize with you, and regret your losses, I am so rejoiced at the escape you have made from the clutches of that rascal, and the ruin that threatened you, that they seem to me almost nothing. It looks to me as if a kind Providence had interfered in your behalf."

" I have no doubt of it, brother; and I wish I could see you putting your trust in Providence more than you do. I will endeavor to live better than I have ever lived, do better than I have ever done, and be more humble, than I have ever been for the balance of my life."

" Why, as to that matter, Anna, I don't see how you are to get any better than you are. I wish I was half as good in moral character as you are. Even your " faults lean to virtue's side"—but like all women, you let your feelings get the better of your good judgment. Your difficulties all spring out of your affections, which blind you to defects in the objects of them, and make you the easy dupe of men, women, and children, whom you love——. Why do you weep? Now is the time you ought to rejoice——. I've left my pocket handkerchief at home—Good morning. I'll stop the advertisement, and pay up both bills for you, and talk to William. He may do well at the new school. Young Smith, his teacher, seems to be a fine young man, and——good morning."

CHAPTER VI.

WE left William Mitten just after his introduction to Mr. Cosby Smith, his fourth teacher. Smith, but recently from college, and coming in competition with Mr. Markham, of course, did not receive much patronage, though few men of his age better deserved patronage than he did. He commenced with sixteen scholars, a fourth of whom were entered by Mrs. Glib and Mrs. Mitten. William, without trouble, and with little study, went immediately to the head of this school ; and he went there only to breed trouble to his teacher, and mischief, vice, and insubordination among his schoolmates. Of all the pests that can be thrown into a school, the smart boy, without a rival in it for talents, and without principle, is the greatest. His talents give a charm to his vices which is irresistible to most of his young companions. School-boys make too little distinction between virtue and vice, anyhow. They never seem to think that their own character is involved in their association with the wicked ; nor that they are under any obligation to discountenance sin, in any of its forms, provided it does not invade their own rights. Hence, the vicious are admitted to all the rights, privileges, and immunities of the little republic, as fully and freely as the most virtuous. Look at the students of a school on the playground—mark their intercourse with each other generally, and you will find it impossible to discover from their conduct which of them stands highest, or which stands lowest, in point of moral character. But you will not find much difficulty in discovering who are the master-spirits among them in their studies. To these there is a marked deference and respect shown, even in their sports. For the most part, their word is law, and whether it be on the side of good or evil, it is equally authoritative. What can be worse than such lawgivers, when their hearts are constantly set on mischief!

For some months before William had entered this school, his applications to his mother, for money, had become alarmingly frequent ; but he always quieted her alarms by representing to her that the funds desired were for some benevolent, or praiseworthy object. His representations brought from her many excellent lectures upon indi-

scriminate charities, and the danger to which his benevolent nature
was exposed from imposters and worthless vagrants, who choose
rather to beg than to work—to which he generally gave substantial-
ly the same reply, namely, "that he was always very particular in
seeing who he gave his money to." In this he told the truth, at
least, since he generally gave his money to one of the Glibs, whom
he had become very particular in seeing too frequently at the card-
table. He had been at Smith's school but a few months, before
the fountains of his charity suddenly dried up; and what may seem
very strange to some, dried up just as he began to acquire the means
of more enlarged benevolence. His growing fortune first exhibited
itself in a profusion of pen-knives, which he carried about him, from
the most costly and elegant down to the cheapest and most worthless
kind.

"William," said his mother, "where do you get those elegant
pen-knives?"

"This one was given to me by Mr. Jones; and this one I found;
and this one was given to me by one of the school-boys." William
did not show his mother his whole assortment, by three or four.

"I hope, my son, that these gifts are but just returns for the many
acts of charity which you have recently done to the poor. One
never loses anything in the end by this kind of charity; but you
should have excused yourself from accepting the last, on the ground
that you had two elegant knives already; and that your young
friend needed it more than you did."

"I did tell him so; but he said I must take it to remember
him by."

"Well, my son, put that away as a sacred keepsake, and never
use it but in case of necessity."

The next signs which William exhibited of his growing fortune,
were books, fishing-poles, shinny-sticks, bunches of quills, breast-
pins, and cakes of divers kinds.

"William," said his mother, "where did you get those articles?"

"They were given to me by the boys for doing their sums for
them; and taking them over their lessons—"

"Oh my son! my son! You surely did not take pay for these
little kindnesses, from your school fellows! I am ashamed of you—
deeply mortified. Where did you learn that groveling sordid spirit?
I would rather have given you twenty dollars, to buy all these things
than to have seen you guilty of such ignoble acts."

"Well, Ma, I didn't wish to take 'em; but they would make me take them."

"No matter what they said, you should not have received them. *As a gift* you might have taken them; but as a *reward* for such little favors as these to your young friends, you should have rejected them."

These were new lights to William; for he thought his mother would be delighted to hear of his superiority over his schoolmates, and that he was already turning his talents to good account.

"And where did you get the two breast-pins?"

"I sold one of my pen-knives, and bought this."

"Not the one, I hope, that your friend gave you "

"Oh, no ma'am; the one I found!"

"Why, William, you surely have not sold a *found* knife! It was not your property, but the property of him who lost it; and you should have kept it, to restore it to him as soon as he could be discovered; and you should have used your best exertions to find the owner, in order that you might restore it to him. I am deeply mortified at this act of yours; and if you have any regard for my feelings, or your character, never do the like again. It alarms me, and pains me deeply to discover such principles in you. Where did you learn them? Not from any who carries the blood of your father or mother in his veins, I am sure. I fear your intimacy with the Glibs is ruining you. Nothing but dire necessity could have induced me to put you to the same school with them; but I charge you, as I have often charged you before, to have as little to do with them as possible."

"Where did you get the other breast-pin?"

William was saved a great deal of trouble and mortification in answering this question, by an exclamation of his sister Jane, who no sooner cast her eyes upon the breast-pin, than she exclaimed: "Why, Ma, that is Flora Glib's breast-pin. Let me look at it William, yes, here are her initials on it: *F. C. L. G.—Flora Claudia Lavinia Glib*. I knew it as soon as I saw it; for I have seen her wear it a hundred times."

"William!" ejaculated his mother, with manifest alarm and indignation, "where did you get that pin?"

"Jeff. Glib gave it to me!"

"Go immediately to him, and return it; and tell him to give it back to his sister."

The truth of the matter is that William had made such rapid im-

E

provement in card-playing, that he had become an over-match for
the Glibs, and he was now indoctrinating as many of his school-
mates into the mysteries of the card table as he could find willing to
become his pupils ; and for the reasons already given, he found nearly
the whole school ready to take lessons from him. Most of his articles of merchandize, (and we have not named all of them) were the
fruits of. his industry in this department of science ; though some of
them were, as he said, rewards for his better services to his fellow
students. It would have been bad enough, had his evil influence
stopt here ; but it did not. He had already become mean enough to
tempt his school-fellows to sin in a hundred forms ; and artful
enough to put them always forward to the post of danger in the
commission of it. The consequence was, that, while he got the
booty, they got the floggings and disgrace.

The iniquities of the school were most unrighteously visited upon
the head of the preceptor, who, at the end of year, was compelled
to quit the village, for want of patronage.

. "And what," said Captain Thompson, to his sister, "are you
going to do with your hopeful son now, Anna ?"

"Heaven only knows ! I fear he will bring my grey hairs with
sorrow to the grave. Brother David, why do you not talk to him ?"

"Talk, the devil ! I have talked to him, in all ways that I
can think of ; and what good does it do ? He has got so of late
that when I talk to him I can hardly keep my hands off of him. I
can see in the looks and actions of the young rascal, that nothing
but fear keeps him from laughing outright in my face."

"Oh, brother, I think you judge him too harshly. I know he has
got into bad habits ; but still, I am sure he respects and loves you."

"And he respects and loves you, too, don't he ?"

"He must be a brute if he does not."

"Well I suppose he does love you ; but I assure you he cares no
more for your counsels than he does for mine ; and that hardly a day
goes over his head that he does not practice some deception upon
you."

"There, brother, I think you judge him a little too hardly again.
. He generally does what I tell him."

"Well, tell him to quit playing cards, pilfering from gardens and
orchards, cursing and swearing, smoking segars, drinking spirits,
frequenting kitch—

"Oh, mercy on me, brother David ! what enemy of my child has
filled your ears with these calumnies ? He is bad enough, I know,

but he is not a devil yet. I cannot believe he is near as base as you represent him to be."

"Very well; what are you going to do with him?"

"I do not know. Will you take him under your charge? for I confess I fear he is getting into bad habits."

"Yes, I'll take him, and clothe him and feed him at my own expense, if you will only give me your word that you will not interfere with my management of him. Will you do it? If you will, I'll perhaps save your boy from ruin and you from a broken heart."

"Where would you send him to school?, To Mr. Markham?"

"I should prefer him; but as I know you object to him, I will engage that Bill shall not be sent to Markham. Indeed, he must be got out of this place; or forty bushels of salt, and as many pounds of saltpetre wouldn't save him. I'll send him to Mr. Waddel. He'll fetch him straight."

"I'm told Mr. Waddel is very severe."

"Not a whit more than he ought to be, I'll warrant you. I am told his pupils generally like him, and improve wonderfully under him. Now, Anna, if I take him, remember the terms. You are to have nothing to do with him. You surely ought to know, that I can have no object in taking charge of him, but his good and your peace.

If, therefore, my conduct seems unkind, or severe to him, don't let your maternal partialities lead you to interfere in any manner with my authority over him. By this time, you are surely convinced of the utter futility of your mode of managing him, and that if some new course of discipline be not adopted towards him, he will bring himself and you to an untimely grave. You must not only make up your mind to give me unlimited control over him, during his pupilage, but you must pledge me your word, that you will show me every letter that he writes to you during his absence from you at school, or I will have nothing to do with him. Why do you weep, Anna?"

"Brother," said Mrs. M., "it is a hard thing for a mother to wean herself from her own child—to tear him from her bosom, and hand him over as property to another. I know, my dear brother, that your intentions are good—that you have the interests of my child deeply at heart, and that all your aims are for his good and mine; but I fear that you have so often been provoked by William, and have become so prejudiced and embittered against him, that you cannot judge of his conduct impartially, you cannot make the due allowances for his faults, and that you will lean as much too far on the side of severity in your government as I have leaned on the side of lenity in mine. Why cannot you act a father's part by him, without usurping exclusive authority over him ?"

"I had a long answer to what you have said, Anna; but your last remark suggests a very brief one, which I think is conclusive. Now all I ask is that you put me exactly in his father's place. Had his father lived, he would have exercised absolute authority over William in all matters touching his education. He would have demanded— or rather you would have freely granted to him, the perusal of all your son's letters to you. In all else you would have ruled the boy conjointly. Now, give me the absolute control of him in the matter of his education, let me see his letters to you, and in all else you shall have unlimited control of him. I need not tell you why I exact these terms of you. They are indispensable to the proper management of your son."

This reply brought Mrs. Mitten to a dead silence; and while she was pondering upon it, very opportunely for its success, in steps Master William, with his beautiful face "pretty considerably" disfigured with bruises and scratches.

"Why, William!" exclaimed his mother, almost at the fainting point, "who upon the earth has treated you in that manner ?"

"Jim Fox," muttered William.

"What did you fight about ?"

"We were *playing* and he got mad, and insulted me, and I struck him."

This was strictly true, but not quite the whole truth. The *playing* was *with cards*, and the *insult* was, "*Bill Mitten, you're the biggest cheat that ever played a card in this town.*"

Captain Thompson said nothing, peradventure, he might at this critical period strengthen his sister's convictions that he was unduly prejudiced and embittered against her son. With the promise to call the next day for her decision upon his proposition, he left rather abruptly.

As soon as he retired, Mrs. M. addressed her son as follows : "William, I'll have to send you away from this village, or wicked associates will be the ruin of you. I find that it is vain to counsel you against keeping bad company, and the only alternative left me is to remove you from it. I have concluded, therefore, to send you to school to Mr. Waddel, an excellent——"

"I'll not go," said Billy, crustily.

This was Bill's first indication, when sober, of open revolt against the authority of his mother, and she met it with becoming spirit.

"Well, sir," said she, "I see you are getting too stout for my government, and, therefore, I will turn you over to your uncle, and see whether he cannot make you go. Now, sir, my word is out, and you know I'll keep it."

"Ma," said William, in a subdued tone, "I'll go any where else but to Mr. Waddel's school. Everybody says that he is the severest man that ever kept a school. He whips boys just for the fun of it, for he laughs all the time he's doing it. You know Uncle David hates me, and he'll put me there just to have me whipped."

"No, William, it is unreasonable to suppose that any man can take pleasure in punishing his pupils. Mr. Waddel's school has a high reputation, which it could not have if he were the man you take him to be. Your uncle does not hate you; but the town keeps him constantly excited with reports of your misdeeds, and, therefore, he sometimes seems cross to you; but he has a kind heart, and desires nothing more than my happiness and your good. Oh! that I had followed his advice sooner!"

"Well, Uncle may take me to Mr. Waddel's, but he'll not keep me there; for I'll run away and come home as soon as his back's turned."

"That matter, sir, I'll leave to be settled between you and him."

Here William saddened and wept; and his mother did likewise.

The next day the articles proposed were agreed to, without qualification, save as to expenses of clothing and tuition, which were to fall on the mother.

CHAPTER VII.

THE articles of capitulation having been ratified, as mentioned in the last chapter, the Captain was anxious to set out immediately with William, for Mr. Waddel's school; but Mrs. Mitten declared that it would be impossible to prepare a suitable outfit for her son, short of a fortnight. "Remember," said she with a filling eye, "my poor child is going among strangers, where he will find none to make or mend for him. He is to be gone at least five months, even if you will permit him to come home in the vacation; or if you will not, then for a year, or it may be"—here Mrs. Mitten's swelling heart stifled utterance. The Captain regarded her for a moment in silence, in thoughtfulness, in petulance, in pity, and then said: "Well, if there be a stranger thing on this green earth than a woman, I should like to know what it is—at least a woman with a smart, pretty, good-for-nothing son. I thought if there was anything in this world that I did know, it was my own sister; but I find that I know nothing about her. A woman! Let her be as good, as sensible, as amiable as she may be, and give her a child, and forthwith her head is turned topsy-turvey. She is as blind to her child's faults as a bat, and she mistrusts everybody who is not as blind to them as she is. I have come to the conclusion that a woman may have a soul before she has a child, but never afterwards—that is, a sound one—a rational one. After that, all is impulse or instinct with her—at least, in all that touches her offspring. She may have a thousand proofs that her indulgence is ruining her child, and she will indulge him still. She will believe him before she will believe any one else; and when his iniquities stand broadly out before her face, she will find an apology for them all. He is '*unfortunate,*' or '*he has been tempted to vice by bad company,*' or '*he is slandered,*' or '*he is the victim of envy,*' or '*prejudice,*' or——"

"Why, dear me, brother David, I don't see what I've said or done to call forth this harangue."

"Why, you are talking and acting just as though I had taken your child from you by force, and meant to afflict him in all forms possible. '*If you will permit* him to come home in vacation, and *if not.*' Do you suppose that I ever dreamed of keeping him away from you during the holidays? Do you suppose that I take charge of him only to torment him?"

"My dear brother, don't be angry with me. I had not the most distant idea of offending you in what I said. I never questioned for a moment your kindly feelings towards me and my child; but have some charity for a mother's love—*folly*, if you choose to call it so. I never was separated from William a fortnight in my.life. He is not *torn* from me, but he is *taken* from me—with my consent—necessarily, I grant, but it is a sore necessity. He is to be carried among strangers, to be treated, I know not how. If sick, to suffer for a mother's care—at least for a time—perchance to die for the want of it. Now, when all these things crowd upon a mother's heart, is it wonderful that it should be depressed?"

"I am not angry with you, Anna, that is—I—believe I am not. I know I don't wish to be; but I am amazed at your want of firmness, your want of resignation to necessities; your surrender of judgment to feeling; your patience under present evils; and your distress at imaginary ones. I am alarmed at the intimations you already give, of the speedy blowing up of our arrangement—not from a breach of your pledge, but from your anxieties, your griefs, your fears, your yearning to be with your son, which will leave me no alternative but to restore him to you, or to see you waste away under their continual corrodings. I pray you nerve yourself up to the exigencies of the case. That William can stay no longer here, you know. That he is in the broad road to ruin here, I know, and you ought to know. That he is getting beyond your control you confess, and in a little time he will be beyond mine. Now, think of these things, and let them reconcile you to any unpleasant issues of our new arrangement. Let this reflection quiet, or at least solace all future anxieties about your son. ' *It is impossible for things to be worse than they are.*' Be cheerful, at least till evils come, and bear them with fortitude when they do come."

Mrs. Mitten promised to do her best, and the Captain continued:

"Don't consume time in gathering up an extensive wardrobe for your son. Let us get him out of this place as soon as possible; for he is rotting here faster than a dead rat in August——"

"Oh, *brother!* How can you speak of your sister's child in that way?"

"Well, I would have used a more delicate comparison, *for your sake*, if I had thought of it; but as for Bill—however, get him ready as soon as you can. A few changes of apparel is all that he needs; and let them be plain and stout. Waddel's school is in the woods, where nobody sees, and nobody cares how the boys are dressed. It is made up, I hear, principally of hardy rustic youths, most of whom, probably, never had a broadcloth coat, a linen shirt, or a pair of store-stockings on in their lives. If therefore, you send your son among them, dressed out in fine clothes, you will expose him to ridicule from his young companions, and to other petty annoyances, which will give him a distaste for the place even greater than he now has. Better for you, and for him, that his clothing be cheap, plain, and durable." Mrs. Mitten promised to get him ready as soon as she could, and the Captain left her.

In the meantime, William behaved himself uncommonly well. He was too much saddened by the prospect before him to relish either amusements or books. He spent most of his time at home in deep despondency; for as soon as it was noised abroad that William Mitten was going to Waddel's school, the reports of Waddel's severities doubled in number, and quadrupled in exaggeration. Any one, to have heard them, as passed among the young ones of the village, might have supposed that he fried a pair of little boys for breakfast, and roasted a big one for dinner every day.

William had heard these reports in all their variations, and they filled him with horror. His mother offered him encouragements with the tongue, but discouragements with the eye, every day, the last, of course, neutralized the first. After twelve days of preparation, Mrs. Mitten informed her brother that William would be ready to take his departure the next day. The Captain visited his sister that night, to make all preliminary arrangements for the commencement of the journey, early the next morning. He found the family alone, for the hour of William's departure had been purposely kept secret, to avoid the intrusion of visitors on this solemn evening. They were all seated around the fire silent and dejected. On the candle-stand, by the mother's side, lay the family Bible open—next to her, in the order of their ages, sat the two daughters, and William rested his drooping head upon the pillar of the mantle-piece. The servants stood around, with their eyes fixed upon him, as if for the last time. They had all just risen from prayers, hurried a little from fear of interruption. The tears which from every eye had accompanied the mother's devotion, had just ceased to flow. A death-like silence reigned throughout the group, broken only by sighs more or less heavy, as they rose from hearts more or less depressed. As the Captain entered, all burst into tears afresh.

"What!" said he, with a feigned indifference to the scene, which he did not feel, "All this mourning at sending a little shaver to school!"

The Captain was not a religious man, but *he was almost persuaded to be a christian;* and the sight of his sister at prayer always inspired him with an instinctive philosophy upon "souls," much more impressive, if not more rational, than the impulsive philosophy which he had recently delivered. He glanced his eye to the candle stand, and took his seat in the circle as mute as the mutest. A minute or more elapsed before another word was spoken; and the first, to the surprise of all, fell from William.

"Uncle," said he, in a grief-stricken, faltering voice, "Uncle—you can—save me—from going to Mr. Waddel's school, if you will. It isn't too late yet—If you *please*, Uncle, don't send me there—I'll go any where else in the world that you choose to send me, and not complain. If you will only not send me to that school, I never will disobey you, or Ma again. I know I've done wrong"—Here the elder sister interposed, kneeling: "Oh, my dear Uncle, you cannot, you will not, resist that—no, your streaming eyes tell me you will not—here on my knees before you, I beg you, I implore you"—"And I, Uncle," said the younger, dropping by her sister's side, "We both beseech you for our dear, our only brother. Why that school, in preference to all other schools in the world?——"

"Girls be seated!" said the Captain; and they obeyed him.

A long pause in the conversation emboldened even the servants to drop a word in William's behalf.

There was but one of the group who did not; and she felt more than all of them together. Under circumstances so trivial, no poor heart ever ran through such a hurricane of turbulent emotions in a few short moments, as did hers. She had never seen her child so moved by fear before. She had never seen him an humble suppliant before; and now, it was to her substitute, not to her! She had never heard such accents of humility and contrition from his lips before. She had hardly ever before seen the manly cheek of her brother moistened with a tear, and never hoped to see it, by the eloquence of her boy. Long sinking hopes rose buoyantly from the scene before her; she "would yet see her first anticipations from her gifted son fully realized"—"her brother's censures would soon be turned into praises; his roughness, to kindness." Anxiety crowded in upon hope—anxiety for the issue of her son's appeal. If successful, "what then? where then?" Alarms pressed upon anxiety. "If he is foiled in this appeal, will he ever make another—will he not be driven to desperation?"

All these conflicting emotions she bore with marvelous composure;

but when the first words of her brother's response fell upon her ear : "God bless you, my dear, dear orphan boy !" her self command entirely forsook her. She crossed her arms upon her Bible, dropt her head upon them, cried "Amen! and Amen!" and sobbed convulsively, loud and long.

"God bless you, my dear, dear orphan boy," said the Captain, "you are now in the right way, my son, and while you walk therein your Uncle will be a father to you—he will love you, he will serve you, he will do any and everything that he can, to make you happy. If he deny you anything, be sure it is for your own good. And now, if you or your Mother will tell me what other teacher I can send you to, with any hope of having you well instructed, and your morals well guarded, I will not send you to Mr. Waddel."

"Can't you send me back to Mr. Markham ?"

"Well, come, your Mother shall answer that question for me."

"In an evil hour, son, I vowed you should never go back to Mr. Markham," said the mother.

"Well, Anna," continued the Captain, "in the present state of things, I think you are released from that vow; but supposing yourself entirely released from it, would you be willing to keep William longer in this town at any school ?"

"Well, as he is penitent, and promises amendment, if I could feel myself free from my vow, I believe I would be willing to see him return to Mr. Markham. But it is not worth while to discuss this subject; I cannot feel myself released from my vow. It is known all over the village, and nobody will believe you put him there without my consent; and every body will think I pretended to turn William over to you, just to shuffle out of my vow. Be this as it may, my conscience is involved in the matter, and I am not going to expose it to any nice questions. If I err at all, let me err on the safe side. I therefore, give no consent to his going to Mr. Markham, and I would rather that you should not expose me to the suspicion of having given my consent to it."

"Well, William," resumed the Captain, "that door's closed. Now, hear me, my son. Don't you remember how sorry you were that I did not have my way with you when you were taken from Mr. Markham? Well, just so it will be by and by, if I do not have my way with you now. You must get away from the bad boys of this town. Haven't they often tempted you to do what you had fully resolved not to do?"

"Yes, sir."

"Now, I know you think you will never be led away by them again, if I let you stay here; but you will be as you have been. You have been alarmed by false and foolish reports about Mr. Waddel's severity and cruelty. If they were true, his school could not be as celebrated as it is. He could not have the number of scholars he has. I am told he has largely over a hundred scholars, some of them the sons of the first men in the State, and that thousands of people from far and near attend his exhibitions. If you'll go there, and get a premium (as I know you can, if you will,) it will be worth having. It will be heard of in two or three States. Come, son, try Uncle's advice this one time. All things are ready now—the time appointed for us to go—if we let it slip, you'll be here doing nothing and worse than nothing, for I know not how long. Cheer up, my boy; you can surely stand a school of such renown, and if you will do your best, you will stand ahead of these big men's sons. Now, what say you, son; will you go or not?"

"I'll go, Uncle," said William, with a promptness and a firmness that astonished all present.

"That's a fine fellow," said the Captain. "I wouldn't take a thousand dollars for my part in you, this day."

William's decision was conclusive upon the family; and the Mother felt herself in duty bound not to disturb it by word, action, or look. She therefore assumed to be pleased, though she was so confident of William's entire and radical reform, from what had just passed before her, that she would have preferred Markham to Waddel, if conscience had been out of the way.

"Anna," said the Captain, "Mary" (his wife,) "and the children will come over with me in the morning to bid William good-bye, and Mary will spend the day with you. I shall be here with the chaise, after an early breakfast, and let all things be ready."

The Captain had anticipated some such scene as that which he had just passed through, and to lighten the burden of it, he would not allow his family to accompany him that night.

CHAPTER VIII

THE eventful morning came, and at an early hour Captain Thompson's chaise was at his sister's door. His family had anticipated his advent some eight or ten minutes. Tom came out to hold his horse, while he went in. "No, I won't light, Tom," said he. "Go and bring out William's trunk, and let us be off, for we have no time to lose." The Captain had no idea of witnessing the parting scene. He waited and shivered for it was cold. "Come on, William, my brave boy—come on; we've a long road and a bad road to travel;" bawled out the Captain to the vacant entry.

No response came, but sobs and blowing of noses.

"Tom ! Tom !" cried the Captain.

Tom was waiting his turn to bid " mas' William " good-by, and mingling his tears with those of the two families, of course, he had forgotten the trunk. The wind began to rise a little, and the Captain began to backslide rapidly from his conversion of the evening before.

"John !" cried the Captain. No answer.

"Sal !" " Lotty !" "Nance !"

They were all around "mas' William;" nothing doubting but that the saturnal of the preceding evening would be extended to the catastrophe of the occurrence which produced it. The wind rose a little higher, and the Captain's impatience rose a great deal higher. At length, it gave way entirely; and, lighting from the vehicle, he bolted into the mourning-hall, with a step, and a tongue, and a passion, exceedingly unbecoming the solemnities of the occasion, and exceedingly opposite to his recent experience. The first object that met his eye was Tom, repeating precisely the part he played the night before, when the Captain was so much affected, i. e. with swimming eyes, and mellowed heart, contemplating William. "You black rascal," vociferated the Captain; "what do you stand sniveling here for ? (John, go to my horse !") Didn't I order you to bring out the trunk?"

" Kigh, mas' David !" said Tom, retiring a little briskly; " Nigger got feeling well as white folks !" You feel, too, sometimes."

" You impertinent scoundrel ! if you aint off for that trunk pretty quick, I'll make you *feel* worse than white folks."

There was a lurking comparison in this reply of Tom, between

himself and "mas' David," decidedly favorable to himself; and a
plain intimation in it that he regarded the Captain as a clear case of
apostacy or inconsistency. But the Captain was in too great a hurry
to analyze, argue, or resent. "I have been out there for a quarter
of an hour," continued he, "freezing, and bawling, and squalling
for every negro on the plantation, and not one could I find."
(*Exeunt blacks, as from patrol.*) "I have now hardly time to reach
old Smith's, before night; and to be caught in the night, on such
roads, will be awful. Anna, is William ready?"

"Just a moment, brother, till I tie this handkerchief over his ears;
the weather's bitter cold."

While the Captain was awaiting this process, ten distinct thumps
from the stair-case fell upon his ear, and then a harsh, raking sound
of terrible import, when Tom announced: "Here's the trunk, mas'
David." The Captain turned, and beheld one of the biggest trunks
of the day. He ran to it and *hefted* it, as the Yankees say, and
grunted furiously.

"Anna," said he, "that trunk can't go on the chaise—it's impossible."

"It is the very smallest I could get to hold the boy's things,
brother."

"What have you got in it?"

"Nothing, but William's clothes, and a few little nick-knacks."

"Well, you'll have to divide them, and put them in two small
trunks—one to be lashed on behind, and the other to go in the foot;
and it's a pretty time to begin that work!"

The Captain was too snappish to be reasoned with; so, by contributions from the girls, the small trunks were soon furnished, and the
unpacking and re-packing commenced.

We will not detain the reader with a detail of the wardrobe. Suffice it to say, that after stopping *in transitu* three shirts, three pair
of stockings, two under-shirts, one full winter suit, and two summer
suits, the Captain saw the two small trunks filled to their utmost capacity with hard pressing; and yet there was a thin layer of clothing
on the ceiling of the basement story of the large trunk; we must
explain. Mrs. Mitten, with Tom's help had placed two blocks of
wood in the bottom of the trunk, upon which she laid a nice, clean,
thin white-pine board, that was so neatly adjusted to the measure of
the trunk, that it divided it into two apartments. The board was
lifted, and disclosed one pound cake, one dozen sugar-biscuits, one
ditto doughnuts, two pounds raisins, two ditto almonds, (shelled,) one
ditto prunes, with chinking of sugar-plums innumerable.

" William, son," said his mother, " I reckon you'll have to leave these; I don't know how you can carry them."

' It seemed to be a hopeless case to all, and Bill surrendered with a long deep sigh, which touched the Captain's heart a little; and casting his eyes to William, who looked like a week's washing of clothes piled together, he said, with a slight smirk : " There's nothing in the chaise-box but a snack, and a little bundle of under-clothing for myself; you can put as many of these things in that as it will hold; but be quick about it !"

This was refreshing. It was regarded as a full atonement for all the petulance, impatience, and crustiness that the Captain had exhibited. One of the girls bounced into the chaise; and by the aid of the rest of the company, she was soon enabled to stow away in the box a goodly portion of all the varieties of nick-knacks just mentioned. In the meantime the trunks took their places, the final kisses were disposed of, and a minute more found the Captain and William on their way. Nothing of special interest occurred on the journey. The Captain gave William much encouragement and good advice, and fretted a little at having to travel a half hour in the night to make his first stage, but, as no accident occurred, he was easily reconciled to it. Four o'clock the next day (Saturday,) found them at the public house, or rather boarding house, of Mr. Nelson Newby, Abbeville District, South Carolina. It was a rude log-house, with two rooms, about sixteen feet square each, and an entry nearly as large, between them. In the rear of it was another building of the same material, somewhat shorter and narrower than the first. This was the dining room. Six or seven small edifices of the same kind scattered around, with little order, served as students' lodges. A rail fence (or rather the remains of one,) three feet high, enclosed the whole. About twenty boys of various sizes, were busily engaged in cutting, splitting, and piling wood, at the doors of their respective tenements—the roughest looking set of students that ever repeated the notes of Homer and Virgil since the world began. The prospect looked gloomy, even to the Captain, and terrific to William.

" Uncle," whispered he, " these can't be big people's sons !"

" Well—don't know—they're pretty rough looking fellows—but —they seem to be very industrious boys." Poor comfort to William. The Captain and his landlord, of course, soon became acquainted; and the first expressing a wish to see Mr. Waddel, the last kindly offered to escort him to the teacher's residence. .

" It is not far out of the way to go by the Academy; would you like to see it ?" said Mr. Newby.

"Very much," replied the Captain.

They set forward, and at the distance of about two hundred and fifty yards from Mr. Newby's premises, they entered a street, shaded by majestic oaks, and composed entirely of log huts, varying in size from six to sixteen feet square. The truth of history demands that we should say, that there was but one of the smallest size just indicated, and that was the whimsical structure of a very whimsical fellow, by the name of Dredzel Pace. It was endangered from fire once, and *four* stout students took it up by the corners, and removed it to a place of safety.

The street was about forty yards wide, and its length was perhaps double its width; and yet the houses on either side did not number more than ten or twelve; of course, therefore they stood generally in very open order. They were all built by the students themselves, or by architects of their hiring. They served for study-houses in cold or rainy weather, though the students were allowed to study where they pleased within convenient reach of the monitors. The common price of a building, on *front row*, water proof, and easily chinked, was five dollars—the chinking was generally removed in summer for ventilation. In the suburbs, were several other buildings of the same kind, erected by literary recluses, we suppose, who could not endure the din of the city at play-time—*at play-time* we say, for there was no din in it in study hours. At the head of the street, eastward, stood the Academy, differing in nothing from the other buildings but in size and the number of its rooms. It had two; the smaller devoted to a primary school of a few boys and girls, over which Moses Waddel Dobbins, a nephew of the Rector, presided. These soon left, and Mr. Dobbins became assistant-general to his uncle. The larger, was the recitation room of Mr. Waddel himself, the prayer room, court room, (see *infra*) and general convocation room for all matters concerning the school. It was without seats, and just large enough to contain one hundred and fifty boys standing erect, close pressed, and leave a circle of six feet diameter at the door, for jigs and cotillons at the teacher's regular *soirees*, every Monday morning.

A delightful spring gushed from the foot of the hill on which the school-house stood; and at the distance of but a few paces, poured its waters into a lovely brook, which wound through a narrow plain, covered with stately beeches.—Venerable old chroniclers of revered names and happy days, where are ye!—It was under the canopy of these beautiful ornaments of the forest, by the side of that whispering brook, that we felt the first gleam of pleasure that we ever derived from anything in Latin. And here are the words which awakened it:

> " *Tityre tu patulæ recubans sub tegmine fagi,*
> *Silvestrem tenui musam meditaris avena.*"

Our party having taken a hasty survey of these things bent their way to *Castle Carberry.* As they journeyed on, Mr. Newby pointed out the ground over which Sam Shanklin and Mr. Waddel had a notable race. Sam had offended " *Old Moses* " (so he were called, even in his prime which he had now hardly left,) and as the latter approached him whip in hand, Sam, took to his heels, not dreaming that old Moses would follow him. But he was mistaken; he did follow him, and gained upon him at every step, a little—Sam, finding his pursuer too fleet for him sought safety in lofty leaping; so he made for a brush heap. Just as he reached it, old Moses fetched him a wipe upon the legs that energized his activity to unmatchable achievement, and he cleared the brush heap at a bound. Here the race ended. The Captain laughed heartily at the story; but William saw no fun in it.

Castle Carberry stood on the highway leading from Augusta, Georgia, to Abbeville Court House, South Carolina, and about equidistant from Mr. Newby's and the Academy. By whom it was erected, we are not informed; probably, by Samuel Shields, an assistant of Mr. Waddel, who had occupied it for two years, previous to the time of which we are speaking, and who was just now gathering up his goods and chattels for his final departure from the place, and for a much more interesting engagement.* Its name was doubtless derived from Maria Roche's novel—*The Children of the Abby,* which had a great run in that day; but to tell wherein the two Castle Carberry's were alike, would puzzle the greatest conundrumsolver that ever lived. Upon the retirement of Mr. Shields, Alexander B. Linton succeeded to his possessions, and James L. Petigru to his office (not as some have most erroneously supposed, the Mr. Pentigall, of the 'Georgia Scenes,') though it was in this very castle that the great question was discussed: " Whether at public elections should the votes of faction predominate by internal suggestions or the bias of jurisprudence?" Mr. Petigru had been in Columbia College, a year or more before the discussion came off.

Some two or three students always boarded themselves at Castle

---

*He soon after married a young lady of Vienna.

Carberry. It served as a nucleus around which other edifices of like kind and for like purposes gathered, all built of the common material. We think its tenants were, in Mitten's day, Alex. B. Linton, Henry Rasenel, Samuel Weir, and William D. Martin.

At Castle Carberry the promenaders re entered the big road which they had left at Newby's, having now seen all of Willington *proper ;* Willington *common* embraced every house within three miles of the Academy. As they entered the road, a messenger called for Mr. Newby to return home on some special business. He gave the Captain directions to Mr. Waddel's, and returned. The directions were simply to keep the road to the next house. A walk of a quarter of a mile, or a little over, brought the Captain and his charge to the residence of the renowned teacher. It was a comfortable, framed building, two stories high, neatly, but plainly paled in—very rare things in that vicinity.

Some six or eight more boys, like the Newbyites, were differently employed about the premises.

" Do you know, my son," said the Captain, addressing one of them, " whether Mr. Waddel is at home ?"

" Yes sir," said the youth, springing to the door, and opening it, " Walk in, take seats, and I will call him."

He disappeared, and in a moment returned with Mr. Waddel.

" Mr. Waddel, I presume," said the Captain.

" Yes, sir."

" Thompson, sir, is my name, and this is my nephew, William Mitten, whom I have brought to place under your instruction."

" It is rather chilly, here," said the teacher, shaking their hands cordially, " walk into my study, where I have a good fire." Won't you go in, David ?" added he to the guide, who was about retiring.

" No, I thank you, sir, said David.

" That's a sprightly youth," said the Captain, as he moved towards the study, " and he is a namesake of mine."

" Yes," said the teacher, " he is a clever boy—the son of the celebrated Doctor Ramsay."

" What ! Doctor Ramsay, the patriot, statesman, and historian— who married the accomplished daughter of the renowned Henry Laurens, President of the first Congress of the United States, Minister to Holland, and father of the gallant John Laurens, the beloved of Washington ?"

F

This was a clear *splurge** for William's benefit.

"The same," said Mr. Waddel.

"Well, I feel myself honored in bearing the boy's name.

Before this conversation ended, all were seated in the teacher's study. It was crowded with books—partly the teacher's private library—partly, books laid in for the students which he furnished at cost and charges on Philadelphia prices.

"Have you studied Latin, William?" enquired Mr. Waddel.

"Yes, sir."

"How far have you gone?"

"I was reading Virgil, when I quit school."

"Well, I have a large Virgil class, which will be divided on Monday. I have found that some of them are keeping others back; and I have ordered them to get as long a lesson as they can for Monday morning. Those who get the most and recite the best, will be put in one class and the rest in another. Now, you can take either division of this class that you may be found qualified for, or you may enter the *Selectæ* class, which will commence Virgil in two or three months. Meet me at the Academy on Monday morning, and we will see what will be best."

"How many pupils have you, Mr. Waddel?" inquired the Captain.

"About one hundred and fifty."

"Where do they board?"

"Just where they please, among the neighbors around. They all take boarders, and reside at different distances from the academy, varying from a few hundred yards to three miles."

"Have the students to cut and haul their own firewood, and make their own fires?"

"Not always. At some of the boarding houses the landlords have these things done for them, and at all, they may hire servants to perform them, if they will, or, rather, if they can; but, as at every house there is at least a *truck-wagon* and horse at the service of the students, and wood is convenient and abundant, and to be had without stint or charge, they generally supply themselves, and make their own fires."

During this conversation, which from the beginning to end, was of the most alarming interest to William, his eyes wide open, were fixed on Mr. Waddel, who was an object of still more alarming in-

* A splurge is a moral *cavort*. Both are embraced in the generic term, *cutting shines. Ga. Vocab.*

terest to him. He had never seen—we have never seen—a man of sterner features than Mr. Waddel bore. From the time that William entered the house to the time that he left it, "shadows, clouds, and darkness" were gathering and deepening upon his mind; relieved only by one faint gleam of light from young Ramsay, whom he regarded as the concentrated extract of all that was august, and great, and gifted, and good in the United States, if not in the world; and an ample verification *per se* of all that his uncle had told him about " big men's sons."

William was entered in due form a student of Mr. Waddel's school; and the Captain having enquired of the post office at which the students received their letters, and pressed Mr. Waddel to give him early information of William's conduct, standing, and progress, he left with his charge for Mr. Newby's. A long silence ensued. At length it was broken by William.

" Mr. Waddel is the grummest looking man I ever saw."

" Pretty sour," said the Captain. " But I don't reckon he is as bad as he looks to be. The boys seem cheerful around him; and David Ramsay seemed perfectly easy in his presence."

The truth is, the Captain was sore pressed for encouragements himself, and it was the luckiest thing in the world for him that he happened to fall in with young Ramsay just when he did.

" I had an idea," continued the Captain, "of proposing to Mr. Waddel to take you to board with him; but it occurred to me that you might prefer to board somewhere else; and I am perfectly willing to accommodate you in this matter."

" Uncle, I wouldn't board with him for five hundred thousand dollars !"

" Well, my son, I will not place you with him. I think the best way will be for you to board at Mr. Newby's, for the present. After you become acquainted with the other boarding houses, you can take your choice among them."

Silence ensued, which we fill up with a more particular account of Mr. Waddel. As he was made a Doctor of Divinity soon after the time at which we are speaking of him, we will anticipate a little, and call him henceforth *Doctor* Waddel.

He was about five feet nine inches high; of stout muscular frame, and a little inclined to corpulency. In limb, nearly perfect. His head was uncommonly large, and covered with a thick coat of dark hair. His forehead was projecting, and in nothing else more remarkable. His eyes were grey and overshadowed by thick, heavy eye-brows, al-

ways closely knit in his calmest hours, and almost over-lapping in
his angry moods. His nose was bluntly acquiline. His lips were
rather thick, and generally closely compressed. His complexion
was slightly adust. His *tout ensemble* was, as we have said, extremely austere; but it was false to his heart; for'he was benevolent,
affectionate, charitable, hospitable, and kind. He was cheerful, and
even playful, in his disposition. Good boys felt at perfect ease in
his presence, and even bad ones could, and did, approach him with
the utmost freedom. He never whipt in a passion—indeed, he
seemed to be in his most pleasant moods when he administered correction, and hence, a stranger to him would naturally suppose that he
took pleasure in flogging. It was not so, however. He hardly ever
whipt, but upon the report of a monitor; and after a year or two
from Master Mitten's introduction to him, very rarely, but upon a
verdict of a jury of students. His government was one of *touching*
" moral suasion ;" but he administered it in a new way. Instead of
infusing it gently into the head and heart, and letting it percolate
through the system, and slowly neutralize the ill humors with which
it came in contact, he applied it to the extremities, and drove it
right up into the head and heart by percussion. He seemed to regard vices as consuming fires, and he adopted the engine process of
extinguishing them. One would suppose that moral reforms, so
hastily produced could not last; but we have living cases to prove
that they have lasted for fifty-three years, and are still fresh and vigorous. It is a very remarkable fact that Doctor Waddel never
flogged a boy for a deficient lesson. To be "turned off," as it was
called—that is, to have to get a lesson over a second time, was considered such a disgrace by the students, that if this did not cure the
fault, whipping, he well knew, would not. He would often mount
his horse at eight o'clock at night, and visit the students at their
boarding houses. Sometimes he would visit them *incognito,* and re-
count his observations the next day to the whole school, commending
such youths as he found well employed, and censuring such as he
found ill employed. And what were the fruits of this rigid but
equitable discipline? From under the teachings of this man have
gone forth one Vice President, and many Foreign and Cabinet Min-
isters; and Senators, Congressmen, Governors, Judges, Presidents,
and Professors of Colleges, eminent Divines, Barristers, Jurists, Le-
gislators, Physicians, Scholars, Military and Naval officers, innumerable.

Captain Thompson returned to Mr. Newby's. His name had been

made known to the boys during his absence. One of them intro-duced himself to him as the son of Doctor Hay, a near and dear friend of the Captain, in times gone by. The youth was made ac-quainted with William—offered him a part of his bed and study, which were accepted. Before retiring to rest, the Captain paid a hasty visit to William's new dormitory. He found him at a table, with three others, who were studying their lessons before a rousing fire. They seemed very cheerful and happy. After a few questions, he withdrew, and left them to their studies. An early hour the next morning found him on his way homeward.

CHAPTER IX.

Monday morning came, and William moved sadly to the Academy. Soon the students of every size began to pour in from every quarter; and soon the whole school was in commotion. George Cary had got a thousand lines in Virgil! He was to leave his class, of course; for such a lesson had never been heard of before, even in Dr. Waddel's school, where the students seemed to take in Latin and Greek by ab-sorption.* As his classmates came in, they compared notes, and not one of them had got more than three hundred lines. "I didn't get but two hundred and ten," said one; "I didn't get but two hun-dred," said another. "Well, I'm at the foot of all," said a third, "I didn't get but a hundred and fifty; so I'm double distanced, and left, of course."

William heard these reports with overwhelming amazement. The largest lesson he had ever recited was thirty-five lines, and the largest he had ever heard of being recited was one hundred. He had been led to believe that his native village was the very focus of in-tellectual illumination and mental vigor, and that he himself was the centre-beam of the focus. He did not suppose that Latin and Greek were made for country folks at all, much less for poor folks; and be-hold, there stood before him homespun,† Gilbo-shod, potato-fed chaps,

---

* George McDuffie afterwards overtopt Cary, for he recited twelve hundred and twelve lines, in Horace, for a Monday morning's lesson.

† We give this name as it was pronounced. We think it was spelled Guillo-bou. He was shoemaker-general for the school, and one of the best that ever lived. The soles of his shoes were about half an inch thick, and the heels three-quarters. The upper leather in exact proportion with the soles. In short, they were brogans in all respects, of the stoutest sort. It took them about a month to show outward signs of an inward foot. Then they began to wrinkle down to something like foot-shape; with only a tolerable greasing, they were good for a year, certain.

even smaller than himself, who had mastered one hundred and fifty lines in Virgil, acknowledging themselves the fag-end of their class, and "double distanced!" His mind was immediately made up to take the *selectæ* class, mortifying as it was to a gentleman of his calibre to have it known at home that he had retrograded; but could he keep up with this class? He had little hope of doing so; but so shocking was the idea of falling two classes below his home stand, that he resolved to try it at all events. He had one consolation, at least, and that was, that none of the school-boys knew of his advancement before he came hither. Withal, he concluded that there must be a something about Doctor Waddel's school that made all the boys who came to it smart, and whatever that something might be, he surely would catch it in a short time. The Doctor soon made his appearance; and William signified to him his choice of classes.

The school was summoned to prayer, and at the conclusion of this service the monitors' bills were handed in, and the dancing room cleared. The Doctor read over to himself the bills, with an affected seriousness, while a death-like silence reigned around him; his countenance meantime assuming all varieties of expressions. It was very easy for those well acquainted with him, to collect from these indications the general character of the bills in hand; and the signs this morning were of things grave, novel, funny and common.

The reading finished, the Doctor began: "Pretty heavy bills! some things new even to me. Garrett Sandige, go and get the *change* to settle off these bills, and see that it is such as has the genuine *ring!*" To a correct understanding of the first case on the docket, it is necessary to premise a little. John Freeman had been exalted for the first time to the dignity of Monitor on the preceding week, and he had over-acted his part a litttle; he was rather too vigilant and authoritative.

To economise time, while Garrett Sandige was collecting the change, the Doctor sounded the docket in a humorously emphatic and pompous style:

Austin B. Overstreet, for being idle repeatedly! What say you, Austin?"

"I deny it, sir," said Overstreet.

"Monitor, speak!"

"Doctor Waddel, almost every day in the week he follows me all about with his Greek grammar in his hand, and goes on in this way: *tupto, tupteis, tuptei,* (of all the monitors) *tupteton, tupteton,* (that I ever saw in my life) *tuptomen, tuptete,* (John Freeman takes the load) *tuptousi,* (rather rousy.) I told him I'd *spunk him*, (report him) if he didn't quit it, and he wouldn't, so I spuuked him."

During these pleadings the Doctor's face put on all sorts of expressions; to maintain the dignity of the Monitor's character, it was of the first importance that he should hear him with the profoundest respect and gravity; and yet there was something so novel and farcical in this case, that he could with difficulty suppress open laughter. He drew his eyebrows to their closest, pressed his lips forcibly together for a moment, and then passed judgment :

"This is a new case—I confess it perplexes me not a little. It seems to be a case in which study and idleness are so equally and intimately blended, that you can't hit *idleness* without at least grazing *study*, nor indulge *study* without indulging *idleness*. If, as soon as Overstreet began to make up his compound, you had informed me, Mr. Monitor, of his experiment, I could have given you a recipe that would have precipitated the feculent matter so entirely from the pure, that we might have dealt with it this morning without danger of disturbing the pure; but as it is, with no antecedent law to meet such a case, and under the maxim that it is best to err on the safe side—the side of mercy—if we err at all, I will let the matter pass for this time; but if you come up again, Austin, with such a mixture of Greek and English in the presence of a monitor, I'll teach you the first future tense of your Greek verb in such a style that you'll never think of mingling English with it again while you live, unless it be the true English."

Before this case was disposed of, Sandige had returned with about a half dozen hickories beautifully trimmed The Doctor took one, drew it through his left hand, found it knotless, gave it an experimental flourish, liked the ring, and proceeded :

" *Garry-Osko-Sapling, for being idle repeatedly !"*

Garry stepped into the ring without defence.

The Doctor gave him one cut and paused—"Garry," said he, very good humoredly, "that doesn't sound right. My ear don't often deceive me." So saying he stooped down and raised up the pants of the left leg, pulled down the stocking, and discovered a tasteful and most artistic binding of the calf and its appurtenances, with long narrow strips of old shirt. The Doctor manifested not the least surprise at this, but very deliberately commenced unwinding. At about every yard detached, he would pause and look up to the school with an expression of countenance which seemed to say, " boys needn't try to fool me." Having unrolled about four yards and a half of swathing from this leg, he proceeded to the other, and did the like. During the whole process the school was a roar of laughter, and few laughed more heartily than Garry himself. Having returned the stockings and pants to their places, "let us have fair play, Garry," said the Doctor! "Fair play is a jewel. Now stockings are fair, and pants are fair, thick or thin. If I can't get through them, why, that's my fault, not yours." So saying, he let Garry have the remaining six with a brilliancy that fully compensated for the lost pleiad.

"Why, Neddy, this is an awful account for one week. Monitor, are any of these charges upon your own observation but the first?"

"None, sir. They are all by order of the boys whose names are to them."

"Explain, James Freer, what is meant by knocking *by* your nose."

"He came by me, and struck his fist as hard as he could, as close to my nose as he could drive it to miss my nose."

"Did you tell him to quit?"

"Yes, sir."

"And did he afterwards repeat the blow?"

"No, sir, but he went knocking by the noses of twenty boys in the same way."

"How was your case, Thomas Murray?"

"Exactly the same as Jim Freer's, sir."

"What have you to say to all this, Neddy?"

"Why, Doctor Waddel, I was just playing with them. I quit as soon as I saw they didn't like it. None of the other boys got mad at it."

"And what's your case, Malory Rivers?"—Malory was the smallest boy in school, save one.

"He come up to me, sah—he came up to me, sah—an' he put his face mos' touchin' mine, and he opened his mouth and eyes jus' as wide as he could stretch 'em—putti'n out his arms over me, too, like he was tryin' to scare me."

"What do you say to that, Brace?"

"I just did it for a little fun—I wanted to see what he would do—and I got the worst of it, too, for he butted me on the nose, and I didn't set him down for it."

"Did you butt him on the nose, Malory?"

"I *give* him a little butt."

"Oh well, the case is easily settled; if you take justice into your own hands, you must not appeal to me. I regard a *little butt* full pay for a *big look*."

" And what have you to say, James Collier, against the defendant? 'Plaguing *with* a dead cat' is a new offence. Explain!" •

" He took a long forked stick," said Collier, " and stuck an old dead cat's neck on it, and swung her up by the head, and swung the stick on his shoulder, and went all about among the boys like he did'nt see 'em, stinkin' 'em up. Sometimes he'd meet a boy, and when he got close up to him, he'd wheel off another way, as if he just thought of something, and swung the dead cat by 'em almost touch'n 'em. I, and Andrew Govan, and Jim Tinsley, and Sam McGraw, and Alfred Hobby, were talking, and I saw Brace coming with his cat, and I hollo'd to him and said : ' Now, Brace, I've seen you scatter two or three parcels of boys with that cat; and if you come here with it, I'll spunk you. He pretended he did'nt hear what I said, and kept coming up, asking me all the time what I said; and he knew what I said well enough. All the other boys run, but I wouldn't run; and he comes to me, and says : '.Jimmey, I've been hunting all over the school to find somebody to help me bury this poor cat : but they are the hard-heartedest set of boys that I ever saw ; wont you help me, Jimmey ?' So without saying anything to him, I went off and spunked him ; and just as I started off he turned round as quick as he could, and whirled his cat almost all round me. And I don't b'lieve there's another boy in the world that could have stood that cat as long as he did, just to have his fun out of the other boys."

• " What do you say to all this, Neddy ?"

" Doctor Waddel, twenty boys will tell you I did ask them to go with me to bury the cat. I don't think Jim Collier had a right to order me away from the other boys he was talking to. If he didn't like the cat and my company, why didn't he go off as the other boys did ? They all thought the cat smelt bad, but it didn't. It didn't smell one bit." Here the Doctor opened his eyes, and showed signs of light which materially changed the aspect of the case. It immediately flashed upon his mind, that the weather had been very cold for a week, and that, perchance, the cat was not offensive.

" James," continued he, " did you smell the cat ?"

" I didn't stay long enough to smell it." •

" But you say he whirled it round you as you went off; did you smell it then ?"

" I think I would have smelt it if I hadn't held my breath."

" Doctor Waddel," said Brace, " he couldn't have smelt it to save his life. Call every boy he says I went to with it, and not one of them will say that he smelt it."

· A· number of witnesses were called, and not one testified that he smelt the cat. Most of them had kept out of smell of it; some held their noses; and others, by whom it had been whipt, remembered nothing about it.

"The case is certainly wonderfully changed," said the Doctor. "Had a single witness testified positively that he smelt the cat, I would not have held you altogether guiltless, Brace; not that I deny your right to shoulder as many dead cats as you please, and to carry them where you please, provided you do not push yourself, with your charge, into the company of others, and to their annoyance. But you have no right to constrain a student to leave his company, or his place, or to endure a stench. As to your pretending to want help to bury the cat, I understand all that perfectly; you wanted no such thing."

"What have you to say, Gilbert Hay, against Brace?"

"He threw a lightwood knot on my foot, on purpose, and hurt it so that I haven't got over it yet."

"Why did you do that, Brace?"

"I declare, Dr. Waddel, I didn't mean to drop it on his foot."

"Yes you did, sir——"

"Address me, Gilbert—not him," said the Doctor.

"Well, Doctor Waddel, he kept carrying his lightwood knot about among the boys, and as soon as he'd come near one, he'd pretend to let it slip off his shoulder, and pretend to be trying to catch it; and halloo, 'take care of your toes—I can't hold it,' and let it fall right by the boy's foot, just to make him jump. He did two or three boys so, 'fore he came to me, and when he came to me, he let it fall on my foot, sure enough."

"Is all this so, Neddy?"

"Yes, sir; but he shows himself I didn't go to do it."

"No, sir, 'you didn't go to do it,' but you went to do what you knew was very apt to do it. So if James Freer, or Thomas Murray, had happened to lean suddenly forward, or been accidently pushed forward just as you were striking by their noses, he would have got a very severe blow; and you wouldn't have went to do that, either. You have no right to sport with the *feelings* of others, for your fun. So I'll give you a little for your *nose-fun*, and *two or three littles* for your *foot-fun*, and the usual price of *idleness* unrepeated."

Ned had a pair of breeches which he called *his Monday morning breeches.* They were very full in the legs—trousers, in fact. In their natural position, they hung tangent to the calves of his legs, or nearly so; but, by catching them near the hips, and pulling them backward, and a little upward, they pressed tight upon the shins, and swung entirely clear of the calves, by at least an inch. Ned had acquired such skill in directing the play of these trowsers, that he had brought his calves through several penal Mondays almost, or entirely, intact. He knew the velocity of the switch, and he gave his twitch just at the instant of its reaching the leg; and at the crack, hands off! the pants were back to their place.

Ned stept into the ring, and received the first cut with his usual success. It was a clear flash. The Doctor, without pausing, went through the motions of the second, but arrested it in its descent, and saw, with a smile, the pants fly back to receive it. "I thought," said he, "that lick made a false report. How was that done, Neddy? You keep your hands a little too much akimbo for the occasion. Hands off, and fair play, Neddy! Big breeches are perfectly fair; but no pulling!" The remaining nine told (as an officer said of a park of artillery in battle,) "with beautiful effect!"

David Murray, for throwing a chew of tobacco in James Nephew's eye!

David, commonly called *Long David*, was the tallest, and, for his height, the slimmest student in the school. He stood full six feet in his stocking.

"How was that, David?" said the Doctor.

"He asked me," said David, "to throw him down a *chaw* o' tobacco, and I *done* it, and it hit him in the eye."

"Where were you, David? Where did you throw it down from?"

"I wasn't anywhere, sir. Because I am tall, all these little fellows are constantly running up to me, and askin' me to throw 'em down a chaw o' tobacco, jus' like I was 'way up in a tree."

"Well, David," said the Doctor, chuckling in spite of himself, "if a boy asks you to throw him down 'a chaw o' tobacco,' I don't think you are responsible for where it falls."

"What!" the reader may be disposed to ask, "did he ever whip grown up young men?" Not within our recollection, because we never knew but one who rendered himself liable to this kind of correction, and that one left the school in quick time after the commission of his offence; but tradition said that he had done that thing; and he used to flourish his hickory with graceful, but terrific vigor of arm, when a little fretted with matters and things in general, and thunder forth, "I'll whip you, sirs, from Robert Pettigrew down to

James Scriven, *inclusive.*" The first was the largest, the last the smallest student in the school.

A number of other cases, besides those mentioned, were disposed of; but there was nothing remarkable in them. They were chiefly cases of idleness in which judgment was confessed; but the sessions closed with a case of contempt of court, which deserves to be reported, *first,* because it is the only case of the kind, we believe, that ever occurred during the instructorship of Doctor Waddel; and, *secondly,* because it shows how he disposed of cases which demanded immediate notice, but which he could not visit with the usual penalty, without violating his fixed rule, never to flog in a passion. The last case on docket was just disposed of, when something that the Doctor said or did, now forgotten, led Brace to exclaim pretty rudely, " *Doctor Waddel, that's partial!*" " What, sir !" thundered the Doctor from a hurricane countenance. He paused a second—then dropt the switch he had in his hand, and seizing Ned by all the apparel that covered his breast, he shook him tremendously. He lifted him high and sat him down emphatically, but not injuriously. He now waltzed him round the ring in the quickest possible time. He then made a path with him, five feet deep, through the boys—brought him back with a double-jerk—took another turn with him as before, and dismissed him at the door with a push that sent him off at a " *half hammond.*" As soon as the impetus had spent itself, Ned stopt, looked back, looked up, looked around, like a man in *delirum tremens,* and then set off at a tip-toe, at a rather brisk gait, like one creeping to catch a butterfly, and discoursing, as he went, in a sort of half whisper: " *The man's mad! The ma-a-ns mad! He's made me drunk, turning me round. If I didn't think he'd kill me, I'll never budge!*"

The morning's exercises were exceedingly interesting to Master Mitten, of course, and he was allowed half a day to muse upon them; for he was without the text book of his class, and could not be supplied until Doctor Waddel went home to his dinner. The forenoon of the day was employed chiefly in taking observations of the costumes, manners, and conduct of the boys; but part of the time was spent with young Hay and three of his classmates, with whom he studied during that day. They construed alternately a sentence aloud, and if the version of the reader was corrected by some one of the listeners, it was considered as properly rendered, and adopted by all. Occasionally, a dispute would arise between them as to the case of a noun, the mood and tense of a verb, or the application of some rule of syntax, and the dispute was invariably settled by an appeal to the grammar, which each one kept always by him in studying his lessons. Herein, he found one clue to a solution of the mystery which had astonished him so, at the opening of school—the prodigious lessons which the boys recited—and before the next day he discovered another which solved the mystery entirely; it was, that the very idlest of the boys studied twice as much as any school-boys he had ever seen. In the afternoon his selectæ was furnished him, and he set in regularly with his class. He begged to be excused from reading in his turn, as the author was new to him. He was indulged; and thus he was virtually carried over his first lesson. One reading of it, to him, was enough to make him as perfect in it as any in the class, and consequently he recited it creditably. He had hardly concluded his first recitation, when the signal for evening prayer was given; the students were assembled, prayer was held, and they were dismissed for the night. Thus ended the most terrific day of William's pupilage. We have been particular in giving its history, not only for its effect upon Master Mitten, but that the reader might have a practical exhibition of Doctor Waddel's government. Terrific as the day was to William, it was the first of a long series of days pregnant with good luck.

CHAPTER X.

By reason of detention at the river, and an accident to his vehicle on the way, Captain Thompson did not reach home until near eight o'clock on Monday night; and at his request the tidings of his return were kept from his sister until the next morning. As soon as they reached her, she hastened over to him, to hear his report from Dr. Waddel's school. "How did you find things, brother?" said she; "I hope you got a good boarding-house, and a comfortable room for William this cold weather; and that before you left, you saw him well provided with bedding, fire-wood, and all the other little conveniences that he needs; for you know he has no idea of providing for himself. Did he seem satisfied with his new school? What sort of a man is Mr. Waddel? Is he as severe a man as he is represented to be?"

"Bless me, Anna!" said the Captain. "What time have I had to prepare answers for all these questions? I got there at four o'clock on Saturday afternoon, and left a little after sunrise on Sunday, so that I had no time to learn much about Mr. Waddel or his school. Oh, Anna, who do you think was the first boy I got acquainted with there! David Ramsay, son of Doctor Ramsay, who married Miss Laurens, daughter of Henry Laurens, President of the first Congress, and Minister to Holland. He seemed to be very well satisfied there—quite cheerful and happy—fine boy."

"Couldn't you have got William into a room with him?"

"Well—I didn't try—he boards with Mr. Waddel, and I thought——" ·

"Oh! brother! I wish you had placed him with young Ramsay, immediately under Mr. Waddel's eye. I should have no fears, then, of his getting into bad habits."

"Well, he can board there yet, if he wishes to, for I only paid his board at Mr. Newby's for one quarter, and I told him to visit the other boarding houses and select the one he liked best, and I would place him at it. I am determined to make him just as comfortable and happy as I can, at Mr. Waddel's. His room-mate is a son of our old friend, Dr. Hay, of Washington—nice youth—fine school, I've no doubt—one hundred and fifty scholars! Industrious, hearty looking fellows, of all sizes! Willington is the finest town in the world, for boys. Anna, I'm a little pressed with business this morning; come over another time, and we will talk the matter over more leisurely." So saying, he retired.

"Sister Mary," said Mrs. Mitten to Mrs. Thompson, "did brother David give you any of the particulars of his trip to Mr. Waddel's? Did he tell you how William liked the school and his teacher?"

"No," said Mrs. T.; "I asked him how William liked the school, and he said he hadn't seen the school, when he came away. I asked him how he liked Mr. Waddel, and he said William thought Mr. Waddel a very grum *looking* man; but that he had had no opportunity of getting acquainted with him before he left. But he (Mr. Thompson,) said that it seemed to him that the man and the place were made for William—that Willington was the most quiet, peaceful little village he ever saw; in a healthy region, with delightful water, beautiful study-grounds—industrious, hard-working, orderly boys, &c., &c."

"Sister Mary, you may depend upon it, brother David was disappointed in the school, or William is dissatisfied with it, or both are dissatisfied with the teacher, or the board, or something else, or he would not put us off with these general remarks. As sure as you're born, there is something there that he knows will not please me. If all had been to his liking and mine, he wouldn't have waited for questions from me, knowing my solicitude about the boy. He would have *spoken* in raptures about everything. How agreeably disappointed William had been—what a charming family, and what comfortable quarters he had got in—what an accomplished, agreeable, fascinating man Mr. Waddel is, &c., &c. What is the use of his trying to conceal these things from me? As soon as I get a letter from William, he will tell me all about them, and brother David had as well let me know about them at once."

"No, sister Anna, he cannot be dissatisfied with the teacher or the school, as is plain from what he has said to both of us. I reckon the living is rather rough up there, for he said it was the cheapest board that he ever paid. Just think of it, sister Anna; ten dollars a month for board, washing, lodging, and firewood! The kindest man in the world couldn't supply boys with dainties at these rates. And all this without making any allowance for damage to room, furniture, bedsteads, bedding, breaking window glasses, plastering, and the like, which is sure to occur in students' rooms; for boys are certain to get into romps and frolics at times, and then everything flies before them. Now, I reckon husband found the boys' fare very plain at Mr. Newby's, and thought, maybe, that it would distress you to know this fact, as William has never been used to such living. As for accomplished, agreeable, fascinating school-masters——"

"Well, sister Mary, it may be so; I hope it is no worse. Learn all you can about the school from brother David, and report to me. Good morning!"

Mrs. Mitten went home, and immediately addressed to her son a letter, wherein, among other things, she said "As yet, I have learned but very little about the school or your teacher from your uncle; but as he seemed to think it promises every thing good to you, I ought to be satisfied. I have always been under the impression that Mr. Waddel's school was in the woods, but your uncle informs us that it is in the lovely, quiet little village of Willington. I have looked for it on the map of South Carolina, but cannot find it put down there. Now, I charge you, my dear boy, not to be running about the streets of nights, to the disturbance of the villagers. You are now, thank Heaven! away from the G—— boys, and I hope you never will again fall into such company. I am happy to learn that you have had the good fortune to become the room-mate of Dr. Huy's son. It is a long time since we had the pleasure of the Doctor's society, but we never can forget it, and we take it for granted that the son of such a man must be all that a son should be. But even the best boys will occasionally have their romps and frolics, and then they are very apt forget their duty to their hostess. I do not forbid you these little pastimes; *but I strictly enjoin it upon you,* if they occur in your room, and any injury results to bed, bedding, bureau, table, washstand, basin, pitcher, looking-glass, window-glass, or any thing else, to go immediately to Mr. Newby, and insist upon his charging the whole damage to you, assuring him that I will pay it promptly and cheerfully. So cheap is the board, that I know he cannot afford to bear the expense of breakage.

"There is another thing upon which I would repeat a caution already given you; you will often be applied to, as you have been, to carry some of your less gifted schoolmates over their lessons. Do these little kindnesses for them cheerfully, and for the honor of your name, do not think of charging *or receiving* anything for them. Study neatness and cleanliness of person. Before you left me, I told you to change your linen every day, but as the number of your shirts were reduced at your departure, and more especially in mercy to Mrs. Newby's wash-woman, and her mistress, I will revoke that order, and say to you, change only three times a week. *Eat what is set before you, asking no questions.*".

Mrs. Mitten added a great many other wise and pious counsels, but as they would be of but little interest to the reader, we suppress them. She concluded her letter, folded it, addressed it to " Master William Mitten, Willington, Abbeville District, South Carolina," and sent it to the post office. As there was no post office at that time in Willington, the letter went to Abbeville Court House, where it remained three weeks from its date before it was called for. At the end of that time it was reported to Dr. Waddel, who took it from the office, and the same day delivered it to William.

Three days passed away before Captain Thompson found it convenient to give his sister a circumstantial detail of matters and things at Willington; and on the fourth he set out for Augusta on business of importance. As soon as he was gone, Mrs. Mitten called on his wife.

"Sister Mary," said she, "have you picked up anything from brother David about Willington ?"

"Not a word, sister Ann. He's always too busy, or too sleepy, to talk upon this subject. Whenever I bring it up, like old Jenkins in the Vicar of Wakefield, with his one sentence of learning, he begins to run on about young Ramsey, as he did to you, but with this difference : that he was serious when he delivered his harangue to you, and he chuckles every time he repeats it—or begins to repeat it—to me. I believe you are right, sister Anna; there is something about Mr. Waddel's school which he doesn't wish us to know; and as for my part, he may keep it to himself till doomsday, for aught I care; I shall ask him no more about it."

"Well, sister Mary, he can't keep us long in suspense, for I have written to William, and I shall get a letter from him in a week or so that will explain everything."

At Augusta chance threw Captain Thompson and Thomas M. Gilmer in the same room of a public house, for two nights. They were made acquainted, and among various other topics of conversation, Doctor Waddel's school came upon the *tapis*. "That school," said Mr. Gilmer, "just fills my notion of what a boy's school ought to be. Plain dressing, plain eating, hard working, close studying, close watching—and, when needful, good whipping."

"You are well acquainted with the school, then."

"Well, not so much from my own observation as from what my boys and my neighbors' boys tell me; for I'm so clumsy, as you see, that I go no where but where I'm obliged to; but every body says the same thing about the school—that it is the best school in the United States."

"Mr. Waddel is said to be very severe with his pupils."

"I reckon not. No doubt, if they don't walk straight he gives them the timber, as he ought to do; but all his scholars that I know like him very much, and they seem to consider all other schools as very small affairs, compared with his."

Captain Thompson after making a sufficient apology for his inquisitiveness, fished out of Mr. Gilmer that Governor Mathews had three or four grandsons at Doctor Waddel's. That Senator Bibb had two brothers-in-law there—that Congressman Early had a brother there—that Judge Tait had a son there. That Congressman Meriwether (David) had a son there. And before the Captain left Augusta, he learned that Senator, Governor Milledge had a nephew there. And last, (and best known of all, among men, women, and children, throughout the State,) that William J. Hobby had a son there. This gentleman was the Editor of the Augusta *Herald*, and in the use of all the implements of editorial warfare unsurpassed by any journalist of his day. A story was current about this time, that a lady, expressing a wish to a female friend to have her infant daughter bear the greatest name in the world—"name her," said the friend, "*William J. Hobby*." Should the reader be disposed to enquire how Mr. Gilmer came to know so many of the grandee pa-

G

trons of Dr. Waddel's school, we answer, that he was connected by blood, or marriage, with all but two of them; and one of the two lived in the same county with him, was as intimate with him as a connection, and had rescued his son George and other boys of this very school from a falling house under which they had taken shelter in a storm; and the other resided in an adjoining county, and was well known to him, and a Judge of the circuit which embraced his county.

The Captain, fully charged with these woman-cooling facts, wended his way homeward in high spirits. His exultation was increased upon reaching home by finding a letter waiting him, from Doctor Waddel.

As soon as he had reached his dwelling, and had taken refreshment—" come," said he, " Mary, let's go over to Anna's, and have our too long postponed conference about Mr. Waddel's."

" If you are going to talk seriously to your sister, to relieve her from her anxiety about her child, I'll go with you; but if you are going to run on with all that stuff about the whole breed of Ramsays, who seem to have turned your head, I will not go one foot."

" Well, I am going to be serious, and to give Anna a full statement of things at Mr. Waddel's as they are. I know it will distress her, and I want you to help me reconcile her to them."

They went, and after the usual salutations, the Captain began :

" Well, Anna, I have come over to tell you fully how matters stand at Mr. Waddel's. My reason for postponing the disclosure was, that I was in hopes of receiving a letter from Mr. Waddel that would help to reconcile you to the state of things at Willington. So brief was my stay at that place, that I really learned but little of the particulars in which you are most interested ; but I saw enough to satisfy me, that to all who would have their sons removed from vice, well instructed, invigorated in mind and body, and early taught self-reliance, there was no better school than this. But all things about it are of the very cheapest, plainest, and roughest kind. There is one framed house in Willington, and that is the head teacher's; all the rest are of logs, and open at that." (Mrs. M. turned pale.) " William's study and bed room are of this kind. He occupies it with young Hay and two others. Its only furniture is two mattresses, (on the floor,) a table, and four split bottomed chairs. The boys cut and haul their own wood and make their own fires." (Mrs. T. turns pale.) " The fare is very plain—necessarily so, from the price of board. Mr. Waddel is a very rigid disciplinarian," (they both turn paler,) " but not tyrannical. His government is strictly equitable. Among all the boys that I saw at Newby's and Waddel's, I did not see one who was as well dressed as your Tom. Even Doctor Ram— however, we'll pass him over. This is as it should be. Boys who cut wood and carry lightwood knots have no use for fine clothes. I need hardly tell you that your boy, among them, looks like a bird of Paradise among so many crows. I wish you had taken my advice in laying in his wardrobe, for I am sure his finery will bring upon him the taunts of his school-fellows. And now I have told you the worst—the very worst. But I have something to brighten this picture a little. And first, read this letter from Mr. Waddel."

" You read it, brother," said Mrs. Mitten, with swimming eyes and tremulous voice.

The Captain reads :

" WILLINGTON, &c., &c.

" *Dear Sir:* On taking leave of me, you requested me to give you early information of the standing, conduct, and progress of your nephew ; and, as my letter will reach you through the kindness of Mr. Jones, the bearer, nearly or quite a week sooner than it would by regular—or rather *irregular*—course of mail, I avail myself of the opportunity to comply with your request. William has been under my instruction just a week to-day ; and though I would not venture confident predictions of him, upon so short an acquaintance, I will give you my present estimate of him, for what it is worth. If I am not grossly deceived in him, he is destined to a most brilliant future. He was a little rusty in the principles of construction at first—no, in the *application* of them—for of the principles themselves, he is master, and he improves in the application of them with every lesson. His class was a week ahead of him in the Greek grammar, when he entered it. He has already made up the deficiency, and now stands fully equal to the best in his class in this study—indeed, in all their studies. He is moral, orderly, and studious, and if he will only do half as much for himself as nature has done for him, he will be the pride of his kindred and the boast of his country. You will not be much more delighted at receiving this intelligence, than I am in communicating it.

" Yours very respectfully,

MOSES WADDEL."

" There," said the Captain, bouncing up in transports and throwing the letter in his sister's lap, " there, sis, what do you think of that ? Now, as you are a good christian, play Methodist for one time, and go to shouting. I begin to believe in shouting, if religion is what it is cracked up to be."

" Brother," said she, " I am just as happy as a mother can be at such tidings ; but what do they signify, when my poor child may be brought home to me in less than a month, a corpse ? William's constitution can never stand the hardships to which he is exposed. A hard mattress on the floor, in an open hut, this bitter cold weather ! Cutting wood !—the boy never raised an axe in his life— carrying lightwood knots ! He never brought a turn of wood in the house in his life. Taunted by rude school-mates for being decently dressed ! My child is worse off than my negroes."

" Don't you suppose there are fifty in that school who have been brought up as tenderly as your boy has ?"

" No, I do not. They are all poor boys and country boys who have been brought up to hard work. I may have erred in bringing him up so daintily ; but it is done, and he is now unable to bear hard usage."

" Do you reckon General Senator Governor Mathew's grand-children are poor boys ?—that the Honorable Peter Early's brother is a poor boy ?—that Senator Merriwether's son is a poor boy ?—that Senator Bibb's brothers-in-law are poor boys ?—that Judge Tait's son is a poor boy ? Is young Hay a poor boy ?".

" How do you know that all these men have sons there ?"

" I learned it from a *bigger* man than any of them, who is kin to them, and knows all about them, and their sons."

" Well, I suppose all their sons were raised in the country and raised to work."

" Do you suppose that Senator Governor Milledge's nephew was raised in the country and to work ? That William J. Hobby's son was raised in the country, and to work ?—that Doctor Ramsay's son was raised in the country and to work ? It is high time your dainty, cake-fed boy was set to work, if you expect him to live out half his days. And when a better time than now ? or where a better place than among his school-mates of rank, who all work ?"   ⸂

" He is under your control, brother," said Mrs. Mitten, burying her face in her handkerchief; " but surely, surely, he is the most unfortunate child that ever was born."

" Yes, he is one of the most unfortunate children ever born, in having a mother whose sympathy for his body makes her forget the interest of his soul—who to save his hide, will ruin his head—However, what's the use of talking to a woman."

"Husband," said Mrs. Thompson, "you don't know how to make the proper allowances for a mother's love. I've told you so a hundred times. That is your greatest fault—almost your only fault—that, and refusing your children little innocent indulgences that every other father allows to his children. I have been mortified to death to see my children along side of their cousins. Because men have no feelings themselves, they think women have none—or ought to have none—"

"Ph-e-e-e-ew! what a gust! what did you come over for, Mrs. Bildad?"

" I came over to comfort sister Anna, who has most as much to bear as Job had."

" I don't think Sarah suffers much by comparison with Ann and Jane—at least if you'd look at one of Sanford's bills you'd think she ought not to."

" Well, I manage to keep her a little decent by enduring a month's grumbling at the end of every year; but compare George and William will you. Till last year and the year before, when did he ever have a new coat—a decent one—to his back? I've been cutting down your old coats and pants for him ever since he was born——"

" He must have gone into pants early."

"That's very witty, I confess ; but you know that every word I say is true. What pleasure it can be to any one to be always mortifying and cowing their children, I can't conceive. You're always talking about making boys work, work, and giving 'em fine constitutions, and George has done no more work than William has, and his constitution's no better. Now, husband, what will the world say to see you sending off your sister's child into slavery, and keeping your own son at home, with all the comforts of life about him ?"

" I thought he was in a dreadful pickle at home."

" Well, so far as his feelings—his sensibilities are concerned he is ; but he's not a mean-fed, mean-clothed, ridiculed slave ; he's not tumbled down, on a hard mattress, on the bare floor, in a negro house, this pinching, freezing weather. I wouldn't expose George to such hardships and insults, if he never got an education during ash and oak."

" I think that very likely."

"Surely, upon the face of the whole earth there can be found some school as good as old Waddel's where boys can be taught without being made niggers of."

" Mr. Waddel is not old, precious ; and it would distress him mightily if he knew that you didn't like his school."

" I don't care whether he's old or young, nor what he likes or dislikes. One thing is certain, and that is that George never goes to
him——with my consent."

" Well, come darling, let's go home! you have comforted Anna
more in a few minutes than I could have done in a month; for you
have dried up her tears and actually drawn two or three smiles from
her. My purpose is fully answered. Old as I am, I never knew
how to comfort women before."

"Brother, I thought you said Willington was a village !"

"So it is, but nobody lives in it but students and one tavern-
keeper."

" I sent my letter there."

" Well, maybe it will go there. You should have sent it to Vienna. Come, sweetest, let's be going !"

" Go on, sweetest; and I'll come when I'm ready."

CHAPTER XI.

FEW men living, have a higher respect for the " American fair"
than we have. We regard them as a thousand times better than
men, and do not feel that we pay them a very extravagant compliment at that. Nor are we blind to the virtues of the men. There
are many splendid specimens of humanity among them; but, as a
class they do not equal the other sex in any thing, that tends to en-
noble the human race. As good as women are, they would be better still, if it were not for the men; and yet, with this confession
on our lips, we are constrained to say that after all, woman is a very
curious thing. In proof of this assertion, " let facts be submitted
to a candid world !"

The reader has seen with what spirit and dignity Mrs. Thompson
reduced her husband to order as soon as he began to cast reflections
upon women generally—how he opened a whole volume of family se-
crets, that the world would have never known but for his over-latu-
dinarian outgivings—with what independence she spoke of " old
Waddel," and his " likes and dislikes "—how sweetly she dismissed
her husband—and how his sister was comforted by all these things.
Now, after the Captain had retired, and the two ladies were left
alone, what think you, gentle reader, was the strain in which she
continued to her husband's sister? Why, of course: " Sister, you
are to patient—too weak—too submissive. Be independent. If we
don't show some spirit men will make slaves of us. Resume your

authority over your child, and take him away from that horrible monster, old Waddel, and his one hundred and fifty white slaves." You are mistaken, kind reader. After a pause, long enough to let the Captain get out of hearing, thus it ran :

"Sister, that is a sweet letter of Mr. Waddel's. How kind it was in him to write so soon. However severe he may be, my life on it, he is a kind man at heart, and takes great pleasure in seeing the advancement of his scholars. It is very hard for a child raised as William has been, to be exposed to such rough usage ; but, after all it may turn out for the best. Every day that I live I become more and more satisfied, that after a certain age boys should be subjected entirely to a father's government. As you know, husband and I have had many disputes about the proper management of George, and I have always found that in the end he was right and I was wrong. We are too apt to let our love get the better of our judgment in the management of our children, especially our sons. I reckon it is a wise arrangement of Providence, that men should not have much love and sympathy—that is, as much as we have—that they may not be led off by their affections into too much indulgence. So much better satisfied am I with David's judgment, than I am with mine, in ruling boys, that I don't pretend to oppose him in any thing concerning them, except in the little matter of dress ; and besides you know him well enough to know that when he once sets his head upon a thing, and puts his foot down, you'd just as well undertake to turn over the Court House with your little finger, as to move him. Now, I see he has made up his mind to keep William at Waddel's, and nowhere but Waddel's, and he is the more bent upon it, because he wants him to contend with those—what was that biggest man of all, that told him so much about Governor's, and Senators, and Judges, and all that?"

"Gilmer?"

"I never heard of him; did you?"

"No."

"Well, it's very strange that we never heard of him—we've heard of all the rest of them. But as I was saying : David thinks there never was such a boy born for mind as William. I tell him I think George has quite as good a mind as William—not such a sprightly mind, but more solid. Don't you think so, sister?"

"George is a sweet, good boy, sister; a boy to be proud of, and of fine mind. I've no doubt but that he will make a more solid, practical, useful man than William ; but———"

"Well, I've told my husband so; but he says as for *talent*, for *genuine, native talent*, George won't do to be named in the same year with William. And that's another very strange thing in men; have you never noticed it? They always think every body else's children smarter and better than their own. What was I saying? Oh—David's head is set upon showing off William to those great folks, in that large school, and have his way *he will;* so I think, my dear Anna, you'd best try to reconcile yourself to it. Don't let it distress you. Surely, if other people's children, raised as tenderly as he has been, can live through it, he can."

"Oh, I could bear it all with becoming fortitude, my dear sister, if I could be sure that William would live through it—that his constitution would not be undermined by it. But the change is so sudden—in everything! If he lives through it, his spirit will be broken down—he will be cowed—his ambition be stifled. I know William's disposition better than any body else in the world knows it. He can be led by kindness, stimulated by praise, and won by words, but he cannot bear harshness, censure, and, least of all, chastisement. Now, is it not strange, my dear Mary—is it not unaccountable, that of all the schools in the world that is the one my poor child should be doomed to at last? When, and where, will his misfortunes end? And now, what shall I do? What am I to do? I have given my child up to brother David's control, and I know his inflexibility where he thinks he is right. There is one thing I know, and but one thing, that will overcome, him, and that is my grief; but I do not wish to afflict him with my anguish of heart. What trouble have I given him! What brotherly kindness has he shown me! How prophetic has been his forecast! How proud he is of my son! How rejoiced when he does well! It is cruel in me to pain him. And yet, when I think of my poor boy, how can I help it? Yes, I will, sister Mary—I will strive to suppress my feelings; at least, to hide them from brother David. I am greatly delighted with Mr. Waddel's letter. I am sure he is not the cruel, merciless man he has been represented to be."

"Well that is right, sister Anna. You be happy, and husband will be happy, and I will be happy, and we'll all be happy. At least, hope for the best, till you hear from William. It will be time enough to grieve when you hear that William is unhappy." With these words, and two emphatic kisses, moistened with the tears of both, the sisters parted.

Now, we could moralize as long, and quite as profitably, upon the character of Mrs. Thompson, as Dickens does upon the characters which he dreams out; but as we detest the repeated interruptions, of a story by long dry homilies from the author, we will take it for granted that when we faithfully delineate a character, the reader can draw his lessons of morality from it as well as we can ; but as it would be doing great injustice to the character of Mrs. Thompson to rest it with the reader upon an occasional interview with her nearest and dearest friends, we are sure that we will be indulged in a word explanatory of her seeming inconsistency in the conversations just detailed.

After long and careful observation of human nature, in all its phases, we are strongly impressed with the idea that there are many women in the world—good women, sensible women, good wives, and good mothers, who are a little *impulsive*—liable, under very trying circumstances, such as masculine wit at femine expense, *he* slurs at *she* sense, man's snuffing at woman's loving, and the like, to become slightly excited ; and then, as they feel themselves called upon to extemporize without a moment's preparation, or a moment's pause, they, of course, do not deliver themselves with a due regard to logical precision, or methodical arrangement. Constrained in their hurry to snatch up any implement of warfare that presents itself, they have no time to consider its fitness, or unfitness, for the contest; consequently, they sometimes seize a battle-axe, with handle so long, that while the blade hits the enemy, the handle knocks down two or three friends at the same time. They send off a petard so maladroitly, that, while it only singes the foe, it blows up whole platoons of allies. It should be remembered, likewise,. that they fight only " to restore the equilibrium "—never for permanent conquest. It would be very strange, therefore, if, under these circumstances, they did not at times seem inconsistent in their words and ways. Now, Mrs. Thompson was one of this class, and one of the very best of this class. While upon this head, let me disabuse the reader's mind of another false impression that he may, perchance, receive from the scene of consolations which he has just witnessed. He may suppose from the Captain's sudden change of note, as soon as his wife took up the soothing harpsichord, that, except in the matter of George, and upon a few very rare occasions, when " he put his foot down," he was under pretty rigid petticoat government. Not so. Foot down, or foot up, whenever a material issue occurred between the heads of the family, his judgment was final and conclusive ; but in matters of minor import both acted independently.

The jurisdictions of each were early defined after the marriage; to the madam was assigned the house, the kitchen, the smoke house, and the garden, in absolute sovereignty; to himself, all other interests were accorded. After children were born to them, all fell under her jurisdiction up to the age of six; then, the Captain assumed a little authority over the males, up to ten, when he reversed the order of things, he becoming principal and she secondary. As to the females, he claimed no privileges, but the very humble ones of grunting and turning up his nose occasionally at their flounces, and of grumbling annually (*vide supra,*) at their store bills. Small as these 'things were, they were unconstitutional encroachments, for which he received the due retributions, to which he submitted with no other signs of impatience than perpetrating a joke, or a witticism, in the midst of them, always under the pain of double punishment— yes, he was guilty at times of other encroachments in the way of certain significant " *Humphs!*" at pale coffee, undone biscuits, burnt meat, and the like, at meals; to which she responded in the following apologetic terms:

" *When your negroes cease to be masters and mistresses of the family, maybe you'll get something fit to eat.*" To which, at the earliest convenient opportunity, she added an amendment, in manner and form following, to-wit:

" *I suppose you* (little Sucky,) *think that because the grown niggers are allowed to run over me, and do as they please,* YOU *can do so too; but I'll teach you better Miss. I can manage you, myself, Miss Empress Catherine!*" Meaning, thereby, that the aforesaid David Thompson had been guilty of *crassa negligentia,* and divers nonfeasances, to the great detriment of the said Mary, and highly unbecoming the Chief Executive officer of the Thompsonian Government. By means whereof the most insignificant subjects of said Government had come to regard themselves Emperors and Empresses, and to deport themselves to the said Mary accordingly.

To these impeachments, the Captain filed no plea; " sometimes pretending " that he was too deaf, and at others too busy to hear them.

Nor did the madam always keep within her legitimate domain. She would, with malice aforethought, stop a plow to send Sarah to a quilting, and then, the Captain's foot would come down in earnest, and he'd " wonder whether there was a woman in the world that wouldn't lose a crop to give her daughter a sugar-tit!" All which, and much more like it, Mrs. T. bore with lamb-like meekness, and speechless submission, her eyes looking out meantime as though she was contemplating evening clouds. The equilibrium was beautifully preserved in the Captain's family.

From all this, it appears that Thompson was no farther under petti coat government than all husbands are, and all good husbands ought to be. He was a very happy man in his family, and his wife was as happy as he was.

Before his wife returned from the visit of consolations, the Captain had finished a short letter to William, reporting Doctor Waddel's opinion of him, the gratification it afforded his mother in particular, and his connections in general—urging him not to disappoint the high expectations which had been raised of him—to be studious —not to mind the taunts of the boys about his fine clothes—to wear them out as quick as possible with lightwood knots, and get plain, coarse ones. "Let the boys see," said the Captain, "that if you do not know how to work, you can soon learn. Beat them in every thing. Beat them in learning, in working, in running, in jumping, in wrestling, in athletic sports of every kind. That is the way to make them respect you." We must not let the reader suppose that the Captain omitted the important matter of diet, though he expressed himself upon it in very coarse terms—withal, they are characteristic: "Don't let your head be always running upon what is to go into your paunch."

The Captain was just folding his letter, when his wife returned. "Well, Mary," said he, "and how did Anna seem when you left her?"

"Why, poor dear soul, it's enough to make one's heart bleed to see her. She does try her very best to become reconciled to William's lot, but it seems impossible. If you could have heard her when she talked about your kindness to her, and how it increased her griefs to know how they afflicted you, it would have filled your eyes with tears. Do, my dear husband, be as kind and tender to her as you can. She says that she will strive to overcome her feelings for your sake——"

"Well, that is all I can expect of her," said the Captain, with suffused eyes—"visit her every day, Mary, and keep her as much as possible from brooding over William's fate. See if you can't persuade her to take a trip of a month or two from home, as soon as the weather breaks—I must away to the post office."

CHAPTER XII.

At the very time when Doctor Waddel was penning his letter to Captain Thompson, teeming with compliments to William Mitten, the same William Mitten was writing another to his mother teeming with phillippics against Doctor Waddel; but as good luck would have it William's letter was about a month in reaching his mother. This may seem strange to the reader of the present day, when communications pass between New York and New Orleans in a few minutes and letters pass between them by the due course of mail in five or six days. But the matter is easily explained. In the good old days of President Jefferson, people were not as much like the Athenians as they are now—that is, so greedy of news that they could think of nothing else; and had they been, they would have deemed it utterly impracticable to send a letter by public conveyance over sixty miles, in less than two days, excluding stoppages. And if Dogfight post office lay on the way, and rain fell between times, the post-boy was commended if he came up to schedule time. But if Dogfight and Possum-town post offices both lay on the way, and a storm intervened, three days to sixty miles was considered but a scant allowance. No mails were carried in Georgia by vehicles, but the mails between Augusta and Savannah; none in South Carolina, we believe, but between Charleston and Columbia. All others were horse mails, commonly in charge of boys under nineteen years of age. These took their rest at night, and took shelter from rain in the day, as their health required. The vehicles called *stages* carried passengers as well as mails. They, too, stopt for the night, and well for the passengers that they did; for Waddel's shaking of Brace was a comfort compared to the shaking and bouncing of passengers in these vehicles, when going over rooty, rutty, and stony ground.

The facetious Oliver H. Prince, who was toothless in front, upon being asked how he lost his teeth, replied, "that they were jolted out by traveling over Georgia roads in a stick sulky." If this were true, teeth must have been scarce among the stage passengers between Augusta and Savannah, sandy as the road was for the most part.*

Besides the tardiness of the mails, there was another more serious

---

* Post Coaches were introduced in South Carolina and Georgia by Eleazer Early, in 1825, we think; and *we know* that the first passengers in one of them were Gen. Thomas Glascock, Major Freeman Walker, and the writer, of Georgia, and Col. Christian Breithaupt, of South Carolina.

obstacle to ready communication between the students and their parents at a distance. The nearest post office to Willington was, as we
have intimated, at Vienna, six miles from the Academy; and in all
Willington *proper* or *common* there was but one horse that could always be had for hire, and that was Southerland's old Botherem.
Now, for a student to wait the revolution of fifty or sixty Saturdays
before his turn to hire old Botherem rolled round, would have been
distressingly dilatory. Withal, to hire him just to mail a letter, was
"*rather fatiguing to the finances*" of the youth of this Institution,
which were exceedingly reduced in those days. To walk six miles to
mail a letter, was out of the question. The only alternative left,
and that which was universally adopted, was to take the chance of a
visitor to the village on business, or pleasure, and the chance of hearing of his intended departure before it occurred, and the chance of
seeing the visitor *ad interim*, and the chance of his being willing to
bear the letter, and the chance of his not forgetting to mail it after he
took charge of it. It might be, therefore, especially with a new
comer to the school, several weeks before all these contingencies
would result favorably to the writer, and so it was with William.
His letter to his mother made his fare even worse than it was, by a
total omission of wheat biscuit at least once in three weeks, and
sometimes oftener, and butter " semi-occasionally," and fresh pork
for middling, every now and then; chicken pie twice or thrice a
year; and turkey as often as old Maner* could kill a wild one, which
happened about once in two years; and venison as often as old *Maner*
could kill a deer, which happened once in three years. Of course,
master Mitten was not to blame for omitting all these things, for
even biscuit-time had not rolled round when he wrote; but it is due
to the kind-hearted landlord and landlady, that Mitten's report
should receive the just qualifications. After descanting upon his
board and lodging, he proceeded as follows : " All I ever heard about
old Waddel, is true. He whips ten times as much as Mr. Markham
does, and twice as hard, and laughs and chuckles all the time he is
doing it, like it made his heart glad to cut boys' legs all to pieces.

" Last Monday morning, one boy named Ned Brace made him
mad, and he caught him by the throat with both hands, and lifted
him up, and slammed him down, and jerked him all about among
the boys, till I thought he would have killed him ; and I wish he
had, for he does nothing but torment me every chance he gets.
Uncle had hardly left here, before he came up to me, and asked me

---

* A fancy shoemaker and great hunter, who boarded at Newby's.

how long I thought it would be before I would blossom? I told him
I did not know what he meant. 'I mean,' says he, 'how long will
it be before your shirt begins to peep out of your breeches and
jacket?' Then he tells me I am the prettiest boy he ever laid his
eyes on, and have got the prettiest little hands and feet that he ever
did see, and that it almost makes him cry his eyes out to think that
my pretty hands will have to touch lightwood knots; and that I never
shall do it, for he will get a nice little pair of tongs for me to pick
up the knots with, and a pretty little band-box for me to carry them
in. The other day he squalled out to me, right before all the boys,
' Oh, Bill Mitten, I have found you out, have I? I suspected it as
soon as I saw you, but I thought nobody would do such a thing.'
"'What do you mean?' said I. 'What have I done?'
"'Why,' says he, 'you have come here in boy's clothes, and you
know very well that you are a girl; and I believe you are the very
girl that looked so hard at me in church last vacation. I knew you
loved me, but I never thought you would follow me here in that
plight. What do you expect me to do? Do you think I would
marry any girl in the world that acts that way?'
" Here, I ordered the monitor to set him down for making game
of me, and telling lies; and I do hope old Waddel will give him
twice the choking and jerking he gave him last Monday. He is
everlastingly tormenting me, and setting all the boys to laughing at
me. * * * * * The boys here are the smartest boys I ever
saw; and they study the hardest of any boys I ever saw; but they
do not seem to like me, and, therefore, I keep away from them, except a few good boys, who are very kind to me. All their amusements are running, jumping, wrestling, playing town-ball, and bull-
pen. The big boys hunt squirrels, turkeys, &c., of Saturdays, and
'possums and coons of nights. Mr. Waddel does not require them
to study at their boarding-houses, though they almost all do it."

This was true from 1805 to 1808, but about the latter period, a
shoal of city youths entered the school, who abused their privileges
so much that they were curtailed one by one, until at length the
students were forbidden the use of fire-arms, were required to retire
to rest at 9 o'clock P. M., if not engaged in study beyond that hour,
to consume but fifteen minutes at their meals, and to rise with the
sun every morning. It is a remarkable fact, that, with two or three
exceptions, no student who entered this school between the years
1806 and 1810, from the largest cities of Georgia and South Carolina, ever became greatly distinguished; while the period including

those dates was the most fruitful of great men of any of the same length, during the whole time of Doctor Waddel's instructorship.*

Master Mitten closed his letter with a most earnest appeal to his mother "to do all that she could to get his uncle to remove him from this school." She forthwith dispatched a messenger to the Captain, who was soon at her side. He found her weeping, of course. The letter was handed to him, and he commenced reading it gravely; but when he reached the complaints against Ned Brace, he began to laugh, and laughed more and more immoderately as he progressed.

"Brother David," said his sister, "what do you find in the letter to amuse you so much?"

"Why, this odd fish, Ned Brace!"

"It seems to me very strange that you can find anything laughable in such vulgar, unprovoked rudeness as he shows to your nephew."

"Oh, Anna, I wouldn't mind these little boyish frolics. There are always some Braces in a school, whom the boys soon get used to, and become amused with rather than angry with. As soon as Bill blossoms, no doubt Ned will let him alone——"

"Brother David, I shall take it as a great favor, if you will not obtrude the refined Mr. Brace's wit on my ear, how much soever you may relish it."

"Well, now, Anna, you have a great deal of the blame of all this to take to yourself. You have raised your child in a band-box—— Oh, come back Anna! I give you my word and honor I had no allusion to Brace's fun. I told you not to rig William out in finery for that school; but you would; and now, he is verifying my prediction. But do not take such trifles so much to heart. William tells you the boys there are the smartest and the most studious boys he ever saw; and Waddel tells you that he is among the most promising of them all. Now, think of these things, and do not let the fun or folly of his schoolmates distress you. He seems to have a fine protector from Brace, at least, in Mr. Waddel. If William does his duty he will soon command the respect of all his school-fellows, even of Brace

---

* We name the following: Wm. D. Martin, M. C., Judge Circuit Court, S. C.; Eldred Simkins, M. C., S. C.; James L. Pettigru, Attorney General and District Judge, S. C.; Andrew Govan, M. C., S. C.; Hugh S. Legare, Attorney General U. S., S. C.; George McDuffie, M. C., and Governor of S. C.; Lewis Wardlaw, Judge Superior Court, S. C.; Francis Wardlaw, Chancellor S. C.; George R. Gilmer, M. C., and Governor, Ga.; George Cary, M. C., Ga.; John Walker, M. C., Ala.; Henry W. Collier, Governor and Chancellor, Ala.; and many others of lower rank. John C. Calhoun and William H. Crawford were Waddel's pupils, of earlier date.

himself. As to his leaving that school, it is out of the question. There are but two contingencies upon which it can be done. His sickness is one, and the other, I shall keep to myself, for the present, at least."

"Did you not say that you left it optional with him to board at Mr. Newby's or elsewhere?"

"I did, and so he may. By going to another boarding- house, he will get rid of Brace of nights and mornings, but not of noons. I have no idea that the fare is any better at the other houses than it is at Newby's. He is now convenient to the 'Academy,' with pleasant room-mates, acquainted with the boarders, his landlord and landlady, and, doubtless, better satisfied upon the whole than he will be any where else. Now, would you put him among strangers, with what kind of a room-mate you know not, and have him walk from one to three miles every night and morning, through winter storm, and summer heat, just to have him a little better fed than he is, and to remove him from the taunts of one waggish boy?"

Mrs. Mitten pondered over these sayings sadly for a time, and then rejoined: "Now, brother, you're always ascribing William's misfortunes to my folly or weakuess; tell me candidly, isn't it bad luck, and nothing but bad luck, that Mr. Waddel's school happens to fall in the woods? That William should be compelled to endure such rough fare? And that he should have fallen into the same boarding house with that tantalizing Ned Brace?"

"Well, as Bill is—that is, as you have made him—I don't know but that his falling in with Brace may be considered rather unlucky; but if he had been raised as he should have been, he would probably have been able to stop Brace's mouth without appealing to Mr. Waddel. But as he is, why doesn't he give Brace as good as he sends? If Brace ridicules his fine clothes, why doesn't he ridicule Brace's coarse and dirty ones! If he admires Bill's pretty face, why does not Bill laugh at his ugly one! If he calls Bill a pretty girl, why does not Bill call him an ugly wench! That's the way to meet such larks as Brace; not to play the girl before him, sure enough.

"As to the fare, I consider that sheer good luck. It's high time that Bill had the cakes, and the sugar-plums with which you have been stuffing him all his life purged out of him——"

"Why, brother! where did you learn your coarse language? Not from your father or mother, I know."

"I learned it from William's bringing up; the like of which you never saw in your mother's family, I know. She taught me, God

bless her! to work, to move quick at her bidding, to eat just what
was set before me—and she generally set before me for breakfast, as
you know, a pewter-basin of clabber, and a pone of corn-bread, a pew-
ter-tumbler of milk or butter-milk, and a pewter plate of fried apples,
'most floating in sop, with three little pieces of clear, curled middling
perched up on top of them, like dried bean-pods. My dinner was
just the same, with an occasional change of meat to squirrel, 'possum,
venison, and very rarely beef. For supper, I had wind and water,
and nothing else. When I was thirteen or fourteen years old, I have
no doubt I should have considered Newby's fare perfectly luxurious—
certainly, it is quite as good as I was raised on."

"You surely don't think of what you are saying, brother. Mother had both china and crockery ware, and some silver ware; and she
was one of the nicest house-keepers and best pastry-cooks in the
world."

"Oh, yes, she had a set of china; I remember it well; though I
never got but three fair looks at it in all my life; and I remember
quite as well having got twice three fair licks, when about seven years
old, for trying to climb up to the upper story of the old buffet,* to
ascertain what those shining things were that peeped out of the dark
garret every time that mother opened the door of the buffet. How
many pieces there were at this period I do not know; but I know that
just seven (counting a cup and saucer as one) survived the Revolution. They came in full view before me, when three officers of the
army stopt at our house for a night. The *supper,* I had not the pleasure of seeing, as mother invited me over to Uncle John's to spend
the evening; but the *breakfast* was prodigious! First, there was a
table cloth spread on the table. This was amazing; and I ventured
to feel it, at the expense of a back-handed lick right here! (pointing
to the back of his ear.) Then came forth six crockery plates, laid
bottom upwards, with knives and forks by their sides, which I had
never seen before. Then was placed at the head of the table a large
waiter with something on it covered over with a shining white napkin.

*The buffet, often called the *bofat,* was a triangular cupboard, or a t-fitted to
the corner of a room, and extending from the floor nearly to the ceiling. The
first shelf in it was about two and a half feet from the bottom, and the space
was closed by a door, or folding doors, with lock and key. This was the depos-
itory of the family groceries. Then, came another shelf, and another, and another, to the top. These were all closed by glass doors, or a single door, after the
manner of a window shutter. The first division was appropriated to the lighter
pewter-ware. The second to the liquors for the day, with their needful accompaniments of honey, sometimes sugar, mint, bowls, mugs, spoons, and occasionally glass tumblers. The third contained the crockery, and the fourth, half-con-
cealed by the cornice of the buffet, the china and silver ware, if any.

H

(Here I got lick No. 2, for peeping under the napkin.) There was set in the centre of the table a pepper-box, and a salt-cellar, the last after the fashion of a morning-glory on the foot of a wine-glass. On either side of said salt-cellar, and equi-distant from it—say nine inches—two table-spoons of solid silver crossed each other, bowls downward, and two more lay, the one at father's plate, and the other where the fried chicken was to be; on mother's side of the first brace, was placed a little glass bucket, like a doctor's mortar, full of rich yellow butter, frizzled all over, pine-burr fashion. Now came in a plate of beautiful biscuit; then an equally beautiful loaf of light-bread; then a plate of new-fashioned corn bread, parceled out by the spoonful, and baked in the shape that the spoon gave it. Then came in a dish of nice fried ham—then another of fried chicken, dressed off with cream, and flour doings, and parsley; then another of broiled chicken, put up as now, with wings akimbo, and legs booted in its own skin; then came two bowls of boiled eggs, the one hard and the other soft—not the bowls, but the eggs. All this accomplished, the napkin was removed, and oh! what a sight was there! A china tea-pot, six cups and six saucers, all real china, and all with red pictures on them, of things I had never seen, and have never since seen! A proud, dandyish, pot-bellied, narrow-necked, big-mouthed, thin-skinned silver cream-pot, strutted out among the china, and turned down its only lip, at everything it faced, most insultingly. A silver sugar-dish, shaped like the half of a small muskmelon, stood modestly by the dapper cream-pot. Mother picks up the little dandy, and turns him bottom upwards, to make him disgorge six silver tea-spoons that he had swallowed. The handles appear, but the bowls stick in his throat. She rights him, gives his seat a pat on the table, and turns him up again; but he can't deliver. She therefore picks out of him one spoon at a time, and lays it in a saucer by the side of a cup. She now orders Silvy to bring in "the *little pitcher* of cream." The little pitcher appears (pure crockery) with half its lip bit off, and the handle gone, and an ugly crack meandering from the upper foot of the handle towards the disfigured lip. The little gentleman is carefully filled from the pitcher, his mouth is wiped clean, and he is set up to make mouths at me till the company comes. The pitcher goes back to the dairy privately. Dick is ordered to bring in the coffee, and it appears in a large tin coffee-pot. The tea-pot is filled out of it, and it is ordered back to the fire in the kitchen. All things are now in order, and I am directed to inform the company that breakfast is ready. And now, Mrs. Anna Mitten, you have had a full display of all the crockery. china, and silver, that your mother possessed from the year 1773 to the year 1787. when the whole disappeared with sister Jane, upon her marriage."

"You surely mistake some things, brother," said Mrs. Mitten. smiling, "and, therefore, it is quite likely you mistake the amount and kind of mother's table-ware. Mother never let us saunter about the table when she was fixing for company. She never sent you in your coarse clothing to call American officers to breakfast——"

"Just stop there a moment, sister, and I'll explain matters to your entire satisfaction. When mother invited me over to uncle's for the evening, she invited me home again at day break the next morning. I accepted the invitation, and was prompt to the time, knowing that ladies always get in a pucker when fixing for company, especially for 'the Quality,' and that it would have been very undutiful in me to add a scruple's weight to mother's disturbance of mind upon such occasions. I know I should have reflected upon it *with pain*, as soon as the company retired. 'Go,' said mother, on meeting me, 'to the spring, and fetch a keeler of water, and take it up in the loft, and wash and dress yourself, and come down to my room; you will find your clean clothes on the bag of dried apples.' I did as I was bidden, and came down in my Sunday suit, and walked into mother's room. She ran her eyes over me, pulled up my breeches, pulled down my jacket, spread out my shirt collar, looked for dirt on my neck and behind my ears, didn't find any, clasped my shoes a little tighter, combed my head, powdered it, and bade me take my seat in the dining room. All this was done, doubtless, that I might have it to say, in after times, that I had seen General Greene, Colonel Washington, and Colonel Williams; that they had supped and slept, and breakfasted, at my father's house; and (perchance,) that I had actually spoken to them, and been spoken to by them. It may be, too, that the good lady, finding me getting a little boorish, was disposed to give me some knowledge of nice entertainments and genteel society. If my improvement was her object—if she designed to inspire me with military order, she missed it. When the officers first took their seats at the table, I was deeply interested in their looks and conversation; but when I saw all the luxuries of the table going under their voracious appetites with a perfect rush, alarm entirely suffocated admiration. The vanishing ham, I didn't care so much about; but as piece after piece of chicken disappeared, and egg after egg, and biscuit after biscuit, till all were gone but two chicken-necks, one hard egg, two slices of ham and three-quarters of the loaf of bread, I became perfectly furious, and a Tory outright; and I said to myself, 'if these are the sort of fellows who are fighting for our liberties, I wish that .Cornwallis and Tarleton (they talked mostly of them) would catch and hang every rascal of them.'

"The same breakfast set was paraded again, near the same time, when Colonel Lee supped with us, and ●ever again until Jane's marriage.

"And now, sister, raised as we have been, where did you get your refinement in love and maternal indulgence from?"

"In your zeal to display all mother's crockery, you put one plate too many on the table, brother."

"No, I didn't; Uncle John was expected to breakfast, and prevented from coming by a shaking ague that very morning."

Mrs. Mitten had her tears turned to smiles, at least by the Captain's account of "the old folks at home," and this was more than he hoped for, after reading William's letter. He begged his sister to give William no encouragement to hope for a removal from Waddel's, promised to write to him himself, and left her.

CHAPTER XIII.

Captain Thompson's design was to keep his nephew at Doctor Waddel's school long enough to wean him from his old associates, and his old habits,.to put at least seventeen years upon his head before he entered College, to prepare him so thoroughly for the sophomore class, that he might enter it with credit, and in the meantime to give him the strength and vigor of constitution, that would sustain him through any amount of mental labor that he might find it necessary to undergo in order to stand at the head of his classes in College. All this was as well planned as it could be. College is no place for a youth given to bad habits. It sometimes happens, that religion finds such an one. there, and reforms him; but it much oftener happens, that he makes shipwreck of the religion of all his College companions who associate with him. Nor should a youth be sent to College until he has acquired some little stability of character and self-control; and seventeen is the earliest age at which these can be hoped for, in youths generally. Well for them if even at that age they have the moral firmness needful to resist the temptations to vice, which are found in all Colleges. One of the best securities against these temptations is a high reputation for talents and scholarship, acquired immediately on entering College. Students will commonly struggle harder to maintain, than to gain a high position in their classes.

But to the success of Captain Thompson's plans, it was indispensable that William Mitten should become reconciled to this school; otherwise he would keep his mother in such a state of mental excitement, that her health must soon give way under it, when no alternative would be left him, but to save the life of the mother, by indulgence of the son. He flattered himself that time would reconcile William to the school, and the sooner, when he saw all hope of leaving it cut off. He knew that the worst must soon be told, and he supposed that if he could carry his sister safely through the successive developments of the first month or two, his ultimate designs would be accomplished. His policy was, therefore, to lighten the first shock of each unpleasant discovery, by diverting her mind from it, with something amusing, flattering, or harmlessly controversial. The critical reader will have learned his tactics from what has been recorded specially in the last Chapter. Having allayed the mother's anxieties for a moment at least, he turned to the son, and addressed to him a letter, in which, with much good advice, he administered to him a stern rebuke for afflicting his mother with his complaints. "Are you," said he, "so inhuman, so brutish, as to try to win me over to your wishes, through your mother's tortures? Are you not well enough acquainted with her to know that she never forfeits her word—that she would sooner die, now, than reclaim you from me until your education is completed? Why, then, do you croak to her? Why do you not make your wants and discontents known to me? I am the only one that can appease them.

"And you are grumbling about your fare already! Why, I carried cakes and sugar things enough with you to last you one week surely; and pray get unstuffed of them, before you begin to grumble about your next cramming. If you had seen your father and me when we were of your age, gulping down ash-pone and cracklings, you would, for the honor of the stock at least, keep your daintiness to yourself. I don't know what Newby gives you to eat; but I have no doubt it would have been a feast to us in our day. What apology have you for grumbling at your diet, when you have the privilege of boarding where you please? If you don't like Newby's, go somewhere else. What better are you than the hundred and fifty boys around you? This much you may take for settled: *that I never will take you away from Mr. Waddel's, just to accommodate your belly.* So quit your grunting about what you are to eat; and if you must grunt, grunt to me, and not to your mother.

"And what does it signify to you, who or how 'old *Waddel*,' as you call him, whips, so long as he does not whip you? '*Old Waddel!*' That is a pretty way for such a chap as you are to speak of a man of Mr. Waddel's age and rank, now is it not? Pray, Master Mitten, where did you learn your manners? From '*uncle Twat*,' or uncle *Sot?* In the parlor, or in the kitchen? Now mark me, young man! The next time you write that name in that way to your mother, or me, I will cut it out and send it to Mr. Waddel, and ask him whether he allows his pupils to speak of him after this manner. I lose all patience, when I think that at the very time when you were speaking thus rudely of him, he was penning a letter filled with the most flattering compliments to you————"

While the Captain was thus writing to his nephew, Mrs. Mitten was busily engaged devising means to raise her son above want and ridicule. She resolved that William never should "blossom," and that in this matter, at least, she would disappoint Mr. Brace. Accordingly she set to work with all dispatch to make him up two new suits; and that they might not attract attention from their fineness, she chose for them the coarsest material that her heart would consent to William's wearing. "Let my son," sighed she, "look like a negro, rather than *suffer worse than one!*" She taxed her mind to find some decent substitute for a shirt, but failing here, she made him up three cotton shirts, of Mrs. Thurlow's spinning and weaving —that is to say—of the best quality of home manufacture. To these she added three pairs of stockings of Mrs. Figg's knitting. All these, with three blankets, and two pairs of *cotton* sheets, were packed in one box; but as they did not quite fill it, she slipped into it one tumbler of plum jelly, and one of raspberry jam. These being nicely surrounded and covered with cotton, the box was closed. Another was replenished with biscuit, crackers, cheese, tongue, sliced ham, sausages, &c., &c., to a large extent; and this too, like the other, was closed rather carelessly. The whole process was kept a profound secret from the Captain; and indeed, from everybody else, but Tom, upon whom secrecy was strictly enjoined. As there was no hope of meeting with a convenient opportunity of sending these cumbrous stores to William, by one going to Willington, Mrs. Mitten determined to forward them without delay *per cart*, in charge of her most intelligent and trusty servant. The reader immediately conjectures who this servant was. But a very ugly difficulty lay between the plan and its execution. Tom did not know the first mile of the way to Willington, and to get directions from the Captain, was just to blow the whole project sky high. Mrs. Mitten took the rounds of the stores, therefore, in quest of the desired information. But few of the merchants or citizens of whom she made inquiry, had ever heard of Willington; and, when she told them that Willington was the place where Mr. Waddel kept his school, they looked at her as if doubting whether she was in her right mind; for every body knew that her son was at Mr. Waddel's school, and that her brother had carried him there. All were too polite, however, to ask explanations of her. From Mr. West, she got a little light. He told her that when her brother went off with William, he met them near Mr. Ellison's, on the Washington road. This was enough to start by, at least; and she knew that Mr. Smith's was the first stage; but she was well aware that it would never do to dispatch Tom upon this information alone. She was constrained, therefore, to resort to her brother at last. She went over to his house early in the afternoon, and found that he had gone to his farm. She awaited his return; and in the meantime made a confidant of Mrs. Thompson, and bespoke her assistance in extracting from her husband such directions, as would guide Tom surely and speedily to Willington. The Captain reached home just at supper time. His sister greeted him with a radiance of countenance and gaiety of manner, that really transported him.

"Oh, my dear sis," said he, "how happy I am to see you so cheerful—so much like your own dear, sweet, former self! What good news have you heard?"

"None, brother. My cheerfulness is not altogether real; but I hope it soon will be so; and perhaps the best way to make it so, is to assume it when I can."

So went the conversation, as they went to the table. When seated, Mrs. Mitten actually began a playful conversation with Mrs. Thompson, by enquiring whether she had heard lately of "David Ramsay, son of Dr. Ramsay, the Historian, &c., &c. &c."

"No," said Mary, "I don't think he'll ever say 'Ramsay' to me again, as long as he lives."

The Captain roared, and all laughed.

"Well, Moll," said he, "if I could always see you and sis in such fine spirits, I believe I should be the happiest man living."

"Well husband," said Mary, "we ought both of us always to be in fine spirits, for after all your teasing and wilfulness, I don't think any woman ever had a better husband than I have, or a better brother than Anna has."

"I can say 'amen' to that with all my heart," said Anna.

"Well, done, ladies!" cried the Captain, pretending to take it all as a joke, "what project have you now on foot? Where are the girls going? How many horses will they want, and for how long? How much money will it take to rig them out, and bear their expenses. It can't be that either of the girls are going to get married : the oldest is a little too young for that."

"Nothing of the kind, husband ; nothing of the kind. It just came in the way, and I spoke out the honest sentiments of my heart."

"And so did I, brother, I assure you."

"Well, ladies, I can only say that I wish from the very bottom of my heart, that all this would 'just come in the way' every day. It would make me the happiest man in the United States, I'm sure."

"Brother, have you answered William's letter?"

"Oh, yes, long ago," said the Captain, looking as if he thought something was about to "come in the way" that was not quite so comfortable.

"Husband, how far is it to Mr. Waddel's?"

"About sixty miles—maybe a little under or over."

"Which way do you go to get there, brother?"

"I went the Barkesdale Ferry Road, because it is a little nearer than the upper road by Lisbon, Petersburg, and Vienna. Look here, good women, what do all these questions mean? Anna, you surely have no notion of going to Mr. Waddel's, have you?"

"Oh, no, not the most distant idea of it—at least till the weather becomes milder."

"You're not going to send for William to come home, surely!"

"No, no, my dear brother, no. Did you ever know me to violate my word? And if I were disposed to do it, do you suppose that I would do it stealthily?"

"That would be quite out of character with you, sister, I confess. But there is something so strange in this catechising from you and Mary, and it goes on with such quizzical looks between you, right upon the heel of a loving fit, that I am constrained to think that there is something in the wind that I am not to be suffered to understand."

"How do you know husband, but that we are paying you back in your own coin? It is fine sport for you to trifle with our curiosity."

"I should expect such pay from *you*, but not from *Anna*."

"Well, sister Mary, as we can't please him either by being serious or pleasant, suppose we go over to my house for the remainder of the evening."

"Oh, no, my dear wife, and my dear sister, don't go away and leave me while you are in such a pleasant mood. I have not had such a refreshing, for two years. Stay, and you may ask me as many questions as you please, and I will answer them with pleasure."

"Stay a moment, Anna, and let's try him," said Mrs. Thompson. "What is the given name of the Smith whom you stayed with the first night?"

"John."

"How far does he live this side of Washington?"

"About three miles—perhaps a little less."

"After you pass through Washington, what is the next town that you come to?"

"No town. But there are two places that bear the names of towns— or names which a traveller would take for the names of towns, though there are not six houses in both of them put together; the first is Rehoboth, and the second is Goshen."

"Well, you have said your lesson so well that we will not examine you any more to-night. And now, sister Anna, he has been such a good boy that I think you ought to sit down and spend the evening with him."

"I would with all my heart, sister, if I could, but business that must be attended to-night, calls me home. Remember, I have been here nearly all the afternoon."

"Well, if you must go, I'll go with you."

"What in the mischief can these women be after?" mused the Captain as they left the house. "If Waddel was a widower, and didn't whip so joyfully, I should think that Anna was going over to lay siege to his heart." The Captain being fatigued, retired early to rest.

As soon as the ladies entered the house, Tom was summoned.

"Tom," said Mrs. Mitten, "I want you to take old Ball and the cart, and carry those boxes to your mas' William. He is going to school to Mr. Waddel, in Willington, over in South Carolina—is Ball shod?"

"Yes. ma'am, new shod. day before yesterday."

"I want you to start at the peep of day in the morning. And now listen well to what I'm going to tell you.● You take the Washington road, the road by Mr. Ellison's, and keep it till you come to Mr. John Smith's. He lives only two or three miles this side of Washington. There you will stop for the night. no matter what time you get there.

The next morning, make an early start, and when you get to Washington, enquire for Rehoboth——"

"Stop, Mis'ess—call that name 'gin !"

"*Rehoboth*—Re-ho-both."

"I got him !" said Tom, with one ear up and the other down, his eyes looking on the ground six feet off, and listening, most vigorously.

"When you get to Rehoboth, inquire for Goshen, and when you get to Goshen, enquire for Barkesdale's ferry; and when you get to Barkesdale's ferry, enquire for Willington, or Mr. Waddel's either; and when you get to Willington, ask for Mr. Newby's, where you will find William—I believe that's all right, isn't it, Mary?"

"Exactly."

"Here is your pass, Tom, in which I have stated where you are going, and for what. If you get out of the way, show that to any one you meet, and he will set you right. And here are ten dollars; take five to bear your expenses, and give the other five, with this letter, to William. Now, do be particular, Tom, for if anything goes wrong, we shall never hear the last of it. I want you to get back before brother David finds out that you have ever been."

"I'll go it, mis'ess, like a streak o' lightnin'."

Mrs. Thompson returned home and slipped into bed without waking her husband. The next morning he watched her very closely, but could discover nothing unusual in her conduct or conversation. After breakfast, he re-visited his farm, and returned to dinner. Having dined, he sauntered down to the business part of the town, where he joined a group of gentlemen in front of Mr. West's store. They gave him a somewhat distant salutation, and eyed him with rather a solemn interest, saying nothing.

"Why, gentlemen," said the Captain, "what makes you all look so serious?"

"Captain," said Mr. West, "have you heard from your nephew, William Mitten, lately?"

"Not very," said the Captain, turning pale. "Has anything happened to him?"

"Not that I know of, but his mother asked me the way to Mr. Waddel's yesterday, with some anxiety, and I didn't know but that something had happened."

"She asked me, too," said a second. "And me, too," said a third. "And me," said a fourth.

"Why," resumed the Captain, "it is the strangest thing in the world! Nothing can be the matter with William, for his mother was at my house last night, and I hardly ever saw her more cheerful than she was, all the time she stayed. And, what was unaccountable to me, then, and is more so now, she and my wife were pumping me all the time about the road to Waddel's."

"I thought it very strange," continued West, "that she did not go to you for information."

"I was not at home in the forenoon."

"Oh, well, that accounts for it."

It was sheer good luck on Mrs. Mitten's side that none of the party knew but that she had gone to consult her brother in the first instance. While the whole company were standing amazed, Mr. Houghton came up, smiling—

"Captain," said he, "as I came into town this morning, I met your sister's Tom about two miles this side of my house, in a cart, with two boxes in it, and about two feeds of fodder and corn. Why, Tom, said I, "where are you going?"

"I'm gwine," says he, "to Mr. Wodden's, who keeps school at Mr. Williston's, in Car'lina." ·

"Well," said I, "Tom, you'll never get to Car'lina this way, till you pass through Augusta."

"Why, ain't this the Washington road, Mas' Josh?" said he.

"No, Tom, you left the Washington road three or four miles back."

"Emp-e-e-eh!" says Tom. "My sign fail me this time, that's sartain!"

"What sign, Tom?"

"Why, you see, Mas' Josh, when I come to the fork of a road, and don't know which to take, I spit in my hand and hit 'um with my fore-finger, so; and which way the mos' spit fly, I take that road. But, bless the Lor', the spit cheat me this time, that's sartain."

A peal of laughter followed this narrative, loud enough to be heard over half the village; but the Captain did not swell it much. He disguised his wrath, however, pretty well. ·   •

"I put him in the right road again," continued Mr. Houghton, "and for fear the spit wouldn't fly right, I advised him of all the forks between my road and the Washington road."

"The mystery is explained," said the Captain. "Anna has sent off a cart load of comforts to her son, which she did not wish me to know about; and now I'll have to go after Tom, for he'll never find the way to Waddel's during ash and oak."

"What did he mean, Captain,",inquired Houghton, "by Waddel's keeping school at *Mr. Williston's ?*"

"The place where Waddel's school is kept, is called *Willington,* and Tom has mistaken it for a man's name."

As the Captain's feelings were not in tune with those of the company, and as every question made the discord more and more grating to his refined sensibilities, he concluded to retire; so putting on an air of perfect indifference to the whole matter, and saying carelessly "I must see Anna," he withdrew very leisurely; but one who saw how his face reddened, and his pace quickened with every step towards his sisters after he turned the nearest corner, might with truth have exclaimed, "The ma-an's mad !"

CHAPTER XIV.

Captain Thompson had ample cooling time before he reached his sister's residence, for it was full two hundred yards from Mr. West's store; "but contrary to the law in such case made and provided," instead of *cooling,* he got hotter and hotter with every step of the way. Business, at home demanded his attention just at this time—the weather was still cold, and might in a day or two turn much colder. When and where he should overtake Tom, and how he should dispose of him and his load when overtaken, were perplexing considerations. Then his sister's unconquerable indulgence of her son, with its probable consequences, coming upon the raw places of his mind which it had already produced, was quite irritating. Nor was he entirely forgetful of the fun of the village already enjoyed at his expense, and likely to be renewed on his return. All these things pressing upon a mind naturally excitable, were not calculated to lull it into repose. The reader therefore will not be surprised to learn that they so completely absorbed the Captain's attention, that he became wholly forgetful of the claims of dignity, and "the poetry of motion," and that he reached his sister's steps in a palpable trot.

As soon as his sister saw him she showed signs of great alarm, for she observed that he was in a state of very unusual excitement. Her alarms had a good effect upon the Captain; they reduced his feelings instantly to a little above temperate.

"What," said he, "was in those boxes you sent off by Tom, this morning?"

"One contained some clothing for William, and——"

"More finery, I suppose !"

"No, not a stitch of finery."

"What then?"

"Two suits of coarse negro cloth, (I may call it) some cotton homespun shirts, and a few home-knit stockings."

This was refreshing to the Captain. "Well, I rejoice," continued he, "that your love for your boy is beginning to show itself in the right way at last. And what was in the other box?"

"Some refreshments——"

"More cakes, raisins, almonds, sugar-pums, &c., &c., of course?"

"No, not a single one of either."

"What then?

She named the contents of the box.

"Well, if he must be crammed, better this than the first lot. Now I've got to pack off after that fool negro, pressed as I am with business, just at this time; for he'll never find the way to Waddel's while the world stands——"

"Brother, I am sure you need not take upon yourself that trouble. Tom is a very intelligent negro——"

"Humph!"

"—— And I have no doubt but that he will go straight to Mr. Waddel's without a blunder. I give him such particular directions that he can't miss the way——"

"*You* gave him directions! Why, there never was a woman—a *town* woman—on the face of the earth, who could find the way to a house fifteen miles from her own, after going to it twenty times; and there never was one who could direct Solomon to a place ten miles off, so that he could find it; and here you've sent off a stupid jackass of a negro to go sixty miles under your directions, and to a place that you've never been to yourself!"

"Well, if he doesn't find the way, it will be all your fault——"

"How the devil will it be my fault?"

"I got the directions from you, and I gave them to Tom just precisely as I received them from you, and sister Mary will prove it."

"I didn't pretend to go into the details, for I did not know what you and Mary were fishing for; and if I had given them, there is not a *Tom* in the world that could have followed them."

"I think, brother, you underrate the negro character, as you are too apt to do with all character, except that of the 'lords of creation.' I must think that there is a little sense in the world that does not belong to them. Perhaps, however, I am mistaken."

"Well, what directions did you give Tom?"

She repeated them.

"And you think Tom can't miss the way under those directions?"

▫ "I am sure he will not, for I have proved him to be uncommonly shrewd at finding roads."

"Well, he did not get ten miles from town before he got lost—took the Augusta road, and told Joshua Houghton that he was going to Mr. Wodden's who kept school at Mr. Williston's, in Carolina!"

"Oh! Mr. Houghton must have misunderstood him. He couldn't have miscalled Mr. Waddel's name, for it has been repeated in his hearing over and over, and over again. Isn't Burke's Meeting-house on the Washington road?".

"Near it."

"And isn't it more than ten miles off?"

"Yes."

"Well, he knows the way to Burke's Meeting-house, for he has taken me there repeatedly."

"Yes, and if you had told him to go by Burke's Meeting-house, he would have gone that far straight, at least."

"I couldn't have told him that, for I didn't know that Burke's Meeting-house road and the Washington road were the same myself."

"I suppose not. But it is not worth while to stand talking about it. I know that he will not find the way to Waddel's in a week, if ever, and I must go after him. Was old Ball shod or bare-foot when he set out?"

"Newly shod."

"Did you give him any money to bear his expenses?"

"I gave *Tom* money."

"Did you understand me to ask whether you gave old Ball money to pay his expenses?"

The Captain, without waiting for an answer to his last question, went home with his "*foot down*," and of course his wife was all meekness and obsequiousness. He did not speak to her at all, but called out in her presence to Dick, "to have his horse ready at the peep of day, for him to puck off after Anna's Tom."

"Master, is Tom runaway?"

"Ask your mistress there—she can tell you."

"Miss'ess is Tom——"

"Go about your business, you black rascal," said Mrs. Thompson, in an undertone."

"Kigh!" whispered Dick, "some 'en wrong here!"

The Captain fell to writing letters furiously—jumped up and ordered Dick to grease the chaise—resumed his pen, and jumped up again and felt in his breeches' pockets—wrote sometime, and jumped up again and jerked open a drawer, looked in and shut it up again—folded up a letter and commenced another—jumped up and ordered Delphy to get him some warm water to shave—wrote again—stopped, punched the fire, and told Suckey to tell Dick to bring in some wood, "plenty of it. for I don't know that I shall go to bed to night." Wrote again—rose, went out and stayed a little while, and came in again. Folded another letter or note, and went to writing again. Finished, another note, and called for the water to shave. Just here, Mrs. Thompson, in a very subdued tone, informed him that supper was ready. It consisted of tea, biscuit, butter, cheese, sliced ham, cold tongue, and a few cold sausages. The Captain took his seat, and looked at them as if they were all laughing at him, and then fell to work upon them, as if he were fighting them for their rudeness.

"What clothes shall I put up for you, husband?" said Mrs. Thompson, tenderly.

"I reckon you'd best put up all I've got, for I expect to wear them all out before I find Tom, and get him safely home again. It will be at the very least, four days before this can be accomplished. Upon this hint the good lady stocked him for a week.

After supper, the Captain shaved, went to the stable to see that old Roan was in travelling order, returned, handed the letters to his wife, and went to bed. The letters were all left open, from which the wife understood prefectly, that her duty concerning them was to be learned from their contents.

And now having put the Captain quietly to bed, we beg leave to indulge in a few reflections upon his conduct towards his sister and wife. We can find it in our heart to palliate, if not wholly excuse his gusts of temper before his lovely sister. The heat of his mind would not cool, even in cooling time. But how can we justify him, in a direct issue between them upon the capacity of the negro race generally, and of Tom, in particular, for ascribing his blunder wholly to stupidity, when he knew and must have remembered, that negro stupidity had nothing to do with it! It was the result, as the reader has seen, of a symbolical delusion (if we may be allowed the expression) and not of mental imbecility. It was not in keeping with the Captain's usual candor to suppress this important fact.

Nor can we find a single apology for the Captain's long protracted crustiness to his wife. He had relieved himself at his sister's of his redundant steam, there was nothing to raise it again on his way home, her playful "fishing" frolic was certainly no offence, and her meekness in his presence should have reduced him instantly to tenderness and kindness. But so it is with these "lords of creation;" they must not only be allowed to become furious, but they must be allowed to spend their wrath upon the dearest object they have on earth. Is it likely that women will continue to marry if such conduct be persisted in? And what is to become of the world when they cease to marry?

Having made no allowance for the six or eight miles that he had lost on the Augusta road, Tom concluded, at the end of seventeen miles from home that he must not be far distant from John Smith's; and that he might not pass his stopping place from ignorance of its location, he determined to keep himself well advised of his approaches to it, from such travellers as he might meet. His mind was no sooner made up to seek light, than an opportunity was afforded him in the person of one who entered his road but a few yards ahead of him.

"Master," said he to the stranger, "how far is it to Mr. Smith's?"

"Which Smith?"

"John Smith."

"*Parson* John Smith?"

"Well, I 'reckon he's a Parson, for Mis'ess is a mighty good Christian, and she told me I must be sure to stay at his house to-night, any how, day or night."

"That's the road to Parson Smith's," said the traveller, pointing to the road he had just left. "It's just three miles to his house."

Tom took the road and went on his way rejoicing. He soon reached the Parson's, and without introduction, or question, to the good man, he commenced ungearing. Mr. Smith, noticing him from his window, walked out and asked him what he was doing.

"Ain't this Parson Smith's?" enquired Tom.

"Yes."

"Mis'ess told me I must stay here any how, no matter what time I got here."

"Who is your Mistress, my boy?"

"Mrs. Mitten—mighty good woman."

"I don't know her—I reckon there's some mistake—Have you any paper?"

"Yes sir," said Tom, handing his pass.

The Parson read it, and said, "Tommy, my boy you've come out of your way. I'm not the John Smith you are seeking. He lives right on the road you left, just this side of Washington."

"Emp-e-e-e-eh! How far is it Master?"

"Why, if you go back to the Washington road it is about fourteen miles, but if you'll take that road that turns around the horse lot, you will save near two miles." Tom took it, fell again into the Washington road and reached Smith's an hour or two in the night.

The next morning the Captain and Tom had an even start; they both left their respective stations as soon as they could see to drive. As it was next to impossible for Tom to miss his way after being set right by Houghton, until he passed little River, the Captain made no inquiries for him up to this point, but employed himself in a close look-out for the tracks of the cart wheels, and of old Ball. Every now and then he would espy traces of a two wheeled vehicle, drawn by a new-shod horse, which he felt pretty sure was the equipage he was in pursuit of; but still he was far from certainty upon this head. He stopped at the first house he came to after he passed the river, and enquired whether a negro, driving a large bald-faced sorrel, in a blue cart, with two boxes in it, had passed that way. "Yes," said the man whom he accosted, "I met him yesterday at the forks of the road up here, axing for Parson Smith's, and I put him in the road to the Parson's."

"*Parson* Smith! who the devil made him a parson? A month or two ago, he was one of the profanest men I ever saw."

"You don't know the man, sir. Brother Smith is one of the most religiousist men in all this country."

"What! John Smith, just this side of Washington?"

"Oh no, not him! *Parson* Smith, who lives over here by Bethesda Meeting House."

Here the Captain, contrary to his habit, let fall a very bad word against Tom, and proceeded:

"What could have put it into the head of that addled-brained goose to quit the plain beaten road and run off into by-ways to hunt up Parsons and Meeting-houses!"

"Stranger, I don't know but that I am to blame for that. He axed for John Smith; I axed him if he meant Parson John Smith; and he said he reckoned he was a Parson, for his Mistress was a mighty good woman, and told him he must stay all night——"

"Well, please direct me the way to Parson Smith's."

"Stranger, I hope you won't think hard of me——"

"Oh, no sir, no! I don't blame you the least in the world. Di-

I

rect me the way to Parson Smith's if you please, for I am in a great
hurry."

"I'm mighty sorry if I turned him out of the way; but he axed
me———"

"I give you my word and honor I don't blame you at all—but I
shall blame you if you don't tell me the way to Smith's as you did
the negro."

"Oh, yes, well I will with a great deal of pleasure. Go on till
you pass a little old field to your left, and you'll come to a road wind-
ing round the *fur* edge of it; take that, and it will lead you straight
to Parson Smith's."

As the Captain turned off, the other continued :

"Stop one minute stranger!"

The Captain stopped.

"Have you ever thought, stranger, of the sin of profane swearing ?"

"Yes," said the Captain, cutting up old Roan. "I never do it
unless I am very angry."

The Captain had no difficulty in finding the road to Parson
Smith's, but he had great difficulty in solving a mystery which presented itself to him as soon as he reached it. As the road was but
little traveled, the tracks of the cart wheels and of old Bald remained entirely unobliterated. They proved to be the same that he
had caught glimpses of on the way, and supposed to be Tom's tra-
cing ; but while they showed plainly that he had gone to the Parson's, there was no sign that he had returned to the direct road from
the Parson's. This perplexed him seriously, and made him wonder
whether Tom had not gone to a camp meeting with the Parson.
There was no alternative, so he determined to go to the Parson's
even at the hazard of getting a more serious lecture from him than
he had already received from one of his flock. He soon reached
the house, and saw a lady standing in the door. He called to her to
know "whether Parson John Smith lived there?" The lady looked
at him intently, but gave him no answer. He repeated the question,
but still received no response. "Why what upon earth does the
woman mean?" muttered he. "If there was a fatal disease on this
earth called ' *The Woman*,' I should die of it, to a dead certainty."
At length the kind woman broke silence:

"Light and come in, and warm yourself."

"No, I thank you, madam, I am not cold, and am in a great hurry. Did a negro man stop here with a cart and a blaze-faced horse,
yesterday?"

The lady made no answer, but advanced slowly towards him. Coming near the chaise she said : "You'll have to speak a little loud to me ; I'm a little hard of hearing."

"Is this Parson Smith's ?" asked the Captain in a pretty loud tone.

"Yes, sir."

"Where is he?"

"He's at the pig pen, sp—— 'tending to his pigs."

"Did a negro man and a blaze-faced horse stop here yesterday ?"

"You'll have to speak a little loud to me ; I'm a little hard of hearing."

The Captain repeated the question louder.

"I think he did."

"Which way did he go ?"

"Sir ?"

"Which-way did-the-negro-boy-go ?" bawled the Captain to the top of his voice.

"Well, I'm not so deaf as all that comes to—I think he went round the lot there."

The Captain wheeled off, soon struck the trail, and "opened on it " loudly.

At the true John Smith's, he learned the history of Tom for the preceding night. Smith told him that he had given Tom such directions as would carry him on his way through Washington.

The Captain pushed on through the village, struck the trail on the Petersburg road, followed it for two miles, and stopped for the night at Mr. Brown's. Brown told him that Tom had passed there early on the preceding morning, and that this was all the information he could give of him, except that he seemed to be getting along very well. A little after night-fall another gentleman stopped at Brown's, whom the landlord greeted with all the cordiality of intimate friendship, under the name of Col. White. "Here's a man," said Brown, "who can probably tell you something about your boy; he lives right on the road about five miles this side of Petersburg. "A boy," continued Brown to White, "in a cart, with a balled-sorrell in it."

"Oh yes," said White, "he stopped at my house and enquired for ' the Hobot,' but I understood him and put him in the road to Rehoboth."

At Col. White's Tom was much nearer to Doctor Waddel's than he was to " the Hobot ;" but he had promised " to go like a streak of lightning," and he was verifying his pledge.

As his game had "doubled," the Captain determined to quit the trail and push directly for Rehoboth. By this movement he had gained greatly upon Tom; but not enough to overtake him that day. We will not detain the reader with further particulars of the chaise, suffice it to say that about two hours by sun on the third day, in a rugged by-way, about two hundred yards from the highway leading from Augusta to Barkesdale's Ferry, and about three miles from the ferry, he came up with Tom under very interesting circumstances. On a washed hill side, Tom, as a classic reader is reported to have said, "in trying to avoid Skilly he had rushed upon Caribogus"— or (leaving the classics) in trying to avoid a deep gully on the one hand he had run over a log on the other; and though he did not quite upset his cart, he tilted it far enough to pour out both boxes in the gully. The top of one of the boxes was so far opened by the fall, that it discharged four biscuits and two crackers in the gully. The top of the other burst entirely off, and the tumblers of preserves were broken, having delivered a part of their contents to the top of the box, part to the package, part to the road, and having retained a part. As the biscuit and crackers were too dirty to be replaced, as the jelly and jam were irretrievably lost to William, and as Tom, from fatigue and long fasting, was very hungry, he rightly conceived that he could make no better use of them than to eat them. As well as he could with a biscuit, he cleaned the package, then the board, (which happened to rest bottom upward) then skimmed the top off what was on the ground, and topped off with what was left in the tumblers. As he did not observe the rule of proportion in eating, his biscuit and crackers gave out before he had dispatched the last tumbler, and he was just wiping it out with his forefinger, and sucking it, when the Captain came up with him.

"Lor gor' a'mighty, Mas David!" exclaimed Tom, as the Captain approached him, " I never was so glad to see anybody in all my born days. These people 'bout here been 'foolin' me all day long—"

" How did you get here, you wooly-headed scoundrel?"

" One man told me I'd save three miles by comin' this way."

As the Captain got to saying bad words again early in the interview, notwithstanding the lecture he had received, and as what farther passed between him and Tom was of little interest, we omit it. They were now but about six miles from Willington and the Captain, very reluctantly, concluded to pilot Tom himself for the remainder of the way. The idea of appearing at Willington, with a cart load of provisions for his nephew, was very annoying; but the thought of lugging them all the way home again, and disappointing his sister, was still more annoying; so he chose the least painful alternative.

Things were righted, and the two set out for the ferry. They reached it and found a wagon waiting the return of the flat from the South Carolina side. His heart leaped at this good fortune, for he knew that the wagon could hardly cross without going through Willington. He was not disappointed. The wagoner lived but five miles from Willington, was going through it, and knew everybody who lived within six miles of it. The Captain took his name, placed the boxes and Mrs. Mitten's letter in his charge, offered to pay freight, but the wagoner would receive nothing, placed Tom's unexpended cash (seven dollars) in his hands for William, dropped a line in pencil to Newby explaining things, and set his face homeward rejoicing. Nothing of interest occurred on the way back. The Captain's good fortune prepared him for receiving Tom's account of his adventures which were wonderful indeed, and which Tom never got done recounting during his life. The moral of it, as drawn by himself, may perchance be of service to the reader: "If I had forty thousand niggers, I'd never sen' one so far from home by he'self 'less he know de road firs' chop."

The Captain reached home early on the fifth day from his departure. He gave the particulars of his trip to his wife and sister by snatches, as he happened to be in the humor, until they were all told. The fate of the jelly and jam was very provoking to Mrs. Mitten who was "sure if she had been there, she could have saved some of it." The Captain was too busy to visit the public square for more than a week after his return; and his visits were very brief for more than a fortnight. But Tom became for a long while a distinguished character on the square.

CHAPTER XV

THE incidents of the last chapter were, upon the whole, fortunate. They cured Mrs. Mitten of sending delicacies to her son, cured William of his complaints for many months, improved his style when speaking of his Preceptor, brought him out in suitable apparel for his place and associates, and sprung all the energies of his mother to reconcile herself to his lot. When so much is said, the reader need not be told that Captain Thompson was also a great gainer by them. Things now went on more smoothly than they had for years. William soon stood a head and shoulders above any member of his class. The Georgians began to brag on him, the Carolinians to emulate him. He began to mingle in the active sports of his fellows, to be cheerful, if not forward, in sharing his part in providing fuel and making fires. His new clothes, to be sure, did not quite reach him before he "blossomed," for he kept the changes of his first supply as long out of sight as possible ; but he was far from being in *full bloom* when " the fruits of home industry reached him. Immediately upon their arrival, he appeared in the handy work of Mrs. Thurlow and Mrs. Figgs, and Brace's lips were closed to all further sarcasm upon his dress. In short, he followed his uncle's advice as well as he could, and forthwith began to experience the practical benefits of it. His new clothes "scratched him mightily at first, but he had got use to them," as he wrote to his mother; but he thanked her for them. The change in his dress was not much more remarkable than the change in his physical constitution.

From a weakly, puny, cowering, retiring, say-nothing boy, he became a muscular, active, sprightly, vigorous youth, who was nearly a match for any of his age, in running, jumping, wrestling, and the active sports of the school; and for loud clamoring at bull-pen, and town-ball, he had no superior. There was but one South Carolinian in the school who could throw him down, and that one was Andrew Govan ; there was not one in the school who could match him in running. From fifty lips the exclamation would come : " Did you ever see a fellow come out of the kinks as Bill Mitten has ?" By the time it came to his turn to make fires in the Academy, (one of the duties of every student,) he was as prompt and skillful in this work as most of his associates. Sweeping out the Academy (another duty) of course was easy. Beyond all this, there was nothing remarkable in his history until the annual examination and exhibition came on. These exercises continued for several days, and they were attended by multitudes—more, by many, than usually attend our College Commencements in these days. The order was as follows: First, the examination of all the classes; which was invariably conducted by the visitors, except when they declined· the task, and this rarely occurred. Then speaking, for which prizes were awarded. And lastly, the performance of one or two dramatic pieces, usually a comedy and farce: but these were discontinued after the first and only public exhibition in which William Mitten took part, and the reading of compositions was substituted for them. The speakers were divided into three classes, according to their age and advancement; the first class being composed generally of the oldest students in the school; the second, of those next in years; and the third, of the youngest, excluding those in the elementary studies. This arrangement was not always observed, however. Sometimes the larger and less advanced were put in the first class, and the smaller and more advanced, in the second class. William's age flung him in the lowest, though his advancement would have entitled him to a place in the second. The examination approached, and William wrote pressingly to his mother and uncle to attend. They did so, and reached Newby's the day before the exercises commenced. William recognized them at the fence, and ran out to meet them. Neither of them knew him, till he greeted them, any more than if they had never seen him. His fine face was there, a little tanned, but that was all of William Mitten that was left. He had grown like a weed, and developed as we have said. The Captain looked at him in triumph—the mother in tears. Mr. Newby was soon at the chaise and introduced to Mrs. M. Five or six ladies were standing at his door, observing the new comers.

"I fear, Mr. Newby," said Captain Thompson, "that you will not be able to accommodate us."

"Oh, very easy, if you can rough it a little for a few days."

"Why, where will you put us? Your house seems full already."

"Oh, we've plenty of houses, as you see."

"But those are the students' houses; what are you going to do with them?"

"Oh, we cotton them upon such occasions as this, if necessary."

"Cotton them?"

"Yes; put 'em all in one hole and ram them tight together. However, I don't think that will be necessary. We've two large rooms in the house, in one of which we will put the ladies, and in the other the gentlemen."

" Well, that will answer very well," said the Captain. "Do you take charge of Mrs. Mitten, and William and Tom and I will attend to the horses and baggage."

" Why, this is a new horse, Tom," said William, as he sprung to unsaddle a horse which Tom had led up. " Whose is he ?"

" He's Mas' David's. He say if you do well while he's up here, he gwine to give him to you. He's a tip top hos."

" Well, I've got him safe," said Bill. " What's his name ?"

" He name *Snap Draggum.*" .(Snap Dragon.)

" Here, Tom," said the Captain, "take this trunk in the house——"

" I'll take it," uncle, said William.

" You can't carry it, my son; it's pretty heavy."

Let me try it," said Bill; so saying, he flung it on his shoulder, and marched off with it, with perfect ease.

" Look ya-a-nder !" exclaimed Tom, as he moved off. " Bless de Lor', Mas' William done got a man 'ready."

The Captain saw him near the door with his burden without a totter, then turned, wiped his eyes twice, and was just blowing his nose the third time, when William leaped the fence, to assist Tom in leading the horses to the horse lot.

" Why, Bill," said the Captain, " I never saw a boy improve as you have in all my life."

The ladies gathered at.Mr. Newby's were all of the first respectability. They soon made Mrs. Mitten easy, and before they parted, several of them and Mrs. Mitten promised to interchange visits most certainly "if ever they came our way." (They never came our way.)

The night shut in and the woods were vocal in all directions with rehearsals of speeches and parts of plays. A very comfortable supper was provided for the guests, (increased by several, after the Captain's arrival) the mattresses were spread, all laid down, the gentlemen talked till twelve, the ladies till two, and all was hush—save here and there "the bubbling cry of some strong" snorer "in his agony." They were all, of necessity, up betimes the next morning, when they declared generally that they had "had a most delightful night's rest." Thus passed a wonderful night for Mrs. Mitten.

The next morning exhibited a complete metamorphosis of the students. It was easy now to distinguish the sons of the Patricians from those of the Plebs, though *turkey-red* and *indigo-blue* predominated largely over nankeen and gingham still.

From seven o'clock till nine, people of all ranks, ages, sexes and sizes, might be seen wending their way to the school house, or rather

to the area in front of it—for the examination was conducted under
the stately oaks of the campus. Some of the first men of the two
States were there. At nine the examination commenced. The students, with very few exceptions, acquitted themselves admirably. In
all the studies of his class, William distinguished himself. On this day
an incident occurred which was absolutely luxurious to all who disliked Brace. The reader need hardly be told that however bright in
wit, or ingenious in teazing Brace might be, he was not very bright in
his studies. He was in one of the Virgil classes, and he had caught
from a student, given to spouting poetry aloud, whenever he had any
in store to spout, the four first lines of Dryden's translation of the
second book of the Ænead. Doctor John Casey was conducting the
examination, flanked on his right and left with an imposing row of
dignitaries. "Begin," said the Doctor to Ned, who was at one extreme of the class in more senses than one, "at the second book of
the Ænead, and read the Latin first." Ned did so to the extent of
six or eight lines.

"Now translate."

Ned proceeded :

"All were attentive to the God-like man,
When from his lofty couch he thus began."

A roar of laughter burst from every one—loudest from the boys;
for two reasons, first, because they gloried in Brace's mortification;
and second, because they wished the company to understand from
this token that they were thoroughly versed in the poetry of all languages under the sun.

"Give us the translation in prose, if you please," said the Doctor.
Ned continued :

"Great Queen, what you command me to relate,
Renews the sad remembrance of our fate."

The laugh was repeated, but the Doctor had no occasion to repeat
his request; for Ned had exhausted his stock of poetry. His *debut*
was doubly unfortunate; for besides exposing him to ridicule, it left
him wholly in the dark as to how much of the Latin his version had
covered. So he began his literal translation two lines back of what
he had already rendered; and Dryden would have been amazed to
discover how he had butchered the Mantuan Bard, according to
Brace's translation.

This day and the next were consumed in like manner. On the
third day the speaking commenced.

A stage of rough plank was erected adjoining the school-house.

On this sat the Judges, of whom William H. Crawford, John C. Calhoun, and William W. Bibb were three. These hardly ever failed to attend the public exercises of Dr. Waddel's school. The two first had been his pupils, and the reader will excuse the digression, to learn that the first wife of the Doctor was the sister of the second.

In front of the stage, large logs were laid parallel to each other on which planks were placed at convenient distances apart, for seats. The whole was covered over with a bush-arbor. It was but a scant provision for the throng that attended upon this occasion; but what provision could accommodate all, when the number fell little, if any, short of two thousand people? The ladies, several hundreds in number, occupied all the seats.

Without going through the details of the exercises, suffice it to say that Mitten took the premium in his class by the award of the judges, approved of by every man, woman and *student* present at the exhibition. He had a part in both the dramatic pieces; and here he acquitted himself, if possible, with more credit than in declamation. When Mr. Calhoun, with a few complimentary words, presented him the prize, the whole assembly applauded loudly and cordially. One pretty little girl, beautifully dressed, quite forgot herself, and kept on clapping after everybody else had done, till her mother, laughing most heartily, stopped her. "Mitten, Mitten, Mitten!" was on every lip. All the ladies, old and young, wanted to kiss him; all the little girls fell in love with him. A thousand compliments saluted the ear of Mrs. Mitten from lips that she knew not. Through Captain Thompson, she had been made acquainted with Doctor Waddel, before the exercises commenced, and through him, with most of the gentlemen who sat as judges, and her acquaintance was still farther extended by the sojourners at Mr. Newby's; but now everybody sought an introduction to her, and everybody congratulated her upon the performance of her son.

Most of the judges waited upon her, and all of them had something flattering to say of William, or to him in her presence, for he was always at her side.

"Master Mitten," said Mr. Crawford, "I am proud to claim you as a Georgian. Cultivate your brilliant talents as a duty and an honor to the State that gave you birth."

"Master Mitten," said Mr. Calhoun, "the United States have an interest in you; and should I live to see you in the prime of life, I shall be sorely disappointed if I do not see you the admiration of them all."

As for Captain Thompson, he was in danger of going off by explosion. He had been filling up with joy, from the first sight of Bill, to the close of the exhibition; and now to find him so far surpassing his most sanguine expectations in everything, to see him standing at the head of his classes in scholarship, and declamation, and ahead of the whole school in dramatic talent, to hear him applauded by all, and specially by Messrs. Crawford and Calhoun, and (though last not least,) to see his sister almost in transports, was really perilous to the good Captain. He had tried to quench the volcano that was in him with rain; that is to say, he had cried six times, twice secretly, and four times publicly; but this gave him only momentary relief. Besides, the fire kept kindling all the time, and he could not keep crying all the time. Whithersoever he cast his eyes he saw something to inflame his ecstacy, and what would have been the consequence it were hard to tell, had not David Ramsay sauntered near him just at the critical moment—" Why, David, my young pilot, how do you do?" said the Captain. " Come here, my son, and let me introduce you to Mrs. Mitten, my sister, mother of William. Anna, this is David Ramsay, of whom you heard me speak!" " How do you do, Master Ramsay?" said Mrs. Mitten, smiling almost to a laugh. " I am very familiar with your name, for my brother could talk of no one else for some time after his return from his first visit to this place."

" I remember Captain Thompson very well; but I cannot call to mind anything that I said or did to make him remember me."

Here the Captain was a little at fault, but he soon rallied, and replied :

" It was your prompt courtesy to us as strangers, David, the coincidence of our names, but most of all, your connections, who are known to all, that impressed you so permanently upon my memory. I no sooner asked if Mr. Waddel was at home than you answered in the affirmative, sprang to the door, invited me in, and brought Mr. Waddel out to see me. This was but common politeness, to be sure, but I did not see any of your playmates offer to do the same thing. But for your kindness I might have had to knock long at the door, and sit long in the cold parlor, before Mr. Waddel would have come to my relief."

This interview was an admirable safety-valve to the Captain. It set his thoughts to running back to times and incidents, well calculated to relieve him from over-pressure of joy.

The conversation with young Ramsay was but just ended, when

Doctor Hay stepped up and greeted the Captain and his sister with a fervor which showed plainly that time had not abated his friendship for them in the least. The greeting was returned with equal warmth. The Doctor expressed his regret that he had been detained by professional business at home until the last day of the exhibition; but added, that he had been amply compensated for his trouble in coming, by the rich entertainment he had just enjoyed—"An entertainment, Mrs. Mitten," continued he, "to which your son was the largest contributor. I deem myself fortunate in having my son in the close connection of class-mate and room-mate with him."

Mrs. Mitten returned the compliment, by repeating what she said upon hearing that her son had fallen into the same room and class with the Doctor's son, only changing the terms of the compliment so far as to accommodate it to the Doctor's ear.

"And now," continued Dr. Hay, "you must tarry with me to-morrow night on your way home. Let us go over to Petersburg this afternoon, stay there to-night, take an early start in the morning, and (barring accidents) we will reach my house by dinner time or a little after. There rest until the next morning, when, if I can't prevail on you to stay longer, I will give you an early breakfast, and set you on your way in time to get home, without traveling much in the heat of the day."

The invitation was cordially accepted, and as soon as one of William's small trunks could be packed with selections from his wardrobe for the summer vacation, and Mrs. Mitten could renew her invitations and promises to the few ladies who had not left, and return her thanksgiving to Mr. and Mrs. Newby for their kindness to her son, and their hospitality to herself, and kiss Miss Thompson because she bore the family name and both knew they must be related, though neither could tell how, and give each of the house servants a quarter of a dollar apiece for being willing to do for her all that Tom did, and a dollar to the wash-woman for extra services, and a half dollar (sent) to the ostler for fear that he might be disappointed and her brother forget him—Mrs. Mitten was ready to depart.

While all this was transacting, the chaise was at the fence, Doctor Hay was sitting in his sulky, Gilbert was mounted on his father's horse, Silverheels, William on Snap-dragon, and Captain Thompson at the door getting comfortable fast.

The Captain escorted his sister to the chaise, she took her seat, the Captain took his, and off went the happiest company that ever moved from Willington. Nothing of interest occurred on the way

to Petersburg; for Mrs. Mitten, having to send back for her veil just
as she reached Dr. Waddel's, was not even attended with inconvenience, as she declared that she could not think of passing by Mr.
Waddel's door without lighting and bidding him good-bye, and
thanking him for his kindness to her son. These little duties consumed exactly the time needful for recovering the veil. It gave the
Captain, too, an opportunity of charging William and Tom to notice
well the road, so that either of them might find it without difficulty
on their return. Doctor Hay's servant, Quash, went back for the
missing article, and strange to say, found it readily. The dusk of
the evening found the company at Mrs. Ragland's, in Petersburg.

The reader will naturally enquire where the immense throng which
attended Dr. Waddel's exhibitions found accommodation. We answer, at all the houses within six or seven miles of Willington, and
at the four villages of Lisbon, Petersburg, Vienna, and Richmond.
The three first were tolerably thrifty little villages at the time of
which we are speaking. Petersburg was quite an active, busy,
commercial little town. It was situated in the fork of the Savannah
and Broad Rivers, and contained some eight or ten stores, with the
usual supplement of grog-shops, and the very unusual supplement of
a billiard-table. Notwithstanding these last, the citizens of the place
were generally remarkable for their refinement, respectability, intelligence and hospitality. The dwelling houses far outnumbered the
stores and shops. It was separated from Lisbon by Broad River,
and from Vienna by the Savannah. Lisbon we believe could never
boast of more than two stores and a groggery, and as many dwellings.
Vienna surpassed Lisbon in everything, but exactly how far, and in
what we are not able to say, except in John Glover's house and store,
which had no match in Lisbon. The road leading to Willington
from Vienna ascended a hill, about a mile from the latter place, which
was crowned with Richmond. This town was very compactly built.
It consisted of one dwelling house, one doctor's shop, one kitchen,
one stable, one corn-crib, and one smoke-house. Its white population
consisted of Doctor Thomas Casey, his wife, one or two children, and
Warler (or Waller) Beckly, a student of medicine.

Neither of the four towns surpassed this in hospitality. Doctor
Casey's house was open to all, and his heart was as open as his
house—so was his wife's. It was a great resort of the beaux and
belles of the neighboring villages; here they were always made welcome and happy. In these villages, the remotest of which was not
over seven miles from Willington, was ample entertainment for all

who attended the Exhibition, and could not procure it elsewhere.

Captain Thompson and Mrs. Mitten spent a happy night at Doctor Hay's, and were at home the next day by five in the afternoon. As they stopped at Mrs. M.'s door, the Captain inquired of William how he liked Snap-dragon.

"Oh! I am delighted with him, Uncle. I think he's the finest horse I ever saw."

".Well, he's yours, my son. So you see if your Uncle scolds when you do ill, he rewards handsomely when you do well."

"Oh! thank you, thank you, Uncle, a thousand times. You never will find me doing ill again, I promise you. I am so glad that you sent me to Mr. Waddel's I am so glad that you would not allow me to leave there when I wanted to—you have been, you are a father to me, and the very best of fath——"

"Well. that'll do, my son—you paid me for him before I gave him to you.' Remember your pledges, as often as you ride him!"

Alas! Captain, where was your usual forecast when you made this present?

CHAPTER XVI.

The cup of Mrs. Mitten's happiness was not yet full. In less than a month after Captain Thompson's return from Willington, he embraced religion and joined the Methodist Church; and in the course of a week his wife followed his example. The story which he told at the first Love Feast which he attended after his conversion, is worthy of being recorded:

"I have had," said he "for many years before me, a most beautiful example of the Christian character in my dear sister. I never could see but one fault in her, and that was 'a fault which leaned to virtue's side:' too much indulgence of her son. She embraced religion early in life; and often when I have seen her at her devotions, my conscience has smitten me sorely. But I always managed to silence its reproofs, for a time at least. Oh, how eloquent is the godly life of a sister! Whether because she was my sister, that the inward monitor would not forsake me, although repelled a thousand times; or because I have had for many years a secret leaning towards religion, which prolonged his visits, or some unknown cause, I cannot tell; but a month never rolled over our heads, that I did not observe in her the gleaming or broad out-shining of some heavenly virtue, which came "like lightning to my soul."

" As some of you know, about a month ago my sister dispatched a servant with some comforts for her boy at school in South Carolina. Knowing that I would bitterly oppose the measure, she kept it secret from me. I found it out, however, and posted off after the servant in a great rage. The blunders of the negro increased my rage. I stopped at a house to enquire for him. A plain illiterate man came out and informed me that he had left the plain large road and gone off on a by-way. In my wrath I cursed outright, and on the trip, I repeated the sin oftener, I believe, than I had in the whole course of my life before. As I turned to leave the good hearted man, 'Stranger,' said he to me, ' have you ever reflected upon the sin of profane swearing ?' I was in no frame of mind for reflecting upon any thing, and in the worst possible, for receiving religious lectures ; but a flash of respect for the good man came over me, which kept me from insulting him, and I replied, that I was not in the habit of profane swearing."

" My pursuit ended and object gained, I now set my face homeward, and on the way had nothing to do but to *reflect*. My mind had hardly resumed its accustomed tone, when the question of my road-side friend, in the rude accents in which he put it (for I have not given it in his own terms) forced itself upon my memory. Associated as it was, with the ignorance, the artlessness and innocence of the propounder, I smiled, and endeavored to divert my thoughts ; but the question would control them, so I let it have its way ; ' Have you ever reflected upon the sin of profane swearing !' No, honest, untutored yeoman, I never have ! What a sin it is ! Every other sin has something to plead in its behalf. The gamester, the cheat, the swindler, the thief, the robber, the pirate, sin in the hope of gain. The assassin for the gratification of revenge—the drunkard to appease a raging thirst—the prodigal, for many gratifications. But thou, oh, profane swearer ! what have you to plead in the extenuation of thy offence ? It is purely gratuitous. In one single, short imprecation, you embody sins enough to damn a world. You insult the Almighty, you trifle with his Holy Name, you violate the law of reverence, the law of love, the law of humanity, the law of peace ! You set God's power at defiance and invoke God's power to crash your *neighbor* and your *brother!* And all for what? What momentary gain do you derive or promise yourself from your sin of sins ? Often, most commonly, you have not even the flimsey plea of *passion* to gloss over your crime. You mingle it in your sports, your revels, your banquets, and horrify it with a laugh !"

" You will not wonder, brethren, that I became alarmed, and re-solved never to swear another oath while I lived. This was as far as I *went at the time;* but it was not as far as I *fell,* by a long, long way. Thenceforward my sins were more constantly and vividly before me than ever, until I sought the pardon of them, in God's own way, and as I believe found it—I am strongly tempted to say, 'I *know* I found it.' "

In religion, the captain was as he had been in every thing else that he undertook : .open, active, liberal, ardent, zealous, laborious, untiring. What some Christians call a *cross,* such as holding family prayer, particularly before strangers of rank, praying in public, and speaking in public on proper occasions, was to him no cross at all ; and we advise those Christians who cannot perform these offices, (and there are such) not to dignify them with the name of *crosses.*

Captain Thompson and his wife led off a great revival in the vil-lage, upon which Mrs. Glib took occasion to deliver her theology very freely.

" Well, well, well !" said she to Mrs. Lark, this is what you call *getting religion,* is it ? Sinning all your life, and then kneeling down there two or three days and then jumping up a Christian !"

" But, Mrs. Glib," said Mrs. Lark, " you don't remember what they say. They say that under Peter's preaching three thousand were converted and joined the church in one day."

" Well, is old Howell, Peter, or is old Sherman, Paul ?"

" No, but they say that they preach the same gospel that Peter and Paul did———"

" Oh yes, *they say, they say,* and they'll say anything to get up an excitement, and to scare people. Now I love religion—real, genuine religion—that kind of religion which a person goes to work calmly, soberly, and deliberately to get. When I get religion, this is the sort I mean to get ; but this wild-fire sort of religion I don't believe in at all."

" But they say you don't get it when and as you want it."

" They do ! I should like to know how they know what I can do, and what I can't. Now, mind what I tell you, nine out of ten of these flashy converts will back-slide before the year's out—you mark it ! You remember we had just such a fuss as this five years ago, and old Groat and John Dunn and Sally Nix, and Polly Pines all got religion and were mighty happy ; and where are they now ?"

" But Mrs. Glib, you must do them the justice to say that a great many more of them than that, held on to their religion."

" Yes, such holding on as it was. Holding on like Sam Strap ; who is mighty sanctified all day Sunday, and slandering people's children all the week—saying that genteel people's children are little better than a den of thieves. That's what you call holding on, is it ? That's what you call religion, is it ? And there's old Turner prosecuting little boys for a little harmless sport—and he a preacher at that ! Don't tell me anything about any such religion as that ! You'd kill yourself laughing if you could see my Flora Claudia Lavinia take them off. Now you know Mrs. Lark, that I don't allow my children to make game of religious people of any sort. But some nights when we come home from these night meetings, she begins before I have time to stop her, and when she begins I get in such a laughing fit, I can't stop her. She takes off old Howell to perfection—his very voice, action, and words—then old 'brother' McBoon's praying—the very twang. And old 'sister' McRea, creeping about among the mourners. And 'brother' Wilson's singing ! It seems to me sometimes she will kill me. I always reprove her for it. I said to her last night, Flora, you naughty girl, you really must quit this, if you don't I shall get right angry with you—they mean well, poor things, and you must not make fun of them."

Nine weeks after this conversation, Mrs. Glib was brought to death's door with the bilious fever; the first man that she sent for to pray for her was Captain Thompson ; the second was "brother" McBoon. The first woman she asked to pray for her was Mrs. Mitten, and the second was "sister" McRea—charging every one of them, while they prayed for her, to pray for her children, also, and for Flora in particular. She professed conversion in two days from the date of the first prayer that was put up in her behalf, and died. Flora never professed conversion. She married, in three weeks after her mother's death, a worthless, silly fellow, named Curt, who administered upon Mrs. Glib's estate because no one else would, took the guardianship of the boys, because no one else would ; hired a man of some property and no principle, named Carp, to go upon his bonds, sold out all the property of the estate, except the negroes, as soon as he could, and moved off with his security, and the whole tribe, white and black, to the frontier of Alabama, to the great relief and greater delight of every body. Nine years afterwards, the younger Glib (Ben.) came back to the village to learn something about the estate. To the amazement of all who knew the family, he was a decent, pious, but ignorant man. His story was that Curt and Carp settled near each other in Alabama. That in a very few years after they got out there, Carp had got from Curt every negro that belonged to the estate, and then moved still farther West. That the elder Glib got into a difficulty with a gambler, who shot him. Of his sister, he could be got to say no more than that he did not know where she was. That his other brother was thrown from a horse in a quarter race and killed. That he himself, seeing nothing but poverty and ruin and disgrace all around him, had sought and obtained religion. That as soon as he did so, a good Baptist man of considerable wealth took him by the hand, gave him employment on his farm, telling him that if he would do well, he would give him good wages till he came of age, and then give him a little start in the world. That his friend had been as good as his word, and that he had now enough to live on comfortably, though he was not rich.

The records showed of what the estate consisted. He took copies, went to the old family mansion, sauntered round it for a time, wept, and left the village forever.

Having gone thus far with the Glib family, we had as well dispose of it finally—it is replete with moral lessons. Carp had played his cards adroitly to avoid responsibility. He knew the character of the boys, and judged that none of them would live long enough to call him to account. He knew, too, it would be an easy matter to wheedle Curt out of all that he was worth individually or representatively, and conjectured that as soon as poverty began to stare her in the face, Mrs. Curt would be setting lawyers upon his trail. He therefore, from the day that they left Georgia, became exceedingly kind and exceedingly attentive to her ladyship. He would often speak to her playfully of her husband's inefficiency and bad management—declare that but for her, nothing could have induced him to become his security; "but I saw," said he, "every body hanging off, nobody seemed to care anything for you or your poor orphan brothers; and I said to myself, well, as for the boys, they will soon be big enough to shirk for themselves—they can rough it; but what is to become of Mrs. Curt? I can't see her suffer, and I'll be her friend if it costs me every dollar I have in the world."

He used a thousand seductive arts to entoil, and he succeeded. He loaned money liberally to Curt, often advising him in the presence of his wife not to take it. "Mr. Curt," he would say, "two per cent. a month will ruin you. I can get that from other people, and, therefore, I don't like to loan for less, and I will not lend it to you unless Mrs. Curt says so."

"How much," said Mrs. Curt, "is *two per cent?*"

"Two dollars on every hundred dollars," said Carp.

"Two dollars on every *hundred dollars!* why that is very little indeed! I'd borrow all the money in Alabama at that price, if I could get it."

"Yes, Mrs. Curt, but you will not like to see your negroes under mortgage to secure the debt."

"*Mortgage!* What's that?"

"Its a pledge of a negro to secure the debt."

"Oh, that's nothing—surely Mr. Curt can pay the little sums that he borrows with only two per cent. on them."

The "little sums" ran up so fast that in a few years every negro that Curt had in his hands was under mortgage. Not all for money loaned, but for corn, fodder, pork, bacon, and other things sold; and for large balances in horse-swaps, carpenters' bills paid, and large outlays for Curt, in erecting a mill; for Mr. Curt having a fine mill seat on his land, said it would never do to let such a fine water-power be lost; so he commenced building a large mill when, as yet, there was nobody in the neighborhood to patronize it, and when his brain was about as well suited to manage a mill, as a claw-hammer is to maul rails with.

About the time that the last mortgage ripened to maturity, Mr. Carp concluded to go "and take a view, as he said, of the *Louisiana* country." He went, and came back so delighted with it, that he must needs move there forthwith. But he could not go until he collected his Alabama debts. Curt and he came to a settlement, when it was found that Curt owed him more by three hundred dollars than the negroes were worth by Curt's own valuation; he agreed, however, as Curt was a particular friend, to take the negroes at Curt's estimate, and give him a receipt in full. Curt felt very grateful for the kindness, and promptly signed a bill of sale of the negroes, drawn up by Carp himself, in which he took every precaution to guard against "*after claps*" as he called them, and which, in *aftertimes* gave a western lawyer very great annoyance. Here it is:

"Whereas, on settlement this day made between myself and John Carp, it appears that I am in his debt for monies advanced to me on my own account, and also as administrator of Mrs. Brigita Glib, and also as guardian of the children of said Mrs. Glib, to the amount of t n thousand dollars; and whereas, I did execute a mortgage to said Jo' 1 f t. w.thin fourteen negroes to secure the said debt, said ne- .r s not being worth by three hundred dollars as much as said debt, at my own valuation, which mortgage is given up on my signing this bill of sale, and whereas said John did become my security as administrator, and guardian aforesaid, and I being willing to make him safe from any loss or losses for becoming my security as aforesaid, do make this bill of sale for that purpose also, for all these considerations I do sell and convey to the said John the following negroes namely:" (naming them, their sizes, sexes, and ages.) "And I warrant them to said John against all claim by me or any body claiming the same as heir of Mrs. Glib or any other person whatsoever, &c., &c."

This remarkable bill of sale Mr. Carp required should be signed by Mrs. Curt as well as her husband, and that Curt should sign it "for himself and as administrator and guardian." Curt expressed his readiness to comply with all these requisitions but the first. As to this he said, " he doubted whether his wife could be induced to sign it." "Well," said Carp, "ask her, and if she refuses, all well, it will make no difference."

Curt went to her with downcast looks and told her all the circumstances. To his astonishment she expressed her perfect readiness to sign it. "Sign it," said she, "yes, that I will. Mr. Carp has been so kind to us, that I can refuse him nothing." The bill of sale was executed to Mr. Carp's wishes. "And now, friend Curt," said Carp, "what are you going to do with no help here? You'd better bundle up and go with me to Louisiana. I'll befriend you to my last dollar."

" What am I to do with my mill and my little household plunder and farm?"

" True," said Carp, pondering—" you can't well leave them—oh, I'll tell you how to manage it. Advertise them for sale two months hence. I'll take your wife and child on, and fix her up by the time you get there. When you've sold out all but your best horse, mount him and come on. Sell for cash, for it will be inconvenient for you to come back to collect money. Pity when I was selling my land to Watson I did not think to put yours in the trade too. May be you can sell it to him yet. By this plan you can come on with no trouble or expense hardly."

Curt said he liked the plan mightily, but doubted whether his wife would agree to it. It was submitted to her, and she assented to it readily ; only charging her husband to come on as soon as possible. In four days after this interview, Carp and all his negroes were ready to take the road. He had provided a nice little Jersey for Mrs. Curt and her child, and for fear of accidents, he promised to drive it himself all the way to Louisiana. Just as the caravan was about setting out, "Stop," said Curt, "where shall I find you in Louisiana?"

"Sure enough!" exclaimed Carp, "Now didn't we like to make a pretty business of it! You will find us in *Chuckiluckimaw* Parish, on the Sabine river. Here, I'll give you the name on a piece of paper—*Tonnafoosky* is the town where the Post office is. If you write before you hear from us, direct your letter to *Tonnafoosky Post office, Chuckiluckimaw Parish, Louisiana.* There, it is all written out so you can't miss it." So saying, the whole caravan moved forward, leaving poor Curt in loneliness, wifeless, childless, helpless, and in money penniless. Carp settled on Buffalo creek, Wilkinson county, Mississippi, where he and Mrs. Curt lived as man and wife for many years. Several children were the fruit of this union. Mrs. Curt had been dead about three months when Glib traced Carp to his hiding place. Her death was awful. When the Doctor told her that she could not possibly live more than twenty-four hours, she raised a scream that was terrific. "Doctor," cried she, "I am ruined, I'm lost. Lost, lost, lost forever!" A minister was sent for and came. "You needn't talk to me, sir—you needn't pray for me, sir—I thank you—but if you knew—oh what shall I do!——"

"If I knew what, ma'am? Is it too bad to be told——"

"It might be told, but telling it will do no good and much harm—It isn't *passed*, it's *now*—yes, it has been for years, it's now, it's all the time."

"Can't you tell it to your husband, or some of us?" said one of the several ladies at her bedside.

"He knows it—he knows all about it. No, my *husband* doesn't know it—he's innocent, poor man—yes, he knows part of it, but not all of it—not half of it, not a quarter of it, not a thousandth part of it—wasn't it a shame to treat him so?" (another scream.) "Her mind's gone," said one. "No, it isn't! I know all that I am saying—I know you, I know everybody here. It isn't anything *passed*, I tell you. It's *now*, I'm dying in it, and what good can praying do? It's too late to get out of it. If I were to get well I couldn't get out of it. My children scare me, my husband scares me, the negroes scare me; my thoughts scare me, everything—send for Mr Carp here, and you all go out of the room. Go clean away, send all the children away, and all the servants, and I'll tell him all about it."

It was done, and Carp entered the room.

"Mr. Carp, see what you've brought me to! I never would have thought of it, if it hadn't been for you——"

"Haven't I treated you well, Flora?" "Yes, better than I deserved; but what does it all amount to? You've brought me to everlasting ruin. It was bad enough in me to leave my poor husband; but to leave him as we did—with nothing to live on—to fill his ears with lies—to make fun of him—to send him all over the country hunting for us!"

"Oh, Flora, don't take on so! Try and compose yourself. Everything depends upon it. Think of your children! The thing's past and gone now, and fretting over it can't mend it——"

"Our children! Our children!——Look there!——Look there! Mr. Carp! Mr. Carp! Mr. Carp"——Another scream—and her mind was gone. She lay for a few minutes in a stupor, during which the company were called back. Then she began in a low, calm tone of voice:

"Ma!——Ma!——Ma, did you tell them——? you're scared—— 'Pray for Flora!'——You laughed——No——No——yes, both—— In the Pulpit——Mrs. McRae (a wild laugh!) Mr. Wilson! (another) There, its bed time——All dead but me! Ben's alive——we'll all meet in heaven——He was so stupid——Sabine!" Another convulsive laugh—and she died.

Carp was asked repeatedly what it was that distressed his wife so much in her last moments. He said she had told him all about it, but that it was nothing of any consequence—she was out of her head.

Benjamin Glib soon explained the mystery. After satisfying himself fully that Carp was in Wilkinson, he went to a lawyer in Natchez, and unfolded the whole history of his case from the death of his mother to Carp's elopement with his sister. Mr. Stark, his Attorney, advised him to remain in Natchez until he (Stark) could go to Wilkinson, and ascertain all the particulars of Carp's history from his settlement in Mississippi to the time present. Two days were amply sufficient to assure him that Glib's story was true in every particular. He immediately took the preliminary steps necessary to the institution of suits against Carp, in behalf of both Glib and Curt's daughter Sarah, now going under the name of Sally Carp. The child's interests could not be secured without letters of guardianship; and Stark assisted in procuring them. He did not allow Glib to apply for them until he had fortified himself with proofs impregnable, to sustain his application. As soon as it was made, all Woodville was thrown in a ferment. Carp's infamy was exposed, and the horrid death of his putative wife disposed everybody to believe it.

Sarah caused some difficulty at first, but as it was much more agreeable to her to pass for a legitimate than an illegitimate child, it was easily removed. The suits were instituted and recoveries had which swept away nearly the whole of Carp's estate. But we must not suppress the history of the bill of sale.

As soon as he was served with process, Carp went to Mr. Smith, a great Attorney of Woodville, to engage his services. "Well," says Smith, "let us take up one case at a time; what have you to say to Glib's case?"

"Lord bless your soul, squire," said Carp, "I've got 'em tied so fast that they can't kick. Turn which way they will, they're headed."

"Well, Carp, I'm glad to hear you say that, old fellow, for public prejudice is very strong against you."

"Just look at that bill of sale, squire, and tell me how they're to get out of that, will you?"

Smith read it, and while reading it, his countenance assumed nearly every variety of expression that the human countenance can assume. When he had finished—

"Well," said he, "of all the Bills of Sale that ever I laid my eyes upon, that beats. If you had come to me and told me to draw up an instrument, in the form of a bill of sale, that at all times, and in all Courts would be equal to a confession of judgment by you, in any suit brought against you, by any person claiming under Mrs. Glib, I couldn't have come within gun-shot of this for that purpose. Burn it up immediately—destroy it—what's your wife's name doing to that bill of sale? Isn't Flora Curt the woman you've been living with as your wife? But it's not worth while to talk about it—destroy it, I tell you, immediately!"

"And then what title will I have to show for all these negroes and——"

"None; trust to the defects of Glib's title, or to his not being able to identify them——"

"Is that the best advice that you can give me?"

"Yes."

"Then I'll get another lawyer. Stark would give me the same advice; I understand it!"

"What do you mean, you cheating, swindling, adulterous rascal?" said Smith, moving to the back room with a stick hunting motion. Carp was gone before his return.

Carp employed a young attorney of Woodville, who confirmed his views of the bill of sale, in every particular. "There's the title," said he, "*plainly* and *distinctly* set forth—not simply upon a *good* consideration, which would have been all-sufficient, but also upon a *valuable* consideration, and, to make assurance doubly sure, upon *divers other considerations.* This title, like the resistless torrent, is sustained by various tributaries from perfectly pure sources. Then it is fortified by a rampart of truth and generosity on your part, Mr. Carp, that must forever protect it from the imputation of fraud. All else is mere surplusage. How such a profound jurist as Mr. Smith is, could have advised you to destroy this all important document, I cannot conceive, unless he overlooked that sterling legal maxim: *Utile per inutile non vitiatur.*"

Carp was enraptured with this impromptu display of legal ability, rejoiced at his change of Attornies, and highly flattered at finding his skill in guarding against "*afterclaps*" so fully avouched.

Far as we have digressed from the direct path of our narrative, we are strongly tempted to follow this bill of sale through the several Courts in which it made its appearance, but in charity to the reader's patience we forbear. Suffice it to say, that as soon as Stark saw it, he took a copy of it, served notices to produce it in all the cases, and never let it get out of Court until it had, as we have said, turned over nearly the whole of Carp's estate to Glib and his niece. This is but one of a thousand instances in which rascality has over-reached itself, and been made subservient to justice.

Glib and his niece returned to Alabama, rich, and both prosperep in life. Curt was lucky. Watson purchased him out entirely, in less than two months after Carp's departure, at tolerably fair prices, and he set out in quest of his wife with three thousand dollars in his pocket. He had not gone far in Louisiana before he learned that there were no such places in the State as Chuckiluckimaw and Tonnafoosky: so coming upon a valuable piece of land, he purchased it cheap, and settled down upon it with two negro women, proceeds of his surplus funds. His land grew in value and his negroes in number, and thus when he died, (a little before his wife,) he left a right pretty little estate, which went to swell the fortune of his daughter. It would have been lost to her, but for a letter which he wrote to a friend in Georgia, just before his death, who three or four years afterwards went to visit Glib.

CHAPTER XVII

As soon as Captain Thompson joined the Methodists, his sister expressed a wish to attach herself to the same church to which he and his wife belonged.

"No, Anna," said the Captain, "I advise you against it. I am sure you cannot be a better christian in the Methodist Church than you have proved yourself to be in the Presbyterian Church. If I can be as bright an ornament to my Church, as you are to yours, I shall deem myself greatly blessed———"

"Brother, you greatly over-rate my piety. I have a great many faults and weaknesses which your eye never sees, but which I see and mourn over, and struggle against, every day."

"I shall hardly be convinced of my error by that kind of proof, my dear sister. One brazen sin would bring your piety in question with me more than a hundred faults and weaknesses hidden in the heart, and mourned over and struggled against every day. But enough of this—stay with your people, with whom you have long held sweet communion, to whom you are endeared by a thousand ties, and who are entitled to the benefit of your influence and example. I am not sure that the division of the Church into sects is not of God's appointment. Some good results from the division, obviously. It secures the Scriptures from interpolation and mutilation, stimulates the several churches to good works, liberality, generosity, and activity in the advancement of the Redeemer's Kingdom ; brings truth to the test of open, fair and able discussion, guards the church from new heresies, if it cannot eradicate old ones, and effectually prevents a union of Church and State in this blessed country, at least. So much good does it, and much more would it do, if each sect would practice, as it should, the heavenly precepts of love and charity taught them by their common Head. If others will not practice them, let us do it, my dear sister ; and be assured, if our example passes unobserved on earth, it will not be overlooked in Heaven."

"Those are sweet counsels, my dear brother, and they have already banished from my mind every thought of quitting my church. It is strange, very strange, but I cannot dispossess my mind of the thought that some heavy calamity is going to befall us. I am too happy for earth. I question whether there is this day a human being this side of Heaven as happy as I am. You once said to me sportively, 'turn Methodist and shout,' and now I could do it with right good will.   I can hardly keep from it——"

"And why should you wish to keep from it?   It is one of the means which Providence has appointed for relieving the overcharged heart, and I do not see why it should be repressed.   I know why it is repressed, very well.   It is regarded by most people as very un-dignified—only, however, when *most people* are devoid of the feel-ing that provokes it.   Let the people, dignitaries and all, witness a closely contested election of deep interest; at one moment it seems to be going one way, at the next the other, and thus the contestants alternately pass each other, until they stand abreast with but two votes in the box—they come out for the same man.   What do you see, then, among the victors?   One weeps outright with joy, another laughs frantically, another vents the long suppressed breath, and smiles; but all applaud, and nine-tenths raise a shout that may be heard for miles.   There is nothing at all undignified in this!   It is perfectly natural.   Now they are all moved by the same spirit; but it manifests itself in different ways according to the different tem-peraments of the crowd.   I suppose if a battery of artillery were bearing upon them, and they were forbidden to shout, under pain of being fired upon, they might suppress it (doubtful if all would); but what would be thought of the man who would recommend such a measure, or any milder one, to prevent this honest outburst of feel-ing?   When 'General Washington passed through the country on his Southern tour, he was met by multitudes at every town and village at which he stopped.   As soon as the throngs caught a glimpse of the approaching hero, they made the welkin ring with their shouts.   As he passed through the streets, women waved their handkerchiefs, and wept; old soldiers wept, but most waved their hats, and shouted again and again, loud and long.   He would have been regarded as a Tory who gave no outward demonstration of joy at such times.   The very next day these same people would go to a Methodist meeting, and sneer at a new convert for shouting.   And what has Washington done for any one of us, compared with what Christ has done for the new convert?   What the liberty which Washington gained for us, compared with ' *the liberty wherewith Christ has made us free?*'   What can we promise ourselves from this great Republic, compared with the Savior's legacy to the soldiers of the Cross?   At His birth the angels of heaven shouted.   His second coming to earth will be her-alded by a shout.   At His triumphant entry into Jerusalem, the whole multitude of His disciples shouted.   The Pharisee (*strict re-*

ligionists) begged him to rebuke 'them. What was His reply? '*I tell you, if these should hold their peace, the stones would immediately cry out.*' But He had not yet died for these disciples. No one is offended at a shout from the dying Christian! In the times of David and the Prophets, it was not regarded as undignified in holy men to shout. I used to laugh at the shouting Christians, myself. I used to be provoked with them, until I learned something of their feelings, and then I was very ready to excuse them. From *excusing* I went to *thinking*, and from thinking to *reading* upon the subject; and the result of my deliberations and research is what I have delivered to you. Now, do not misunderstand me. I do not say that Christians ought to shout, much less that shouting is an infallible test of Christianity; and least of all, that there are not just as good Christians who never shout, as there are who do. I do not believe that there is a better shouting Christian in our Church than you are; but I do say that it is the most natural thing in the world that Christians of some temperaments should shout, if I understand anything about religion; and that ridicule of it comes with ill grace from a shouting world, or a non-shouting Church."

"But brother, how does it happen that there is shouting in no other Church in the world but the Methodist?"

"Just because the Methodist is, (in one sense) the newest church in the world. When we join a church we as naturally drop into the ways of its people as we do into its creed. I know very well where they all began; it was in such a scene of excitement and clamor as amazed the lookers-on, and led them to mock, and to say that the converts were full of new wine. But all churches will, in process of time, conform themselves to the opinions and manners of the world, just as far as they can, without compromising their principles. Prudence or policy may dictate this course—to avoid persecution, ridicule and contempt, or to gain popularity. Never did the world show any mercy, not to say charity to religious excitements. The Methodists have hardly yet passed the fiery ordeal through which all zealous, self-denying God-serving, world-defying Christians must pass. The marks of violence are still upon their humble meeting houses, and derision meets them at all their services. As yet, they have no church etiquette (if you will excuse the term), no thought, and very little knowledge, of the world's dignities; for they are mostly poor and illiterate; no idea that joy should be disciplined, or transports suppressed. They, therefore, give the rein to their feelings just as nature prompts them. They are happy, very happy, and they express their happiness in the natural way, without fear of startling their brethren, offending their pastors, or provoking sinners. But it is not to be supposed that our church will be exempt from the common lot of churches. With a penniless Ministry, fervid, zealous, devout, persecuted, traversing the country from the mountains to the seaboard, and preaching the Gospel to every creature, white, black, bond, free, rich, poor, at their own doors, it must grow, and as it grows it will increase in *dignity*, science, fine preaching, fine dressing, fine eating, fine stations, fine circuits, fine music, fine churches, and strong *voting*. Of course, it will then become, especially with the most respected office holders and office seekers, very respectable. There will be religion in it, sterling religion in it still—religion armed for giant work, and well employed; but there will be no shouting in it, no fraternal embraces in it, no out gushing of hymns from a thousand voices, eloquent of the heart's heavenly inspirations, no 'brothering' between great preachers and poor members. Or if these distinctive features of primitive Methodism be not entirely effaced, you will have to seek them, to find them, in some poor brother's circuit, in the gorges of the mountains, the wilds of the West, or the negro quarters of the rich."

" Verily, brother, you have said more in defence of shouting, than I supposed could be said; and most certainly, if I never shout myself, I shall always, hereafter, look with the greatest indulgence upon those Christians who do."

" That is the lesson that I would inculcate, my sister. And when you learn what may be said in defence of it, tell me, what think you of that Pastor of a church who requested a good sister of his flock to leave the church, because, under his own glowing description of Heaven, or under something else he said, that filled her heart with joy, she relieved it with a shout? Think of her, if you please, perchance the holiest of his charge, retiring from the house of worship —from the sermon which refreshed her, under the eye-shot of the congregation, shamed, subdued, depressed, disgraced!"

" Oh, my dear brother! Surely such a thing never happened?"

" Surely such a thing did happen, if a credible witness is to be believed. It may be that that woman paid more, for her means, to build the church from which she was ordered—paid more, for her means, to support the Pastor who so deeply wounded her, than any other member of his congregation. She never shouted again, in his church, you may be sure, nor did any other one of his flock; and the consequence was, (I conjecture, not without some reason), he had ever afterwards a very quiet, orderly, Laodicean Church. Charity, my sister! let there be charity among the churches. Instead of looking for faults in each other, let them be looking for what is good in each other, and let them reciprocally interchange the good, and reject the faulty. In this way, all might be improved—all would be more endeared to each other than they are."

" You have so well defended shouting among Christians, that perhaps you can give me some new views upon another usage of your church, which has always seemed to me much more objectionable than shouting. I allude to your altar scenes in times of revival. Some are singing, some are talking to mourners, and two or three are praying aloud at the same time, and when to all this is added the shouts of the converts, the whole scene is one of utter confusion, it seems to me. What can you say in defence of all this?"

" Nothing. It is not only indefensible, but it is positively unscriptural. Each and all of these exercises are proper in their place ; but to have them all going on at one and the same time is little better than to set all the rules of order, human and divine, at defiance. The honesty of intention and benevolence of purpose with which it is done, are all that make it tolerable, even to the most charitable ; but these are very poor excuses for those who are presumed to have read Paul's Epistles, and yet encourage such things. And here, a very pertinent illustration of what I have just said, presents itself: If at revivals in your church, your people would borrow a little more fervor from ours, and ours in like circumstances would borrow a little more order and solemnity from yours, I think both would be improved. Dignity, gravity, and order well become the christian ; but love, joy and zeal, much better become him ; and if they cannot all be harmonized, why, let the first give way, I say, and let all give way to *love*, if it be possible to separate joy from it! And when love and joy abound in him, let him be indulged in his nature's way of manifesting them, even to the interruption of a sermon for a time ; and if the feeling become general among the flock, why, let the sermon go; there is no better preaching, at times, than the rejoicing together of many happy Christians. These are my crude notions, sister ; take them for what they are worth."

" I thank you for them, my very dear, dear brother, and I am sure that they will be of service to me. Oh, how much happiness I have lost from your delay in embracing Christianity !"

" Not so much, perhaps, from want of my counsels and religious opinions, as from want of that deference and respect which I should have shown to your piety, and that tenderness of address that I should have shown to a sister."

In the main, things went on smoothly and happily in the two families, during the vacation; but before its close, both the Captain and his sister had their quiet a little disturbed by William's over attention to Snap-dragon. It was a natural curiosity that prompted him to enquire carefully into Snap-dragon's capabilities, accomplishments, predilections, and tractability. By close observation and experiment, he discovered that a little needless whipping improved him wonderfully—(such the difference between a teacher and a disciple.) It made him move airily, and infused life, grace and activity into both his extremities; that he could trot eight miles an hour—that he could beat Billy Figg's Nicktail, Billy Pine's Catham, and Bob Maston's Flying Nelly easily; that he stood the firing of a gun on him very well; that he could clear a six-rail fence at a leap; that by tickling him in a particular way in the flank (which he called the "grabble-tickle") he could make him kick amusingly, that by applying the "grabble-tickle" to his back-bone, just behind the saddle, he could carry him through a variety of most interesting evolutions—tail-switching, warping, biting, (backwards, at nothing,) polka-dancing, and furious kicking. One thing he taught him which was perfectly original, and that was to stop at the cluck or chirp, and go at the word "wo!" To teach him all these accomplishments William had to devote nearly his whole time to him. He had to ride him far and near; and in so doing it was just as well to call and see all the planters within seven miles of the village, and rest awhile with them, and entertain them with all the wonders of Doctor Waddel's school, as to ride that far and return without dismounting. Every gathering in the county he was certain to attend; by means whereof he had a fine opportunity of studying human nature, in some of its most interesting aspects. He saw how petty elections were conducted—how electioneering was carried on—how much rum it took to elect a Captain and a Justice of the Peace. He saw justice administered by magistrates in their shirt-sleeves, and heard stiff quarrels between them and the suitors—he saw card playing in its most unpretending humility and simplicity, to-wit, by a couple of the *sovereignty*, seated cross legged on the ground, with a dirty cotton handkerchief between them for a table, and a half deck of dirtier cards. (Here was the introduction of *'squatter sovereignty*" into the country; but who could have supposed that it would ever make such a fuss in the world as it has made !) He saw cock-fights occasionally, dog-fights often, and men-fights regularly—now and then he was entertained with a quarter race and a foot race—upon one occasion he took up a banter of "the universal world" for a foot race, by a youth both older and larger than himself, and gained the victory handsomely. His competitor said, "if he couldn't beat him a running, he could whip him." Bill "pitched into him," as the saying is, without a parley, and flogged him, beautifully, and to the delight and admiration of every-body, who thought it mean in him to pick a quarrel with a boy who had fairly beaten him, just from shame of his defeat. These feats gave William great renown in the county. Perhaps no youth in the land ever made greater progress in "the study of human nature" than William did in the short space of two months. But without Snap-dragon, where would he have been? Confined to the darkness of his own village! And whoever heard of any human nature in a village, save at Court times, general elections, and general parades? The Captain often heard of his progress, and often counselled him. "William," he would say, "I fear I committed a great error in giv-ing you that horse; I am sure I did. It was one of the most im-prudent acts of my life."

"Why, uncle?"

"For many reasons. He takes up all your time. 'I never see a book in your hand; you have hardly attended a religious meeting, except on Sunday, since the vacation commenced. You are too young to have control of a horse. He is a spirited horse; and if not managed with care he may break your neck—"

"Uncle, he can't throw me to save his life."

"I'm glad to hear that; my main design in giving him to you, was to make you a good horseman; but he may run away with you, carry you under the limb of a tree, and knock your brains out. If you will be careful with him, there is no danger, for I know him to be a very gentle horse, though spirited—but youths of your age are so thoughtless. I hardly ever see you in the day time; where do you keep yourself?"

"Just riding about in the country, Uncle."

"But sometimes you're gone the live long day, and surely you are not riding all the time without your meals?"

"Oh no, sir! sometimes I take dinner at Mr. Love's, sometimes at Mr. Tod's, sometimes at Squire Mattoxes, sometimes at Mr. White's, and Curtis King's——"

"Why, William, my son, you ought not to visit people's houses in that way——"

"Uncle, they always tell me they are glad to see me, and always beg me to come and see them again."

"To be sure they do; but because they are kind, you should not tax their hospitality all the time. At times, I am sure you must fall upon them very unseasonably, and give them no little inconvenience. When they see you in town here, and ask you to come and see them, why, then go; but don't thrust yourself upon them at all hours, un-invited.

"I'll obey you uncle."

Again the Captain would renew his complaints and advice:

"William, your mother is very uneasy about you. She says you constantly come home charged with news from all the gatherings in the county. Surely, you don't frequent such places? What interest can you take in them? What do you promise yourself from such resorts? I charge you under pain of my sore displeasure to abandon them."

"I will do so, uncle."

William's victories happened to be reported to the Captain by Mr. Moore, in the presence of William, and in the way of congratulation to him!

"Why, William!" exclaimed the Captain, "is it possible that you have been running foot races and fighting——"

"Oh, don't blame him," said Mr. Moore; "I supposed you knew all about it, since it is talked about everywhere. But don't blame William, for he never did a better thing in all his life, and never will do a better while he lives. He was at the Court, at old man Haralson's, and there was an uncommonly large gathering for the occasion. There was a fellow there, a forward, noisy chap, named Jake Black, who was cutting up high shines. He said he could beat anything of his weight and inches in the universal world at a foot race. 'I can beat you,' said William. 'You!' says Black. 'I can run round you three times in fifty yards and then beat you.' 'Well,' says William, 'suppose you try it.' The match was made up, a hundred yards were stepped off, and all on the Court ground went to see the race. At the word they started, and William beat him a clear light of at least seven yards. There was a general shout as they came in, and many had something digging to say to Black. One told him he oughtn't to run against anything but grub-worms and terrapins. Another told him his belly didn't give his legs fair play.

' I saw your thighs,' says he ' hit your belly every step you made. If you can only manage to hook up your belly just three quarters of an inch before you run, so as to give your legs full sweep, you'd beat Bill Mitten thirty yards in the hundred, I know you would.' 'Oh,' says a third, ' his stomach had nothing to do with it—at least it wouldn't have had, if he had been in good keep ; but he was in no order to run. I saw him eat two water *millions* and a peck of peaches, not an hour before the race. Take that weight off of him, and where would Bill Mitten have been ?' ' Well,' said the second, ' that's just what I say. He only lacks three-quarters of an inch of beating ' the universal world,' I thought his belly was *nat'ral.*'

" This kind of chat," continued Moore, "made Jake very mad, and as William stood laughing with the rest, Jake stept up to him, and said, ' If you can beat me running, I can whip you mighty easy.' You know that hard place in the road between old man Haralson's house and the Court room ? He was standing there ; and the words was no sooner out of his mouth than William seized him, fetched the hip lock upon him, and gave him the hardest fall that I ever saw a boy get in all my life. Before Jake could recover from his fall, William was on him, giving him bringer. He very soon ' told the news ' (cried ' enough !') and William got off of him without a scratch. I don't suppose there ever was a people more rejoiced and surprised than they all were at William's doings.' Jake had no idea that a boy dressed as fine as William was, could fight at all, nor did anybody else believe it ; but, Lord bless your soul, Captain, he walked over Jake in the highest style of fighting ! I tell you what, sir, he's as active as a cat and as bold as a lion. So you see he was not to blame."

" And now came the tug of war," (*intestine war*) with the Captain. Before Moore had proceeded four sentences in his narrative, Captain Thompson's countenance lost every trace of amazement and indignation, and assumed a rather unchristian placidity. The next transition was to a benignant smile ; then to an expression of wonder and delight ; then to a laugh of triumph ; and so it went on, stronger and stronger, to the end of the chapter ; so that when Moore concluded, it was manifest that " brother" Thompson had no more thought of religion in him, than he had of the tattling of his countenance ; and no more thought of the tattling of his countenance, than if he had been all the time in profound sleep. But the time had come for him to speak, and what could he say ? Bill had followed his counsels to the letter, and had exhibited the very fruits

K

from them that he had anticipated and desired. Should he now rebuke him? . That would not do. Should he applaud his conduct?
That would not do from a Christian. Should he remain silent?
That would be a tacit sanction of all that William had done. But
say something he must, and that something must be extemporized;
so he began, in a very cool tone, that might be taken for the composure of religion, or the composure of gratification :

"Why, William, I'm astonished at you!"

Very true, but very equivocal.

"I don't think, *in any view of the case*, that his saying simply,
that he could whip you, justified you in attacking him——"

"But, Uncle, I saw that he was mad, and bent upon picking a
quarrel with me, or backing me before all the company, and I thought
that as I would have to fight or back out, I'd best take a running
start on him; for the first blow in a fight is half the battle, they
say."

"Well, that is true—that is—arguing *upon worldly principles;*
and supposing fighting in any case to be justifiable; for by that
course you are certain to get some advan——However, worldly principles are not always to be trusted; indeed, never to be trusted when
they come in conflict with religious principles. The longer I live
in the world, the more dissatisfied I become with its ways and notions. Four or five months ago, I would have given advice that I
would not now give—at least without very considerable qualifications.
Vigor of body, strength of constitution, unflinching courage—*moral*
courage—are certainly great things—great things in many points of
view—but then, like all good gifts, they may be abused. And here,
William, let me give you a caution. You have a very good apology
(our friend Moore thinks) for engaging in those contests with Black.
Now, take care that your victories over him do not lead you to seek
contests merely to show your prowess—merely for the praise of victory, and the terror of your companions. Oh! of all the disgusting
things in this world, a mere bully—a man who forces his fellow being into a fight with him, merely for the vile fame of whipping him,
is the most disgusting. I have seen such men, and I have despised
them. They pretend to take as insults what they know was meant
in friendship, or in fun. They wantonly assail feelings, play insuf-
ferable pranks with men, and then assail them for speaking harshly
of what they say they meant as innocent sport. They take occasion
from a man's dress, his features, his person, his carriage, to worry
him into resistance of some kind, and then flog him for resisting.

Can anything better mark a devil than such conduct as this? Now, William, I don't blame you for fighting (that is, *upon worldly principles*) under the circumstances; but I do blame you for going to such places—not for going to Mr. Haralson's, for he is a very worthy man, and has a very worthy family, but ,for going there in Court times. I have been there often and I don't remember ever to have seen one of his sons in the crowd of Court days, in my life. And I blame you for running a race, at such a time and place."

Now if the reader can extract from this long harangue, what were the Captain's views of the case of Mitten vs. Black, upon *Christian principles*, he is certainly much wiser than the writer. Whether it was becoming in *him* to discuss the case so generally upon "*worldly principles*," without drawing a line of distinction between them and *Christian principles*—whether it was right in him to say what he would have advised four or five months ago, that he would not now without any specifications that might enlighten his nephew, as to whether he meant to take back any of his counsels upon universal excellence, are questions which we will not undertake to settle. But we will venture to say, that Master Mitten inferred from it, that the Captain was highly delighted, (*but of course only on worldly principles*) with his achievements, and that he need never fear the Captain's wrath for fighting, provided he would always fight at the right time, in the right place, and for good reasons in Mr. Moore's judgment.

In the course of his observations, Master Mitten discovered two other things through the aid of Snap-dragon, which we must not omit to mention; the one was, that six or seven months abstinence from strong drink, had not entirely abated his relish for it; and the other was, that the squatter sovereigns committed many errors in their games that he could have rectified with success. It was the custom of not a few heads of families at this time, to make up a mint-julep of peach or apple-brandy, every morning, and to give a little to every member of the family, old and young, blacks excepted. It was a much more invariable custom to make a large bowl of egg-nog every Christmas, of which the whole family were expected to take a little more freely, and it was considered rather a laughing than a serious matter if some of the children got intoxicated. No one ever entered a house to tarry for a half hour, without being asked "to take something to drink," and with the plainer people of the country, this invitation was extended to boys hardly in their teens, and was accepted without exciting any surprise. Not many years before the times of which we are speaking, probably down to the very times, a still more remarkable custom prevailed among some, if not all Methodist Preachers;—which was to ask a blessing upon every glass of toddy they took.   Should this statement be questioned, we have authority for it, at hand, which no man in Georgia will question.   How this custom originated it is easy to divine; the discipline of the Methodist Church enjoined upon its members to do nothing upon which they could not invoke God's blessing, and as they never dreamed that there was anything sinful in taking a glass of toddy, or as it was more commonly called *a little sweetened dram*, they "said grace over it."

While such customs were rife in the country, it is not to be wondered at that Master Mitten had frequent opportunities of indulging his early formed relish for ardent spirits, even without the help of Snap-dragon—with his help they were quintupled.   He however took care never to appear at home, or in the presence of his Uncle, "*disguised with liquor.*"   But as the Captain saw that he was doing no good, he feared that he was doing much harm, and he rejoiced greatly when the time arrived for his return to school.   A little before this time, the Captain informed William overnight that he wished to borrow Snap-dragon for a short ride the next morning, as all his own horses were in use.   William gave a cordial assent, of course.   "Send Tom over with him directly after breakfast, I'm only going to Doctor Wingfield's," said the Captain.

The Captain lived on the street that led directly to Doctor Wingfield's and near the edge of the town.   As William had never seen his uncle on Snap-dragon, and felt a deep interest in his performance under the saddle of his kind benefactor, he took his position in the inner lock of a fence on the street, under cover of some high weeds, whence, with a little change of position, he could have a full view of the Captain's house, and two or three hundred yards of the street and road leading from it.   Tom got to the house with Snap-dragon, about the time that William got comfortably seated.   Snap was soon saddled, and the Captain was nearly as soon by his side, ready to mount him.   Snap showing signs of impatience to get off.   "What makes that horse do so, Tom?" asked the Captain.   "I don't like his motions."

"He's gentle, Mas' David," said Tom.   "He only do so till you start him."

The Captain placed one hand on Snap's neck and the other on the back of the saddle to mount; this hand happened to slip and fall a little rudely on Snap's back. Snap, nothing doubting that this was the beginning of the "grabble tickle," commenced with the preliminaries of the polka.

"Why, that horse is ruined," said the Captain. "I wonder he hasn't knocked William's brains out long ago."

"Mas' David I tell you tho' an't nothin' the matter with him. This is nothin' but some little foolnish Mas William larn him. He's gentle."

In the mean time Bill was rolling in the weeds, "*enthused*?"* with delight.

The Captain made a second attempt, and mounted.

"Tom, tell your Mistress—Wo!" said he to fidgetting Snap, and away went Snap "to the tune of eight miles an hour!" "*Wo!*" repeated the Captain more emphatically, and Snap put off at half speed, at which gait he passed Bill in an agony of laughter. The Captain immediately conjectured that Bill had been running Snap, and that the horse took "*wo*" for "*go!*" and he did not repeat the word again. Snap soon became pacified, and the Captain brought him to a halt. He studied awhile whether it would be best for him to go on or return. He concluded he would try Snap a little farther any how; so he clucked to him to proceed; but so far from proceeding, Snap settled himself in more dignified composure than he had exhibited during the whole morning. He clucked again, with no better success. He chirped, but these changes of note operated upon Snap like a seranade.

"Why, did ever anybody see such a fool horse since the world was made!" mused the Captain. "What's a body to do with him? How is he to be made to go on, or stop? If I ever give another chap a fine horse, he may give me a thousand lashes, and I'll thank him for it. It certainly was the *unluckiest* act of my life to give Bill this horse!"

Upon the whole, the Captain concluded it would be best for him to get out of temptation as quick as possible, by returning home. Just as he made up his mind to this course, Mr. Foster met him:

"Good morning, brother Thompson!" said Foster.

"Good morning, brother Foster," said Mr. Thompson.

"Which way are you going?"

"I *was* going to Doctor Wingfield's, but I've got on my nephew's horse, which the boy has so completely spoiled, that there is no doing anything with him, so I'll go back with you."

---

*This word, of very modern coinage, is now getting into pretty general use, in some parts of the country.

All of the proceedings up to this moment convinced Snap-dragon that he had been brought out that morning for no other purpose in the world, than to beat Mr. Foster's horse in a quarter race. His conjectures were fully confirmed, when in answer to Mr. Foster's question "don't you own him?" the Captain, as he paced about, answered emphatically "*No*.●

At the word, Snap dashed. The Captain soon took him up, and waited till brother Foster came up. As he approached, the Captain clucked to Snap, and he stopped crustily.

"Bless your soul, honey," said brother Foster, "that's a mighty good looking horse, but he's a mighty foolish one."

"He was one of the finest horses in the land——*Wo!*" cried the Captain, (forgetting himself,) to Snap, in rage to beat Foster's horse, and away he dashed again. He was stopped as before.

"Why, brother Thompson, that horse seems to go when he ought to stop, and stop when he ought to go."

"Exactly so," said the Captain; and Snap bristled considerably at the last word, but was chirped to a halt instantly.

"Why bless your soul, honey, I never did see a horse take on after that sort in all my life. I wouldn't give this pipe for him, if I had to ride him."

"No," said the Captain, (Snap bristled,) "nor I neither."

In this way, between stops and starts, and sidles and snorts, the Captain reached home greatly to his delight, and the still greater delight of William.

The lecture he gave his nephew at their next meeting, we leave the reader to conjecture.

CHAPTER XVIII

WHEN the time came for William Mitten to return to school, he begged his uncle to allow him to keep his horse at Willington. He thought "that if he boarded two or three miles from the school house, and rode to school and back to his boarding house every day, his health would be greatly improved." He said, that " if he had a horse to ride to the post office he could get and mail letters speedily —that he often wished to go and hear Mr. Waddel preach at Rocky River Church; but that he had no means of getting there—that it would cost nothing hardly to keep a horse at Willington. That several times during the summer he had suffered from head-ache, occasioned by hard study and want of exercise, and that unless he could take more exercise in the summer months than he had been taking, he feared his health would be ruined. That in the winter it was not so bad; for the exercise of getting wood, and the active plays of the school, at this season gave him plenty of exercise; but in warm weather, he sometimes got so weak that it seemed to him he would faint."

Mrs. Mitten said " that she would cheerfully bear the expense of the horse, if her brother would consent to William's keeping him at Willington. That the idea of his constitution being shattered by severe study was distressing to her. That she had suffered no little in mind herself from the difficulty of hearing from William often through the mails, and that there was something delightful in the thought of her son going to sacred service with his preceptor. She could conceive of nothing more likely to produce reciprocal endear-ment between the two than this; but that if brother David thought differently she had nothing to say."

" William," said the Captain, " you perplex me not a little. The horse is yours, and I do not like to interfere with your right of pro-perty in him; and yet, to allow you to take him off to school with you, and keep him there, knowing as I do how you have used him, seems to me little better than wilfully putting your life in jeopardy, encouraging you to idleness, pushing you into difficulties with your preceptor, and periling all my bright hopes of you at once. What could have possessed me to make you such a present as that! Yes, I know what possessed me; I wished to show you my gratification at your progress—to encourage you in your studies; to prove my affection for you ; to give you confidence in my counsels, and to give you healthful, agreeable, and useful exercise, during your vacation. ——Why didn't I think to reserve the right of taking him back, if you abused or misused the gift !——"

"Uncle, you can take him back, if you wish to."

"No, I will not do that ; but I'll tell you what I will do : he cost me one hundred dollars ; now I will give you for him, one hundred and twenty dollars in any property you will name—but a horse. That sum will get you a very pretty little library, that will be of use to you through life. Or your mother will add to it, I know, a hundred and eighty more, and that will get you a nice waiting boy— or anything else that you prefer. But mind, I do not wish you to make the trade merely to gratify me, or merely to appease my anxieties, or quiet my apprehensions. Act without fear or constraint in the matter. You will not offend me if you reject my offer."

"Why, William," said Mrs. Mitten, "surely when you see your Uncle's solicitude——"

"Stop, Anna ! My solicitude has nothing to do with the matter——"

"I was only going to call to William's mind how sound your judgment had been in everything touching his interest——"

"Well, all that at another time. William's judgment in this matter is and ought to be his guide. In considering my proposition, forget that I am your Uncle ; forget all the good that I have ever done you, and decide upon it with perfect freedom of will. I'll put it in the right view before you : Suppose that Mr. Cunningham was to come and make you precisely the offer which I make you ; what would you say to it ?"

"I would refuse it from *him ;* but———"

"That's enough, my son———"

"But, brother, I don't think that because he would refuse the offer from Mr. Cunningham, it follows by any means that he would not freely and voluntarily accept it from you."

"No, Uncle ; Mr. Cunningham has never done me the favors that you have ; he's no relation of mine ; I do not respect his judgment as I do yours ; and to prove what I say, I now tell you that though I never was as much attached to anything in all my life as I am to Snap-dragon, I freely and voluntarily, and of my own judgment alone, accept your proposition ; and you shall say whether the pay for the horse shall be in books or a negro boy."

"No, my son ; I admire your kind feelings towards me ; they are a full return for all that I have done for you; but I can't base a trade upon them. You are willing to accommodate *me;* but you are not willing to part with *your horse*—though you think you are. He is yours, my dear boy, and I will not purchase him from you upon any other considerations than those which would influence you in a trade with a stranger."

" Why, brother, that seems to me a very strange refinement."

" I don't think so, sister. Suppose I had opened the proposition in this way: ' William, I regret that I gave you that horse. Now, I gave him to you unasked for; I am your Uncle, who loves you; who has done a great deal for you; to whom you owe a large debt of gratitude, but for whom you would never have gone to Mr. Waddel's school, and by consequence must have lost all the honors you have gained there; in all which, as in many other instances, you have seen how much better my judgment is as to your true interests than yours; now, in my judgment, the horse will do you more harm than good ; yield, therefore, to my judgment—return my love and kindness, by giving me back the horse.' Would you think all this right ?"

" No, certainly ; for that would be just working upon the child's feelings, to get from him his horse for nothing; but you propose to give him more than the value of the horse, and in better property."

" Then there is no difference between the case at hand, and the case put, but in the return that is offered to him for the horse. It is right to work on his feelings in any way I please to get his horse from him, provided, I give him for him what *you* and *I* think a fine price! Is that your doctrine? Don't you think that William ought to have a will in the matter ?"

" Oh, pshaw ! The cases are not at all alike. You havn't gone on with all that string of appeals to his heart; you would not let me even speak of your better judgment ; you forewarned him not to let his decision be governed in any way by his relation to you or your kindness to him. He's not a man to judge of prices, and of what will be best for him."

" Nevertheless, he has all the rights of a man in trade. It would be very silly in him to refuse five thousand for his horse; but if he chose to do so, I don't think you would force him to take it, and I am sure I would not————"

" Well, if he was such a simpleton as to refuse five thousand dollars for his horse, I don't know but I would force him to take it. I certainly would advice him strenuously to take it.   But what has all this to do with the case?   Have you forced him?"

"No, but he is acting upon precisely the feelings that my supposed appeals to his sensibilities would have produced."

"And are they not praiseworthy feelings, brother?"

"Highly praiseworthy, sister!   Too praiseworthy to be abused; and it would be an abuse of them in me, to avail myself of them to deprive him of a piece of property which he does not wish to part with.   And now, my dear boy, I withdraw my proposition; and let it not distress you the least in the world, that I have done so.   Do not suppose that I will blame you, or harbor any unkind feelings towards you for your reluctance to part with him——"

"But Uncle, I tell you again, I am willing to part with him *to you* —perfectly willing——"

"Well, my son, I think the more of you for that; but let us drop the matter.   Keep your horse, son, but don't think of taking him to Dr. Waddel's.   I have not yet fully made up my mind whether I have authority to forbid your so doing—I incline to the opinion that standing as I do in the place of a parent to you, duty requires me to interdict positively your keeping a horse at Willington; but I hope you will not force me to decide that question by attempting to take him.   I have many things to say against it, but let these suffice: You've spoiled that horse—he is dangerous to others, if not to you—you will have fifty students on his back, and some of them may get hurt—perhaps killed by him.   He will be a useless expense to your mother—the summer months are now gone—he will interfere with your studies—dispatch of letters between here and Willington is of no consequence, and the weather will be too cold for you to go off to preaching with Mr. Waddel."

"Now, brother," said Mrs. Mitten, "don't understand me in what I say, as interfering in the least with your authority over William, or as opposing my judgment to yours, or as raising the slightest objection to your dealing with him in this matter as you think best; but simply as asking an explanation of you.   William offers you his horse on your own terms; you refuse him because he does not offer him from the right motives, or the right feelings, or something else that I don't understand, and yet you doubt whether you will allow him to use him as he wishes to.   How do you reconcile these views?"

"It will be time enough to reconcile them when I come to act upon them; but should I deem it my duty to forbid his keeping a horse at Willington, I should reconcile them just as you would in giving a toy to your child, and forbidding him to use it to the annoyance of your household, or to the injury of himself."

"But William is not now a child, and I am sure that he would obey your directions strictly in the use of him."

"Yes, Uncle; you may just lay down the law, and I will obey it strictly in every thing."

"But I cannot anticipate all the ways in which you may mis-use him."

"Brother, will you take it amiss if I venture a word of advice here?"

"No; by no means. I will always hear your views in reference to your child with pleasure; and what is more I will always take it, if I am not *confident* that it will operate to the prejudice of your son."

"Well I know that you take a pleasure in indulging him in every thing you can, that you do not think will be injurious to him."

"True!"

"And I am equally sure that William has reaped too many benefits from obedience to you, ever to disobey you again in anything. Now, this plan has occurred to me: September, though a fall month is always a warm, relaxing, sickly month in this climate; and as he has been much on horse-back, during the vacation, it may injure his health to break off suddenly from this exercise, and set himself down to severe study. I know he has made rather a bad use of his horse during the vacation, but he can't do so at school. You have enumerated the evils you apprehend from his keeping a horse there, and that will be sufficient to guard him against them; for he has told me over and over again, that he believed he had the best Uncle in the world; that you had only to tell him what to do, and he would do it if it were to go to the earth's end. Now give him any other orders or cautions about the horse that you think proper; let him keep him only while the weather continues warm, and as soon as it turns cool, I will send Tom for him and fetch him home, if you say so. The short vacation at Christmas will soon be here, and if he keeps him till then, he can ride him home, and save us the trouble of sending for him. But no matter for that, if you say send for him before, it shall be done. As for the expenses of keeping the horse, it will cost no more to keep him there than here, nor as much; and there, he will be of some use, and here he will be of none. But the great benefit I promise myself from it, is William's delightful improving trips with Mr. Waddel to his preaching places."

" William," said the Captain, " retire a little, while your mother and I discuss this matter a little farther."

William retired.

" Do you know, Anna," continued the Captain, " that nothing has fallen from William in three mouths, which has pained me, not to say offended me, so much, as that Rocky River plea for keeping a horse? Here he has been in the midst of preaching, and various religious exercises for three or four weeks, and except on the Sabbath, he has hardly ever darkened a Church door in the day time, and never at night, unless you pressed him into your service; and now all of a sudden he has taken a wonderful yearning to accompany Mr. Waddel upon his preaching excursions."

" Brother, I think the day has gone by when William would deceive; and I am very happy in having it in my power to explain this thing to your satisfaction. I talked to William about his taking so little interest in the meetings, and he said that he wanted recreation after his hard study, for the long term. That he would soon have to renew his studies for ten long months, with only two weeks vacation at Christmas, and that if he did not improve his health in the vacation he would break down. That he had been to preaching in the country several times when there was preaching in town, because he could take exercise in going there. Now at school the state of things will be just reversed. He will be kept constantly employed except on Saturdays and Sundays, and he would be desirous of exercising on those days and doing good at the same time."

The Captain looked doubtingly, and said no more upon that head; but he returned from the episode :

" Anna," said he, " I am very anxious to accommodate you and William, but I have awful misgivings about this horse affair. There is much weight in what you have said; but it does not satisfy me. What a world of trouble one false step may give a man ! What eternal vigilance must a man keep up, both upon himself and his charge, who has the government of boys ! Now, if I refuse to comply with your wishes, and by any chance in the world William should happen to get sick, you will ascribe it to my needless rigor, and carelessness about his health. I erred in giving him the horse, and I am not absolutely certain that after having given him, I ought to control his use of him, simply upon my apprehensions that it will be mischievous. Perhaps no evil will grow out of it for one short month, or a month and a half at farthest, for surely we shall have frost in that time, and by giving William proper precautions, it may be that all will turn out well at last. You and William will be accommodated, my doubts will be removed, (if they can be called doubts) about interfering with his right of property in the present state of things, and possibly his health may be improved, or at least preserved by it. Call him back and let me give him my charge."

William came.

"I have concluded, son, to let you keep your horse at Mr. Waddel's, upon these conditions : You are to ride him no where but to the school house and back to your boarding house, except on Saturdays. On those days, you are to ride him to no grog shops, gatherings or frolics, nor more than six miles from Willington, anywhere, except to Vienna, and there, only to mail *your own* letters—don't forget this condition. *You are never to go to Vienna unless you go to mail a letter of your own, addressed to your mother or myself.* All your letters to others, you must carry to the office when you go to mail your letters to one of us. You are not to go simply to enquire for letters—enquire for them when you go to mail your own. When you go under these restrictions, you may of course carry letters and bring letters for your school-mates—you are not to ride your horse at all on the Sabbath, except to accompany Mr. Waddel to some preaching appointment. You are to loan him to no student—I'll give you a paper to show them, that will excuse you to them for not loaning your horse to them. When your mother sends for your horse, you are to give him up without a murmur, and if you keep him till Christmas, you are to bring him home and leave him here."

William subscribed to the terms cheerfully, and showed by his countenance that he suffered no distress from his Uncle's over-refinement in trade. On the second of September he and Tom took the road to Willington—Tom with saddle-bags which bent upwards with stuffing. On reaching Willington, William selected for his boarding house one of the remotest from the school house that he could find, with any students in it. It contained two pretty wild fellows. A single day here convinced him that he had made a great change for the better, in boarding houses. The eating was better, the sleeping was better, than at Newby's, and here he understood he would not have to cut his own wood and make his own fires. "Why didn't I come here at first?" thought he. "Smith," said he, "does Mr. Waddel ever come round here of nights?" "No," said Smith, " it's too far off for him to come *boguing* about to, of nights; and if he was to come one time, he wouldn't come again, for I'd make him smell the face of a brick-bat."

As there were no *brick-bats* about Willington, we infer from this remark that Smith was a city gentleman.

"And you've no Monitor here?" enquired William.

"No;" said Jones, "Old Moses is got more sense than to make Smith monitor over me, or me over him. He knows we'd never spunk one another."

William was in transports with his new location. His appearance at school on horseback, created quite a sensation among the students; divers of whom got spunked "for looking at William Mitten's horse in study hours"—in short for being idle, but in detail as just stated. As Doctor Waddel was about mounting old Hector, at 12 o'clock on the second day after William's return, he saw William riding Snap-dragon, to water, and he joined him.

"William," said the Doctor, "have you quit boarding at Mr. Newby's?"

"Yes sir."

"I'm sorry to hear that. Did Mr. or Mrs. Newby say or do anything to offend you?"

"No sir, but Uncle allows me to board where I please, and I preferred boarding at Mr. ——'s."

"Is that your horse?"

"Yes sir."

The Doctor cleared his throat sadly and prophetically, and proceeded:

"That horse, William, is going to bring you into trouble, and I advise you to write to your mother immediately to send for him and take him away; and I advise you to get back to Mr. Newby's as soon as possible."

"I don't expect to keep him long Mr. Waddel—only till the weather turns cool."

"That may be quite 'too long. William I have been keeping school many years, and I declare to you, my son, that no student under me has ever done anything to fill me with such fears, anxieties and griefs as you have, in these seemingly small matters of changing your boarding house, and keeping a horse here. What day of the month is this? The fifth, isn't it?"

"Yes sir."

"Is your name upon either of these beech-trees, William?"

"Yes sir."

"Come show me which."

"There it is," said William as they approached a beech.

"Very prettily carved. Do you keep a pocket-book, William?"

"Yes sir."

"Write down in your pocket-book the year and the day of the month, in which you and I took our first and last look together at your name on that beech."

"Why, Mr. Waddel, I haven't done anything wrong, have I?"

"Nothing morally wrong my son, nothing morally wrong. I have a deep interest in you William, and so has your country. Hundreds will regret to be disappointed in you. Lay to heart the advice I am about to give, and follow it as you respect me, as you love your Uncle, as you love yourself, as you love your mother, as you love your country. Till you send home that horse, be more studious than you have ever been, more strict in observing the rules of the school, more watchful of what you say and do, more careful of where you go, than you have ever been. And as soon as you dispose of the horse, come back to Mr. Newby's—Mr. ———'s is too far for you to walk."

"I've paid my board for a quarter."

"No matter for that. Get back to Newby's as soon as you can, and I'll arrange the matter of board with Mr. ———."

"Mr. Waddel, X. Jones and Z. Smith board at Mr. ———'s."

"I know they do, but—they keep no horse. Good day! Remember the fifth of September and the beech tree!"

William did not move from the spot where Doctor Waddel left him, for five minutes. He was alarmed, he could not tell why. "What," thought he, "can there be in keeping a horse, that is so horrible to Uncle and Mr. Waddel! It's the strangest thing in the world!"

CHAPTER XIX

It was a common remark of Doctor Waddel, "show me a school boy with a horse, dog, and gun, and I'll show you a boy who will never come to anything." We can look back through the vista of fifty years, and we cannot point to the man, living or dead, whose history disproves the remark. We can point to many in verification of it. But Master Mitten had as yet only a horse, and at worst according to Waddel, he was only one-third of the way to nothing. Why, then, was the Doctor so much afflicted by his horse? And why did it distress him so much more to find William boarding at Mr. ——'s, than Smith and Jones?

He saw at once that William had changed his lodging only for the pleasure of riding his horse every day. That his horse would necessarily employ much of his time, that might be much better disposed of, and be constantly engaging him in pleasure rides, or vice-rides, when he ought to be at his books. He felt almost certain that ere long that horse would bring him on the monitor's bill, and he disliked exceedingly to give a promising boy his first whipping; because he knew that half the stimulus to close study and good order would be taken from him by his first whipping. But the great source of the Doctor's uneasiness was his room-mates. Jones and Smith were among the few students of the Doctor's school, who disliked him, and they cordially despised him. And yet, strange as it may seem, he had never flogged either of them, he had never said a cross word to either of them. They feared whipping, and demeaned themselves well enough when at school, to keep off the monitor's bills, and recited well enough to drag along with their classes. "Why, then, did they despise him?"

The reader must ask the Devil to explain that matter. We acknowledge our utter incompetency to do it. Yes, we can go a little way into the explanation of it, and as it is one of the paradoxes of human nature, the philosophic reader is entitled to all the light that we can shed upon it. If it were possible we should say that Smith came into the world hating Doctor Waddel; for he seemed to bring his hatred with him to the school. At their very first interview, he showed palpable signs of it, already up to a red heat. Now if it be possible for a rational being to hate furiously at sight, then Smith's hatred commenced with this interview. But if this be mor-

ally impossible, at what period of his life can we better place it
than at his birth?

As to Jones, his hatred, though curious, and smoked a little with
the unnatural, is nevertheless traceable. From his introduction to
the Doctor, to the day of his becoming Smith's room-mate, he
seemed rather to like the Doctor; but on the evening of that day,
the most wonderful transition of feeling took place in him, that perhaps ever occurred in the history of mind. As the two took their
seats, at their study-table, Jones observed, "Old Moses is a pretty
tight old fellow, but 1 can't help liking him." "He's a d——nd
old tyrant!" said Smith. Whereupon Jones' countenance made
proclamation of the workings of his mind in this unmistakable language :—"Why,—La me! I never thought of that! But it's so!
I see it plain enough *now!* What an escape I have made! A little
more, and I might have been precipitated into the bottomless abyss
of love!" Jones covered his ignorance and weakness in the usual
way, by pretending he was in fun, and to prove it, fell to cursing
the Doctor luxuriously. The most of their recreation hours of evenings, were spent in brotherly contests for supremacy in hating and
abusing their excellent preceptor. Let no man say that such cases
never occurred. They are to be found in every school of a hundred
boys in the land—not exactly, to be sure, in the features which we
have given to them, but exactly in substance. Ye protestors against
the doctrine of native depravity, explain this matter, if you please.

Doctor Waddel knew well the feelings of these youths towards
him, and their worthlessness of character ; and he was pleased that
they had selected a residence which cut them off almost entirely
from communication with the other students, save when they were
under his eye. No wonder that he had most gloomy forebodings
when he saw a youth of William's tender age, and bright promise,
placed in daily and nightly intercourse with them.

Young teachers may caution a good, amiable, highly gifted boy,
against associating with a low, vulgar, abandoned youth of his school,
but an old one never does ; for the plain reason that ninety-nine in
the hundred good boys, instead of thanking the teacher for his kindness, holding his counsels in confidence, and improving them, will
go right off to the profligate and tell him all that his teacher has
said about him, render him ten times worse than he was before, in-
furiate his parents, and spread the spirit of rebellion through the
whole school. Well for the kind man if he does not get his head
cracked by the father, his character cracked by the mother, and his

L

chair cracked by his patrons or trustees. All this, kind reader, in
answer to your question, "Why did not Dr. Waddel tell the boy
frankly that Smith and Jones were unfit associates for him, and that
they would ruin him, if he did not leave them immediately?" Doctor Waddel well knew "that there were things," not only "in heaven
and earth," but in schools, "which never were dreamed of" in 'the
world's "philosophy." We must not, however, take leave of Smith
and Jones without doing them the justice to say, that there were
two amiable, excellent, intelligent men, and as many women of like
character, whose opinion of them differed *toto cœlo* from ours : these
were their fathers and mothers.

On the evening of the fifth, William Mitten reported to Smith
and Jones all that had passed between the Doctor and himself;
wondering how the Doctor could be so much concerned about his
horse and his boarding at Newby's.

"I understand it," said Smith, with expletives, which we omit,
"he and Newby are in *cahoot*. He knows you're good pay; and
another thing—he wants you there near him, where he can be poking his grey eyes and club nose through the crack of your house, of
nights, without much trouble. If I stayed there and he was to
come peeping into my house, I'd take a sharp stick and punch out
his old peepers. I was always taught to despise eaves-droppers, and
so I do."

"Oh yes," said William, "I see into it. He thinks if he can get
my horse away from me, rather than walk so far to school, I'll go
back to Newby's; but he misses it just as much as if he had burnt
his shirt. I ain't going to quit the good eating here, and the good
sleeping and easy living and go back there, to eating and sleeping
and working like a nigger, if my horse was gone."

"Bill," said Jones, "did you ever play cards?"

"O yes," said Bill, "many a time."

"I wish we had a pack," said Smith. "We burnt up ours, at the
end of the term ; but if you'll lend me your horse Saturday, I'll go
to Petersburg and get a pack."

"Read that paper," said William.

Smith read it.

"Well, how will your Uncle know that you lent him?" pursued
Smith.

"But I promised my Uncle solemnly to obey his orders about the
horse, and I hate to violate my word. It would distress my mother
to death, if I was to do so, and she find it out."

"Well, are you going to use him Saturday?" said Jones. "If you ain't, I'll tell you how we can fix it elegantly; you just leave him in the stable, and I'll take him, without your lending him."

"I thought I'd go, next Saturday and Sunday, with Mr. Waddel, if he goes, to Rocky River Church; I must go one time——"

Here William's words were drowned, by most obstreporous laughter from his companions.

"But hear me, hear me!" continued Bill. "Let me explain! You see, Uncle disliked my bringing my horse very much; and after giving him all the reasons I could think of to let me bring him, I told him I would like sometimes to go with Mr. Waddel to Rocky River Church! When I said that, I saw something in Uncle's looks, which made me believe he thought I was telling a lie——"

"And who the devil is your Uncle!" said Jones. "Do you belong to your Uncle?"

"Jones, you mustn't say anything against my Uncle—he's one of the best men in the world, and——"

"Oh, go on Bill; I didn't mean to say anything *against* your Uncle."

"Well, as I was saying, I want to go with Doctor Waddel one time, and if I can go before I write my first letter, and tell 'em of it when I write, it will convince Uncle I told the truth, please Mother, and make them very willing for me to keep my horse till Christmas. But if I don't, my Uncle, who watches everything like a hawk, will have a boy here after my horse as soon as the weather turns cool."

"Oh, well," said Jones, "that's not so bad; but take care of old Mose, by the way, or he'll have you back to Newby's Monday morning, to a certainty."

"But," said Smith, "suppose old Wad. does not preach at Rocky River, what will you do with your horse Saturday and Sunday?"

"I shall ride him to Vienna, to mail a letter—"

"That'll do; when you get to Vienna, go over to Petersburg, and buy a pack of cards."

"But my orders are not to ride my horse further than Vienna, except to preaching."

"Well," said Smith, "you needn't *ride* over to Petersburg, you can go there afoot."

"That's it," said Bill, snapping his fingers joyously.

The evening passed off with but little study.

William's class usually recited to one of the Assistants, but the next morning it was called before Doctor Waddel. The Doctor arranged the order of recitation, so as to throw the last part of the lesson to William. He had not been over it, and he bungled shamefully.

"Why, William," said the Doctor, "what's the matter with you? I never knew you to recite so poor a lesson. I'm afraid you don't study at your new boarding house as well as you did at your old one."

William was excessively mortified, and his classmates no less surprised.

After the class retired, William enquired of Doctor Waddel, whether he preached at Rocky River, the next Sabbath.

"No, my son," said the Doctor, "but I preach there the Sabbath after. Why do you ask? Do you think of accompanying me?"

"Yes, sir."

"I am very glad to hear that. Now you are going to make a good use of your horse. If you never make a worse use of him, you will do well."

Saturday came, and William, at an early hour after breakfast, was off to Vienna to mail a letter. As the letter was written only to be mailed, it of course was not written in his usual diffuse, florid style ; but what it lost in beauty, grace and polish, it gained in conciseness, nerve and point. Here it is :

WILL'N, Sep. 7.

"Dear Mother :—I just write for fear you will feel uneasy if you get no letter from me by this mail. Tom can tell you all about me. Delighted with my boarding house—Fare much better than New's. Health good—Told Mr. Wad'l I wished to go to preach'g with him, if he went to-day, but he don't go till next Sat'y—Best love to all.

In haste your af'te son,   WM. M."

After mailing his letter, he went over to Petersburg, and bought a pack of cards, a tickler of peach brandy, and a plug of tobacco. "My son," said the merchant as he handed him the articles "these are ugly things for such a youth as you are to buy."

"Oh, I don't buy any of them for myself, I buy them for Mr. Smith and Mr. Jones, who live about nine miles from here."

The merchant knew William at sight as the youth who had distinguished himself so much at the exhibition, and he naturally felt pained to see a boy of his talents engaged in such a dangerous traffic. Hence his remark, which produced from William one lie and two truths, in consolidated form. He bought the cards for himself, the brandy for Smith, and the tobacco for Jones.

He returned immediately to his residence, and spent the afternoon and till twelve at night, playing cards and drinking peach brandy. The next day he was sick. On Monday he went to school, was called again to recite to Doctor Waddel, and knew nothing of his lesson. It was rarely the case that the Doctor called one of the lower classes to recite to him two mornings in succession.

" What," said he to William, " with all Saturday, and all Monday morning to get your lesson in, come up here and know nothing about it, sir! You don't study, sir!"

The Doctor enquired of Mr. Dobbins how Smith and Jones recited that morning. "They didn't recite at all," responded Dobbins, "Smith said he had been sick from Friday evening till Monday morning, and Jones came up with his jaw tied up in a handkerchief, and took on as if he was raving distracted with the tooth-ache. He disturbed the class so that I excused him from attending recitation."

Tuesday they all appeared at school, as well prepared for recitation as usual, but the Doctor heard none of them.

On Wednesday they were not noticed until after prayer in the evening. This service over, he hauled a tickler out of his pocket, and said :

" William Mitten come forward!" William just had strength to step forward, and that was all.

" Do you know this tickler, sir :"

" Ye-e-s, sir!"

" Whose is it?"

" It's Smith's, sir."

" You took it to Petersburg last Saturday, didn't you, sir; and got it filled with peach brandy?"

" Yes, sir."

" Who did you get it for ?"

" Smith, sir."

" Whose pack of cards is this?" asked the Doctor, drawing a pack from his pocket."

Bill did not require an inspection of it, to give the answer :

" It's mine, sir."

" You and Jones and Smith sat up late on Saturday night, playing cards and drinking peach brandy, didn't you ?"

" We—I—Jo—I did, sir."

" *You* did, sir. Did you play cards by yourself till late at night ?
—and drink all Smith's brandy yourself ?"

" No sir ; they drank some."

"And did they sit by and help you drink, while you played cards
by yourself ?"

" No, sir ; they played too——some."

" Perhaps you may think that I got my information of your dealings at Petersburg, from the merchant who sold you the cards, brandy,
and a plug of tobacco. I have not seen him, and no man in Petersburg or Vienna told me a syllable about it. Alexander B. Linton,
bring me six tough hickories in the morning, suited to the occasion.
In the language of Rob Roper's composition, ' the apple of discord
has been cast in among us, and if not speedily snipt in the bud, it
will inevitably explode and shroud us in the pitchy night of anarchy
and confusion, and deluge the country with fire and sword.' As
that apple is as dangerous to schools as it is to the country, I'll try
to nip it in the bud effectually, in the morning. You are dismissed."

As for Jones and Smith, nobody cared for them, but the whole
school sympathized with William. They laid all his faults to them,
(rather more than was due to them by the way,) and rejoiced at the
retribution that was in reserve for them. Gilbert Hay accompanied
him for about a quarter of a mile on his way to his lodgings. To
this point they walked hand in hand. William leading his horse,
and both weeping bitterly.

Here they stopped, and William broke silence :

" Gilbert," said he, " nothing gave me so much pain in leaving
Mr. Newby's as parting with you. How happy we were in talking
together, working together, playing together, and studying together !
I'd give ten thousand millions of dollars if I hadn't left you——"

" Will, come back now."

" It's too late now—I'm disgraced, I'm ruined—I wish that my
horse and Jones and Smith were all tumbled together in the flames
of Hell !——Stop Gilbert ; don't leave me !"

" I will leave you, William, if you talk in that way ; and, much as
I love you, I must drop your acquaintance, if you use such language."

" Forgive me, Gilbert, I hardly know what I say. You have no
idea what I suffer"—

" Why, it's no killing matter, to get whipped by Mr. Wad——"

" Whipped ! I don't mind the whipping at all, severe as I know
it will be. If cutting my legs to the bone would just put me back

to that happy night I spent at your house, I'd take it willingly."

" Then what is it that distresses you so ?—You are not the first boy that Mr. Waddel has ever caught playing cards and drinking liquor, I know."

" If I should tell you, you never would own me as a friend or acquaintance again."

" Well, it can't be worse than I'll think it is, if you don't tell me."

" In less than one short fortnight, I have deceived the best of mothers, the best of uncles; forsaken you, the best of friends; despised the advise of the best of teachers; drank, gambled and lied—disgraced myself in my class, as you know, and disgraced myself in the eyes of all who applauded me at the examination and exhibition. They will hear of it——Why, here's Tom ! What's the matter at home, Tom ?"

" Mas' David is very sick. He thinks he's going to die, and he wants to see you before he dies. Here's a letter from Missis."

" Lord have mercy upon my poor soul !" half shrieked William. " Can't I die! Can't I die ! Read it Gilbert !"

By the dim twilight he read :

" *My Dearest Boy :* Two days after you left us, your Uncle was attacked with bilious fever. The attack is very severe, but we hope not fatal. Last evening he begged that you might be sent for. Come as quick as you can, in mercy to your horse. The Doctor says there is no probability of his dying in four or five days; so do not peril the life of your horse, in your haste to get here.

Your affectionate mother, ANNA MITTEN."

"Oh Gilbert ! Gilbert ! How shall I face a dying uncle and an afflicted mother ? Show the letter to Mr. Waddel. Tell him I thank him for all his kindness to me—that I never shall forget the beech ——"

" The beech ! What does that mean, William ?"

" He knows—he will tell you. Farewell, my dearest, best classmate !"

Gilbert went immediately with the letter to Doctor Waddel, and delivered it with William's message The Doctor listened, read, and walked the floor in great agitation of mind. After a few strides backwards and forwards, he spoke : " It is awful, awful to think of such a star as that being eclipsed just at its rising ! A breath may change the destiny of a youth for time and eternity. If ever there was a boy

of more brilliant promise than William Mitten, three months ago, I
don't think I ever saw him. And where is he now! Why is it that
in the contact of virtue and vice, vice always gets the advantage—at
least with the young?"

"Mr. Waddel, what did William mean by *the beech?*"

"I'll take you to it and explain, to-morrow at twelve; but I little
dreamed that the catastrophe was so near at hand! At a proper
time, I will write to his uncle,—or mother, to send him back. His
heart's in the right place still, and he may yet be the pride of his
mother, the boast of his teacher, and the glory of his country."

"If you write, Mr. Waddel, tell him I love him yet; and that
the front side of my bed is waiting for him yet."

William wended his way to his boarding house, slowly and sadly.
On reaching it, he went in and informed the landlord of the distressing tidings from home, and that he would leave at the dawn in the
morning. He refused supper, and walked towards the study, near
the steps of which Smith and Jones were standing.

"Well," said Smith, "you've stayed so long we thought you'd
run away. You've got us into a hell of a scrape, and you may well
look sheepish."

"Smith, that boy has just come for me—my Uncle's at the point
of death——"

"You're d——nd lucky, to have a sick Uncle just at this time."

The words were hardly out of his mouth, before the onset of William's fight with Black was renewed precisely; but not with precisely the same results. In his fall, Smith's head struck the corner
of a step, and he came senseless to the ground. Jones, supposing
that he was only a little stunned by the fall, and that he would soon
rally and give William a tremendous beating, (just what he desired)
did not interpose. William supposed so too, (*i. e.*, that he would
soon rise,) and he resolved to improve the interim to the best advantage. Such language, at such a time, from such a character, set his
whole soul on fire, and inspired him with supernatural strength and
inhumanity. He dealt blow after blow upon the face, neck and ribs
of the unresisting Smith, with a force and rapidity that horrified
Jones, and would have astonished any one. It was in vain that
Jones cried out "for God's sake, Mitten, stop, he's dead!" "If he
isn't dead, I'll kill him," said Mitten. Rising from the body, he
stamped Smith in the face with his heavy nail-pegged shoes, and was
in the act of repeating the injury, when the landlord and Tom both
seized him and forced him into the house. As they dragged him

away, "Stop" said he, "let me give Jones a little, and then I'll be
satisfied." He was given in charge of Tom, while the landlord and
Jones took care of Smith. His head was cut to the bone, and the
wound was clogged up with blood and dirt. His face was like nothing human. He was washed, undressed, and put to bed; but he did
not recover his senses, though he breathed, and his pulse beat. There
was no physician within miles of the place, and the landlord did
not suppose it necessary to send for one so far off, as he deemed it
certain that Smith would die or be out of danger before he could
get there. In a half hour's time William became cool, and surrendered himself to grief again. A bed was prepared for him in the
house, his trunk was brought in, he washed, changed his bloody
clothes for clean ones, packed such as he needed in the saddle-bags,
sent Tom to attend to the horses, and threw himself on the bed to
wait, in tears, the coming dawn.

In the meantime, Jones and the landlord were at the bedside of
Smith, in a state of the most intense anxiety. The former was in
the deepest agony. He and Smith had agreed to run away from
school the next morning. It was further arranged that Smith
should give Mitten a sound dressing over-night, because he had not
managed his purchases in Petersburg with sufficient cunning; because he had not extemporized lies according to his talents, under
Waddel's examination; because he had told the truth where he
ought to have told lies, and bungled even at the truth, and because
"he wanted whipping anyhow." There was a short debate between
them as to which should have the pleasure of chastising William.
Smith said that he was so much over Bill's size and age, that it
would look a little mean in him to do it.

"Now you, Jones," continued Smith, "are just about his weight,
and you are but a little older than he is; if you would fan him out,
there would be some honor in it."

"Oh, I can whip him easy enough," said Jones, "and will do it
if you insist upon it, but he will be certain to bung up my face a
little at the beginning of the fight, for you know he can throw me
just as fast as I can get up, and I hate to go home with my face
scratched and bunged up. It will be hard enough for me to make
peace with old John (his father) anyhow. But you can tie him—
you can flog him without a scratch, and don't hurt him much. It
would be mean in a boy of your size to hurt him much; just whip a
little common sense in him."

The matter was arranged accordingly; but instead of Smith's

whipping a little common sense into Bill, behold Bill had knocked a great deal of *very common sense* out of Smith.

To run away and leave Smith in his present condition was not to be thought of. To remain with him until after prayers the next morning, would be certain to awaken Doctor Waddel's curiosity concerning the state of his health, as early as old Hector could bring him hither; and as his old prejudices had greatly strengthened that day, he had no disposition to encounter him anywhere. From what had passed between him and Smith, there was a fair implication that if Smith did not whip William, he would; and though Smith might not hold him responsible for the implied pledge, he would be very apt to hold him responsible for allowing William to beat him while he was in a state of insensibility. William's retiring remark, too, made him feel very uncomfortable; for though he had done nothing to incur his wrath but sympathise with Smith in everything, and drop one disrespectful remark about William's uncle, already atoned for, it was plain that William's mind was not in a condition to allow the proper credits, in closing up his uncle's claims. He was very certain that William would sleep none that night, and if he should conclude to come out a little before day and give him a parting blessing when all were asleep but the two, it would be—very ill-timed, to say the least of it. So that, upon the whole, none of the household spent a more uncomfortable night of it than poor Jones did. To have got rid of the troubles of that single night, he would have been perfectly willing to sign a written pledge to love " old Moses " all his life, *elegantly*, and to accompany him to Rocky River Church monthly, during the term of his pupilage.

Smith did not come fully to himself until about twelve o'clock. When he recovered his mind, and saw with but one eye (for he could not open the other, and one not fully,) Jones and the landlord keeping watch over him, his shirt all bloody, and found himself in pain all over, " Why, what's the matter with me?" muttered he from two hideously swollen lips.

" Never mind," said Jones, " lie still and be quiet till morning, and we'll tell you all about it."

While Jones was talking, Smith was feeling his face and head.

" Why, how did I get in this fix?" enquired he, " I'm in a dreadful fix—my back, hip, head and face all pain me awfully. Jones, tell me who treated me so. Have I been out of my head? What o'clock is it?"

" Never mind, Smith—never mind," said Jones, " you'll soon be

over it if you'll be quiet. Lie still till morning, and we'll explain
all things to your satisfaction."

"Didn't Mitten clinch me? Did he strike me with a stick? He
couldn't——"

"Oh, go to sleep, go to sleep, Smith, and quit talking. A bad
accident has happened to you, and you must be quiet, or there's no
telling what'll come of it."

"I don't recollect anything after he clinched me; but it's impossible he could have hurt me so bad. Is he gone?"

"Yes," said Jones, "he's gone long ago—he didn't do it—it was
an accident, I tell you, and you must be quiet, and not talk, or you
may lose your life."

In this way Smith was quieted, dropped to sleep, and did not wake
until an hour by sun the next morning, when William was ten miles
on his way homeward.

By ten o'clock Doctor Waddel was at Mr. ———'s. The whole
matter was explained to him. He told Jones to stay with Smith,
and nurse him until he was able to walk to school. Jones did so;
but instead of walking to school, they walked home—or rather
walked to where they could get horses to ride home. It was the
Doctor's habit to follow runaways and bring them back, but he was
too glad to get rid of these gentlemen to do so in this instance.

William's purchase in Petersburg soon became the town talk, for
almost everybody in town knew him as the bright boy of the exhibition, and everybody deplored the indications of ruin that his purchases gave. The talk soon spread from Petersburg to Willington,
and from Willington to Doctor Waddel's ears. He went immediately to Mitten's room, where he found the cards and tickler uncon-
cealed, and surprised Mitten with them, as we have seen. Thus did
he possess himself of the few facts, from which he drew out of William all that the trio had done after the cards and brandy reached
their room. He explained to young Hay, according to his promise,
William's reference to the beech, the import of which William fully
understood after his disgrace. What a lamentable thing it is, that
there is no way of inducing the young to follow the counsels of the
old!

CHAPTER XX

Captain Thompson breathed his last but a few minutes before William reached his habitation. We need hardly say that he died happily—he died triumphantly—not shouting, simply because in his last moments, he had not strength to shout, but whispering "Glory, Glory, Glory !"

William's entry into the death-chamber, served but to embitter the griefs of all who filled it. A little while before Captain Thompson expired, he said, "I have been looking anxiously for William— I wished to give him my last counsels, as I have given them to the older children, [his own and his sister's] but it is now too late. Tell him, Anna, my last words to him were, ' Love, honor, cherish and obey your mother.' " These sentences were uttered amidst rests at every three or four words.

Deep and all-prevailing as was the grief around the death-bed of the uncle, the entry of the nephew startled every one, and nearly overpowered his mother. Anguish of mind, loss of sleep, abstinence from food, and fatigue from travel, had wrought the greatest change in his appearance, that perhaps ever had been wrought in a youth of his age, unvisited by disease. He walked, or rather tottered to the corpse, kissed its cold lips, covered his face with his hands, shrieked, and sunk to the floor. The Doctor who had not yet left the room, raised him up, advised that he be removed from the scene of grief to a bed in another apartment, and he assisted in effecting what he advised. He returned and reported to Mrs. Mitten that William needed medical aid, for that "he was quite unwell." She hastened to his bed side with the physician, and found him in a high fever. He was prescribed for, and carried home as soon as possible. Her forebodings of some great calamity had been realized in the death of her brother; but she now believed that her son would soon follow him; and her agony of soul can be better conceived than described. Still she bore her afflictions like a christian ; with no other demonstrations of grief than streaming eyes, deep-drawn sighs, and saddened countenance.

A few weeks before Captain Thompson's death, he and five or six other gentlemen of the village had, upon Mr. Markham's suggestion, agreed to furnish the means for giving John Brown a collegiate education. Mr. Markham, after having taught John gratuitously from the day that he acquitted himself so creditably at the exhibition, set

on foot this benevolent enterprise, and was himself the largest contributor to it. How this excellent man came to enlist so warmly
and efficiently in John's favor, is worthy of record. A short vacation followed the exhibition, and at the opening of the term John
was missing from school. At twelve o'clock, Mr. Markham went to
his mother's to learn the cause of his absence. He found John seated on the door-step, weeping bitterly.

"Well, John," said he, "what's the matter, son ?"

"Mammy says she can't send me to school any more."

"Why, that's bad ; but I reckon you wouldn't study much, if she
was to send you again."

"Yes, sir, I would ; I'd study harder than ever I did in all my
life. You should never have to whip me again, as long as you live."

"Why, that would be a wonderful improvement, John, for I've
generally had to whip you at least twice a week, ever since you first
came to me."

"I know that, sir, because I didn't care about going to school at
first; but now I want to go to school; and if I could go back, you'd
never have to whip me again, I know you wouldn't."

By this time, Mrs. Brown was at the door.

"Walk in, Mr. Markham !" said she, "I never did see a boy take
on so about going to school, as John has all the morning, in all my
born days. 'Twas much as I could do to get him off to school before ; but now he takes on at sitch a rate to go to school, that I can't
help feeling na'trally right sorry for him."

"Well, why won't you let him go, Mrs. Brown ?"

"Well, Mr. Markham, ra'lly the truth is, I an't able to pay his
schoolin'. You know mighty well what my husband is, and therefore
'taint worth while to be mealy-mouthed about it ; he jist na'trally
drinks up, e'en about every little that I can rake together, that he
can lay his hands on. He's a good hearted, clever, hard-working
man, when he's sober; but he's all the time drunk——'tan't worth
while for me to be tryin' to hide it from you, Mr. Markham ; every
body knows it. 'Cept the time Judge Yearly put him in jail for
gwine into court drunk as a jurior, he's hardly drawn one sober breath
since, and you know, Mr. Markham, it's mighty hard for one poor
lone woman like me to get along with three little children, and a
drunken husband besides. Seems to me sometimes that I should
na'trally jist give up. And I b'lieve I——Oh yes, I know I would—
ha' give up long ago, if it hadn't been for your wife, and five or six
other good ladies in town, who've holp me mightily. But after all I

could do, I couldn't do more than jist rake up money enough to pay
for what little schoolin' I could give him, since he's been to you. I
think Johnny would take larning mighty well if he had a chance.
You know he did mighty well at your—at your—show. People took
on mightily at Johnny's doins' that day, and I wish he could have a
chance to git more larning, but I an't able to give it to him—it's a
fact—I an't able to do it, Mr. Markham, and I may as well jist 'tell
the plain, naked truth about it."

"Well, Mrs. Brown, your's is really a right hard case. How long
could you spare John to go to school, if it cost you nothing to send
him ?"

" Oh, la messy ; that would be the onliest thing in the world for
Johnny. I'd be mighty willin' for him to stay till he gets clean
through for my part, and be glad of it. It would be a mighty great
thing if Johnny could git larnin' enough to keep a school himself,
now wouldn't it, Mr. Markham ? You must make a heap o' money
at it, havin' so many scholars as you always have, and gittin' your
money every quarter ?"

" But if I take John to teach him, won't your husband take him
away from me before he gets through ?"

" Oh, la, no! He has nothin' to do with the children, no how,
poor drunken creater ! Besides, he shouldn't do it."

" But how would you prevent him !"

" I could prevent him easy enough. Do you think I'd let him,
who don't do a hand's stirrin' towards feedin' and clothin' my children, take one of them away from gittin' larnin' for nothin' ? No,
sir, he'd no more dare to do it than he'd put his hand in the fire."

"Well, Mrs. Brown, if you'll promise me that you won't take John
away till he gets through, and that your husband shall not, I'll take
John, and if he will behave himself, I'll make him a great scholar—
able to keep any sort of a school. I'll furnish all his books for him,
and teach him, and it shan't cost you a cent."

" Yes, that I do promise for both—— *Behave himself !* If he don't,
I reckon you know how to make him ; and if *you* can't, jest send
him home to me, and I'll give him such a cawhallopin', that I'll be
bound he'll never misbehave again while his head's hot, to a man
that's done so much for him."

" Well, send him over to school in the morning, and we'll see what
we can do for him."

While this conversation was in progress, John's eyes expanded
from a couple of cracks to a couple of pretty respectable key holes,

aud, at the conclusion of it, he commenced patting his foot and
snapping his fingers in unspeakable delight.   As Mr. Markham was
retiring, "Stop a little, Mr. Markham," said Mrs. Brown.   He
stopped.

"Where's your manners, sir," continued she to John.   "Make a
bow to Mr. Markham, and thank him for what he's gwine to do for
you!"

John gave Mr. Markham a bow of his own teaching, excellent for
the stage, but quite too formal for the signal of private thanksgiving, under Mrs. Brown's dictation.   He delivered himself, however,
in his own language:

"Mr. Markham, I'm very much obleeged——"   ,

"Obliged, John."

Mrs. B.   "What, have you been gwine to school all this time
and don't know how to call words yet!"

Mr. M.   "John's is a very common mistake."

John, conceiving that his bow and his thanks had got too far apart,
repeated his bow as before, and commenced again:

"Mr. Markham, I'm very much *obliged* to you for your goodness.
I always said you was——"

"*Were*, John."

"I always said you *were* the best man I ever seen."

"*Saw*, John."

Mrs. B.   "Why, that boy don't know no better how to talk than
me, who han't had no schoolin' at all."

"Well, never mind, never mind, John," said Mr. Markham, fear-
ing John would go back to his bow and begin again.   "Your heart's
right, my boy, and I'll soon set your tongue right.   Mrs. Brown,
you're going to see John a big man some of these days."   So saying,
he retired in haste—in *haste* for two reasons: the one was, that he
might relieve himself from the laughter with which he had been
filling up from the beginning to the end of the interview; and the
other was, to disembarrass John, who, between his corrections, and
his mother's comments, was likely to become inextricably bewildered.

John was the first boy at school the next morning; and thenceforward Mr. Markham never had cause to correct him, or even to reprove him.   He soon became one of the best scholars in the school,
distinguished himself at every examination and exhibition, and in
a short time became such a popular favorite that when Mr. Markham
proposed to the citizens to unite in raising a fund to give him a liberal education, he had not the least difficulty in finding the requisite
number of contributors.

Just before Captain Thompson's last sickness, the arrangement had been made for David Thompson, George Markham and John Brown, to leave for Princeton College, N. J., on the 10th of the ensuing November. Princeton was, at that time, in the South at least, the most renowned College in the Union. Captain Thompson appointed Mr. Markham one of the executors of his will, and authorized him to appropriate any sum out of his estate that he might deem necessary, to the education of John Brown, not exceeding one hundred dollars per annum. He also appointed Mr. Markham testamentary guardian of his two sons, David and George, until the completion of their education; directing that "in all matters touching the education of his two sons, should a difference of opinion arise between his wife [his other representative] and Mr. Markham, his judgment should be decisive."

After an illness of two weeks, William Mitten recovered, and at the end of four, his health was entirely restored. About this time, his mother said to him:

"William, isn't it time for you to think of returning to Dr. Waddel's?"

"Mother," said he, "I can never go back to Dr. Waddel's."

"What!" exclaimed she, horror-stricken, "Oh, my dear, departed brother! Is this affliction to be added to the thousand that thy death has cost me?"

"No, mother, if uncle were alive, he never could induce me to return to Dr. Waddel's. I feared him, I loved him, I adored him, to the day of his death. If I could have saved his life by having my right arm chopped off, I would have done it freely; but uncle could never have induced me to go back to Willington."

"William, in mercy to me, tell me quickly, why?"

"Because I have disgraced myself there."

"*Disgraced yourself there!* Oh, how little we poor mortals know what to pray for! Would that you had died on the bed from which you have just risen!—No, my heavenly Father, pardon me!—In disgrace you were not fit to die; in disgrace you are not fit to live. William, let me know the worst—don't keep me a moment longer in suspense, if you have any respect for me—I may be able to survive the disclosure, if you make it immediately: I may not be able to survive it, if you keep me a few days in this agony of suspense."

"I have lied, I have gambled, I have drank, and been detected in all, and exposed before the whole school——"

"Is that all?—is that the worst!"

" Yes, ma'am, that's the worst: and I don't know what could be worse."

" Bad enough—bad, indeed; but it might have been worse. I have nothing to say in defence of these sins; but how did you rush into them so speedily, after your return ?"

" That infern—, that abominable horse !"

" How could he have involved you in this series of offences, in so short a time ?"

William gave his mother a full and truthful account of all the difficulties in which his horse had involved him. When he had concluded, she resumed:

" I was sure that things had been going wrong with you, from the brief letter you wrote, and which did not reach me until some days after your return. It bore the marks of great carelessness and want of feeling."

" That letter was part of the deceit which I began to practice on you and Uncle before I left here, and which I was carrying on, when I was detected by Mr. Waddel."

" Well, William, you have learned from short, but sad experience, the consequences of vice ; and now abandon it forever. I am under inexpressible obligations to Mr. Waddel, for his vigilance in arresting you in it, before it could become a habit with you. And, now, my advice to you is, to return to his school, do your first works over again, and retrieve your character, as you soon will, where you lost it."

" No, mother, I cannot go back there ; I'd rather die than do it."

" Well, what will you do, my son ? What school will you go to ?"

" I don't care about going into any school. If you are willing, I will go into a store as a clerk ?"

" Mercy on me, William ! Close up all your bright prospects—bury your brilliant talents among goods and groceries ! No, my son, I never can consent to that."

"Why, ma ; almost all the merchants in town began as clerks, and see how rich and respectable they are !"

"But Providence has given you talents above this calling !"

" My talents have done me very little good as yet, and I doubt whether they ever will do me any. What good will Latin and Greek do me ? Nobody speaks Latin and Greek. I don't see any good in anything hardly, that we learn at school. I think I had better stay here with you, and take care of you, and be trying to get an honest living, than to be running off to school, where I will be constantly under temptations."

M

" Well, my son, there is a good deal of force in your remarks. It will cost a hard struggle to give up my fond hopes of your future distinction ; but I can easily reconcile myself to your position in life as a respectable, wealthy, private citizen. It will be a great comfort to have you all the time with me. But let us think a while longer before we decide upon this matter."

While it was held under advisement, Doctor Waddel's promised letter arrived. After tender expressions of condolence with Mrs. Mitten and her brother's family in their recent bereavement, it continued :

" But the main object of this letter is to offer your son encouragements to return to school. He left here under great depression of spirits, and under the impression that his character was irretrievably lost. No one in this vicinity, in or out of the school, thinks so. Now that the story of his misfortunes is fully understood, every one attributes them to a train of untoward circumstances which surrounded him, on his return hither, rather than to depravity of heart. Indeed, he has some noble traits of character, which almost entirely conceal his faults from the eyes of the public and his school-fellows— I say the *public*, for though it is a very uncommon thing for the public to know or notice school-boy delinquencies, yet so wide-spread was William's reputation from his performances at our last Examination and Exhibition, that every one who knows him takes an interest in him, and every one, I believe, regards him with more of sympathy than censure. All would rejoice, I doubt not, to hear of his return to the school, and his return to his good habits. Gilbert Hay, his room-mate and bed-fellow, bids me say that he loves him yet, and that the half of his bed is still reserved for him; and the feelings of Gilbert Hay towards him, I believe, are the feelings of nine-tenths of the school towards him. For myself, I shall give him a cordial welcome. But you will naturally ask, what will be my dealings with him, if he return ? I answer the question very frankly : I shall feel myself bound to correct him ; though in so doing I shall not forget the many circumstances of extenuation in his case. Had he been guilty of but one offence, and that of a veneal nature, I should freely forgive it, as is my custom, with the first offence. But he has been guilty of several offences, and though none of them are very rare in schools, they are, nevertheless, such as I have never allowed to go unpunished in my school, and which I could not allow to escape with impunity in this instance, without setting a dangerous precedent, as well as showing marked partiality. I have reason to believe that William would cheerfully submit to the punishment of his faults, even though it were much severer than it will be, if that would restore him to his lost position ; now, I can hardly conceive of anything better calculated to have that effect, than his volunteering to take the punishment which he knows awaits him on his return, when he might perchance avoid it by abandoning the school. But with or without the punishment, he has only to be, for ten months, what he has been for nearly as many, to regain the confidence of everybody. Nothing but the peculiar circumstances of this case, and the very lively interest which I take in the destiny of your highly-gifted son, could have induced me to write a letter so liable to misconstruction, as this is. But brief as is our acquaintance, I think you will credit me, when I assure you, that my own pecuniary interest has had no more to do with it, than yours will have in deliberating upon its contents. Verily, the loss or gain of a scholar is nothing to   Your sincere friend and ob't serv't,

MOSES WADDEL.

CHAPTER XXI.

So delighted was Mrs. Mitten with the first part of Dr. Waddel's letter, that she rushed with it half read to her son, and recommenced the reading for his edification and comfort. With the close of almost every sentence, she would ejaculate, " *Dear, good man !*" " *How kind.*" " *Such a man is a national blessing !*" " *Who can help loving him !*" But when she came to the whipping part, she was unable to read without comments, and with becoming composure. Having finished the perusal, " Well," said she, "upon the whole, it is a sweet letter; but I cannot see the necessity of his whipping a boy of your size a month after the offence is committed, and when he himself admits that there are so many circumstances of extenuation in the case. If everybody else is ready to forgive and forget, why might not he ? But, William, as these are the only terms upon which you can get back and save your credit, I think you had better go. I will write to Mr. Waddel, informing him of your deep contrition, and begging him if he can possibly pass over the offence without correction, consistently with his sense of duty, to do so ; but if not, then in the midst of justice, to remember mercy. Surely, under all the circumstances of the case, the purposes of justice would be as fully answered by two or three stripes, as by——"

" *Two or three* stripes !" said Bill, " why, he gives double that for simple idleness; and if he were to let me off with two or three stripes, I'd bring home the marks of them next July. I'd rather take ten such as he commonly gives in the summer time, when the boys wear thin breeches, than three such as he gave one boy named Sapling, when he found his legs wrapped up with strips of shirt. If I go back, and he lets me off with less than ten peelers, or fifteen of the common sort, I shall think myself lucky."

"Oh, William, you make Mr. Waddel a perfect enigma; how could a man of his kindness of heart, be so inhuman!"

• "He doesn't think it inhuman to whip students who violate his laws; but it is not worth while to talk about it, ma, for I'm not going back to Mr. Waddel's. As to the whipping, I shouldn't mind that, so very much, if I could believe that I would be put back to where I was before I committed the offences; but I know that that can never be."

"Well, my son, I hardly know what to advise. You surely were born under an unlucky star. Always, always there is something which obstructs the way which seems best for you to pursue. How unfortunate was it that your uncle gave you that horse! How much more unfortunate, that you did not accept his offer for him before your return to Willington! Oh! were he now in life I would surrender you to his government, and never have an opinion of my own upon it, during your minority. But in this single instance of giving you the horse—and there he soon saw his error, and did all that he could do to correct it—his views have always proved right, while mine, however carefully taken, invariably turn out unfortunately."

"Well, ma, you may console yourself with this reflection, that if Uncle David were alive, he could not force me back to Mr. Waddel's."

"Yes, William, if he were alive, and felt convinced that your future destiny hung upon it, you would have to go. He would have reasoned with you, he would have persuaded you, at first; but if he found these means unavailing, he would have carried you back to school at all hazards. But it is in vain to talk of supposed cases. I cannot do what he might have done. What say you, will you go back or not?"

"No, ma'am; never, never, never!"

"William, my *feelings* are against your going, but my *convictions* are strong and pungent that you ought to go. Something whispers me that if you go, you will be great; if you do not, you will be ruined. Will you submit to Mr. Markham's advice in the matter?"

" No, ma ; I've thought the matter all over, and I've made up my mind, coolly and deliberately, never to go back to Mr. Waddel's."

Now the truth of the matter is, that though Master Mitten, while suffering the first tortures of his exposed guilt, and supposed disgrace, would very readily have submitted to a severe whipping, to have regained his lost ground ; as he became more familiar with his disgrace, it began to set very easily on him, while the *whipping* assumed a new interest in his cogitations, and became more and more imposing, as the disgrace became less and less distressing : so that when the consultation occurred which we have just noticed, the whipping crowded clean out of Master Mitten's mind, every other consideration. It brought him, therefore, to a very decided judgment from which nothing could move him which lay within the range of his mother's devices. And yet there was a lady living within three hundred yards of Mrs. Mitten's house, a beneficiary of hers, who did not know A from a deer's track, who would have managed the case to perfection without the help of Mr. Markham. That woman was no other than Mrs. Nancy Brown, mother of John Brown, surnamed *Partus*, which is by interpretation, *Pink-Eyed*. We opine that if Mrs. Brown had been in the place of Mrs. Mitten, and Master John in the place of Master William, she would have given him, the said John, such a " cawhalloping," that Dr. Waddel's best " fifteen" would have been a Charlotte-russe to it. We have no doubt that John would have given his " cawhalloping" for the "fifteen," and made one of his best bows to Dr. Waddel, to boot.

No alternative was now left to Mrs. Mitten but to procure a clerkship for William in some store of the village. Two of the merchants, Mr. Sanders and Mr. Dillon, had been enquiring for clerks, a little while before Mrs. Mitten took the rounds in her son's behalf.

She went first to Mr. Sanders.

" Mr. Sanders," said she, " don't you wish to employ a clerk in your store ?"

" Yes, madam," said Mr. Sanders, " very much indeed."

" Well, I would be very glad if you would take my son William——"

" Your son William, Mrs. Mitten ! why surely you are not going to take such a smart boy as that from school, to make a clerk of him !"

" He has quit school——"

" Quit school ! Why, how did that happen ?"

" He got dissatisfied, and wished to get into some employment, and desires a clerkship——"

"Dear, dear, dear! How thoughtless boys are! Why, Mrs. Mitten, you oughtn't to allow him to quit school. That boy was cut out for a great man—yes, for a very great man——"

"Well, Mr. Sanders, his talents will not be in the way of your employing him, I hope."

"Oh, no, ma'am, no! I prefer a smart boy to a dull one, certainly; but it does look like such a sacrifice to put such a boy as that behind the counter! If he's determined to quit school, he ought, by all means, to study law or physic."

"He's too young for that."

"Oh—ah, yes. He's too young to go into any sort of business. A store, in such a place as this, is a very dangerous place for a youth of William's age. I never could forgive myself if I should take him into my store at his tender age, and he should turn out badly—"

"But he will be constantly under your eye and mine, Mr. Sanders."

"Ah, there's the difficulty, Mrs. Mitten. He will not be constantly under my eye. I have long trips to make to the North twice a year—repeated trips to Augusta and Savannah. But, Mrs. Mitten, if you are disposed to risk it, such is my regard for you and your family—but he is too young—entirely too young!"

"Why, Mr. Sanders, he can't be younger than young Dally was when you first took him; and he did well while he was with you, and went out of your store to preaching."

"Very true, very true, Mrs. Mitten. But young Dally was the son of a widow——and—so is William; and thus far the cases are alike. But Mrs. Dally was a poor widow, with a number of sons, and you are a rich widow with but one son. It was a charity (somewhat) to take her son, but it would be no charity to take yours. And, you see, moreover, besides, Mrs. Mitten, you would never be satisfied with the wages for William that I gave young Dally——"

"I don't care, Mr. Sanders, if you give him no wages at all——"

"Oh, bless my soul, Mrs. Mitten, that would never do! I couldn't think of taking your boy for nothing."

"Well just give him what you think proper. It is not for the pay that I wish to put him under you, but simply to acquaint himself with the mercantile business. I will board him and clothe him myself, and if you choose to give him anything, very well; it will go to him, and he won't care whether it is much or little."

"Ah, there you are mistaken, Mrs. Mitten. William would never be satisfied to see other boys in town, not half as smart as he is, get-

ting two or three times as much as he gets—and I shouldn't blame
him at all. Besides, I can't think of fixing his wages myself. If I
take him, it must be under contract with you, in which his wages
must be settled to our mutual satisfaction. William must have nothing to do with it. Now what would you be willing to take for his
services?"

"Why, bless my soul, Mr. Sanders, I know nothing about such
matters. I'm willing to take anything you choose to give."

Mr. Sanders looked down, scratched his head, and said rather to
himself, than to Mrs. Mitten : "How shall we fix this thing. I dislike very much that any obstacle should stand in the way of my getting the services of such a brilliant youth as he is. But, stop, stop,
stop. Does William understand Arithmetic pretty well? If he
doesn't, you know it would be impossible for me to employ him."

" I presume he does ; he was considered very smart at figures by
his teachers here."

" Well, if that's the case, I reckon we shall be enabled to get along.
Send him to-morrow morning, Mrs. Mitten, at nine o'clock precisely,
and I will try him a little at figures, and if he does well, why then,
that will take away the only insuperable obstacle to employing him."

Mrs. Mitten promised to send him over at the appointed time, and
retired.

The Mr. Sanders of whom we have been speaking, was Mr. D.
Sanders, who was doing business with his brother, Mr. B. Sanders,
under the copartnership name of D. & B. Sanders. The last, however, was little more than a dormant partner.

The conversation just detailed was hardly ended before it reached
Mr. Dillon's ears, who, at precisely nine o'clock the next morning,
closed doors, and " absquatulated," as Billy Munford would say, alias
" vamoosed," alias was " taken with a getting away."

William was prompt to Mr. Sanders' appointed hour.

"Well, William," said Mr. Sanders, "your mother tells me you
are going to quit school, and take to clerking. Is it so?"

" Yes, sir, I am bent upon that."

" Dear me, dear me, what a pity! Why, William, you were cut
out for something greater than a counter-hopper. I earnestly advise
you, my son, to go on and finish your education. Everybody says
that if you only take the right turn, you will be one of the greatest men that Georgia ever produced. Now, are you going to disappoint us all ? I want a clerk badly, but I had rather do without a clerk a twelve month, than be the means of turning you aside

from the glory which is before you, if you only improve your talents in the right way.   So reluctant am I to offering you any encouragement to give up your fine prospects, that I am really afraid your mother took up the idea that I didn't wish to employ you.   Now, William, take an old man's advice; return to school, complete your education, study law, be studious, be moral, and by and by you'll never get done thanking me for stopping you in the course you are now pursuing."

"Mr. Sanders," said William, "I've heard my talents spoken of and praised ever since I was a child, and instead of doing me any good, they have done me nothing but harm——"

"Oh, my son, the time hasn't come yet for you to reap the benefits of your talents.   Look at lawyer M——, and lawyer C——, and lawyer J——, who had nothing to depend upon but their talents; where are they now?   All on the high road to fortune and to fame!   Now I don't believe either of them had as bright talents as you have."

Just here Mr. B. Sanders, who was rarely seen about the store, rode up, dismounted, and walked into the counting room.

"My mind is made up, Mr. Sanders," said William, "and if you will not employ me, I must seek a place elsewhere."

"Well, if you are determined to go into a store—which store would you prefer?"

"I prefer yours greatly to any store in town."

"Well, however desirous I may be to employ you, you know yourself, my son, that I can't do it unless you understand figures pretty well."

"Of course not," said William.

"Well, here take the slate and pencil, and let me try you a little.   How much will five and a half yards of cloth come to, at five and a half dollars a yard?"

The question was no sooner asked, than William answered it by his head without touching pencil to slate.   Mr. Sanders took the slate, ciphered it up, found the answer correct, rubbed out his calculation, and returned the slate to William, saying, "Very well done, my son; but that's head-work, and it won't do to keep merchants' accounts by the head; do it on the slate."

William did it on the slate in less time than Mr. Sanders did it.

"Very well.   How much will eighteen pounds and three quarters of sugar come to, at eighteen and three quarter cents a pound."

William gave the answer promptly, not by his head, but according to Pike.

" Very well, William ! ·Very promptly and quickly done ! How much will five-eighths of a yard of cloth come to at five eighths of a dollar a yard."

William soon presented the answer.

" It isn't right my son," said Mr. Sanders.

William reviewed it.

" Yes, it is right, Mr. Sanders," said William.

Sanders looked over it again and acknowledged his error.

" Well, William," said Mr. Sanders, " I will put a few more questions to you and then release you. How much will seven and a quarter yards of cloth come to at one pound, seven shillings and sixpence ha'penny sterling a yard ?"

William gave the answer correctly.

" Well, let me try you a little at interest." He put down upon the slate " 85671 ", and handed it to William. " There," said he, " give me the interest on that sum for a month and a half, at eight per cent."

William took the slate, placed a dot to the right of the first figure and handed it back, saying " there's the answer sir—six dollars, sixty-seven and a quarter cents."

Mr. Sanders went over the sum in the common way, while William stood chuckling. When he brought out the result just as William had it, he looked at him with perfect amazement. " Well, William," said he, " I believe you are the smartest boy at figures that I ever saw in all my life."

Here Mr. B. Sanders stepped in. " Why, brother," said he, " have you turned school master ?"

" No," said Mr. D., " I was trying William on arithmetic, to see if he would answer for a clerk for us."

" Why, I've engaged a clerk," said Mr. B. Sanders.

" You have !" said Mr. D., " who is it ?"

" John Dally, brother of our old clerk."

" Why brother, there never was a Dally to compare with William Mitten at figures ! I verily believe he is better than both of us put together. Couldn't you get off from your engagement with Mrs. Dally, so that we may employ William ?"

" I suppose I could, if I were to ask her to let me off, but that's not my way of dealing."

" Well, William," said Mr. D. Sanders, " you see how it is—we shall have to give you up. Tell your mother, that I was not only satisfied with your knowledge of arithmetic, but that I was delighted with it—amazed at it; but that my brother, knowing that we wanted a clerk, had employed one."

William went home and related all that had passed between him and Mr. D. Sanders.

"Well, was there ever such an unlucky mortal born, William, as you are!" said Mrs. Mitten. "It seems almost supernatural."

On Mr. Dillon's return home, which was two days and a half after his "*absquatulation*," Mrs. Mitten waited on him to know if he would not employ her son. But Mr. Dillon had just engaged a young man, who had been highly recommended to him.

Mrs. Mitten now made application to every other merchant in town, but they were all supplied with clerks; they all spoke, however, in the highest terms of William's talents.

"And what will you do now, my son," said she, "seeing your favorite plan is broken up?"

"I really don't know, mother; I am at the end of my row."

Mr. Markham, hearing of her disappointment, called upon Mrs. Mitten and proposed to her to let William go on with his cousin David, George Markham, and John Brown, and fit himself for college under Doctor Finley, a celebrated teacher at Basken Ridge, New Jersey. "If," said Mr. Markham, "William will apply himself closely to the study of Greek and Mathematics, (the only studies in which he is deficient,) he will be able to enter the Freshman class in six months with ease, I am certain."

The proposition was readily embraced by both the mother and the son; and while she commenced his outfit for the journey, he commenced the study of Greek assiduously.

CHAPTER XXII

ABOUT nine days before the time appointed for Masters Thompson, Markham, Brown and Mitten-to leave for the North, Mr. Beach, a celebrated manufacturer of vehicles, in Newark, New Jersey, came to the village, on a collecting tour through the State of Georgia. He was well known to Mr. B. Sanders, who suggested to him that the four youths just mentioned were about leaving for his State, and that he would confer a very great favor on their parents, by taking charge of them, at least as far as his residence. Mr. Beach very cheerfully and kindly offered to do so, provided they could delay their departure until the fifteenth of the month, and meet him at Augusta on that date. Mr. Sanders sent for Mr. Markham, introduced him to Mr. Beach, and the arrangement was made to suit the convenience of the latter. On the fourteenth, Mr. Markham was in Augusta with the four youths, where he found Mr. Beach ready to take charge of them. They were placed under his care, and left with him for Jersey, via Savannah, the next morning. On the evening before their departure, Mr. Markham addressed the four as follows :

" I cannot part with you, my young friends, perhaps forever, without giving you the benefit of my experience and observation in the way of counsel. Bear with me if I occasionally play the woman in delivering it, for I speak from a heavy heart. Was ever man placed in precisely the relation which I sustain to you all! I can with truth say, that I never felt the delicacy and responsibilities of it, in all their force, until this moment. When I left college, I had no higher ambition than to be a good and a useful man ; and I saw no better way of attaining these ends than by devoting myself to the instruction of youth. I determined to engage in this vocation—greatly to the disappointment and mortification of my only surviving parent, who, mother like, far over-estimated my gifts and attainments, and regarded them as certain passports to high political or judicial distinction, while in consonance with a miserably perverted public opinion of that day, (not yet entirely reformed,) she esteemed the calling of the ' School Master ' as hardly respectable. I saw the importance of it, and the bitter fruits of this debasement of public opinion, (that it was throwing the sacred business of instruction into the hands of the worst of characters) and I determined that, to the extent of my ability, I would elevate the character of the teacher and rectify the popular error. I opened my school at first in this place, and afterwards in the village where I now reside. I soon acquired the confidence of the villagers—at least of all whose confidence was worth having. I appreciated it highly, and studied to retain and strengthen it by a faithful discharge of my duty as an instructor, and the performance of good offices as a man. The consequence has been, that trust after trust has been devolved upon me through a long series of years. I accepted them simply on the score of friendship, benevolence or humanity, thinking nothing of the responsibilities attached to them, until I found myself occupying the place of a parent to four youths of fair promise, of different means, tempers and dispositions, at the most critical period of life, on the eve of their departure from the parental roof, for two, three or more years. Verily, my position is an unenviable one; but it will be a source of future rejoicing to us all, if you choose to make it such. That you may make it such, listen to the last counsels that I expect ever to give you; remembering that there are others much more deeply interested in your observance of them, (with but one exception) than I am.

"Hitherto you have had wiser heads to shape your course, to correct your errors, to check your wanderings, and to guard your morals, than your own. From to-morrow you must be thrown mainly upon your own resources, and that too amidst scenes of novelty, temptation and trial, to which you are entire strangers. Fortunately for me, and more fortunately for you if you will be advised, I am enabled to anticipate the more serious evils to which you will be exposed during your sojourn abroad, and to fortify you against them. Come safely through these, and your character will survive all others, though it may be smartly chafed by them. To these, however, I shall not confine my counsels, for my purpose is, not simply to save you from ruin, but to exalt you to honorable distinction.

"I begin with your duty to Mr. Beach, who has laid us all under obligations to him which we can never repay. He has kindly promised to take you to his house upon reaching Newark, to retain you there for two days, until he can dispose of a little pressing business, then to accompany you to New York, and devote two more days to showing you the city and as many of its curiosities as can be seen in so short a time, and then to see you all to your destination. Now, whether we are indebted to his native goodness of heart for these unusual and unlooked for kindnesses, or to his friendship for Mr. Sanders, they certainly demand your profoundest respect and your warmest feelings of gratitude. Let him see that you are sensible of them. In your intercourse with him be modest, but not bashful; easy, but not forward; familiar, but not pert; and at all times and under all circumstances, show him the most marked deference and respect. When he speaks, give him your attention. Arrest always your conversation with each other, to hear what he has to say. Should he use an ungrammatical expression, or betray ignorance of any of the very few things which you know, you are not to evince by word, smile or interchange of look, that you notice or know of his defects. Anticipate his wishes, and relieve him of the burden of you as much as possible. Take care of your own trunks and of his, (if he will allow you to do so) under his direction. Whatever opinions he may advance, you are not to object to them; much less are you to debate them with him. These rules should be observed in your intercourse with your elders generally, more especially are they to be observed in your intercourse with a benefactor.

"In the course of your travels, you will sooner or later be thrown in company with every variety of character; the grave, the scientific, the facetious, the ignorant, the profane, the vile. Be not forward in obtruding yourselves upon the notice of either class. A modest and diffident approach to men of rank and learning, you may make, with propriety and improvement; but take care to let them always lead in the conversation; and as soon as they turn their attention from you to another, cease to be talkers, and become listeners. Let others entertain the wit, not you. To the ignorant be charitable, not rude. Ignorance is no crime. Show no countenance to the vulgar and the profane. I do not say that it is your province to rebuke them; but it is your duty to yourselves to exhibit no signs of approbation to anything that falls from the lips of such characters. And do not suppose that you will gain credit for purity of heart, by simply abstaining from vulgarity of lip yourselves. Let me see how you receive it from the lips of others, and I will tell you exactly how far you differ from them in moral character. Does it absorb your attention? Does it excite a smile? Does it raise no blush upon your cheek? Does it receive from you an impulsive hint? You are no better at heart than the retailer of it. The only difference between you is, that you are a little more prudent than he is, in your choice of times and places of relieving your hearts from this moral feculence.

"Do not allow yourselves to contract the habit of profane swearing.

Aside from its sinfulness, it should be eschewed by every man who desires to become fascinating in conversation, or renowned in elocution. I never saw the *very* profane swearer, who was a *very* eloquent *extemporaneous* speaker. The reason is plain : such an one, always accustomed to filling up his sentences with oaths, cannot command the appropriate terms to supply their places when they are rejected.

"When you enter college, you will be presented with a copy of its laws : read them attentively, and resolve to obey them. Indeed, you will be required to sign a written pledge to do so. A word upon this pledge. It is called the matriculation pledge, and imports the formal admission of the student into the Institution. How it comes to pass I know not, but so it is, that not one in twenty students regard this solemnly recorded vow as of any force whatever. A large majority do not violate it—at least in any important particulars—but whether their conformity to it is from respect to it, or a proper sense of its obligations, is very questionable. It is certain, that in the four years in which I was in college, I never heard it adverted to as a ground of obedience to the rules of the Institution. One day, a very grave, pious student said to a rather wild one, in my presence, 'How does it happen that so many students treat the matriculation pledge as a nullity?' 'Oh,' said the other, 'when I took the pledge, I understood it to mean that I would keep the law, or endure the penalty' (!) I see you all smile at this stupendous discovery in moral philosophy, and well you may. If every official oath, and every private promise were to be interpreted in this way, no government could last a year, and every ligament that binds man to man would be severed in less time. Officers might do as they please, and 'endure the penalty!' Husbands might forsake their wives, and wives their husbands, and 'endure the penalty!' I might desert you here, and take your funds to myself and 'endure the penalty!' Mr. Beach may desert you in Savannah or New York and 'endure the penalty!' But I forget myself—you see the absurdity of this doctrine as plainly as I do. If you mean to disregard your matriculation pledge, tell me so now, that I may save you from the sin of taking it. If you mean to keep it, all further counsels from me would seem unnecessary. Not, so, however : nine-tenths of those who take it, mean at the time to keep it ; but from temptation, want of caution, or some other cause, they violate it; and then they think one violation as bad as a thousand, and become desperate, or quiet their consciences with some such miserable appliance as that to which we have just adverted. Now, this is all wrong. One breach of duty can never justify another; and there is almost as wide a difference between a deliberate fault, and one committed under severe temptation, as there is between innocence and guilt. If, therefore, you should be betrayed into a breach of your pledge, do not consider yourselves as released from it, but as instructively admonished to guard with quickened vigilance against the associations or train of events that led you into it.

"But, my young friends, there is a condition attached to that pledge—an implied one, to be sure, but none the less obligatory on that account—which Professors are apt to forget; but students, never: It is, that the members of the Faculty discharge their duties faithfully to the students. And here is the prolific source of many difficulties in Colleges. One duty of the Faculty students always see very clearly; and that is, that every member of the Faculty is bound to treat them with tenderness, courtesy and respect, and this duty they not only exact with unreasonable rigor, but treat a breach of it in the most unreasonable manner that human ingenuity could devise. They hold the Professor bound to this duty, no matter how they may treat him. This is bad enough, but their mode of dealing with the offending Professor is ten thousand times worse. The injured party, instead of mildly and calmly laying his grievances before the Professor, and asking an explanation of him, which in ninety-nine cases out of a hundred would produce a reconciliation, spreads his grievances through the College. His class (perhaps two or three classes,) espouse his cause, visit the Professor with every species of insult and indignity, set all the laws of the Institution at defiance, rage like the Bacchantes of old, get themselves expelled by the dozen and suspended by the score, and then come to order.

"There was but one row of this kind while I was in College; and though I really sympathised with the student whose wrongs produced it, I took no part in it, because I could not see what good end was to be accomplished by it. And had I not seen such things with my own eyes, I could not have believed it possible that any human being out of Bedlam could act in this way. I was blamed for my neutrality while the uproar was in progress, but never afterwards. Now, should either of you feel yourselves aggrieved by anything said or done by any member of the Faculty, after allowing cooling time for yourself and him, go to him and lay the grounds of your complaint before him privately and temperately. If he does not give you satisfaction, appeal in like manner to the Faculty. If they give you no redress, appeal to the Trustees; and if they give you no redress,

appeal to me, and, if your cause be just, I will procure for you an
honorable dismission, and remove you from the College. This course
will be much more creditable and profitable to you, than to tax the
friendship of your fellow-students with your vindication, when it is
impossible that they can gain anything by it, and certain that they
will lose incalculably. All this upon the supposition that you are
actually maltreated by a Professor without any fault on your part—a
case which hardly ever occurs. Take care that you do not construe
the *duty* of a Professor into a *fault*. The laws will show you what
he is bound to do; and all that he does in obedience to the laws, do
you submit to without murmurs or complaint. It is no ground of
objection to him that other Professors are more remiss in the discharge of their duties than he is. The comparison between him and
them will be altogether in their favor while you are *in* College, but
altogether in his when you come *out* of it, especially if you ever
become the Trustee of a College.

"The greatest danger to which you will be exposed, is from the
shocking system of ethics which prevails in Colleges. It is admitted
on all hands, that a student should not become a voluntary informer
against his fellow-students. But even to this rule there ought to be
some exceptions; and the exceptions should cover all cases where
the information is given from a principle of benevolence to the
students themselves, and there is no other means of securing the
end in view but by information lodged with authorities of the College, or of the State. A student, for instance, knows of a contemplated duel between two of his fellow-students; he uses his best
exertions to stop it, but fails; is he to be branded with the infamy
of a common informer, because he puts the Faculty in possession of
the fact? Surely not. *A fortiori*, where the intended crime would
produce irreparable injury to a person, and subject the student himself to the pain of death, as murder, arson, treason, and the like.
True, none of these crimes but the first mentioned (the duel,) are
likely to ever occur in a College; but should they occur, it is very
doubtful whether the informer would find any quarter among his
college companions.

"But let us come to a case very likely to occur. It is a rule in
some Colleges, (in most of them, I believe,) that if a student is
charged with an offence, and another is called on to testify in his
case, and refuse, he shall be dismissed. Every student who enters
the College pledges himself to keep this law; and yet, in the judgment of seven-tenths of the students, it is considered basely dis-

honorable to testify, if his testimony would prove the guilt of the accused! The culprit himself has not the magnanimity to confess his guilt, and save his innocent friends from punishment, but, shielded by this miserable abortion of College comity, he avoids detection, sees them disgraced, driven off and robbed of man's richest boon, (a liberal education,) while he quietly retains his place, and ultimately pockets his Parchment! And yet, black, rotten and foetid as he is, some of the unimplicated congratulate him on his escape, and many of them hold fellowship with him, not only without nausea, but with an agreeable relish!! The dirty lump of humanity should be turned over to the scavenger, by the unanimous verdict of the College, and pitched into the remotest sewer from it. Now this case has actually happened, and it may happen again while you are in College. If so, and you are cognizant of the offence, (*not a participant in it,*) and summoned as a witness against an offender, go to him and tell him to confess his fault, or you will become a witness against him. If thus forewarned, he refuses to confess, testify against him. His friendship is not worth having, nor is the friendship of a legion of students, who would cut your acquaintance for so doing. I know it is hard to bear the derision and contempt of your College companions; but bear that, or even martyrdom, rather than forfeit your word, incur disgrace, be driven from the walks of science, and have your fairest prospects blighted, to favor a villain.

"That students should suffer themselves to be punished, in order to conceal the guilt of an offender too vile to own his guilt—that a rule should obtain among them, which makes it better to be a culprit than a witness, safer to sin than to see it, more honorable to profit by magnanimity than to practice it, and more graceful in the malefactor to divide his responsibilities among his friends than to bear them himself—is marvelous indeed. But the wonders of College ethics do not stop here. Another principle of the school is, that no member of the fraternity is to exculpate *himself* from a crime committed by one of his fellows; because, forsooth, if all who are innocent, avow their innocence, the guilty one must be discovered if he be a man of truth! By the law of all Colleges, I believe, if a student stands mute when questioned as to his participation in an offence, he is to be regarded as the perpetrator of it, and to be visited accordingly. Students, innocent students, stand mute and endure the penalty! They virtually acknowledge a fault, of which they are not guilty. Who is to be benefited by their self-sacrifice, they know

N

not—or may not know! Whether any crime at all has been committed by a fellow-student they do not know, and do not enquire! Whether the consequences which they apprehend, will follow from their exonerating themselves, they cannot know! Their course of conduct will save the offender, or it will not. If it save him, he escapes and they are punished; if it do not save him, they share his fate without doing him any service! Why this is monstrous! Young men, you are not to forfeit the inestimable blessings of a liberal education, for any such refinements as these. You are not to encourage the idea that you are evil-doers, when you are not! You are not to lacerate your parents' feelings, to conciliate the blind votaries of a preposterous dogma! I know that you must have a will of iron and nerves of steel, to withstand the sneers, the jibes, the taunts, the scorn of your college compeers. You can have no idea of their potency until they begin to threaten you. Why are such conservative agencies abused to the encouragement of vice and the terror of virtue! How has it come to pass, that *wrong* receives more favor in schools and colleges than anywhere else? How happens it, that every code of morals, human and divine, is reversed in these Institutions? It is amazing, it is unaccountable! But, my young friends, there is majesty and power in virtue, if she will assume her prerogatives, which will command respect and awe down opposition, even in colleges. Put yourselves under her guardianship, and with head erect and heart unawed, boldly meet the champions of vice, and you are certain of victory, and of victory's richest spoils: a quiet conscience, approving teachers, rejoicing parents, mental culture, public favor, and lasting honor. Stand together as one man in the maintenance of right, be led by neither to espouse the wrong. Cultivate the friendship of the orderly, the pious, the studious, the intellectual. Have no fellowship with the idle, the dissipated, the boisterous, the prodigal. Treat them politely, but distantly. These are the characters who breed all the mischiefs in College. From such as these must have sprung up those moral monstrosities of which I have been speaking. The best code of morals for them is, of course, that which indulges vice and repudiates virtue. Take care of them; the Faculty will judge you by the company you keep; and if you would avoid the trying dilemmas of which I have spoken, keep away from the vicious and the lawless. These are the ones who are arraigned for outbreaks, and their companions are the witnesses, if not the accomplices. Let cards alone; let intoxicating liquors alone! If you disregard everything else that I have told you, burn these seven words into your memory : *' let cards alone; let intoxicating liquors alone !'* Let your recreation hours, *and only your recreation hours,* be spent mainly in female society; preferring the pious and intellectual, to the light and volatile. Write home often, and when temptations assail you, think of home. Do not get in the way of neglecting your College duties; remissness is the first step to degradation. You all have your Bibles ; read them often—if not from a better motive, read them for your mothers' sakes. And now, bow with me in prayer to God, that He incline your hearts to keep these precepts, and His own, which are far better, conduct you safely to your destination, preserve you, and bless you, during your sojourn at the seat of Science, and return you to us, endowed with its richest treasures !"

The prayer was offered up, and the following morning Mr. Markham bade his young friends a tearful farewell, saw them on their way to Savannah, and then turned his steps homeward.

CHAPTER XXIII.

THREE days' staging placed Mr. Beach with his charge in Savannah, and an eight days' voyage landed him in New York. He proceeded immediately to Newark, whence he wrote a letter to Mr. Sanders, concluding as follows : " Report our safe arrival all in good health, to Mr. Markham. He told me that the boys were raw, untraveled youths, whom he feared would give me much trouble ; but I assure him that they gave me no trouble at all. So far from it, they sought every opportunity to relieve me from trouble. They seemed to contend for the pleasure of serving me. They are four of the most genteel, well-behaved, clever boys I ever saw. Instead of giving me trouble, they were a pleasure and delight to me all the way. As they were from the South, used to be waited on, and not used to work, (as I supposed,) I did expect to find them all a little lazy ; but they were ready to turn their hands to anything. On board ship they were all very sick, and as they had all been so kind to me, I took great pleasure in waiting on them. In two or three days they were all well, and ever since have been as hearty as bucks. They are now at my house, quite the delight of my family. To-morrow and next day I shall take them over to see New York according to promise, and the day after go with them to Basken Ridge and Princeton."

This letter of course went the rounds of the families most inter-

ested in it, and gave unspeakable satisfaction whithersoever it went.
Mr. Beach fulfilled his promise. Markham, Thompson and Brown
entered the Sophomore class without difficulty. It was exceedingly
mortifying to William to find himself under the necessity of going
through a preparatory course in order to enter the Freshman class,
when his old schoolmates were all honorably admitted into the next
higher class; and he determined to make amends for lost time by
assiduity in study. The weather and the place favored his resolution, at least for several months, for he was kept in-doors from the
cold, and there were few, if any, dissolute youths at Basken Ridge
to tempt him to vice. His first letter to his mother spoke in highest
terms of Mr. Finley and his "charming family;" and the first letter
of Mr. Finley to Mrs. Mitten was not less complimentary to William.
At the end of five months, his teacher pronounced him fully prepared for the Freshman class, put in his hand a very flattering certificate, and dispatched him to College. Instead of presenting his
certificate to the President, and making application for admission
into the Freshman class, he excogitated a brilliant scheme, not altogether original, to be sure, but highly creditable to his ingenuity,
whereby he was to get into the Sophomore class without the needful
preparation for it. Thus thought our hero: "If I apply for the
Junior class, they will have too much respect for my feelings to put
me away down in the Freshman class, if they can possibly avoid it.
Even for the Junior class, they will, in all probability, examine me
upon those studies which I have been over, and here I shall acquit
myself so handsomely, that they will readily compromise matters,
and let me into the Sophomore class." Accordingly he reported
himself to the President with an air of great self-possession, as a
candidate for the Junior class. The President, after gravely taking
his dimensions with the eye, to the manifest terror of Master Mitten,
said: "The *Junior* Class, now more than half advanced! How far
have you advanced in Latin and Greek?" William answered. "In
mathematics?" He answered again. "Have you studied Chemis-
try, Astronomy, Natural and Moral Philosophy and Logic?" "No,
sir!" "Under whom did you prepare for College?" "Mr. Waddel
and Mr. Finley." "Mr. Waddel of South Carolina and Mr. Finley
of Basken Ridge?" "Yes, sir." "We have four students now in
College, from Mr. Waddel's school, and ten from Mr. Finley's, all
of whom entered without difficulty. Did either of your preceptors
advise you to apply for the Junior class?" "No, sir, but I thought
may be I could enter that class." "Well, Master Mitten, *I* think,

'may be' you can enter no class in College. I will give you a trial, however, for the Freshman class, if you can bring down your aspirations that low." "Well, sir," said William, with a spirit of accommodation truly commendable, "I'll try for that class." Here William's usual *bad luck* attended him, for his ingenuity had exposed him to agonizing mortification, betrayed him into a falsehood, and, as he well knew, made the President's first impressions of him very unfavorable.

He was examined, and admitted without difficulty. The President was curious to learn what sort of an examination he stood, and enquired of the examining Professors. "Admirable!" said they, *una voce.* The President smiled, but said nothing.

William followed Mr. Markham's advice strictly through the Freshman year, and for four months of the Sophomore year, and the consequence was as usual; he stood at the head of the class. His letters to his mother were in the highest degree gratifying. He spoke gratefully of Mr. Markham's last counsels to him, and promised to obey them to the letter; he expressed his admiration of the Faculty, particularly of those members of it who had charge of his class, in terms bordering upon the extravagance of praise—rejoiced that he had been defeated in his attempt to procure a clerkship; and rejoiced still more that he now saw the error of his ways, and had radically reformed. One of his epistles he concluded in this language: "When I think, my dearest mother, of the trouble I have given you—how I abused your goodness, and disappointed your reasonable expectations, my conscience smites me, and my cheeks burn with blushes. How could I have been such an ingrate! How could I have sent a pang to the bosom of the sweetest, the kindest, the tenderest, the holiest, the best of mothers! Well, the past is gone, and with it my childish, boyish follies: they have all been forgiven long ago, and no more are to be forgiven in future. That I am to get the first honor in my class is conceded by all the class except four. These four were considered equal competitors for it until I entered the class, and they do not despair yet; but they had as well, for they equal me in nothing but Mathematics, and do not excel me in that. The funds that you allow me ($500 per annum) are more than sufficient to meet all my college expenses, and allow me occasional pleasure rambles during the vacation. What I have written about my stand in College, you will of course understand as intended only for a mother's eye.

"Your truly affectionate and grateful son,

WM. MITTEN."

William's report of himself was fully confirmed by his fellow-students of the village. He wrote also an affectionate letter to Doctor Waddel, thanking him for his many kindnesses, approving of all his dealings with him, and censuring himself for his rejection of his counsels, and disobedience to his rules. Before this letter reached his old Preceptor, William's fame and prospects in College had reached the school, where all considered themselves interested in his reputation, and all rejoiced. At his home the rejoicing was more intense, and all the merchants of the place, and Mr. Sanders in particular, congratulated themselves that they had offered him no encouragement to become a merchant. There was one exception, to be sure, to the general rejoicing, in the person of old Stewey Anderson; and he only suspended his joy; for he offered, " to give his promissory note, payable twelve months after date, for double joy, if Bill Mitten held on that long."

"Billy," said Stewey, " is a Belair colt; he beats everything for a quarter, but he can't stand a long run, I'm afraid; he's entered now for the four mile heats, and I think he'll break down about the second or third mile, sure." There was something, too, that chilled the ardor of Dr. Hull's delight, though no one knew what it was. But that he partook of the general feeling to some extent, was manifest; for he never took a chew of tobacco and grunted when William was praised.

Up to the close of the fourth month of Master Mitten's Sophomore year, he had almost entirely neglected Mr. Markham's advice touching his recreation hours; indeed, he hardly allowed himself any recreation hours: but occasional visits to a beautiful little Princeton lassie, by the name of Amanda Ward, reminded him forcibly of his remissness in this particular, and he resolved forthwith to amend his ways. Miss Amanda was not pious, but she was sprightly, witty and graceful; and for her age (for she had hardly "entered her teens,") she was not wanting in intellectual culture. William's interest in her increased with every visit to her, and his "recreation hours" began to increase with his interest. The necessary consequence was, that his *study hours* became more arduous. Still he maintained his reputation and his place in his class, with only a hardly perceptible change, in the promptness and fluency with which he disposed of his recitations. Soon after his first visit to Miss Amanda, William's talents were made known to her, as well as his fortune, which was represented to be something under the square of what it really was. She was quite too young and too ro-

mantic to have anything venal in her composition, and, as his handsome person, brilliant talents and interesting conversation began to
win upon her affections, she became touchingly pensive. By as
much as she lost her vivacity, by so much did William's interest in
her increase. He loved her before, and now he sympathized with
her deeply and tenderly. It was a floating sympathy, to be sure,
seeking, like Noah's dove, a resting place and finding none; but it
was none the less sincere on that account, and none the less appreciated by the lovely object over which it hovered, and diffused its
grateful incense. Often from the gloom which overshadowed the
dear Amanda, would she send forth mellow twinklings, like those
which sport upon the bosom of an evening cloud, and which would
irradiate the countenance of her anxious friend for a moment; but
he could not persuade her to reveal the cause of her depression.

Under the combined force of love, sympathy, anxiety and suspense, William's spirits forsook him, he became sad and gloomy, and
study became irksome to him. Late sittings with Miss Amanda,
and then much later sittings to make up the lost time, began to
make inroads upon William's health, and all his fair prospects would
probably have been blighted before the close of the term, had he
not determined to act upon conjecture as to Miss Ward's anguish of
mind. He judged, not without good reason, that it proceeded from
love to him, and that she was wasting away under the consuming
passion, because she supposed that it was not reciprocated. He resolved, therefore, with becoming frankness to unbosom himself to
her and offer her his hand. Accordingly, at their next interview,
he thus addressed her :

"Miss Ward, you know that I am not blind to your despondency,
and, by a thousand proofs, you know that I am not indifferent to it.
Believe me, that my oft repeated enquiries into the cause of it were
prompted by a purer and holier motive than mere idle curiosity. No,
Miss Ward, that heart which is not touched with the griefs of the
gentler sex, must be insensible indeed ; such an one, I am sure, was
never reared in the genial clime of the sunny South. He who could
obtrude a selfish curiosity into the hallowed sanctuary of woman's
sorrows, never breathed the balmy zephyrs which waft the odors of
the magnolia and the orange. 'Twas sympathy, Miss Ward, which
prompted my questions—an honest desire to share your griefs, if I
could not relieve them. Your generous nature will appreciate my
motives, and pardon one more question—the last, if answered nega-
tively : Am I in any way, directly or indirectly, connected with your
mental perturbations ?"

Torrents of tears from the eyes of the fair Amanda relieved her gallant suitor's suspense, while she struggles for utterance with her irrepressible emotions. At length she spoke:

"Mister Mitten, your noble nature assures me that I may trust the dearest secret of my heart to you, without fear that you will ever betray the trust, under any changes of feeling, time or place. I frankly own that I am and have *long* been most ardently attached to you——I have sometimes thought—hoped—that our attachment was mutual. Yet, why did I hope it? when I knew that we never could be united?"

"Know that we could never be united, my dearest Amanda?"

"Never, never, never!" exclaimed Amanda, burying her face in her handkerchief, and sobbing convulsively.

"Then I am doomed to wretchedness for life!" ejaculated Mister Mitten. "Amanda, you are my first love——"

"And you are mine, William. My first, my last, my only love. When you return to the land of birds and of flowers, object of my adoration, send back a thought to your poor, unfortunate, heart-broken Amanda!"

"Amanda," said William, in tears, "you said you would entrust the dearest secret of your heart to me: tell me then what insuperable obstacle there is to our union?"

"I never violate my promise, dearest William, I am told that you are very, very rich; and never can I consent to marry a man with whom I cannot be upon an equality,—a man who must ever feel that he stooped to take his partner's hand; and who may suppose that the poor trash of earth, called *wealth*, had some influence upon her choice. I should be the most miserable wretch upon earth, to discover in the being I adore, anything going to show that he considered me his inferior, or capable of loving him for anything but himself."

"These noble sentiments," responded Mister Mitten, "exalt you higher, if possible, in my estimation, than ever. Know, then, thou sweetest, purest, noblest of thy sex, that I am not rich——"

"Not rich! Don't trifle with my feelings, William!"

"I assure you, upon the honor of a gentleman, that I am worth nothing. My mother owns a very pretty estate, which, when divided between her three children, will only give a comfortable living to each of them."

"Oh, happiest moment of my life!" exclaimed Amanda. "William, there is my hand, and with it a heart that idolizes you, if you choose to take them."

"I receive them," said William, "and exchange for them a hand and heart equally warm and unwavering."

Their vows were plighted, and they separated in ecstacies.

Fortunately for William this interview occurred on Friday night; or it would have played the mischief with his next day's recitation.

The next day William visited Miss Amanda to arrange for the nuptials; and however indiscreet and rash we may consider the engagement, everybody must accord to them the highest prudence in settling the preliminaries of the nuptials.

The arrangement was that *Mister* Mitten (so we must now call him, as he is engaged to be married) should go on and complete his education, return to Georgia and spend two or three months with his family, then go to Litchfield, Connecticut, and attend Judge Reeves' Law Lectures for one year, revisit Georgia, get admitted to the bar as soon as possible, return to Princeton, and consummate the marriage. Could old Parr himself, and a lady his equal in years, have ordered things more wisely! As soon as matters were thus happily arranged, Mr. Mitten said:

"I have reflected a great deal, my Amanda, upon matrimonial engagements, and I have brought my mind to the conclusion long ago, that there is a radical error in regard to them, too common in the world. Let us reform it—at least as far as we can. I allude to the secrecy with which such engagements are kept by the parties to them——"

Miss Amanda started——"Why, if the parties are sincere and mean to be constant to each other, should they object to the world's knowing of their engagement? Were it generally known how few matches would be broken off! What man of honor would pay his addresses to a lady whom he knew to be pledged to another! What woman of honor would receive the addresses of a man whom she knew to be engaged! For my part, I shall make no secret of our engagement, and then if any man dare to pay you particular attentions, I shall hold him personally responsible——"

"Oh, William, my dearest William, do not think of such a thing! Our engagement must not be breathed to a human being—not even to father, mother, sister or brother. If our parents knew of it, they would certainly break it off if they could, on the ground of our age—— Break it off! No, that can never be. Sooner will the moon cease to shed her placid beams upon the earth, sooner will this heart cease to beat, than your Amanda forget her vows, or human power make her break them. But think of the troubles that may follow the disclosure!

Oh, William, I cannot bear a frown, I cannot bear even a cold look from my dear, sweet parents ; and how would it rend my heart to see them frown on you or receive you distantly——"

"And does Miss Ward suppose that her parents would object to our alliance?——"

"No, no, William: I'm sure they will be delighted with it, at the proper time ; but think how young we are! I have heard my father say that the man who has grown daughters in Princeton occupies a very delicate position. To forbid them to receive the visits of students, would be to forbid them from receiving in the main, the very best society that they could have, and to violate the laws of hospitality; but to encourage students in making love to their daughters, was injustice to the students, and treason to their distant parents. Now, if he knew that we were engaged, he would be almost certain to send me away to some boarding school—and what pain would that give us! And suppose another should address me; does my William think that there is another in this wide world who can make the least impression on his Amanda's heart? Can you doubt your Amanda's constancy? Can you fear that anything on earth could chill her first, her only love, in a few short years? No, William, whether you remain true or false, never, never, can I love another. The very thought startles me like an electric shock. The keenest pang I ever felt, was at hearing my mother say that my father was not her first love—I ought not to have mentioned it—I have never breathed it to another; but to you I may entrust it, for we are soon to be one—— From you I can conceal nothing. But what agony did the disclosure give me——you'll never mention it, William?"

"Never, Amanda."

"I felt for days, weeks and months, as if I were an orphan. Oh,. how my heart sympathized with my dear, sweet father! He knew it when he married mother. They live happily together. But it seems to me, the cruel. bitter thought must sometimes present itself, ' this heart was once another's—this heart was not always mine,' and oh, what pain it must give ! And what is married life, if there be anything in it to interrupt, even for a moment, the constant stream of heavenly bliss which it promises to hearts united in the silken cords of pure, ecstatic, first-born love ! There, William, you are entrusted with every secret of my heart."

Mr. Mitten was so charmed with Miss Amanda's sentiments, and enraptured with her eloquence, that he entirely forgot the text. He soon recovered it, however, and after thanking Miss Ward for her confidence, and promising to keep it sacred, he said:

"Under all the peculiar circumstances of the case, my Amanda, I will consent to keep our engagement a secret; but, as a general rule, I think there should be no secrecy in such matters."

Mr. Mitten's mind being now disburdened, he resumed his studies with alacrity, and maintained his place to the close of the Sophomore year. The vacation ensued, and the first five weeks of it Mr. Mitten devoted to Miss Amanda. He took her out almost daily on pleasure-rides, lavished presents upon her, of the most costly jewelry, books, engravings, and love-tokens innumerable; and strange to tell, Miss Amanda received them without rebuking this ill-advised waste of his humble patrimony. Nor was Mr. Mitten less attentive to the decoration of his own person, than of Miss Amanda's. He laid in a profusion of coats, vests, pants, gloves, stockings, boots, shoes, pumps and under garments, all at the highest prices, and in the most fashionable style. To his other purchases he added an elegant watch, chain, seals and key, and a handsome diamond breast pin. Many of these things were purchased upon a short credit, to be paid for as soon as he could get remittances from home. With all his accomplishments there was one wanting to make him perfect in Miss Amanda's eye, and that was, "the poetry of motion." Herein Miss Amanda excelled, and she urged him to put himself under Monsieur Coupee, to add this to his many graces. She said that she was very fond of cotillon parties, but that they had lost all interest to her since she learned that he did not dance. He took her advice. As "the poetry of motion," cotillon measure, consists entirely of anapests and dactyls, performed with alternate feet, Mr. Mitten soon mastered this accomplishment. Thus went off the first month and a quarter of the vacation.

With all his expenditures he had taken care to reserve money enough, as he supposed, to spend a few days in Morristown, a week in Newark, and a week in New York, without exhausting his funds. At the commencement of his sixth week, of the vacation, he set out for Morristown. Here lived a class-mate of his, who insisted upon his spending a week with him. Mitten consented. A round of parties ensued, all of which he attended, and at all of which he played havoc with the hearts of the girls of Morristown. From his class-mate the report soon spread through the village, that he was the first scholar in his class, and immensely rich. These things conspiring with his fine person, graceful manners, and agreeable conversation, made him absolutely irresistible. Now there happened to be in Morristown at this time, a young lady from South Carolina, of the

Bethlehem School, who was spending her vacation with a relative of the village, or rather making Morristown her headquarters for the vacation. Her name was Louisa Green, she was behind Miss Ward in nothing, and one hundred thousand dollars ahead of her in point of fortune. Miss Green and Mr. Mitten being both from the South, naturally formed a strong partiality for each other ; *of course it did not amount to love on William's part,* but it amounted to love palpably, on Louisa's part. As she was from the South, William felt himself bound to pay her particular attentions. Accordingly he did all that he could to make her time pass agreeably during his stay in Morristown. He could but observe the tokens of her favor, and they awakened in him a tender compassion. She had appointed to visit a school-mate in Elizabethtown, five days after the time when he was to leave for Newark. He offered to wait and accompany her. This threw him five days longer on his friend's hospitality, than he contracted for, but he was welcome. She accepted his offer thankfully. They went—he was introduced to her young friend, who prevailed upon him to spend two or three days in Elizabethtown. He consented—parties commenced on the second day after his arrival, and were kept up with but short intervals for nine days. The scenes of Morristown were renewed. He had set every day for the last six, for leaving Elizabethtown, but something or other always delayed his departure. The school-mates of Elizabethtown planned a visit to a third, in New York, for a few days. As this jumped with William's plans exactly, and promised to make his visit to New York pleasurable infinitely beyond his anticipations, he proposed to accompany the young ladies. They accepted his proposition with pleasure. It required three days to prepare the young ladies for their contemplated trip, and these embraced the opening of the college term. Time had run off so merrily that he had not kept count of it, and he was thunderstruck when a question put to him about the college, reminded him that the term opened on the day before he was to leave with his fair companions for New York. What was he to do ? Violate his pledge to the young ladies ? That would never do.

He determined to conduct them to New York, and hasten on to College. When he came to settle up his bills in Elizabethtown, he was thunderstruck again ; they were four times as large as he anticipated, and in counting up his cash, he found that he had barely enough left to take him to New York and back to Princeton. The ladies were delayed a day beyond the appointed time by some accident. Mr. Mitten was in torments. It was certain that his funds would give-out before he reached Princeton; and here in a land of strangers, what was he to do? In this emergency, it had just occurred to him that he had been very remiss in not paying his respects to Mr. Beach, and he concluded to spend a part of the spare day with this kind friend. Mr. Beach hardly knew him when he presented himself at his door, so changed was he in every thing. After a visit of an hour, "Mr. Beach," said William, "I have been out spending the vacation, and my expenses have been so much heavier than I expected, that I have got out of money; could you favor me so far as to loan me thirty dollars, and I will give you an order on Mr. Sanders for the amount, or I will send it to you as soon as I get back to college." "Certainly, William," said Mr. Beach, "I will take the order, and if you pay it when you get to college, I will send it to you. The money was loaned, and William returned to Elizabethtown rejoicing. On their way to New York he suggested to Miss Green that the college term, had opened and that on the day after their arrival in New York, he would be compelled to return to college. She expressed her regrets that they must part, probably never to meet again, but hoped that they would renew their acquaintance, after their return home. William proposed a *friendly* correspondence *ad interim.* She said she could not promise that, as the pupils of her school were forbidden to correspond with young gentlemen; but if he chose to write to her she had no objections. On their arrival in New York, the news greeted them, that on the evening of the next day two of the greatest tragedians of the age were to appear in the principal parts of Shakspeare's Othello. William had never seen a play acted by professed performers, and "as he had overstayed his time any how, and one day more could not make much difference," he determined to prolong his visit that far, and take the ladies to the theatre. He procured tickets for the three young ladies, but as the father of the one whom the others were visiting, chose to accompany them all to the theatre, and furnish tickets himself, William had two on hand either to use or throw away at his option. He was transported with the performance. Hamlet was announced for the next night; but as the ladies declined going to the theatre two nights in succession, he went alone. Macbeth was announced for the next night; and as all the girls must see this play, they went as before; William accompanying. The day following he left for Princeton, and reached there with just seventy-five cents in his pocket.

His class-mate of Morristown (*Johnson* by name) brought down his history to his departure from that village. "He went off," said

Johnson, "after a beautiful accomplished South Carolina heiress, worth a cool hundred thousand in cash, with *kinky-heads* according; and he has only to stretch out his hand to her and she'll snatch at it; for everybody sees that she is over head and ears in love with him, as indeed all the girls in Morristown are ; for Bill is death among the pullets." This report mitigated the anxiety of his Georgian companions concerning him, but did not entirely relieve them ; for they feared the consequences of William's change of habits, not only upon his stand in College, but upon his future life.

We have said that he had four competitors for the first honor, but there was only one of them that he had cause to dread, for though the five were equal in mathematics, there was but one who approached him in the other studies. This one was Taliaferro (pronounced *Toliver*) of Virginia. When at the opening of the term, the class appeared to recite in mathematics, and Taliaferro found Mitten absent, his countenance kindled with delight. His delight increased with every recitation in this study, until it came to the fifth. As he retired from this he said triumphantly, "I've got him safe—I've got this brilliant young Georgian just as the owl had the hen, so that he can neither back nor squall. With his head full of girls and fortune, if ever he keeps up with the class, and makes up five lost lessons, he is a smarter man than I think he is, and I think he is the smartest I ever saw." Taliaferro thus spoke because he well knew that a lost recitation in mathematics is almost as fatal to farther progress in the science, as the loss of one of the nine digits would be to enumeration. And yet if William had determined to do it, he could have made up his deficiencies before the end of the Junior year, and thrown Taliaferro far in his rear in the Senior year. Why he did not, we shall see. When called to account for his absences he said "*he was necessarily detained.*"

Having followed Mitten's movements during the vacation, let us now unveil some of his thoughts and reflections accompanying these movements. "Here it is now," mused he on the fifth day of his acquaintance with Miss Green. "If Amanda had not made me promise to keep our engagement secret, I could now tell Louisa of it, and let her understand the true ground of my attentions to her ; but as it is, I must either be distant to her—which would be unpardonable in me as she is from the South—or I must encourage her attachment which is plainly visible and growing. Amanda will hear of my attentions through Johnson, and suppose I am after Louisa's fortune. No, dear girl, fortune shall never make me sacrifice my word and my honor."

On the seventh day: "It was very indiscreet in Amanda to exact that promise from me, I don't know how to act under it."

Ninth day: "Hang that silly promise! I'll keep it, but I fear I shall never feel towards Amanda as I should have felt if she had not extorted it from me. I was too hasty in making it—in fact I was too hasty in the whole matter. Well, whatever may come of it, I shall not forego duty to a Southern friend, far from home, because I happen to be engaged."

On the day he visited Mr. Beach: "What a botheration it is to want money—I doubt whether Amanda will ever be satisfied to live in Georgia. I wish she was not quite so romantic. It was very imprudent in her to speak of her father and mother as she did to me—I don't believe one can love truly but once; I believe I could love Louisa just as ardently as I love her, if I would allow myself to do so."

On the day he left New York: "One hundred thousand dollars! I wish I had fifty of it now. What a sum it is! Enough to last a man's life time, and satisfy every desire of his heart. One hundred thousand dollars, and a beautiful intelligent lovely *Southern* girl to boot! Amanda ought to adore me for resisting such a temptation for her sake."

On reaching Princeton, he went immediately to see Amanda and found her in deep distress. She said "she had been meditating suicide, but she could not leave the world without one more last, longing, lingering look upon her William." Upon his assuring her, however, that he was not engaged to Miss Green, that he had not proposed himself to her, and that he would have informed her of his engagement, if he had not been forbidden to do so, Miss Amanda was greatly comforted, insomuch that she concluded to postpone the suicide to a more suitable season. She entertained him with a melting narrative of her soliloquies and tears over breastpins, lockets and the like, which, as it came just at the time when he was terribly pinched for money, produced a double sympathy—or rather an oscillating sympathy, which played so equally between himself and Miss Amanda, that she could not understand it, and took it for coldness. They parted, however, with renewed professions of love.

Markham, Thompson and Brown, had together paid a short visit to Philadelphia, Trenton and Monmouth, early in the vacation, and

---

*At this time Jersey bank bills were just as current in Georgia as gold and silver.

The first one dollar bill that ever was seen in Georgia was from a Jersey bank.

returned to Princeton. On their return, Brown enclosed a fifty dollar bill* in a letter to Mr. Markham, saying: "I have saved this much out of my allowance without stinting myself in the least. If you think it would not be wrong to appropriate it to my mother's necessities, please deal it out to her as she needs. Apply all of it but what is absolutely necessary to keep my mother above want, to the schooling of my two little sisters. But if you think that I have no right to use the money in this way, please return it to the kind gentlemen who raised it for me; and tell them that it is more than I need, and I think in justice it ought to be returned to them." We need hardly say that this letter made John's patrons feel much more like doubling than reducing their contributions to him.

From New York William had written a letter to his mother, setting forth that he had greatly miscalculated, in saying that five hundred dollars per annum would be amply sufficient to pay his College expenses. Traveling expenses, he said, far exceeded his expectations—that he had set out from Princeton on a vacation ramble, with money enough in hand, he thought, to pay his expenses three times over, and after visiting only three places, he was in New York with hardly money enough to pay his reckoning, and get him back to Princeton; and there his board and tuition would have to be paid in advance. He concluded by begging her to send him on two hundred dollars as speedily as possible. Here was the very place for him to have informed his mother that he had borrowed money from Mr. Beach, and to have informed Mr. Sanders through her, how he came to draw on him. But he knew that it would mortify his mother exceedingly, to learn that he was repaying Mr. Beach's kindness by taxing his purse; and he intended to stop the draft from going to the drawee, by payment of it. Brown's letter had a fortnight or more the start of William's, and its contents were known to everybody in the village in three days after it had reached Mr. Markham. When William's letter therefore reached home, it alarmed and distressed his mother exceedingly. She gathered the money as soon as she possibly could, (borrowing a part of it) and dispatched it to William, with a letter eloquently expressive of her feelings. "How is it, my dear boy," said she, "that John Brown, with his limited resources, can visit Philadelphia, Trenton and Monmouth, and yet send hither fifty dollars out of his income, to assist his poor mother, and school his little sisters; and you cannot visit as many places without exhausting your funds and requiring two hundred dollars over?" The whole letter would fill every reader's eyes with tears;

but we have not time and space for it here. By the shortest possible course of mail, William could not receive an answer to his letter in less than a month from its date. In the meantime he must be shut out of College, if he could not raise the tuition fees at least. His only course was to borrow. He went to his cousin David, who loaned him fifteen dollars, all " he had over," as the merchants say. He went to Markham, and he loaned him twenty, saying " this is all I have, but go to Brown, I know he has over fifty dollars, for wo compared notes when we got back to College." He went to Brown and asked the loan of fifteen dollars. " William," said Brown, " I would loan it to you with a great deal of pleasure, but I have it not —here are three dollars, all I've got, which you are welcome to, if it will be of any service to you." William looked on him furiously and said—" Brown, if I don't raise fifteen dollars, I can't get back into College, and I know you have that much, and three times that much." " William, I give you my word and honor I have but three dollars in the world. How can you suppose that I would not loan it to you if I had it? If there's anything I have, by sale of which you can raise the amount, go take it and sell it, with all my heart ———"

William wheeled off in a rage, and hastened to Thompson and Markham, saying " Who could believe it possible, that John Brown would see me shut out of college, rather than loan me fifteen dollars! He says he has but three dollars in the world——" " John Brown says so!" exclaimed the two. " Come," said Thompson, " let's go and bring him face to face."

Away they went and Brown seeing them coming turned pale as a sheet. " Look at his countenance," whispered William. " John Brown," said Thompson, " did you tell cousin William that you hadn't fifteen dollars in the world?"

" Yes, and I told him the truth———"

" Didn't you tell George Markham and myself that you brought back from your travels money enough to pay tuition and board, and leave you over fifty dollars in hand?"

" Yes I did; but I have disposed of fifty dollars of it."

" How did you dispose of it?"

" I do not wish to tell, but in a way that all of you would approve off if I were to tell you—indeed I do not know myself as yet, how it went——"

" Did you ever hear such chat," said William, " from anybody but an idiot since you were born! Disposed of it as we all would approve, and does'nt know himself how he disposed of it!"

The boys wheeled off indignantly.

"Stop, boys," said Brown, with streaming eyes, "and I will explain——"

"We want no explanations, sir," said William. "Dig a mole out of the dirt and stick him on a steeple, and he'll be a mole still."

No pen can describe John's agony. He saw himself deserted by the sons of his benefactors—he knew that they all believed that he had lied; and he knew that before the morrow's sun, it would be trumpeted all through the College that the bright Mitten was kept from his class by his meanness. In the midst of his horrors, the bell summoned him to recitation. The class was arranged alphabetically, and his name was the first on the list. The Professor called on him; he rose tried to suppress his emotions, but could not; and he resumed his seat, his bosom heaving, and his eyes streaming as though his heart would break. The class stood aghast, and the Professor looked sad; for Brown had not been remiss in a single College duty. Keen as was his anguish, it would have been aggravated heavily, but for George Markham's prudence.

"Boys" said he, "it isn't worth while to spread this thing through the College—at least let us wait awhile before we do it. Remember that he is a Georgian, has been our intimate friend, and it will be flung up to us upon all occasions. And after all, I never knew John Brown to tell a lie in my life, and he may be enabled to explain the matter."

After some debate they agreed to keep the matter to themselves. That very day John received tidings of his father's death, and as no body thought of enquiring as to the precise time when he received the intelligence, it was regarded by the class as the cause of his emotion in the recitation room, and by his three friends as an additional inducement to deal tenderly with him. Thompson borrowed the fifteen dollars for William, and he joined his class.

Thus stood matters when Mrs. Mitten's letter was received. As soon as William read it, he hastened to Thompson and Markham's room with it, handed it to his cousin, flung himself into a seat, dropped his forehead, hands-covered on his knees, and wept bitterly. Thompson read it, and passed it in sobs to Markham. He was not so much affected, and spoke first:

"The Lord be praised that we kept our notions of John's conduct from the college. Why this, and our coldness, and his father's death all coming upon him at once, would have killed the poor fellow. He's almost heart-broken, any-how. What a warning is this to us against acting hastily in such matters! Let us send for him, and relieve both him and ourselves immediately." He was sent for, and as soon as he entered the room, they all rushed to him and embraced him together. "Oh, John," continued Markham, "we know what you did with your fifty dollars, and we are all ashamed of ourselves."

"John," said William, "I beg your pardon ten thousand times—"

"And I."

"And I."

"John," said William," "how could you say, you didn't know as yet how your money went?"

"Because I didn't know that it would be right in me to take money raised for my education, and apply it to the use of my mother and sisters; so I sent it to Mr. Markham and told him, if he thought I had no right to use it in this way, to return it to the gentlemen who raised it for me, and I don't know which way it went, even now, for Mr. Markham said nothing to me about it in the letter reporting my father's death."

"John," continued William, "I never shall forgive myself for my treatment of you. I had some apology for suspecting you of insincerity, but I had none for that vile, unfeeling, brutal remark of mine—"

"What remark, William?"

"About the mole."

"I didn't hear that."

"You didn't! Thank heaven, that you did not, but it's none the less mean on that account."

William paid the sums borrowed and his board; and now the merchants, tailors, shoe-makers and jewelers began to press him. They always press at the opening and close of terms, because students are then commonly full-handed; but they had other reasons for pressing in this instance. The balance of his two hundred dollars, save fifteen reserved went in less than a fortnight, without paying more than fifty cents on the dollar of his debts. Youth-like, he thought more of the annoyances of creditors than of their respective claims upon his honor, and Mr. Beach was postponed to the most ravenous. Some of these, all of whom understand well the art of milking students, said "that they were not in the habit of crediting students, but that everybody represented Mr. Mitten as such a brilliant, high-minded, rich and honorable young man, that they would have trusted him for

half their goods." Others said, "that relying certainly upon payment at this time, they had contracted debts on the faith of it, and
if disappointed, they did not know what was to become of them."
Another said, "If Mr. Mitten couldn't pay him all, he would be very
glad to get half the amount due, to keep his wife and children from
suffering." Thus they went on with every variety of experiment
upon his feelings, until he began to think that his own character, the
character of the South, and all Princeton, were likely to sink together in one common grave of indiscriminate ruin. Most of Mr. Mitten's debts had been contracted within the past three months, and
many of the students, well posted in such matters, testified with becoming indignation, that such a thing was unheard of in the history
of Princeton, as dunning students for debts but three months old;
and two or three proposed, in vindication of the time-honored usages
of the place, to stone the windows of the importunate creditors; but
Mr. Mitten, partly from the lights of Mr. Markham's counsels, and
partly from his own good sense, opposed all violent measures, as he
could not see how these would sustain his credit or cancel his debts.
But there were two specialties, which hurried the creditors; the one
was, that Mr. Mitten had promised to pay them at the opening of the
term, and the other was, that Miss Amanda, either from love of truth,
or the truth of love, had corrected the popular opinion of Mr. Mitten's vast wealth, and represented him, upon his own authority, as
not only not very rich, but *very poor.* The torments of creditors
abated considerably the rapture with which Mr. Mitten was wont to
view the ornaments of Miss Ward's person, interfered with his studies, and set his thoughts to running upon filthy lucre. He commenced his friendly correspondence with Miss Green. His first letter was
exceedingly friendly. He waited the proper time for an answer, but
received none. He wrote another, still more friendly, but received no
answer. He wrote another in the very agony of friendship. To this
he received the following answer:

"All your letters have been received. They have given the Principal of the School great uneasiness, and me great delight. He
knows only whence they come—know you whether they have gone
into the most hallowed chamber of my heart. Mail your letters
anywhere, but at Princeton; my answers will be returned through a
confidante in Morristown.   YOUR LOUISA."

Thenceforward Mr. Mitten could hardly do anything but write letters. The two friends soon became so much attached to each other,
that they interchanged pledges of perpetual union. The " hundred

thousand dollars" were now safe, and college honors sank to insignificance in the estimation of Mr. Mitten. He studied only to graduate, and in the short space of four months, dropped from the head below the middle of his class. The "hundred thousand" were a good way off, and his demands for money were immediate and pressing. To meet the exigencies of the time present, he concluded to try his skill at cards with the "Regular Panel" of Princeton. He was very successful, but still he forgot Mr. Beach. The club, of course, had refreshments, to counteract the effect of sedentary habits and constant watchings. They met at Mr. Mitten's room, and as he had been very successful, he was very liberal in his supplies of good cheer. The young gentlemen enjoyed themselves quietly until about one o'clock A. M., when they became rather troublesome to a Professor in an adjoining dormitory. The Professor rose, dressed himself, and went to Mitten's room door—listened awhile and knocked. "Walk in," said Mitten. The Professor attempted to open the door, but it was locked. A shuffling of feet, a moving of chairs, a rattling of glasses were heard, and the door was opened. The Professor stepped in, found a table set out in the middle of the room, with two candles on it, burnt down nearly to the socket—two fellows on Mitten's bed with all their clothes on, *fast asleep*—two more in his room-mate's bed, covered over with a counterpane, except as to the heel of one boot—another just undressing to go to bed under same counterpane (at least he was near that bed)—another seated at the table studying the Greek Lexicon—while Mr. Mitten, who opened the door, was pacing the room in manifest indignation. Though not exactly intoxicated, he had stimulated his nervous system up to an unwonted degree of independence—while the Professor was very coolly making his observations, (for he was a man of nerve.) "Well, sir," said Mitten, "I hope you have nosed about a dormitory in which you have no business, to your satisfaction." (Here one of the sleepers, whose face was to lights, turned abruptly over with a sleepy snort: and the Greek student saw a funny word in the Lexicon at which he gave a little chuckle. "Not quite," said the Professor, calmly.   •

"Well, sir," continued Mitten, "I think I can convince the Faculty,.and if not the Faculty, the Trustees, that you have no right to be poking about another Professor's dormitory of nights."

"May-be so," said the Professor coolly, still "poking about."

This was the Professor of Mathematics, who had repeatedly provoked Mr. Mitten, by pressing questions upon him at recitation which he could not answer. This is considered very impolite in all Colleges.

CHAPTER XXIV.

ALAS! for the instability of human happiness! Just before the fatal vacation of which we have spoken, Mrs. Mitten was as happy as she could be on this earth. Her two daughters had married men of worth, position and fortune, and were comfortably settled in counties adjoining that in which she resided. Her son, already distinguished, was on the high road to preferment, and her mind was at peace with her Maker and the world. What changes a few months more wrought in her destiny!

The events with which we concluded the last chapter, occurred on Friday night, running into Saturday morning. On Monday morning the Faculty met and Mr. Mitten was summoned before them.

"Mitten," said the President, "you are charged with keeping a disorderly room—with keeping intoxicating liquors in your room—with drinking intoxicating liquors—with playing cards, and with insulting Professor Plus on Friday night last."

"May I be permitted," enquired Mitten, "to ask upon what evidence these charges are brought against me?"

"I do not think," said the President, "that you have a right to demand the evidence, until you deny the charges."

"I hope," said Professor Plus, "that I shall be permitted to put Mr. Mitten in possession of the evidence upon which the charges are founded, before he is required to answer them." The President nodded assent. "About twelve o'clock or a little after, on Friday night last, I was waked out of sleep by a noise in the dormitory adjoining mine. It was not continuous, but fitful, and therefore the more annoying; for with every intermission I flattered myself it would cease, and I would just get into a doze, when I was roused by it again. I endured it for about an hour, when I rose, dressed myself, went out, and found that the noise proceeded from Mitten's room. I approached the door, and paused for a moment; just as I reached it, I heard five thumps on a table in quick succession, followed by a yell and profane swearing. 'But for Mitten's Jack of Hearts,' said a voice that I took to be Johnson's, 'I should have taken the pool. He plays the devil with *hearts*.' 'Rabb,' said one, 'you were looed.' 'No, I wasn't,' said Rabb, 'I didn't stand.' 'It's Mitten's deal,' said another. 'No, it isn't,' said a third, 'he dealt last time.' Here I knocked and was told to walk in, but I found the door locked. After much shuffling and rattling of glasses, I was admitted. Upon entering the room, my olfactories were assailed strongly with the fumes of wine and brandy." The Professor proceeded with the details which we have already given the reader.

"President S****," said Mitten, "suppose a Professor of this Institution should take up a strong prejudice against a student, should seek all opportunities of mortifying him and wounding his feelings, and in order to bring him before the Faculty, plainly and palpably violate the laws of College—has the student any redress, and how?"

"Mr. Mitten," said the President, "our time is too precious to be occupied with the discussion and settlement of hypothetical cases; but if you have been thus aggrieved, you should seek redress of the Faculty, and if you do not find it here, you should appeal to the Trustees."

"So I supposed," said Mr. Mitten, "and I am now ready to answer the charges brought against me, and to lay my complaints before the Faculty."

He now delivered a flaming speech, in a remarkably fine style for one of his age. As to the first charge, he said that "*keeping* a disorderly room," certainly implied something more than having disorder in his room for a single evening. So of "*keeping* intoxicating liquors in his room." As to "*drinking* intoxicating liquors," he said he would answer that with the last charge. He admitted there was card-playing, but asserted positively that there was not a bank bill, a piece of gold or silver staked on the game—that the pool spoken of consisted of nothing but button-molds—"

"Mr. Mitten," said the President, "didn't those button-molds represent quarters, half dollars or dollars, or some other denomination of money?"

"Really, Dr. S****, I cannot see how little bits of bone could *represent* money. A bill *represents* money, because it contains on its face a promise to pay money; but—"

"Go on with your defence, Mr. Mitten," said the President.

"Before I answer the last charge," continued Mitten, "I beg leave to read a law of the College: '*One of the Professors shall room in each dormitory, whose special duty it shall be to visit the rooms, and keep order therein.*' Now, *gentlemen* of the Faculty, (I only address such,) you perceive that Professor Plus had no right to visit rooms out of his dormitory. My dormitory was in charge of Professor Syncope, a man not more remarkable for his gigantic intellect than he is for his courtesy, kindness and easy familiarity with the students. *He* heard no noise, '*continuous or fitful.*' *He* was not disturbed, and it is very strange that one *out of the dormitory* should have been annoyed and disturbed by noises kept up for near an hour, which one *in the dormitory* heard nothing of. I know that one Professor may have much more sensitive nerves than another, and be much more given to *watchings* and other *imbecilities*, but these differences will hardly account for the wonderful fact, that the one should have been kept awake an hour by noises, which the other, more likely to be disturbed by them, should not have heard at all. But, admitting that Professor I'lus was disturbed by the noise, and admitting that the noise was twice as loud and twice as long continued as it was, I deny his right to come into another Professor's dormitory to suppress it. The law is clear upon this point. The law says, there shall be *one* Professor in each dormitory; Professor Plus says there shall be *two*—at least when he takes a nervous fit. How far his interference with Professor Syncope's prerogative comported with courtesy and delicacy, it is not my province to determine; but I have a right to see to it that I am not injured by the intrusion. While Professor Plus was in that dormitory, I regarded him as no Professor at all—as having no right to enter my room. No one has a higher respect ,for the Professors of this institution, than I have; but when a Professor so far forgets his high and dignified position, as to turn persecutor of those over whom he is placed as a protector and instructor, to trample the laws of college under foot, to usurp authority which does not belong to him, to forget the comity due to his associates, to pretend to superhuman powers of the 'olfactories,' in distinguishing the odor of liquors assailing them at one and the same time, to consort with owls, bats, wolves and hyenas——"

"Stop, Mr. Mitten," said the President, " I cannot sit here and hear a Professor so grossly insulted without interposing for his protection."

" I mentioned no names," said Mitten, " and if the cap fits——"

"I hope," said Professor Plus, smiling in common with the other Professors, " I hope that the young gentleman will be permitted to finish his speech. I speak candidly and sincerely, when I say that I have rarely, if ever, had such an intellectual entertainment from one of his years. I will thank him, however, to explain to me, wherein I assumed the character of a 'persecutor.' All the rest of his speech I understand perfectly, but as to this part I am wholly in the dark."

" You have called upon Marshall, Morton and myself to recite oftener, than any other three students in the class," said Mitten.

".I was not apprised of that," returned the Professor, "though in all probability it is true. The class is alphabetically arranged, and I commonly begin the recitation first at one extreme of the list, then at the other, and then at the middle. It is frequently the case that there are not propositions enough to engage the whole class, and whenever that is the case, those near the middle will have to recite, no matter at which end I begin. Now as Mitten's name stands right between Marshall's and Morton's, and in the middle of the class, I commonly begin at him, if I do not commence at either extreme, and if I go up from him, Morton will not be called—if I go down, Marshall will not be. This will explain the matter, and I am very happy to find that you have no other ground to base the charge of persecution upon than this. Time was, when Mitten regarded it no persecution to be called on often to recite."

" How much oftener have Marshall and Morton been called up than the rest of the class?"

" Once."

" And you?"

" Twice."

"Mr. Mitten," said the President, "you will retire if you please." He did so, and in a few minutes he was recalled to receive the judgment of the Faculty, which, without a dissenting voice, was, that he be expelled. In delivering the sentence, the President addressed him very feelingly—deplored the abuses to which he was subjecting his extraordinary mind, and exposed the absurdity of any student's supposing that a Professor could take up a prejudice against a moral, orderly student. He referred to a law, which Mr. Mitten had entirely overlooked, making it the general duty of all the Professors to preserve order in the College, and see that its laws were obeyed. The President having concluded,

" Dr. S****," said Mittten, " will you favor me so far as to tell me what I am expelled for?"

" Certainly," said the President; " for keeping—or if you like the term better—for *having* a disorderly room ; for *having* and drinking intoxicating liquors in your room, for gambling in your room, and for grossly insulting a Professor in your room, and still more grossly before the whole Faculty."

" Was there any proof that I drank liquor?"

" No positive proof, but quite enough to satisfy our minds of it."

" *Gambling* implies that we played for *money*—was there any proof of that?"

" Abundant proof; but we have not time now to give the reasons of our opinion upon the several charges. Suffice it to say that you have not denied a single one of them; and as for this one, we are constrained to believe that six young gentlemen would not have set up till one o'clock in the morning playing for button-molds."

" But four of them had actually gone to bed, and another was undressing to go to bed when Professor Plus entered."

" Yes, but they must have sit up very late; for they were so completely exhausted that they could not take time to undress; and so sleepy, that between the knock at the door and the opening of it, they all fell sound asleep. They monopolized all the beds in the room, too, leaving you and your studious companion no place to sleep; which was exceedingly impolite, to say the least of it And here, Mr. Mitten, is the end of questions and answers."

Mitten retired very much incensed, and appealed, not to the Trustees, but to his fellow-students, for justice. Nine espoused his cause. They disguised themselves, serenaded Professor Plus with tin pans, horns, and other noisy instruments, broke his windows, broke up his black-boards, and placarded him in various ways and places. Six were detected and expelled, of whom David Thompson was one. Three escaped for want of proof against them. Thus far Thompson had been hurried on by blind impulse; but now the hour of sober reason had returned, and he was overwhelmed with the troubles which gathered upon him. He was disgraced near the close of a creditable Collegiate career. He had not money to bear his expenses home. He looked towards home with horror; for his mother was no Mrs. Mitten, and Mr. Markham was a faithful representative of his father, and there was the mortification of meeting his many friends and his father's friends as an expelled student. As his troubles increased, so did his indignation against his cousin. " William," said he, "had you followed Mr. Markham's advice, you would have taken the first honor in your class; but instead of that, you have disgraced yourself, disgraced me, and got five more of your fellow students expelled. Two of the three ringleaders in the scrape have escaped, while the rest of us who did nothing more than join in the serenade are dismissed. Had Mr. Markham been inspired, he could not have foreseen our difficulties clearer, or advised us better about them than he did. What benefit has our frolic been to you? How much has it injured Plus? You were justly punished, and you know it; and I know it; and suppose you had been unjustly punished, how could such foolery as we went through better your case? Bad luck attends every one who links himself to you. What am I to do? I've not money enough to carry me home——"

"I've got nearly enough to carry us both home, and I can borrow ——"

"And where did you get it? You won it; and I will not touch a cent of it—————I'll tell you what I'm going to do: I'm going to acknowledge my fault, promise a strict observance of the rules of the College for the future, and beg the Faculty to restore me——"

"Is there a man in whose veins the Thompson blood runs who can let himself down so low as that?"

"Yes, and I am that man. I have done wrong, and why not confess it? I will confess it to everybody else who cannot help me; why not confess it to the Faculty who may help me?"

"Well, if you can truckle to men who have treated your cousin as the Faculty has treated me, you can do so; but if you do, I can never feel to you again as a cousin ——"

"Well then, we shall be even, for I certainly do not feel to you as a cousin ——"

"You don't?"

"No, I don't."

"Then, good morning, Mr. Thompson. You can shape your course as you please, and I'll do the same."

Thompson followed his better judgment; and the Faculty, in consideration of his previous good conduct—that he had never been charged with an offence before—and that he was nearly related to Mitten, and therefore exposed to peculiar temptation from him, commuted the punishment from expulsion to three weeks' suspension: He rejoiced at his good fortune, and thenceforward improved it through life. Two of his companions in guilt tried the same experiment; but as they had nothing to recommend them to clemency, their sentence was unchanged.

"And there is Nassau Hall justice," said one of them. "Two students in precisely the same predicament, one expelled, and the other suspended for three weeks! A glorious College this!"

Mr. Mitten waited on Miss Ward, and informed her of "the injustice that had been done him."

"It only gives me, dear William," said she, "an opportunity of proving the sincerity of my attachment. As the ivy clings to the beauteous column, whether erect, careening, or prostrate, so my heart's affections cling to my William, through all the changes of life. There is a sweet comfort mingled with the bitterness of your misfortune, my idol: it is, that the hour which is to unite our hearts in the golden chain of wedlock, will be hastened a full year and a half or more."

William looked up to the ceiling, as if he expected to see the gold chain up there; and Amanda took his upturned eyes as an indication of heavenly aspirations, and wept.

"I must tear myself from you, Amanda," said William, presenting his hand and lips. She threw her arms around him, and then he threw his arms around her. They kissed.

"Another," said Amanda.

"And yet another."

And then a long, long, " farewell !"

She dropped her head upon his bosom and wept. William covered his face with his handkerchief, blew his nose twice, sympathetically, heaved theatrically, and waited a sign that the tragedy was over. But as no sign came, he said:

"We must part, Amanda. I never shall forget you—your all-confiding nature, your tender, warm-hearted love."

Here an honest tear filled his eye, conscience stung him, shame reddened his checks, and he gave her a strong, remorse-forced embrace, and *tore* himself from her, in truth. As he left the door, he muttered:

"Love like that deserves a better return. How sincere, how ardent! How sweet her breath, how fervid her embrace, how eloquent her grief! And yet they made no more impression on me, until I began to utter literal truths and mental lies as a return for her affection, than the dew-drop makes upon the flinty rock! Heavens and earth! What progress I am making in iniquity! I am already a very devil! A deceiver of those who love me most—my mother—Amanda—I must not reckon up my iniquities, or they will addle my brain, or drive me to suicide."

He reached his room, paced it awhile in anguish, then seated himself and wrote:

"My dearest Louisa—Ill health drives me from college ——"

"Another lie!" said he, flinging down the pen and rising furiously. "How sin begets sin," continued he, with hurried strides over the room.

It was long before he could return to his letter; and when he did, it was only to add:

"To-morrow, I leave for Georgia, whence you will hear from me more fully and more affectionately, on my arrival."

" There," said he, " there is my last lie, at least. I'll go home, reform, marry Louisa, and lead a new life."

He set out for Georgia the next day, and reached home without delay or accident. The Sanford draft had preceded him just two days. His mother paid it promptly, and had just closed a long, tear-bedewed letter to him, when he rushed into the room, and advanced to embrace her. He did embrace her, just in time to save her from falling to the floor, for she had swooned at the first sight of him. Assistance was called, and she was put to bed. She revived, embraced her child and swooned again. The doctors advised him to retire from her bedside, until she recovered strength to receive him. So long did the second paroxysm continue, that even the physicians began to fear that life was extinct. She did revive, however, like one awaking out of a sweet sleep. Casting her eyes around the room, she whispered :

"Have they taken him away from me already ?"

"He is near at hand, Mrs. Mitten," said a physician, "and will be introduced again as soon as you become a little more composed."

"I am perfectly composed now," said she, in the same subdued tone, "let him come in. Do you know what brought him home so soon ?"

" No, Mrs. Mitten, your physicians know better when you will be prepared to receive him than you do, and we hope you will put yourself under our direction."

"Certainly I will, Doctor. I am a poor, weak woman. I try to do right, but I am always doing wrong. Let it be as soon as you can, Doctor; but don't yield your judgment to mine. for I have no confidence in my opinions. I followed brother's advice while he lived, and Mr. Markham's after he died, and I don't know what better I could have done. I feel a great deal better now, Doctor; don't you think I am? I think I could see him now calmly; if nothing had brought him home."

One of the physicians withdrew to William's room :

" William," said he, " for your mother's sake I enquire of you, what brought you home so soon ?"

" I was expelled from College," said William. " I need not try to conceal it, for it must soon be known."

" William," continued the Doctor, " if you tell your mother that, I'm confident she will not survive it an hour. She has been declining in health for several months, and your sudden appearance to her, has brought her to the very brink of the grave——"

" Then, I suppose, to the long list of my lies, I must add another to a dying mother."

" Why, William, you shock me!"

" I wish heaven's lightning would 'shock' me, even unto death. What I came into the world for, I don't know, and the sooner I go out of it, the better for both the world and myself, I reckon."

" Compose yourself, William, and if we send for you, approach your mother with as much self-composure as possible——"

Just here the Doctor was sent for in haste. He returned to Mrs. Mitten, and found her sinking, and begging to see her son. He was sent for, and approached her with marvellous self-command.

She reached forth her arms to him, and he gently bent himself to their embrace. She held him long to her bosom, a flood of tears came to her relief, and she brightened wonderfully. Releasing and gazing on him for a moment, she said :

" My dear boy, you are wonderfully improved in appearance."

By this time the room was thronged with visitors. The Doctors requested them to withdraw, in order that Mrs. Mitten might be undisturbed, and if possible, gain sleep.

" Let William and Mr. Markham remain," said she.

The rest retired.

" Mr. Markham," said she, " I am very weak. I do not think the Doctors know how extremely ill I am. Be as you have been for a few years past, and as you would have ever been but for my folly, a father to my boy ; and, William, regard Mr. Markham as your father, and follow his counsels in all things. Mr. Markham, pray with us. Give thanks for the safe return of my boy, and that I have been permitted to see him once more before I leave the world. What fortune brings him home so suddenly I know not, but it is good fortune to me, for without it I am sure I should never have seen him again. Give me your hand and kneel, William. Pray, Mr. Markham."

As they bowed, William thought of Mr. Markham's parting prayer, and the counsels that preceded it, of his abuses of those counsels, and the bitter consequences ; and his bosom heaved with indescribable emotions. His mother gave his hand a quick emphatic pressure at every petition, which she would have him notice particularly. These signals of attention became less and less sensible as the prayer progressed, till just before its conclusion they ceased entirely—her grasp relaxed, and her hand lay motionless and almost lifeless upon that of her son. Mr. Markham and William rose, turned their eyes to the gentle sufferer, and saw on her countenance every mark of immediate dissolution. They called for the Doctors—they came, and reached her bed just in time to hear her last words:

"William—meet me in——"

The sentence was never finished. The sweetest, the kindest, the gentlest, the holiest of the village was gone! We will not pretend to describe the scenes which followed. Her daughters and sons-in-law came but to pour tears upon her mortal remains, as they reposed in the coffin. The elder sister and her husband took charge of the house; the other two remained a few days, and left for their residence. William took his room, and never left it for near a month, save to tread pensively the walks of the garden. At the end of a fortnight, he addressed a letter to Miss Green, reporting his mother's death, and telling her that she was the last and strongest tie that bound him to earth, and his only hope of heaven. In due time he received an answer, expressing the tenderest sympathy for him in his bereavement, and concluding as follows:

"I have been tormented by strange reports concerning you which I cannot, I will not believe, until they receive some confirmation from your own lips. I will not aggravate your griefs by repeating them now, farther than just to say, that if true, your last brief epistle from Princeton was untrue. With unabated love,

YOUR LOUISA."

CHAPTER XXV.

MISS GREEN's letter filled Mitten's bosom with horror. "What a thoughtless fool I was," said he, "to write that useless lie to her! I ought to have known that she would soon learn the true cause of my sudden departure from Princeton! Why did I not forestall public report by a frank confession of the truth, and offer such justifications of myself as I could? True it is, that when a man turns rogue, he turns fool, and no less true is it, that when a man turns liar he turns fool. It will almost take my life to lose Louisa; but I deserve to lose her, that I may learn what it is to have one's holiest feelings and brightest hopes trifled with. I will write to Louisa, make a frank confession of my errors, vow an eternal divorce from them, and promise to be anything and everything that she would have me to be, if she will remain steadfast to her engagement." He did so, and indeed, made the most of his case that could be made of it. The answer came:

"MR. WILLIAM MITTEN—Sir: Your dismissal from College, and your misrepresentation to me, I could forgive; but I never can forgive your addresses to me, while you were actually engaged to Miss Amanda Ward.   "Your abused   LOUISA."

"All is lost!" exclaimed he, flinging down the letter. "How did she find out the engagement? Amanda herself must have inform- ed her of it." This was not true: The engagement came to Miss Green's ears on this wise: Mitten's attentions to Miss Ward were notorious; and her disrelish for any society but his was equally no- torious. From these facts, the inference was drawn by many that they were engaged. What was stated at first, as a matter of infer- ence, soon began to be stated as a matter of fact. As it was contra- dicted by no one, it came to be regarded as a thing universally ad- mitted. So Rumor bore it to Miss Green's ears. The mischievous jade was no less cruel to Miss Ward than she was to Miss Green; for she reported to her that Mr. Mitten was in regular correspondence with Miss Green from his return to Princeton, to his departure for Georgia. Amanda drooped under the tidings—became sedate and pensive, gave her heart to One who better deserved it than her lover, fixed her adoration on the proper Object, moved among the poor and afflicted like an angel of mercy, lived to be universally beloved, kind- ly rejected many a wooer, and died smiling, where Mary sat weeping.

The report went abroad that William had broken his mother's heart. This was nearly, but not quite true. Mrs. Mitten's health had begun to decline before William's troubles began, and it is pro- bable that she would not have survived a month longer than she did, had William remained at Princeton. But she had become uneasy at the silence of his College companions, concerning him, for some months past. The tone of his letters had changed alarmingly. Then his heavy draft on her for money, increased her alarms. Then the Sanders draft added poignant mortification to her distressing fears and anxieties. All these things were wasting her away rapidly, when his abrupt appearance to her filled her with emotions which her feeble frame could not endure. His conduct certainly shortened her days; but it could not with propriety be said that he broke her heart. Still so went the report, and it gained strength from his re- marks to the Doctor, which were overheard by a visitor, and went forth with exaggerations. The consequence was, that when he be- gan to mingle with the villagers, there was something so cold and distant in their greetings, so formal and cautious in their conversa- tion, that he recoiled from their society, shut himself up in his room, brooded over his misfortunes for a time, became enraged at the treatment of his old friends, and with a heroism worthy of a better cause, he resolved to retaliate upon them. He went forth boldly among them, treated all coldly, and some rudely ; made advances to no one ; stepped loftily and independently, and resolved to hold every man personally responsible to him, who had taken the liberty of using his name, otherwise than with the profoundest respect. The young gentleman had undertaken an Herculean task, but he deemed himself adequate to it, and acted accordingly. He called the Doctor to account for circulating remarks made by him "under great excitement and distress, which any man of common humanity would never have thought of repeating." The Doctor declared that he never had repeated them. Mr. Mitten told him that "it was not worth while to add the sin of falsehood to the sin of brutality, for no one else could have mentioned them."

Anderson's remarks also became town talk, as soon as it was known that Mitten had "backed down" in the "third heat." He went to Anderson in a great rage.

"I understand, sir," said he, "that you have been making very free with my name in my absence."

"No, Billy, I only said——"

"Don't call me *Billy* sir——"

"Well, *General Washington*——"

"Stop sir ! But for your age, I'd give you a caning. And, now listen to me sir: If ever I hear of your mentioning my name in any way, I shall forget the respect due to age, and give you a chastising, let it cost what it may. If you must expend your race-course wit, expend it upon some one else, not on me."

"When you undertake to chastise me," said Stewy, "you'd better appoint your executors : for they'll have to wind up the business."

Thus Mr. Mitten went on rectifying public opinion, and purifying private conversation, until there were but five persons in the village or its vicinity who could venture to be upon terms of intimacy with him. These five, two old men and three young ones, conceived a marvelous attachment to him. They forced themselves into his affections by a thousand kind sayings of him, and as many harsh ones of all who kept aloof from him.

"Never mind, Mitten," said one of the ancients ; "as soon as you get possession of your property, these very men who are shying off from you now, and whispering all sorts of things about you, will be truckling to you like hound-puppies. They hate me worse than

P

they do you, just because I always take up for you. I see how they
look at me, every time they see me with you. I despise those old
men who forget that they were once young, and make no allowance
for a little wildness in young men."

"Well," said a young one, "I'm glad to see Mitten's independence. He is not beholden to them for anything, and I like to see
him going his own way, and taking care of himself."

"Mitten," said a third, "we are going into Thew's back room to
amuse ourselves with a game of cards for an hour or so ; where shall
we find you when we come out ?"

"Why," said William, "I'll go in with you."

"You'd better not," said two or three voices at once. "You
might be tempted to play," said Old Fogy, "and when once a young
man begins to play cards, he never knows where to stop. Could you
do as we do, just set down and amuse yourself for an hour or two,
and then get up and quit, why that would be all well enough ; but
young people are not like old folks."

"Well," continued William, "I'll go in and see you play, but I
will not play myself, for I have suffered enough from card-playing
for one lifetime I know."

"Oh well, if you'll do that, no harm done."

William went in, and kept his word.

The same scene was repeated for a number of days. At length
William began to spend his opinion upon the play of one and
another, demonstrating by the doctrine of chances that they were
injudicious.

"Its lucky for us, Mitten, that you don't play, or you'd soon leave
us without a stake. We know nothing about book-learning, and
just thump away after our old plantation way. Old as I am, I'd give
the world if I only had your education."

Day after day rolled away in like manner.

At length, said William, "let me take a hand, and see if my theo-
ry holds good in practice."

"Oh, no !" exclaimed half of them, "He'll beat us all to death.
What do we know about the doctrine of chances !"

"Mitten," said Old Fogy, "don't play. I'm an old man, and
though I don't know anything about chances, I know that the cards
run so sometimes that there is no counting on them. Now, you are a
high-minded, honorable young man, and if you should happen to
lose largely, you would be strongly tempted to refuse to pay, plead
infancy, the gaming act, and all that sort of thing; even when you

got able to pay, and I wouldn't lose my good opinion of you for all the money in the county."

"I hope, Mr. Fogy, you don't think I'd do that."

"No, I know you'd die now before you'd do it, but temptations are hard things to get over. I talked just so to young Tickler, as honorable a young fellow as ever was born, and what did he do? Why, he won of me day after day, and week after week; but when the cards took a turn in my favor, he refused to pay the little, nasty sum of one thousand dollars, when he was worth forty thousand. I never asked him for it till he got his property in hand, and then he said I tempted him to play and cheated him, and I don't know what all. I wouldn't have lost my good opinion of that young man for double the money."

"Well," said Mitten, "I am not anxious to play." And he did not.

Mitten's company and back-room sittings coming to the ears of Mr. Markham, he warned William against his associates. He told him that they were a set of sharpers who would certainly ruin him if he did not abandon them.

"Mr. Markham," said William, "these are the only men of the village, (yourself excepted,) who have treated me with any respect and kindness since my return home. You mistake their character. They play cards, it is true, but so far from tempting me to do the same, they advise me not to do it; and consequently I have not thrown a card since my association with them. I should be an ingrate and a fool to abandon the only friends who stood by me when all the rest of the world abandoned me"

Mr. Markham told him their friendships were pretended, their professions unreal, and their counsels hypocritical. In short, he used every argument and entreaty that he could to withdraw him from these men, but all was unavailing.

About this time his college companions returned, having completed their course. Brown had taken the first honor in his class, and Markham the third. Thompson graduated creditably, but took no honor.

The day after their arrival, Thompson presented Mitten a beautiful box.

"And who sends this?" said Mitten.

"Open and see," said his cousin.

He opened it, and saw all the jewelry that he had given to

Amanda. On the top of it lay a small note of velvet paper prettily folded. He opened and read :

"Let them follow the heart of the giver.

AMANDA."

"How did she seem, David, when she handed it to you ?"

"Heart-broken."

"Yes, poor girl! Had I remained true to her, she would not have forsaken me, as all my colder friends have done. In a little time, now, I could have made her comfortable and happy, and for all time she would have made me happy."

Tears rolled rapidly down his cheeks as he spoke.

Mr. Markham turned over his school and the profits of it to his son and Brown—he only retaining such a supervision over it as to pass it as his school. The first studied medicine, and the second law, while teaching. In a little time Brown fixed up a comfortable little residence for his mother, and furnished it neatly. He gave his sisters the benefit of a good Female Academy, and extended their education by his own private instruction. David Thompson became the head of his father's family, and trod in the footsteps of his father through life. William continued his *unlucky* associations.

One day, while he was looking on at the game of his friends :

"Here, Mitten," said one of the seniors, "play my hand for me," rising and going out. On his return another addressed him, saying :

"Look here, old man, take your seat there and play your own hand we can't play with Mitten."

Mitten had won ten dollars while representing his old friend.

"Lord," said another, "what a benefit an education is in everything !"

William now proposed to take a hand for himself.

"Well," one said, "we needn't object on his account, if we don't object on our own, for there is no danger of his losing."

William played, and won a little. So did he for five or six sittings. Then his winnings and losings began to balance each other pretty equally. Then he began to lose regularly, but in small amounts— then in larger amounts.

About this time Mr. Mitten made divers remarkable discoveries, to-wit : That whenever he lost, one of the old ones and one of the young ones lost, but that they won in regular succession, so that, at the end of a week's play, he owed (for they "played on tick,") each of them almost exactly the same amount. That though they often played against all the doctrines of chances, they were very sure to win. That the young one would frequently relieve himself from the fatigues of the game by playing the fiddle and walking round the table, and that so long as he played the fiddle, he (Mitten) was certain to lose: That the other two young ones lost and won occasionally, but in the long run were like himself, losers; and that their losses, like his own were the equal gain of the other three.

Now prudence dictated that he should quit this clique, but he was largely over a thousand dollars in debt to the trio, and he could not gain his consent to do so, until he recovered his losses. At a convenient season he took his fellow-sufferers aside, informed them of his discoveries, and proposed to them that they should play in co-partnership against the other three "only till they got back their money." They readily assented to his proposition, and William in-doctrinated them in a set of signs, offensive and defensive, that in a better cause would have immortalized him. He cautioned them to wait the signal from him before they put any of their plans of *attack* in operation, and in the mean-time, to act wholly on the defensive.

The parties met, and old Fogy entertained the company with an account of his early adventures at the card-table, in which was this passage: "I lost, and lost, and lost. Dollar after dollar went, and negro after negro! I bore it all like a man until I had to sell my favorite servant, Simon. This was tough, but I had to sacrifice him or my honor, so I let him go."

The club took their seats. Two hours rolled away, and the seniors gained nothing from the juniors. The fiddler got fatigued and took his fiddle. The Juniors, as if by accident, hid their hands every time he walked behind them. He soon got rested, and resumed his seat. At twelve o'clock at night, the Juniors being a little winners, Mitten got too sleepy to set any longer, and the game closed. Five sittings ended nearly in the same way to the utter amazement of the seniors.

"The young rascals have found out our signs," said Old Fogy, "we must make new ones."

They did so. Mitten discovered it in three deals.

"This is a piddling sort o' business," said Fogy; "let's play higher."

William had not only concerted his signs in a masterly manner, but he had a way of communicating to his partners the most import-ant signs of their adversaries as soon as he discovered them. While he was making his discoveries his party lost a little.

"I don't like to raise the stakes when I'm losing," said William, "but luck must turn soon, and that will be the quickest way of getting back my losings, and I believe I'm willing to play a little higher."

Old Fogy put up the stakes very high, and William gave the signal for *attack* with all his armory. In less than an hour, the *corn* (representing money) was streaming from the Fogy party in a perfect sluice. Mitten lost to his partners two hundred dollars, and the Fogies lost to them from five hundred to a thousand each. At one o'clock, A. M., Mitten rose from the table saying: "That his brain was so addled he couldn't play; and that if he could, such a run of luck would ruin the best player in the world."

It would be both interesting and instructive to the young, to trace Mitten's progress step by step in gaming, until he became a most accomplished blackleg; but our limits will not allow us to do so. He was in rapid progress to this distinction, when Miss Flora Summers, daughter of Col. Mark Summers, who resided five miles from the village, returned home from Salem, N. C. She was an only child, handsome, agreeable in manners, of good sense and well improved mind. William visited her, and so did John Brown, now admitted to the bar and practising with brilliant promise. The Colonel received Brown with great cordiality, and William with distant civility. Flora reversed things exactly. The Colonel was not surprised at her preference, but before it had time to ripen into love, he thus addressed her: "My daughter, it may be that Mitten and Brown will become suitors of yours. I do not say to you, in that event marry Brown, but I do say to you do not marry Mitten, if you would save yourself and me from misery intolerable. You know his history in part. If he did not break his mother's heart, he hastened her death. He has rendered himself odious to all good men, and become the associate of gamblers. And yet he is a young man of handsome person, fine address and fine talents. These endowments are apt to win upon a girl's heart; but surely my daughter can fortify her heart against dangerous impressions from such a man as Mitten."

"Yes, Pa," said Flora, "I can and will. I assure you that I will never give my hand to William."

"Then, without feigning an attachment that you do not feel, give him the earliest opportunity of declaring himself, and let your refusal be respectful but decisive."

"I will. It will cost me no difficulty to refuse Mitten; but I don't think I ever can love John Brown. Dear me, Pa, he is so ugly!"

"Well, my child, be that as you would have it. I certainly shall not urge you to have Brown or any body else. Your choice will be mine, provided your choice does not light upon one of despicable character."

Mitten repeated his visits, and was received more warmly by the Colonel than at first. In process of time he declared himself and was positively rejected. Brown continued his visits too, but at much longer intervals. His fame in the mean time was constantly growing. His manners were not wanting in polish, and in intellectual endowments he now far outstripped Mitten. His visits for five or six months seemed only of a friendly character. He read well and talked well, and was both a wit and humorist; but he never wounded by his sallies. Flora soon became satisfied that John had no idea of courting her, and she threw off all shyness and came upon terms of easy and agreeable familiarity with him. John spoke freely and playfully of his own homeliness; told amusing anecdotes about it, and spoke of it in such ways as made Flora laugh heartily. A single example: After they had become as intimate as brother and sister, there was a pause in the conversation one day, and John after a deep sigh said, " Well, I'd give a thousand dollars just to know for one hour how an ugly man feels." Flora laughed immoderately. " Well, John," said she, "I think you might for a dollar know how such an one feels for a life time." Then John roared. Thus matters went on until Flora began to feel that John's society was a very important item in her life of single blessedness. She met him with smiles and parted with him—not exactly in sadness, but with an expression of countenance and " good-bye," which seemed to say, " John, it's hard to part with you, you pleasant, ugly dog."

Still John never whispered love, while everybody spoke his praises. About this time Col. Summers got into a lawsuit, that alarmed him greatly. He employed Brown, who disposed of it, on demurrer, at the first term of the court. At his next visit to Flora, she expressed her gratitude to him very tenderly, and added, "John, I hope some day or other we will be able to repay the obligation that we are under to you."

" Why, Miss Flora, said John, " it's the easiest thing in the world for you to cancel the obligation and make me the willing servant of you both——"

" How, John?"

" Why just let your father give his daughter to me, and you ratify the gift."

Flora looked at him and blushed, and smiled, looked serious and said :

"Are you in earnest, John ?"

"In just as sober earnest as if I were preaching."

"John, I don't believe you love me."

"Yes, I do, Miss Flora, as ardently as ever man loved woman, but. until recently I believed my love was hopeless, and therefore I concealed it, or tried to conceal it, for I know you often saw it."

"Why, John, you astonish me.!—Go, ask Pa, and if he gives me to you, I'll ratify the gift. I might get a handsomer man, but I never could get a more worthy one."

"As to my beauty," said John, "why that's neither here nor there. One thing is certain about it, and that is, that it will never fade."

"Well, John, if we live ten years longer, I am sure *I* shall think you handsome ; for your features have been growing more and more agreeable to me, ever since you began to visit me."

"Well, Miss Flora, if they are *agreeable to you*—*tolerable to you*, it is a matter of perfect indifference to me what any one else thinks of them. Another great advantage you will have in marrying a homely man, and that is, you will not be exposed to the common torments of the wives of handsome men."

"I'm not so sure of that, John. Splendid talents, renown and fascinating manners are much more apt to win the admiration of our sex than a pretty face."

"If you see all these things in me, Flora, you see more than I have ever seen. As you are getting in a complimentary strain, I'll thank you to ask your father in ; for though I bear compliments with great fortitude, they always embarrass men, and when coming from you, they give me a peculiar drawing to the lips that utter them."

"Well, how do you know but *they* would bear the drawing with great fortitude, too?" So saying, she bounced to her room and left him alone, saying as she flitted away, "I'll send my father to you and *listen* how you draw to each other."

The Colonel soon made his appearance.

John looked at the Colonel, put his right leg over his left, took it down again and patted his foot. The Colonel took a chew of tobacco, cleared his throat and looked at John. John cleared his throat too, coughed twice, blew his nose and looked at the carpet. "John," said the Colonel, "Flora said you wished to see me."

"Yes, sir," said John, "I have long had a warm attachment to your daughter—and I thought if I could gain your assent to address her——''

" To *address* her ! Why, she says you are engaged, and only want my consent to get married. If that is the case, you have my consent freely. There is not a man in the world that I would prefer to you for my daughter." So saying, he retired.

Flora immediately re-entered, laughing immoderately. " Well John," said she, " I don't think you had much of a '*drawing*' to Pa."

" Confound this asking for daughters !" said John, " I'd rather ask forty girls to marry me, than one father for his daughter. I never acted like such a fool in all my life !" Three weeks from this date, John Brown and Flora Summers became one, and remained one in the best sense of the term, through life.

Mitten surrendered himself to cards ; distinguished himself among gamblers for his shrewdness, and actually made money by his calling, until he was arrested in his career by that disease so common to gamblers, and so fatal to all, consumption. When he found the disease fastened incurably upon him, he took his room, his mother's bed room. The old family Bible was there. She had often said, that at her death she wished it to go to William, and there it was left for him. He opened it, found in it many traces of his mother's pen, scraps of paper with texts of scripture, holy resolutions, prayers, Christian consolations, and the like, written on them. He closed the book, pressed it to his bosom, and wept bitterly. " Dearest, best of women !" soliloquized he. " What a curse have I been to thee ! what a curse have I been to myself ! One fault thou hadst, and only one —— No, I must not call it a *fault*—one *weakness* shall I call it ? No, that is too harsh a term for it. One heavenly virtue in excess, thou hadst too much tenderness for thy son. But why do I advert to this ! When I reached the age of reflection and self-government, this very thing should have endeared thee the more to me—should have made me more resolute in reforming the errors, which thy excessive kindness produced. But oh, how impotent are human resolutions against vices which have become constitutional ! Tom, go for Mr. Markham."

Mr. Markham came, and found William with his head on his mother's Bible, bedewing it with tears. He raised his head, reached his hot hand to his friend, and after some struggles for utterance, said :

" Mr. Markham, you have known me from my childhood to the

present moment, you have marked my every step in the pathway of ruin—you have seen me abuse and torture the best of mothers, reject the counsels of the best of uncles, and the best of friends, multiplying sins to cover sins, insulting men for disapproving of what my own conscience disapproved, avoiding the good, and consorting with the depraved, prostituting heaven's best gifts to earth's worst purposes—in short, assimilating myself to a devil, as far as it was possible for me to do so; now tell me, my dear friend, do you think it possible for such an abandoned wretch as I am to find mercy in heaven ? In making up your answer, remember that I never thought of asking mercy, and probably never should have thought of it, had I not seen Death approaching me with sure, unerring step."

" Oh yes," said Mr. Markham, " you are not beyond the reach of mercy ; provided you seek it in the way of God's appointment.'"

" Be pleased to instruct me in that way ; for I am lamentably deficient in knowledge of the Bible."

" Well, in the first place, you cannot expect mercy unless you ask for it. If you ask for it you cannot expect to have your request granted, unless you perform the conditions upon which such request is to be granted. Now these conditions are (the essential ones,) that you show mercy to every human being that has offended you——"

" That is but reasonable."

You must freely, and from your heart forgive every one who has trespassed against you. You remember your infantile prayer."

" Yes, but I never understood it until this moment."

" You must seek to be reconciled to every one who has aught against you."

" The hardest condition of all. I can forgive those who have injured me ; but how shall I ask peace of those whom I never wronged?"

" God never wronged you, did He ? And yet He asks you to be reconciled to him."

" Wonderful !" ejaculated William, thoughtfully.

" You would not come to me, William, and ask a favor of me, and at the same time say, ' I ask it, but I do not believe you will grant it,' would you?"

" No, that would be to insult you to your face."

" Neither must you ask favors of God, believing that He will not grant them. You must ask, believing in His goodness, His word, and His promises, i. e., you must ask *in faith.*

" Perfectly just !"

" If you were to ask a favor of me, and I should say come again, I cannot grant it just now; would you turn away from me in despair, and never ask me again ?"

" Surely not."

" Then do not show less confidence in God than you have in me.. If he does not answer your prayers as soon as you expect, pray on and bide His time."

" Well, God helping me, I will follow your counsels this time, to the day of my death. Pray once more for me, thou heaven-born and heaven-directed man."

Mr. Markham prayed with him, as if his "lips were touched with a live coal from off the altar."

William, now gave himself to prayer and reading the scriptures. He sent for all within his reach whom he had offended, or who had offended him. Freely forgave, and was freely forgiven Two, three, and four months the disease spared him; but he found little comfort. At the beginning of the fifth he found peace; rejoiced for a month more, preached powerfully to all who came to his bedside, and with his last breath cried, " Mother, receive thy son !" and died.

www.ingramcontent.com/pod-product-compliance
Lightning Source LLC
Chambersburg PA
CBHW020113030726

47498CB00006B/2077